FOREVER GONE

A LEE DANFORTH SUSPENSE NOVEL

R. S. HAMPTON

For my Family
Seni çok seviyorum

1

———

Jack is dead. Finally.

I can't bring myself to go inside St. Philip's Church for his funeral. Clenching the steering wheel, I close my eyes and imagine leaving the air-conditioned car to join the steady stream of mourners trudging through the muggy heat. Only visualization combats the constant anxiety, a condition I blame on the dead man inside.

Fiddling with my hair, I ignore the mirror. I don't want to see the fine lines on my forehead and the faint crow's feet that sprouted three years ago at thirty-five. I tuck an errant curl behind my ear as I fight the memories of his world swirling in my head.

A sharp rapping on the car window jolts me, and I slam my knee into the steering column. A woman from my church peers at me through the window.

"M. L. Danforth, what are you doing in that car? Get out here and get in the cool church before you fry your brains."

I grin, pointing to my cell phone as if on a call. The lady bobs her head as she turns and marches toward the church's front doors.

My black sheath dress, freshly highlighted blonde hair, and pleasant Charleston-honed demeanor are ready even if my heart and soul are not. Releasing my seat belt, I straighten the top of my dress and open the car door, ensuring my modest heels are solid on the cobble-stoned pavement before I stand.

My stomach continues its familiar flip-flopping. I haven't felt this nervous since my first oral argument ten years ago. But this isn't just nerves. Trepidation wraps around me like the thick Lowcountry humidity of Charleston.

I am opening a padlocked door to my past that should remain fully bolted.

Jack Marshall, the dead man, was my employer at fourteen. He progressed a year later to mentor and with a slow, careful seduction, by age seventeen, after the risk of statutory rape had passed, was my lover. Mama would have keeled over dead then if she'd known that the well-regarded Christian man she held in such high esteem seduced her precious daughter. At least now the sonofabitch is dead, although I refuse to believe it until I see him prone in that casket.

Jack's wife, Victoria, teeters by my car on too-tall pumps. Her thin form is topped with a tiny black fascinator perched to one side, black netting covering her face. A stab of vicious hatred hits deep in my chest. The lawyer part of me insists I be here, even though the rest of me is fighting it. Because he was such a giant in the community, I cannot skip his funeral without raising more than a few eyebrows.

Pushing my shoulders back, I mentally don my lawyer armor, the attitude and confidence that carries me through the terrors of equity courtroom interactions, conferences with vapid clients I loathe, and the long, dreary docket calls where I am one of the few women in a room full of men. I take a deep breath to quell the ever-present nausea and follow the crowd into the sanctuary.

The leaded glass windows that light the building's main cathedral are in full glory, and the standing vases of long-stemmed white roses at the end of each pew catch the streams of colored light. Jack's funeral should have been at the tiny church on Wadmalaw Island, where he grew up, not here. This is all Victoria's doing.

And Jack hated roses.

In the middle of the entry, I am struck with a vivid memory, and I stop, causing the woman behind me to hiss under her breath when she bumps into me. Snapshots of daffodils and narcissus flood my mind. At nineteen, I was painted naked by Jack in a field of them.

A wave of disgust floats up my throat.

I shift to the side of the entrance to sign the guest book, then change my mind and drop the pen back into its holder. That witch will know soon enough I am here. There is no reason to make it a permanent record. The church fills quickly as I walk down the center aisle, taking the first open seat. The mourners talk in low voices, and the antique pipe organ exudes soft tones that float to the massive arched ceiling.

Victoria sits in the first row, her black hair streaked with gray pulled into a chignon, the feathers in her ridiculous fascinator bouncing like a dancing rooster. Seated to one side is her daughter, a young woman with dark blonde hair whose name I can't remember. On the other side is her son, Brad. Displayed on an easel as if surveying his domain, is a framed head shot of a smiling, happy Jack.

I glare at his photograph. Twenty years of anger twists in my soul, desperate to be free like a genie escaping a bottle, followed by a hurtful pang in my heart. I remember all those mornings working side by side as his office assistant followed by the illicit afternoons filled with heat and lust. He was a grown man teaching me, a young girl, of sex and love.

And I hate him for it.

The music stops, and a junior minister appears at the front. I guess Victoria couldn't afford the big guns. I tune him out, surrendering to the scenes running through my mind until the congregation's laughter snaps me out of it. My stomach rolls from the cloying odor of funeral flowers. I pray for the massive organ pipes to begin their music again, stopping the man in front of me whose words reveal he never knew Jack.

I shift forward in the pew to leave, but the church is packed. Walking out now will brand me as a pariah in a world where everyone loved Jack. He basked in that hero worship, especially from the women. Yet I knew the *real* Jack. The righteous, irreproachable Victoria would be mortified. Her husband was a hot-blooded artist boy-man inside, with blasphemous questions about God and a penchant for the deviant—and the father of the child I'd been forced to give up for adoption.

Yet all I can think of now is how Jack, instead of apologizing to me for his errant first kiss, turned from me and apologized instead to God. It is all I can do not to grasp one of those ridiculous vases of roses and throw it against the wall.

As the attendant moves down the aisle, he reaches my row. The people next to me stand to go either toward the casket and the receiving line or toward the exit. I look at Jack's photo again and freeze.

I cannot do this.

Collapsing onto the pew, my legs block the people behind me. Mutters float over my head as mourners jostle past me out of the pew. After several more rows file past the casket and head toward Victoria, I finally get the courage to join them. I need to finish this.

At the casket, I lean forward to look carefully at Jack's face. Something isn't quite right. I pull back in disgust at the odor of stage makeup, moth-balled clothing, and chemicals that cloak the body. His face has been molded back into shape as if he were a victim of a horrific car accident instead of a heart attack.

I stand there, uncaring of the whispers floating around me. A surge of hatred rises in me like a boiling pot, the likes of which

I've never felt. Before I can stop myself, I hack up spit and let it fly. It lands on Jack's cheek and runs down his face, exposing the pallid skin underneath and leaving a half-inch trail of ghostly white in the undertaker's makeup.

My words are loud and crisp as if I'm standing before a judge in a Charleston County courtroom.

"I hope you rot in hell, Jack."

2

Her. Marjorie Lee Danforth. The one person who could bring it all tumbling down in an instant. The one person who should not be at her husband's funeral and who, in front of a church full of people, just spit on his dead body.

For a second, Victoria froze, unsure what to do. Marjorie Lee knew things no one else did, from the beginning of Victoria and Jack's tumultuous marriage to things about Jack that no one should know, not even God. There shouldn't be a scene, especially here.

But it was too late.

Oblivious to what was happening behind him, the next man in the receiving line stuck out his hand and leaned toward her to kiss her cheek.

"Victoria, we are so sorry for what happened to Jack. If there is anything we can do..."

Victoria ignored the man. Marjorie Lee stood there glaring at Jack until a cough from someone in line behind her broke the silence. Looking up, she realized she was the center of attention.

"Brad, Janine, I'll take care of this. You stay here. She leaned close to her son and daughter, motioning for them to come closer. "Brad," she said softly, "be sure you remind Deacon Haggers how much we appreciated his last check. See if you can get another one, or even better, one every month."

Victoria caught Janine rolling her eyes and ignored her daughter's typical response to anything related to donations, money, or the farm business. Her father's daughter. It didn't matter. The girl would be on a plane to California in a few hours. At least she lived and worked in San Francisco, as far across the country as possible.

Brad gives Victoria a wink as his hand extended toward the next person in line. This was the final act of Jack's death, the reminder to all of Charleston that his family was still here and the farm still needed their money.

As Marjorie Lee pivoted toward the main doors, Victoria shoved through a group of mourners, ignoring their gasps and words of alarm. Angling toward Marjorie Lee, she blocked the woman's way.

"What do you think you're doing?" Victoria grasped the younger woman's arm.

"Get your hands off me," Marjorie Lee responded, batting her arm away.

Victoria felt a wave of raw hatred radiating from the woman as Marjorie Lee stepped around her and headed for the exit, kicking off her heels and snatching them up with one hand. The cathedral doors slammed behind her, but not until Victoria saw her running barefoot down Church Street.

Victoria followed, even though she had no idea what she would do if she caught the woman. Ahead, Danforth wrenched her keys from her purse and squeezed the remote. The Audi's headlights blinked twice, and the woman grabbed the door handle, slid inside, and slammed the door. Victoria stopped as the engine roared to life, catching herself before she let out a scream in front of mourners on the sidewalk.

Brad barreled past her, stopping only when Danforth slammed the car into drive and sped down Church Street to the stop sign. Standing in the empty parking space, Brad's hands were on his hips as the Audi turned right on Queen Street, almost plowing over three tourists exiting an art gallery.

"Mother, we need to finish the receiving line," Brad replied, his voice concerned. His eyes cut to the people watching them.

"Yes, we should." Yet she does not dare miss this opportunity. Brad turned toward the church, and as Victoria reached for his arm, she swooned. Pretending to faint on the sidewalk, no one heard her murmured complaint as she fell.

"Damn it, Jack. This is all your fault."

3

Halfway to my office on Archdale Street, I jerk as my cell phone rings through the car's stereo system with the final crescendo of *Barber's Adagio for Strings*. I shift into work mode and accept the call on speakerphone.

"M.L. Danforth."

"You need to figure out who did this, and why." The voice is older, female, and a bit strange. "Before someone else gets hurt."

First nerves, then trepidation, now this. I hit the brakes to stop myself from hitting a pedicab pulling out in front of me, the cyclist standing on his pedals to avoid a collision.

"Who is this?"

"Now's your chance to redeem yourself, and maybe help dozens of girls caught up in this mess." The voice is electronic. I am talking to a computer.

"I'm hanging up unless you tell me what you want."

"Just look at the text. You'll figure it out. I'll be in touch."

"What...?" The phone dings with an incoming text.

I pull into a loading zone on Queen Street, leaving the engine running and the air conditioning blowing at full blast. A horse cart filled with tourists clops past me. I shiver. The summer is too hot for me to be this cold.

I look at the photos the caller has forwarded. Taken from five feet away, blood covers Jack's face. His forehead is mangled. Another close-up photo shows a gunshot wound in the center of his chest.

I open the following message, which contains a link to a voice memo labeled "Press Conference." Chancing the repercussions of opening something from a sender I don't know, I click the link. The familiar voice of Clint Harbin, the Charleston County Solicitor, booms out of the speaker.

An unfamiliar voice questions whether Harbin is considering criminal charges against the principals of Timberline Farm. The accusations appear to be against Brad. I know from my work in high school at Timberline Farm—Jack and Victoria's farm for abused, neglected, and unwanted children—that each year, social services brings a half dozen young girls to the farm, either as orphans or by families incapable of caring for them. Even though the facility is for boys, the farm never turned girls away, and eventually, a different location was built for girls.

Clint evades questions about allegations of child abuse, and then murder charges. Voices then talk over each other as questions are shouted, and Harbin deflects them all.

As an attorney, I can read between the lines. Something nasty has happened at Timberline Farm, and Harbin is trying to side-step. I can guess what happened because of my history with Jack and Victoria.

My nausea rises, this time with the force of a volcano, and I wrench open the door only seconds before I am sick, my earlier lunch splattering the pavement outside the car. Most days, I can stop it, but today is proving to be one where I can't. Using the steering wheel to right myself, I dig in the glove box. After a wet wipe, mouthwash, and repetitive calming breaths, I force myself to listen to the audio file again.

Jack is dead, someone having murdered him for me. I am finally free, and the problems at Timberline Farm are those of someone else. Except they are not. I was the first person abused there, and from questions thrown out at this press conference, there are others. For years, I shoved my abuse to the back of my mind, hoping it would go away.

But it didn't. And now, someone is expecting me to do something about it.

Grabbing another tissue and chewing gum, my mind churns. There are most likely plenty of victims to create a long list of suspects for Jack's murder. Those numbers are the probable reason for Harbin's avoidance. Yet, his statements give no sign he is investigating at all. Why not do his job?

And why do I care? I don't want to care. Murder is way out of my lane, and as long as Jack, my abuser, is dead, my problem is solved.

Squeezing my eyes closed, I travel through bits and pieces of images as they float through my mind, guilt building with every memory. A smile here, a kind word there—little gestures and tiny gifts given to others younger than me by Victoria and sometimes Jack. Little bribes.

Staring at the dashboard, a trickle of sweat rolls down my neck. I close the car door and turn down the air conditioning. The voice on the phone might be one of those children. There was so much hatred unhidden by the electronics. Until today, I had myself convinced I was the only victim.

A lie.

BACK AT MY OFFICE, my practice manager, Clarice Richardson, steps from the kitchen with what is most likely her tenth coffee of the day. The woman has coffee running through her veins. She is not just my office manager but my sounding board, right-hand jack-of-all-trades, and best friend.

Clarice follows me into my office, a large room with window-paned French doors that look out over the planted rear garden I saved from demolition in the remodel. Tall and lithe, I admire my friend as she dresses like a fashionista every day. Gray filters through her short cap of hair. Today, she is wearing her favorite canary pants, with a floral sleeveless blouse that sets off her smooth mocha skin. Her toned arms from countless hours at the gym remind me I must use my membership or cancel it.

Most of my success as a lawyer is because of Clarice. I am too much of an introvert. She is the one who schmoozes the realtors, builders, and bankers that make up the client base of my practice.

Plopping down in my desk chair, I remove my heels with relief. Clarice sits close by, ready for gossip. "Well, how was it?"

"Brutal. Especially at the end."

Her forehead wrinkles in concern as I unload half my purse on the desk, hunting for my cell phone. Finding it, I allow myself to stop, closing my eyes for a second, wishing the past—and what I'd just done at St. Philip's—to disappear.

"Lee, what's wrong?" Clarice's hazel eyes grow wide. As my eyes open to meet hers, she places her cup on the desk and waits.

I say nothing, so she tries again. "Don't blow me off. I can tell this is important. What happened?"

"I'm pretty sure Jack was murdered. His face looked bad in the casket, and then on the way home, someone sent me some photos and a link to one of Harbin's press conferences."

"Any idea who did it?"

"No. There's more, but..."

"But what?"

"I spit on him."

Clarice chokes out a laugh. "Come again?"

I open my eyes and bend forward, pounding my head on the desk several times before sitting back up.

"I couldn't hold it back. Everything had built up for so long." I stand and walk to the window overlooking the garden. The daylilies are in full bloom, in various shapes and colors, as they reach for the sun through the shade of the old oak tree.

"It just happened. After I spit on him, I told him how I felt about him, right there at the casket, turning into a fire-breathing dragon. I made a fool of myself in front of half of Charleston. And her."

"I think this deserves something stronger than coffee." Clarice tugs my sleeve and heads toward the antique cabinet that holds the liquor. Pouring two fingers of a fourteen-year-old scotch whisky into a crystal glass, she motions for me to sit beside her on the couch.

"Now start over and spill. Who is *her*?"

"Clarice, I know we've been together for years, but there's a lot I haven't told you. Especially about Jack. I've tried to put all that behind me." I take a big sip of the scotch, a present from my grandfather that Clarice and I try not to touch except in an emergency.

Today would be such an emergency.

Her eyes are sympathetic, and Clarice pats my arm. "Everybody has secrets. Is yours with Jack Marshall?"

"Yes." If I start blathering about Jack now, I won't stop for a week. "I'm not sure I can discuss this."

"I won't pry. You can tell me, but only if you want." She sits back and crosses her legs, getting comfortable on the overstuffed chintz couch, her glass of scotch cradled in her hand, waiting. Regardless of her words, I know she will sit there until Christmas to hear the details.

"Let's just say we were closer than we should have been."

Clarice breaks the silence when I refuse to elaborate. "When was this?"

Looking at the floor, I wanted it to swallow me whole, right in the middle of the medallion of the Turkish carpet.

"When I was a kid," came my soft reply. To her credit, Clarice's gaze never changes.

"I thought he was married." Expecting disdain, I look up. My friend's face holds sympathy instead, and with a rush, everything tumbles out.

"Yes. His wife's name is Victoria. They were married just after college. That is the "her." She was, of course, at the funeral."

"How long did this last? With you, I mean."

"Seven years." I exhale and look at the ceiling. "As bad as it sounds, we were only friends until I reached seventeen. Then, our relationship bloomed into a full-blown affair. We even had our own love nest a few hours from here."

What am I doing making excuses to my best friend? Particularly since Jack's first kiss was when I was barely fifteen. I had hidden this my entire life and the embarrassment would not allow me to say the truth.

"It doesn't matter how I try to frame this, Clarice. It was wrong, and on his part, it was horrible. I was a kid who thought she knew what love was. But it's taken me twenty years and a lot of therapy to understand how sick our relationship was."

Clarice takes a sip of her scotch, and I upend my glass, unable to hold the cough at the end as it burns fire down my throat.

"It was bizarre for a man supposed to be the epitome of virtue. He had two distinct lives, and I was one of them. I was young, naïve—oh, I don't know—stupid, I guess."

Clarice's face is incredulous as she rises from the couch, reaching to pull me from the chair and into her arms. Her voice is soft as she holds me tight.

"You never told me this."

I squeeze her and step back to sit again, refusing to meet her warm gaze.

"I only told the Judge and only because I had to."

Judge Thomas Augustus Rhineholdt married my grandmother

when I was nine. It was a second marriage for both. Grandmama passed when I was in college, and Mama a few years ago, so the Judge is my last living relative. Even though not a blood relative, the Judge is most decidedly my grandfather. A Scot, he lives on Sullivan's Island, a half hour from my office in downtown Charleston.

"Then there's the call." I run my finger around the edge of my glass to steady myself. "I mean, after the funeral. There was a strange call from an electronic voice. I thought it was a woman, but it could be anyone."

"Weird spam call?" Concerned, she sets her glass on the side table.

"Weird, but not spam. Photos and an audio file." I hesitate, then retrieve my phone. "They probably embedded a virus in my phone, and I fell for it. I guess we need to wipe it and start over again. You'll have to call Angus and Nikki for me."

"What were the photos?"

I hand her my phone.

Her face scrunches as she winces. "Who is that?"

"The illustrious Jack Marshall."

She makes a disgusted face at the gore, then swipes back to look again.

I point to the phone. "Go to the next text and start that audio file."

She clicks and then increases the volume. I shake my head as the shouted questions on the clip blare across the room.

"Will you ever get hearing aids?" I ask.

"I'm fifteen years older than you, but I still have all my faculties." Clarice's face twists in a grimace. "It's not my fault I loved rock' n' roll as a teenager."

When the recording ends, she crosses her arms over her chest, the concern on her face now uneasiness. "Are you involved in any of this?"

It wasn't the first time Clarice had accused me of causing

trouble, but my unfortunate tendencies had to do with my loud mouth, not murder.

"Where Jack was concerned, I thought about it." I hesitate in admitting this to Clarice. I should have admitted my affair to her years ago. "But I didn't kill him."

She squints as she looks at the wall, thinking. She knows me too well. "Why are they sending you this?"

"Because someone knows I had a relationship with Jack and thinks that his murder would matter to me. And others, like me, were abused. But that's the responsibility of the sheriff's department, and it's up to Harbin to prosecute. I don't care one way or the other what the Solicitor does. Jack's dead and out of my life forever."

"Then stop doing whatever's in your head," Clarice replies. "It was a long time ago. It's over. And now that he's dead, you can't have him prosecuted, something you probably should have done a long time ago."

"I know." I don't tell her I tried several times but could never go through with it. I can't meet her gaze, but Clarice is never one to mince words.

"What is going on in that head of yours?" She leans toward me with that look she gives me as if she can read my soul.

I clench my glass so as not to throw it across the room. "I'm just embarrassed by all this."

What does Clarice think of me now? A man sexually assaults me, and then I stay with him for seven years? There is no telling what the rest of Charleston thinks. I begin shuffling things on my desk, and Clarice gets the hint. I am finished talking. Life has to go on.

"Then let's get going. You have new clients coming in, and as you can see..." Clarice points to the stack of files on my side desk. "We have a lot to do."

4

———

The next afternoon, I collapse into my too-comfortable desk chair. It was a long day before an uncooperative judge and belligerent opposing counsel, all over a real estate case that should have been simple. My chair was a present from my grandfather, and it cost a fortune. Given to me as a graduation gift after law school, the chair is soft black leather, luxuriously padded, and ergonomic. On my to-do list, I make a note to call the Judge and confirm our standing brunch for Sunday.

The Judge is the only reason I continue to practice law in Charleston. Some days, I swear the entire bar in the tri-county area gives me a difficult time just for fun. Since I attended college and law school outside the state, no matter how many years I practiced here, I will always be a foreigner in the insular world of Charleston. To say I was tired of it was an understatement. But because of the Judge, I will not quit. I can't do that to him.

My elbow hits the tall stack of files and correspondence, and I grab the pile before it hits the floor. The top letter in the stack is open and ready for my review. Clarice's loopy handwriting in Sharpie fills the hot pink post-it note. She is all about color.

Wow. I don't know what to say here.

I laugh, pulling the sticky note from the thick bond writing paper, its handwriting in a familiar spidery cursive.

Dearest Marjorie,

Your actions at the service have given the family cause for concern over your mental well-being. It has been years since we have seen you, but we have followed your career and remember you fondly. We were remiss at the funeral in not extending the continuing hand of friendship in Christ we know you deserve. Given the circumstances of Jack's death, we would be most pleased, as would God, to receive a prayerful contribution in an amount sufficient to reflect your contrition. This contribution would go a long way to soothe the ruffled feathers in our family caused by your callous action against my deceased husband. Should questions arise, your contribution ensures we will hold our tongues against you. After such a long relationship with me and my husband, we hope you will appreciate our silence.

Please know we have prayed for you and hope that whatever ill will you feel toward Jack may be reconciled between you and the Lord now that Jack has passed. We hold no hardness against you for your actions and pray that you will find peace in the coming days.

In Christ,

Victoria Marshall

I SNORT, then begin to laugh and cannot stop. When I get to the hiccup stage of my laughter, I grab a water bottle to make them stop. Clarice's voice booms around the corner

"Who in their right mind puts something like that in writing? It's extortion."

I reread the letter. Victoria doesn't care if I spit on Jack. This is a greedy warning for me to stay out of her way. I smash the letter into a wad and flip it across the room. It hits Clarice in the chest as she appears in the open doorway, then drops to the oriental carpet and rolls to a stop.

"Don't take it out on me." She hesitates in the doorway, hands on her hips.

Chagrined, I smile. "I'm sorry. I didn't know you were there."

"Are you going to pay that woman?" she asks. "I mean, you did spit on him."

"Have you lost your mind?" I pull a file from the stack and open it, trying to change the subject.

She sits in one of the guest chairs in front of my desk, her right leg crossed over her left, the ever-present coffee cup resting on the top knee.

"Dani and Glenna were here," she said.

"Were?" I asked.

"They raided the snacks, as usual, but I told them you were very busy and not to knock on your door."

Dani is Clarice's niece. Even though spoiled by her aunt and grandmother, she is a lovely young woman. She is off to college in another year and plans to attend the same university as her best friend, Glenna, their high school track star. The teenager is a duplicate of Clarice, tall and willowy with beautiful mocha skin. I met her at five, a short, curly-haired princess, at a Unitarian trick-or-treat party. I can't believe she is almost an adult now.

"I'm sorry I missed them," I say.

"You've had a difficult day. I didn't want them to interrupt you. There will be other days."

Clarice shifts forward in her chair as she cocks her head to one side as if she's waiting for something, her face unreadable. I shove away the file folder, unable to escape Victoria's clipped, controlled taunts that roll around in my head—those of a right-eous Christian woman, correct in everything and never to be disputed. And now she wants hush money. For what? Spitting on Jack? Or for her version of the past? Anything released about me would harm Victoria two-fold. I agree with Clarice. The letter makes no sense.

"I'm not sure what Victoria's thinking." I flip through several pages of the file.

"Well, think about it. Between that tape, the murder photo of Jack, and now this letter threatening you, there's something serious going on here." I do not look up.

Getting my message, she heads back to her desk, closing my door. I plow through the prep for the week's real estate closings and equity hearings. My practice is a narrow one. I only handle real estate closings and disputes because no jury is involved. I hate juries. They can make severe errors. I would rather have a qualified judge decide my cases any day. And trial work is stressful. A therapist I no longer see advised me to stay far away from trial work. Based on today's events, I think about calling her office to get an appointment, then change my mind.

Jack is dead and gone, and I refuse to give him or his family one more second of my time and not one "red cent," as Mama used to say. They can shout whatever they want from the rooftops.

FINISHING up at the end of the day, I stand before the French doors. The corner of the flower garden's riot of black-eyed susans and confederate jasmine made me think about the days in a field of flowers that led to Jack's paintings. Had I still been a child at seventeen? In my grandmother's time, women were married with children much earlier. But there are laws against that now.

Will this guilt ever let me go?

A triple-rap sounds on the door.

"Come in."

I focus on a red cardinal perched on the fountain, searching the tree where he lives with his camouflaged partner. Did they mate for life? Have I subconsciously mated to Jack for life?

The door opens. "You still here?" Clarice asks.

"Yeah, just winding up for the day. Thinking." She learned long ago that I think better on my feet, a habit from law school. Many people pace. I stand. Some of my best thinking time is at the Judge's house on Sullivan's Island, ocean water just above my knees, waves crashing around me.

"Taking stock is always a positive attribute." Her footsteps move to the couch, followed by creaking and a sigh as she relaxes and settles in. I turn and look at my friend. How much can I unload on her before she gets disgusted and is no longer my friend?

Strange, subtle things have always divided our lives. Skin color in the South has a way of doing that. But over all these years, she has become an essential part of my life. Knowing it is true for Clarice, too, makes all the difference. Even when we're mad, we love each other.

I sit back at my desk.

She tilts her head to the side. "Still thinking about the dead man?"

"Yes." I run my finger over the top of the empty glass that had sat there since this morning. "And that text and that message. What are they trying to tell me? I don't think his murder is the point."

Clarice's eyes follow my movements. "I told you I won't pry, but it's more than that, right?"

"When did that ever stop you?"

She makes a rolling motion with her hand.

"Why don't you start at the beginning and just get it all out? Get it off your chest." She leans forward from the couch as if about to watch a reality TV show. Maybe it *is* time I let it go.

I HEAD for the scotch again, looking at Clarice with a question. She shakes her head, her right eyebrow giving me that telltale arch. Knowing she is right, I grab a bottle of water and sit in one of the overstuffed chairs across from her.

"Victoria hired me to work in the office at the ranch. She got Mama's permission, but I never knew what she told her to get it. As did everyone else, Mama thought these two people were God's gift to the community. They took in kids, mostly boys, with nowhere else to go."

"How old were you?"

"I started attending bible studies at the ranch in the eighth grade, so I was thirteen or fourteen. When Victoria offered me the job, I was almost fifteen. The ranch was twenty miles from home, and even though I didn't have a driver's license, I commandeered Daddy's old truck. Mama just looked the other way."

"You were a child." Her voice is almost a whisper. "But we won't speak about your dead mama."

I take a deep breath and force myself to keep talking.

"No, we won't speak about Mama." I visualize my mother, her gray curly hair and thick plastic-rimmed glasses.

Clarice remains silent, waiting for me to continue.

"Victoria hired me to do general office work for two or three hours each afternoon after school. Jack would leave me notes of what to do, and if I had questions, Victoria was around to answer them."

I can't bring myself to say the nasty things Victoria did. It began with her constant condescension toward me, then progressed to loud fights with Jack in the kitchen, where I could hear every word she said about me. It made no sense to me then or now. Why hire me to help if she didn't want me there? Unknown to Jack, she locked the door from the office into the house, requiring me to go to the bunkhouse to use the toilet and endure the leers of whatever ranch hand was around.

"Jack was always having to get me out of scrapes. I was undisciplined, a kid on my own, with little oversight. Don't blame my mother—she was lost after my father died, and now that I'm older, I understand that. Jack became my mentor, the person I turned to for help. He ran the bible study, worked at my high school with the Fellowship of Christian Athletes, and taught me responsibility. I became his right hand. Then, almost overnight, it seems, I became more than that. I'd been involved in an automobile accident that scared us both, a couple of incidents at the farm...then there was the guy who tried to kidnap me and take me to Vegas..."

"What? Wait... what? Kidnap?"

"That's a story for another day. Anyway, Jack saved me and called the sheriff to Timberline when the guy showed up. That day changed everything."

"And you were how old?"

"I had just turned sixteen."

"Did Victoria know all this then?"

"Victoria knew everything. And she had her own criminal enterprise—she tried to groom me into a snack for wealthy donors. She taught me how to dress, act, and speak, insisting it helped increase the money they brought in at the charity events when a young girl was around. Since I didn't know any better, I believed her."

Clarice's forehead furrows as her glass hits the side table a little too hard, but she doesn't say anything, so I continue.

"Her training," I use air quotes for the two words, "really did a number on me. I still find myself saying or doing misogynistic things. I'm pretty sure she hates women, but I don't know why. She tried to pass that along to me.

"I grew up quick then. College was too expensive even though I was second in my class. Jack and Victoria took a group of us to look at the big universities. Jack got the school counselor involved and helped with the applications. When I got a scholarship, I took it."

"Forgive me for saying," Clarice interjects, "but these opportunities were a bribe. Victoria Marshall groomed you for older men. Do I understand you correctly?"

I am too embarrassed to respond and stare at the slip-on flats I wear in my office between clients.

"What happened when you went to college?" Clarice continues.

I hesitate. I had confessed none of this to anyone except my grandfather, and only then when I got in over my head. But I trust Clarice more than anyone. Still, the nerves begin their dance, and I feel the skin below my right eye twitch.

"The ranch manager, Morris, was Jack's best friend from college. He lent Jack the use of his mother's house, which is not too far from Savannah. She died several years prior, and he never used it. At first, it was our place to meet away from Charleston. But later, it became more important to me than anywhere else."

"Why?"

"I learned to keep house there. I learned to—" I hesitate to discuss my sex life, even with Clarice, even though I'd heard my fair share of her intimate life with Brooks over the years. "On the weekends, we had our own life, our own world."

Clarice's voice is sad. "Was he ever going to leave his wife for you?"

"I had hopes..." I pause, letting out a long breath. "... even though Victoria had him trapped."

I detest the pitiful way Clarice looks at me.

"You've been single the entire time I've known you. Is it because of him?" Her face scrunches. "Have you guys been together all this time? Is that why you're so upset he's dead?"

I shake my head. "Oh no. Everything ended when I graduated from college. I tried to reach him for several weeks right before graduation. When I finally could talk with him, it was as if a television evangelist had embodied him. Overly religious and spouting scripture, he cut me off cruelly and coldly, telling me it was over. I crumbled and took a gap year after college to recover."

I cannot bring myself to talk about the child I gave up. "Thanks to the Judge, I got into law school. And now we're here."

I am gutted and, for the first time in a very long time, vulnerable. I toe the corner of the Turkish carpet as I wait for the inevitable next question.

"That's why you became a lawyer?"

"What do you mean?" Her question catches me by surprise. My being a lawyer has nothing to do with Jack.

"So you could untangle him from the mess you say his wife got him into?"

I clench my teeth. Has Jack's hold on me been that insidious? I can't answer her.

"I don't know. Even with all the therapy, this isn't something I've considered."

Clarice stands and casually stretches. "Why don't I call Brooks and get him to feed himself tonight? I don't think you should be alone right now."

Clarice's and Brooks's boys are adults now, one in Philadelphia, the other in Houston. "Plenty of lasagna in the fridge. He'll be fine. Let me call him while you open that bottle of red you've been saving for a while. You need to celebrate your life. I don't think you know how lucky you've been since that man left you."

I have to admit she is right. Other than the fleeting sense of freedom after the funeral, there will be no peace unless I get the hatred for that man out of my head.

5

"I don't give a rat's ass what you think, Mother!" Brad stomped his foot like a child.

Victoria smoothed her deep green satin skirt as she watched her middle-aged son pace to the opposite end of the living room. He would wear a hole in her new Swedish rug if he did not stop.

"Don't you dare talk that way to me," she responded. "Just because Jack is no longer here doesn't mean I will tolerate poor behavior on your part."

Brad whirled to face her. She forced herself not to slap his petulant face.

"She had no business spitting on Daddy that way. I don't know why you aren't more upset." He dropped into a white modern leather chair and began playing with the abstract marble piece on the side table. "There has to be something we can do to her. She shouldn't get away with such a disgusting display."

"I told you I would handle it. And I have," she answered, keeping her anger in check.

He snorted as he returned the marble piece to its stand. "A

letter will do nothing. She won't pay a dime. You should have threatened her somehow."

"Threaten her how?" Victoria asked. "The woman is a lawyer, Brad. Did you forget?"

He rose to his feet and began pacing again, silent for a few minutes as she waited, checking her watch and wondering how long this rant would last. With his back to her, she took several seconds to straighten her spine and shift to the front of her chair, crossing her legs at the ankle as she'd been taught at boarding school. Brad faced her again, his index finger prodding the air like a knife as he spoke.

"It has to be a criminal offense for someone to spit on a dead person. Send Uncle Clint after her. Make her sit up and see things from a different perspective. A little warning from him, maybe."

"Brad, leave Clint out of this. Enough gossip already floats across the county after your father's death." She omitted the truth —that Brad's actions were the real reason for all the gossip. In the end, it would not matter. The people in Charleston would believe whatever she wanted them to believe.

He stopped pacing at the floor-to-ceiling window with a bird's-eye view of the farm's hundred acres. Running both hands through his hair, he gave his bangs a little flip with his head before shoving his hands into his back pockets. Marching to the sideboard, he pulled out a bottle of bourbon and poured four fingers into a crystal glass.

Victoria looked to the ceiling and sent a private prayer, asking for help. The drink of the devil resolved nothing. Why did her son walk so closely with Satan? Her daughter never acted this way. Jeanine received a scholarship and was at the top of her class at Berkeley. After graduation, she was employed with no help from her parents. It was as if the girl was not their child. Or as if Brad belonged to someone else.

Each family had to have a black sheep, and Victoria was very tired of hers.

Sweat rolled down one side of Brad's face. Something had him nervous, and she intended to wait him out. He could never keep a secret and always had to look like the big man, knowing everyone's business and flaunting his own. He took the art of manipulation and reversed it, and she had stopped trying to correct him.

His voice was loud, his face red. "That old biddy stirred this up."

Finally.

"What is this about, Brad?" she responded, letting out a weary sigh.

Victoria thought she might not want to know. Since Jack's death, Brad had been even more unsettled than usual. Jack had been away for so much of Brad's life. Why was his death any different?

Boys. At least girls could be used to an advantage. Yet Marjorie Lee, that trashy slut, had seduced Jack, upturning all Victoria's plans for her future. Then, to make it worse, Jack insisted he loved the twit and that Victoria leave the girl alone. When she'd refused, he'd moved out. What an idiot. Now that her husband was dead, Marjorie Lee Danforth would pay for seducing Jack, one way or another.

"Some woman went to Clint's office alleging rape," he confessed.

She toyed with the gold bracelet on her arm. He expected her to be outraged and insistent on resolving his latest screwup. His entire life, he had expected others to fix his problems. If someone had accused him of rape, it was probably true. Most things her son had been accused of had been true. It was too late to change him now.

She adjusted her face, trying to include the expected outrage in her voice. "What? When was this? Why didn't you tell me before?"

Brad stepped toward her, his face expectant as she appeared to take his side, just as he had done at age ten when he'd *accidentally* killed his new Christmas puppy by snapping its neck, and Jack had been apoplectic.

"It just happened this morning. This is my first opportunity to talk to you alone."

She was unsuccessful no matter how she tried to rid him of the devil and his ways. She thought it was a miracle that Brad made it this far. She knew the rumors, his line of disgruntled women so extensive, they couldn't all have been voluntary.

"Who accused you of rape?"

"I don't know, damn it. Clint refused to let the woman tell him what she knew."

"As your best friend's father, I think he'd be smarter than that." She would need to call the man when alone for the details. Clint Harbin had been Jack's college roommate, one of his best friends, and a groomsman at her wedding. After law school, Clint followed in his father's footsteps as a Solicitor. His son, Dan, was in law school, and Victoria expected him to follow in the family's "business."

She had cultivated—and exploited—the closeness of Jack and Clint's relationship. With a slight grin, she mentally patted herself on the back at how easy it had been to make Jack's best friend her lover.

"Dan's not been much of a friend if you want the truth." Brad's irritating whine made her bite her tongue. "I'm surprised his father told me anything at all," he said as he stared down at his shoes.

This was a change. Dan and Brad had been drinking buddies and skirt chasers since high school.

"Why is that?"

Never raising his eyes, he continued. "We've just drifted apart.

Busy. You know how that goes." His hand slid down his face as if smoothing an invisible beard. She didn't know where he had picked up that nervous habit and the hair flip. He copied others' behavior and had done so since he was five. He was a pleaser. Until now, most of his imitation had been of his Uncle Clint.

She asked her next question, knowing the reply would be a lie. Even as a child, with fur and slobber coating his fingers after he had killed his own dog, he was able to look her in the eye and deny that he'd done anything wrong. With Brad, nothing was ever his fault.

"Any truth to this allegation?"

"Well—since I don't know what she said, I can't tell you that, now can I?" His sarcastic tone grated. His constant disrespect had grown since college and had been intolerable over the past week.

"Brad, you know what I mean. You're no saint, but your father and I raised you better than that. Is there some girl that might hold a grudge against you?"

"You know how girls are, Mama. I can't make any of them happy."

She and Jack had tried to straighten the boy out, putting him in excellent schools and ensuring he was at church every time the doors opened. Nothing worked. He was bad through and through, and for the life of her, she had no idea why he was this way.

6

____

Victoria's letter continues to irritate me like an unreachable mosquito bite. On the way home, I call my grandfather. He is my port in a storm, and even though I don't want to involve him in my mess, he might see something I am missing. It's how we work.

The Judge answers on the third ring, his habit as a retired circuit court judge—to always check caller ID before answering.

"*Mo Ghràdh.*"

In his childhood Scots language, he always calls me a term of endearment, this time *my darling*. His deep voice is warm but deceiving. To hear my grandfather on the phone, one might think of him as a giant. Physically, however, he is not much taller than my five foot seven. Yet when robed and sitting on the Circuit Court bench in downtown Charleston, that voice shows the reality. In the legal world, he is omnipotent.

Something extraordinary happens deep within me when he speaks to me in Scottish Gaelic. It dawns on me that I never ask him about his homeland. We always focus on me. I need to change that.

"I just needed to hear your voice."

"Oh? Is everything all right?"

"You know Jack Marshall is dead."

"Yes, praise the Almighty." His hatred is almost as intense as mine.

"I went to the funeral."

"Yes, I know. The entire town knows you were there and what you did. Have you lost your feckin' mind?" My grandfather rarely uses foul language unless he is well into his glass. Or angry. Today, I vote for the latter.

He lets out a long breath.

"You should not have attended the funeral, Lee," he says.

"I needed to see him in the casket—I don't know what possessed me. I was just angry."

"As you should be, but he's good and dead now. You can put that behind you."

"Someone murdered him."

"Nae, he died of a heart attack." I hear the clink of a glass through the phone.

"I have proof that says otherwise."

"What proof?"

"A photo of him shot multiple times."

"Where did you get that photo?"

"An electronic voice called me after I left the funeral."

"Could it be fake?"

"Possible, but I don't think so. I'll have Angus look at it." One of my investigators is the Judge's great-nephew from Scotland, my second cousin through marriage. He is an expert in electronics and deep-fakes and can determine if the photo is real. His wife, Nikki, is even more talented, especially in forensic accounting.

"You need to stay far away from anything related to that man's death." The Judge's tone shifts to concern.

While I'd rather discuss all this over brunch the following Sunday, I can't wait that long. "Can I come out to the island?"

"Of course. I'm in the same place I was the last time you saw me."

I head out of Charleston and over the Ravenel Bridge. A massive cargo ship, so large I think it will clip the bridge's underside, passes beneath me at the same time I cross, giving me an otherworldly feeling. The wide bridge is still new to me, its cables rising taller than most cable bridges on this side of the world. I learned to drive when the old Grace Bridge was still in existence, a two-laner so narrow and rickety that I was terrified, even when opposing traffic came across the separate Pearman Bridge.

On Sullivan's, I head down Jasper Boulevard toward Breach Inlet, turning toward the ocean just before the bridge. Sullivan's being a barrier island, it changes almost daily. The sand accretes and erodes, and flocks of birds come and go depending on the presence or absence of hurricanes.

Many mornings, I drive out to the island and stand, sand between my toes, and watch the sunrise with my coffee. My grandfather purchased the lot years ago, building the big white barn of a house after he married my grandmother. We celebrated most of my holidays and summers here. This house is my definition of home.

I find the Judge sitting at the "front" of the house, the ocean side, on the covered porch, watching the tide. The beach at this end of the island is narrow and shaped by repeated hurricanes. Each wave crashes close to the house with a boom.

"High tide is in twenty minutes. Grab yourself something and sit with me."

The Judge makes it a point to sit each evening on the porch, most delighted those nights when the tide is at its highest. I hope he is no longer with us when the resulting rise of the water from climate change swallows his beloved home. I know my heart will undoubtedly break.

I retrieve a tumbler and sit with him, taking just enough scotch in my glass to discolor the bottom. I dive right in.

"When I was in high school, did you know Jack well?"

"To see the man socially, yes. To know him, no." He takes another sip of his scotch as he watches the waves.

"And Victoria?"

Her name brings a look of disdain. "The same. Why?"

"You mentioned something to Mama when I was a kid, insisting I no longer work at the ranch. What was her response?" I throw back the liquor, resting my glass on the porch floor.

"Shouldn't we let that lie?" His voice is so soft I have trouble hearing him over the waves. "Nothing served by dragging your dead *màthair* into anything."

I take his free hand in mine. "There were things between me and Jack that shouldn't have happened. Were you aware of the things involving Victoria?"

He turns to me, a look of confusion on his face. "What things?"

"Judge, just answer the question, please."

He smiles at my commanding tone. "No, counselor, I know Victoria is a spoiled socialite from Columbia if there is such a thing in that town. I was not aware of her biases toward malice until recently. But that relates to an incident that has nothing to do with you."

I will pick his brain on that "incident" another day over brunch.

"What did you tell Mama?"

My grandfather focuses on a sandpiper running in and out with the waves. The humidity falls with the evening's arrival as we watch the sunset behind us reflect the oranges and pinks in the sky. The waves crash as the tide crests, then begins its slow retreat.

"*Seanair*?" I hope addressing him in his language will bring a response.

"Aye. I was remembering your mother."

It is my turn to be silent, waiting for him to continue. The sandpiper stops to grab a morsel on the beach as a wave almost covers the tiny bird with its ferocity.

He squeezes my hand. "You were not the warm young lass you were as a child. At first, I thought your behavior change was an aspect of growing up. With so many boys in my family, I'm nay used to girls. But as you got older and progressed to the upper school, I realized you reacted to men differently than women."

"In what way?"

"Reserved, as if you dinna trust them. You were always pleasing, mind you, but not the happy, carefree child you once were."

His observations of those years are correct, but Victoria was primarily responsible, not Jack. Her rules of how to behave around—and seduce—men completely changed how I looked at them. So, I avoid them now whenever possible, especially in my personal life.

"When did you go to Mama?" The sandpiper is gone, having enough of the rising tumultuous water.

"After that automobile accident before you received your license. I will never know why your silly goose of a mother allowed you to drive that day." He releases my hand, taking another sip of his scotch. "Your *leannan* appeared almost immediately, *saving you*, your mother said," his fingers make air quotes around the words, "wrenching you from the car after you'd hit that poor family and wrapping you in an embarrassing embrace."

My grandfather stares out at the Atlantic, forcing himself to continue.

"I talked to the police officer myself to ensure there were no loose ends. The man was very uncomfortable with how Marshall treated you that day—like you were his possession, his wife. At not even sixteen, that concerned me. And, of course, I chewed on your mother a bit for allowing you to drive with no license. You were so unsupervised, I worried."

The Judge swallows his scotch as my memories are revived in technicolor. I will never forget how Jack grabbed me from the front seat of Daddy's truck. I was in shock, and Jack's strong, safe arms wrapped around me as I trembled.

My grandfather's expression lets me know there is more.

"And? Please tell me what I need to know without me having to drag it out of you. We've always been honest with each other."

He places his glass on the adjacent small table and faces me. "Your mother turned a blind eye toward Jack and Victoria Marshall. I insisted they were showing too much influence over you, and she needed to step in and stop it."

My fists clench. "What did she say?"

"She said you were growing into a lovely Christian woman, and the Marshalls supervised you way better than she could. She forbade me from interfering." He shakes his head and focuses on the open ocean before him. "What tripe."

"What did you do?"

"I watched more carefully. But I should have done more. I tried to talk with you several times, but you froze on me like an iceberg."

He is right. I wanted no one to know what was happening to me at that place, especially him. I was terrified that I would lose him then if he knew the things Jack, and especially Victoria, put me through.

"When did you know for certain things were going on that shouldn't be?"

Taking in a large breath, he slowly releases it. "When you finally came to me for help."

I'd hidden it well. Twenty-one then, a senior in college—seven years from the day things started, and had just learned I was pregnant. I turned to my grandfather for help with the adoption process for the baby, especially when, before I could tell him we would be parents, Jack wanted nothing further to do with me.

I lock eyes with my grandfather. "I'm not blaming you for anything."

He pulls me from the rocking chair as he stands, enveloping me in his arms.

"You should blame me." His voice is so soft I can barely hear him over the waves. "We were adults, your mama and me. And, for that matter, Jack and Victoria Marshall. You were but a child. I'm forever grateful you don't hate me for it."

7

Clarice hands me a file the minute I walk into the office. Standing behind her desk, her face is perplexed.

"The girl in the conference room is sweet, but I can't get her to tell me anything about what happened to her. She will only talk to you." She drops into her chair and cocks her head toward the conference room. "She's ready, but you'll see most of the file is blank."

I grab the file from her and head toward the kitchen for coffee when Clarice tosses another zinger.

"And she's a kid. Says she's eighteen but doesn't look it."

"Are the parents here?"

"There aren't any." Her voice is low. "She's from Timberline Farm."

I stop and turn back to her. "What happened to her?"

"Like I said, I don't know, she won't tell me. But my gut says this will not be good, Lee."

"You need to update me on Lauren after this appointment." The first-year law clerk I'd hired kept more to herself than I liked. I need my team to be active and work openly with me. "She doesn't seem to communicate well."

"I've loaded her a bit," Clarice replied. "Actually, I buried her in paper to get her caught up with things. I'll take a pulse and see how she's doing while you're in with the new client."

In the conference room, the girl has the unmistakable patina of a consignment store. One sleeve of her blouse is frayed, and a button is missing at the neckline. Yet she radiates calmness even though her hands twist a worn cotton handkerchief. With thin, dirty blonde hair to her shoulders, she wears no makeup, and the brown freckles across her nose compete with the purple half-moons under her eyes. Instantly I am desperate to find the girl something to eat.

"Ms. Danforth."

"Please call me Lee. There's no need to be formal here."

"All right." The girl twists the handkerchief again until she notices I am watching her. "My name is Beth Swindle." Speaking to her lap, her voice is so low I lean forward to hear her speak. "Until a week ago, I lived at Timberline Farm."

Hearing her say the name of the farm, my stomach twists violently. As usual, Clarice is right. This will not be good, and I have no business talking with this girl. While my practice exudes a calm environment where prospective clients feel comfortable confiding what happened to them, it is not enough today for either of us.

I scrutinize Beth as she stares at her rough pink hands. Her nose has been broken at least once, and there is the yellowish tinge of a fading bruise above her left eye. She has a secret she is hiding—a big one.

I'm one to know.

I keep my voice even. "Anything you tell me here is confidential."

For the first time, Beth meets my eyes. "That place is just hard for me...."

Damn Timberline Farm. And damn Jack.

I need her to talk to me even though every red flag possible is flashing in my head. If this interview is close to what I suspect, can I even represent this girl? Not without an inch-tall stack of disclosures. Because of my involvement with the Marshalls and their farm, there is a significant conflict of interest should I decide to represent Beth. But I'm way ahead of myself. I have no idea why she is here. Just because I was abused at that ranch does not mean that is what happened to her.

Yeah, right.

"Can you tell me why you're here today?" I ask, understanding how difficult this has to be for her. I am not prepared for the venom in her response.

"Rape." Beth spits the word out loudly as if it is a hot pepper, her face bright pink.

My spine stiffens at the word, and I lay my fountain pen on the desk, taking a long, calming breath.

"Rape is a criminal charge brought by the Solicitor's Office. It's not something you can file through a civil lawsuit," I say to her. "There are two basic types of law: criminal and civil. The first asks for punishment for someone breaking the law, and the latter, the kind of law I practice, asks for money or something worth money. The head attorney in a South Carolina district that practices criminal law is called the Solicitor.

"Yes, I've been told that." Beth enunciates her words. "Mr. Harbin informed me of this. I spoke to him yesterday. He refuses to investigate Timberline Farm or Brad." Her words pick up pace, as does her anger. "Because his son Dan and Brad Marshall went to college together, the man had the nerve to tell me I was crazy. Said I was malicious, un-Christian, and out to smear the farm and Brad for no good reason. He said he'd have no part of it and had his secretary escort me out of his office."

She tugs hard at one end of the handkerchief, and I wait for it to rip.

This is not Clint Harbin's usual *modus operandi*. The man can be overbearing and opinionated. As the Solicitor for Charleston County for eight years, his father had been the previous Solicitor for twenty. Yet, I know Clint, in most cases, to be fair. He looks at the facts and makes the right decision, but that opinion is not based on first-hand knowledge. My clients are white, middle-class homeowners, realtors, bankers, and wealthy developers. Clint's world is the opposite.

"I'm sorry this happened. Can we back up a minute?" I ask. "Tell me exactly what you told Clint about what happened to you. Who raped you? Brad?"

Beth begins to speak, then stops. Her eyes blink rapidly, and suddenly, the tears start. I pull the tissue box from the credenza drawer and slide it toward her.

"I gave the details to a young lawyer. Once I mentioned Brad's name, the girl suddenly excused herself. A few minutes later, she took me into the Solicitor's office. Mr. Harbin was pretty angry. He refused to let me give him any information at all. He waved the intake form at me, ripped it to pieces, and said he wouldn't want anyone else's name associated in his mind with this craziness, so he ushered me out the office door." The girl's tears streamed down her face, and I gave her a few minutes to compose herself. "I don't think I've ever been that angry before."

I study Beth. Her bangs fall in her eyes, and she has the worn-down look of most farm girls. Yet Beth's eyes, when they finally meet mine, hold an unexpected fierceness, something beaten out of many children from the system.

"Beth, I'll help you if I can, but I'll be honest, criminal law is not what I handle." I reach behind me for the local attorney directory. "I can refer you to several excellent attorneys."

Beth shakes her head. "No. I don't want another lawyer, so put your book back in the drawer. Everyone, especially Buddy, says you're the best."

Buddy runs the grocery at the corner of Queen and Logan

and makes the best deli sandwiches in Charleston, but he's never been my client. A former professional wrestler, his endorsement is nice but useless. I wonder who sent this girl to me, and who is "everyone." Something smells wrong about what Beth tells me, but I can't turn this girl away.

"Look, Beth, if, after hearing the full story, I decide to take your case, you'll have to sign a release stating that you understand I am not your best choice for a lawyer." I stand and head toward the door. "Let's take a break, shall we? You can relax right where you are, and we can talk further. That sound okay?"

Beth's body relaxes. I make sure she has water and more tissues and shut the door.

"Clarice, can you get us all lunch while I get organized and join us?"

"What did she—"

"Not much, then she broke down. She needs a break and needs to eat. She's so thin."

Clarice immediately picks up the phone. "Buddy's ok with you? Since he referred her?"

"Sure."

Later, I know I will regret even considering taking this case. Working at Timberline Farm in high school does not make me a criminal lawyer. Everything in this mess depends on the proof Beth has against Brad and what I can dig up that will allow me to file a civil case while pressuring Clint to prosecute criminally.

While Beth picks at her sandwich, Clarice talks about anything other than Timberline Farm. Afterward, once the wrappers and drinks are taken away, as my Mama said, it is time to fish or cut bait. Pad and pen ready, a pleasant smile is on my face.

"Beth? Are you ready to tell me what happened?" I keep my voice upbeat and pleasant.

"Can Miz Clarice stay in here with us?" Beth asks, looking between Clarice and me. Her double blink tells me Clarice has no objection.

"Yes, of course. You understand the confidentiality rules?" I asked.

"Yes." Beth replies, as she looks to Clarice. "She was clear on all of this when I first got here. What I tell you in this room stays between us, and if we have to use it for any lawsuit, you'll discuss it with me first."

"I will. And you know I have investigators that will need to know what you've told me to do their jobs?"

"Yes, ma'am. Miz Clarice was clear on that, too."

"Then start from the beginning," I say. With Clarice in the room to take notes, it frees me up to concentrate on the girl before me. Suddenly reserved, Beth looks away from me, focusing on a passing pickup truck out the window, its speakers blaring country music, two four-by-six-foot US flags whipping behind. A minute ticks by. Then she speaks.

"I was thirteen..." Beth's voice falters.

I pour her a glass of water and wait, knowing how hard this is for her.

Her words come out as a whisper. "I was thirteen when it all started, almost fourteen. I'm not sure of Brad's age."

"How old are you now?" I soften my voice to match hers. Even though Clarice told me her age, I want to hear it from Beth.

"Eighteen. I left the farm last week. They have to release you when you get to legal age."

When I worked at Timberline Farm, Jack and Victoria's then spoiled toddler had been shuffled back and forth between a nanny and his wealthy grandparents. Always into something, the kid exhibited more than a case of the terrible twos. I calculate Brad's approximate current age in my head.

I circle the number thirteen on the yellow pad. In South Carolina, the cut-off age for statutory rape is fifteen or younger, and it is called "criminal sexual conduct with a minor." For additional charges of sexual assault and battery or criminal sexual assault, there is no cap on when a person can be charged.

My past slithers around me like a large black python. Our ages are almost the same: one is the father, the other the son. The first girl taken advantage of at that place, I am most likely the catalyst for what was done to Beth. Guilt overwhelms me with the knowledge that Jack and Victoria started something I could have stopped.

"I used to love riding the horses at the farm," Beth continues. "We care for the horse assigned to us. Mine is—well, was—Snowflake. I love that horse more than anything."

Another similarity in our lives. I picture Betty, the horse Jack always saddled for me on weekends, the falling leaves of the hardwoods in the fall, and the swim across the lake in the summer.

"Brad waited until I was alone, helping me clean the barn, even though it was a kid's job. He told me it was his thinking time." Beth let out a clipped laugh. "What a joke. Who likes to shovel horse shit? It sounded silly, but he said it grounded him and made him realize how fortunate he was."

I reach for the sweater draped on the back of my chair to ward off the shivers. Brad's father said similar things in the rustic sunroom he used as an office. I was vulnerable from Daddy's death and Mama's inattention, and Jack capitalized on both.

I see what attracted Brad to this girl. While worn down and beaten, there is an air of confidence and intelligence, a young woman neglected by the system who refuses to let it drag her under. Had Victoria seen something similar in me? Or Jack? A worn, grief-ridden child who needed someone to look after her, like Beth. I shove my memories away and focus on Beth.

"Each week, Brad came to the barn on the night I handled Snowflake. He talked to me as he worked, treating me like an adult, asking my opinion, and requesting my thoughts. After several months, he began putting his pitchfork and shovel aside and pulling me to sit on a hay bale while we talked. He put his arm around me one night, and I got nervous. He told me not to be afraid. He was there to protect me.

"For some reason, I believed him." Her words, now flat and monotone, continue. "One night, just after I turned fifteen, Brad came to the barn as usual. He headed straight for me, grabbed the curry comb out of my hand, and hooked it on the tack wall. Silently, he took my hand, pulled me out of the stall, and down the walkway to the hayloft ladder."

Beth suddenly sobs, her voice halting every few words, "I didn't resist... I froze. I wish now that I had done something, anything, but I didn't... know... what he was gonna do... I was so stupid."

I rise from my desk and kneel before Beth, taking her hand and slightly squeezing it. Clarice moves her chair closer to us both.

"You weren't stupid. You were just a young girl. He convinced you that you were safe, and you didn't know any better." She stops crying, and I wait for her to look at me before I continue. "Beth, this is the hard part. You don't want to tell me the rest, but I need to know the details. Don't be afraid. It's in the past."

She blinks, then wipes her eyes.

"We climbed into the hayloft, and he patted a hay bale like always. This time, though, I couldn't do it. There was something different about him. Something angry. When I said no, he snatched me up like a tornado. He had me flat on my back in the hay, my panties ripped off, and his pants down to his ankles. When I went to scream, he clamped his hand down over my mouth."

Brad's actions met the textbook definition of sexual assault and battery. But unless there is a witness or video, especially given how long ago the act occurred, it would be her word against his.

"He told me if I made another sound, I'd be out on the street, or even worse, he would give me to Breaker. I bit the inside of my lip so badly to keep from screaming that it hurt for a week. But, of course, that wasn't everything that hurt. I couldn't walk too well that night, and I had to throw the bloody underwear into the dumpster behind the barn before I got back to the house."

"Did you report him to the police?

"This is the first time I've ever told anyone." Beth's red-rimmed eyes look into mine, then shift over to Clarice.

Without an initial police report or other evidence, this case is a basic "he said/she said" fight for credibility in the courtroom.

"Is that the only time it happened?"

Beth's scornful laugh filled the room. "You've gotta be kidding me. I couldn't leave there until I was eighteen. What do you think?"

"How many times, Beth?"

"I don't know, but it will all be in my journals. Two to three times a week. It tapered off after I got to seventeen. I'm pretty sure I got too old for him. I worried he would take it out on the other girls at the farm if I didn't keep it up. That's why I waited and never ran. If he focused on me, he'd leave the others alone."

"What did you do about birth control?" Clarice asks. "Or was there a child at some point?"

The thought of the young woman having to give up a child reminds me of my own and whether Beth was as heartbroken as I was having to give up my baby.

"There was no way I could ask a house parent for birth control pills. I never got pregnant, but honestly, I should have."

I breathe out my relief and look down at my notes. "Will you let us look at those journals, Beth?"

She does not answer, only opens her cloth bag and slides out a tattered stack of college-ruled notebooks.

Bile from my stomach crawls up my throat as I flip through several of the notebooks. While the details are different, the sexual assault is the same with one important distinction. Beth stayed to look out for others. I only looked out for myself, convincing myself I was in love to escape the guilt.

Clarice looks up, pausing with her notetaking, staring at me. I motion my hand for her to ask whatever she wants to know.

"You were too old for him at seventeen?" Clarice asked Beth.

Beth simply nods her head. Her despair breaks my heart. The girl needs a break—and so do I.

I walk into the garden, breathing in the sweet perfume of confederate jasmine covering the brick wall. Pink clusters of crepe myrtles stand sentry at the corners. After a few minutes, the door opens behind me, and Clarice loops her arm through mine.

"Is Beth okay?" I ask. The girl shouldn't be left alone.

"She wanted a few minutes." Clarice points to the window. "I can see her from here. So, what do you think?"

Even though I have not smoked since law school, I long for a cigar and a glass of something to calm my anxiety. I bump her arm with mine in response. "You go first. What do you think?"

She turns her body away from the window in case Beth is watching. The gold bangles on her right arm clatter as she shakes her fist in front of her chest. "I never used to think much of Clint Harbin. Or his daddy. Now I know *he* is the worst individual this town has ever seen."

I let her anger slide away and the calmness of the garden wash through me. It would not help Beth if I let my anger take over. Clarice was not bound by the same rules, though. She could rant as much as she wanted—to me.

She shifts to face me, her face incredulous. "Well, don't you?"

"I do. But without proof, I can see why Harbin won't prosecute, even though he never got so far as to find out if there was or wasn't any proof."

"He refused to talk to this girl from the get-go. She has journals, four years' worth."

"Agreed. And we'll scrutinize the journals, but they may not have the proof we need. And think, Clarice, what happens when we put all this before a jury? Reading a thirteen-year-old's diary. What if the jury thinks she made it all up? What will that do to Beth? Then, there is Brad and Victoria's civil countersuit for defamation. This could spiral out of control rapidly."

"It's clear Clint knows what Brad has done, so he quickly shut it down."

"Possibly. But I can't deal in possibilities, and you know that."

"Even though you just spun a list of possibilities." Clarice puts her hand on her hips and waits for my retort.

Instead, I walk to the bird feeder Clarice installed in the spring, adding several scoops of feed from the small metal garbage can she keeps under an azalea.

"My mind is spinning. How do I sort this out? And think of poor Beth. At least, when I was there, things were voluntary with me. I could always have said—"

"Said what? No?" Clarice's anger spills out. "You don't know that. What would Jack have done if you had said no? Probably the same thing that Brad did to Beth. Regardless, you cannot compare what happened to you with what happened to Beth. She was coldly and brutally raped over and over. That's not what I understand happened with you and Jack."

That awfulness caused my gut to twist in pain. I winced and bent forward. Clarice put her arm around me, and I straightened again once the pain passed.

"We need to get back to Beth and talk about me later. See if she wants to continue or come back tomorrow. What's on the calendar tomorrow?" I start walking to the door. "We are just at the beginning, and this will take time."

"This is too close to home, Lee. She needs someone else as her lawyer." Clarice's words float after me. "And you need someone besides me to talk about this with. I'm not a therapist."

"Yeah, no. I had one of those, and it was a nightmare. And Beth made it clear she doesn't want another lawyer. Regardless of the details, we are in the second generation of this right now.

Even though neither of us wants to be involved, I already am. You can bow out, Clarice. Victoria will ensure this gets ugly for me, and you don't need to be tainted with this."

Her face is warrior-strong as she steps toward me and puts both hands on my shoulders.

"I'm not going anywhere."

8

The next morning, fresh coffee and Buddy's pastries are waiting. I look at Beth. Her hair is washed, and with a bit of makeup, her confidence has returned.

She smiles at me. "Let's get started." I look at Clarice. She smiles her readiness.

"Rape in South Carolina, depending on the facts, is some form of sexual misconduct. If you want me to avoid these words, let me know."

"I won't fall apart like I did yesterday." Beth shook her head. "Say what you need. It's a fact."

"All right. What other adults worked at Timberline Farm when Brad raped you that first time?"

In a civil lawsuit, I can cobble something together that won't be as effective or punitive as throwing Brad in jail, something that will withstand an initial motion to dismiss or a later motion for summary judgment. Additionally, I need something to bribe Harbin. Since I play it safe with my career, I have nothing slimy hidden up my sleeve to do this.

Beth shakes her head. "In the five years I lived at the Timberline Farm, we had six sets of house parents. House One, where I lived, was the 'training house.' The new parents trained there then would take over another house."

She looks at Clarice. "I'll try to remember all their names and make a list for you." She turned back to me. "In House One, we had half boys, half girls. They expanded a few years before I left, building a girls' home in Berkeley County."

She twisted the fresh white linen handkerchief in her hands as she spoke. "House One was the largest, full of the worst kids in one place. The new house parents came in all cheerful, loving, and Christian. But they wore down and fast."

"A new set of parents would arrive?"

"If they had one. Sometimes, it takes a while to get a new set. They don't make much, not near enough to put up with the crap in that house."

"What were they paid?"

"Well, they get a place to live and food. Their money isn't much. Not even twenty thousand, I was told."

"Who told you?"

"One of the house mothers. I don't remember which one."

"What if there were no new parents?"

"A farm hand lived with us then."

"What was that like?"

"I don't want to talk about him," she snaps. "I'm here about Brad."

I place my hand on her arm. "I need to know his name, Beth. Now's the time to get it all out. I need to know what I'm dealing with here."

A single tear rolls down one cheek. Clarice reaches over and takes her other hand.

"His name is Marion Cavanaugh, but he goes by Breaker. A real cowboy from Montana."

I write the farm hand's name and circle it. Hearing the clacking of Clarice's laptop, I know she is most likely reaching out to our investigators. When she stops typing, she retrieves several water bottles from the mini-fridge.

"Unusual nickname," I say to Beth.

"Not really," she replies. "It's what he does—break things—horses, dogs, people..." She waits for several breaths and then continues. "Kids come in from the outside. Many have had no supervision, no parents, nothing to tell them how to live in the world. It's Breaker's job to break them as if they are wild animals. He does other things on the farm like dealing with the horses and cattle but breaking the kids is his main job. And trust me, he's no horse whisperer. He breaks things the old way. The harsher, the better."

"Give me an example."

Beth takes a sip and carefully places the lid back on the bottle.

"Little kid, only eight. His name was Brent. The story is that he watched his parents kill each other right in their kitchen. The father sliced the mother with a knife. Before she died, the woman had enough life within her to shoot the kitchen and her husband full of holes. They put the kid in the system. Mr. Jack saw the story in the newspaper, tracked him down, and brought him to the ranch."

"Seems like something Jack would do," I say, remembering a similar incident when I worked there.

Beth snorts. "It was a publicity stunt if you ask me. He just wanted the money."

I shift to the original subject, not wanting Jack's name to skew my objectivity. "What did Breaker do to the boy?"

"Breaker was in charge of House One when Brent came to live with us. If you misbehaved, you had to clean the toilet with a toothbrush. If that didn't get you right with Breaker, you had to do other worse things—clean out the pig pens for a week, shovel horse manure, clean up the dog mess in the yard, not just of our house, but all the others; anything gross, the more disgusting, the better."

"Did the discipline work?"

"Mostly. It was when it didn't work was the problem."

"What do you mean?"

"It didn't work with Brent. He would stare at the floor and do nothing. If pushed hard enough, he would break down into the most pitiful sobs I'd ever heard from a little kid. He needed help, not punishment."

"What did Breaker do?"

Beth's face turns a funny shade of gray.

"Beth?" I softly prod.

"That house has a basement." I can barely hear her response.

The frayed edge of her skirt catches her attention, and she lifts it to inspect it, then toys with it.

I move cautiously. "What was in the basement, Beth?"

"I've only been down there once. I got into trouble for talking back to Breaker. After what he did to me then, I made sure I never went back down there. It was dark, and I wasn't sure what much of the stuff was for except the chains attached to the floor. That was just a small part. Over half the basement looked like a prison with bars and cots to sleep on."

"A prison?" I can't stop the shock in my voice.

Beth's eyes lock once again on mine. "You don't believe me?" Redness crawls up her neck.

Leaning forward, I squeeze her shoulder. "Of course, I believe you. I'm just surprised, is all." I hesitate, unsure if I want to move forward. "What did Breaker do to you?"

"Beat me, scared the shit out of me. He threatened to rape me, but he never did. Said I was as skinny as a bird, and he wasn't interested. Said he liked his women plump and juicy."

I sit back and take off my reading glasses, tossing them on the desk as I squeeze the bridge of my nose.

Rape, abuse, torture. No wonder Clint took a hard pass. He doesn't want to get involved. Is his son also a part of this? Or did Clint have a personal connection? And why is Harbin protecting Brad? Disgusted, I wonder what else I will discover once things get rolling.

Twisting the ring on my middle finger, I force myself to continue. "So, what happened to Brent?"

"After Breaker took him to the basement, we never saw him again."

"What do you think happened to him?"

Beth looks at the street, speaking to the window. "He's probably dead or..." She bursts into tears.

Clarice is on her feet, tissues in one hand, a soothing caress with the other. Beth's crying increases until she shifts to hiccups. She looks at us with the most sorrowful expression I've ever seen.

"I'm sorry. I ugly cry when I get nervous or upset. I promised myself not to do it again today, but it's sort of uncontrollable."

"There's no reason to be sorry." I look at Clarice, then back to Beth. "Did Clarice tell you?"

"Yes, ma'am. You have some problem, too, she says."

"I toss my cookies whenever I get stressed, so crying is nothing. Do you want to come back tomorrow? Have some time to feel better?"

"No, ma'am. Let's get this over with."

"Okay," I say. "Stop me any time you need a break. Let's go back to the basement. What else did Breaker use it for?"

"For the running, I think."

"I'm not following you."

She stares at me with angry, ice-green eyes. "If they find out I told you, they'll kill me."

"Beth, I have to know." I have to protect her and the other kids from these animals.

"The girls. They got them ready down there."

"Ready for what, Beth?

"To be sold."

Clarice's eyes widen, then squint as her forehead scrunches with concern. Timberline Farm is the largest private childcare facility in the state. I cannot believe a non-profit religious organization is running a trafficking ring.

"How many kids know what's happening at the ranch?"

Beth stares out the window. "The older ones not adopted—six of us. The younger ones who passed through House One on to other houses don't know. If they heard, they wouldn't believe it, anyway."

"Leave the six names with Clarice. What did you tell Clint Harbin about the trafficking?"

"Nothing. Once I brought up Timberline Farm and threw in Brad's name, he shut it down quickly, but honestly, I could tell he already knew something."

"How so?" I ask.

"When I said the name of the farm, he flushed bright red." Beth smiles and then gets serious. "When I mentioned Brad, he slammed the paper on his desk and got to his feet. He knows something, even if it's not about me."

Clarice glances at me as I write Harbin's name in a block in the upper right corner of my yellow pad, circling it several times. At least Beth's trust meter isn't broken like mine seems to be.

"Tell us how Brad gave you those recent bruises," Clarice says. "Isn't that what you told me yesterday?"

Beth let out a sigh. "It's my fault."

She is beaten and believes it is her fault?

"I went to see Brad before I was released."

"You sound like you were being released from prison," I say.

"Well, that's what it was."

"We need to get photos of your face."

"Sure."

I motion to Clarice, who retrieves the digital camera from her desk and returns, taking multiple photos of Beth's face.

How can a small town private home for children go from a

safe place to something Beth feels is a prison? While twenty years is a long time, her story makes me realize either I'd worn blinders the entire time I worked there, or something significant had happened after I left.

"Go on." I sit back, my hand circling for Beth to continue after Clarice finishes with the photos.

"He was in his new office at the administration building. It was approximately 4:30 p.m., and no one was there but him and me. An Uber was coming to take me to the halfway house. My house mother let me use her credit card because it's thirty miles to town."

Beth looks reluctant to continue, giving the handkerchief in her hands a workout.

"Beth, whatever you said or did, just tell me."

She throws back her shoulders then, and her face takes on a look of determination.

"It was stupid. I called him an assho—anyway, I told him I would do everything I could to bring him down. I never should have let him know I'd be coming for him. And it sounded stupid, I know, coming from a kid."

Two corrupt men protecting each other isn't new in this state. That might explain Harbin's behavior if Brad had given him a heads-up.

"What did he do?"

"He shoved me, and I lost my balance and hit the side of my head on one of the extra chairs he had in front of his desk." She points to the bruise on her face.

"Did you scream for help?"

"Wouldn't do any good. He always makes sure it's his word against mine." Her face twists in a sneer. "He said I was just a scrawny orphan who would clean toilets the rest of my life."

After a few seconds, Beth laughs. "I made it worse when I laughed at him. Told him I knew the names of all his precious donors, and I'd already contacted a few of them. Of course, I was bluffing. His face got all red, and that's when he slapped me again. Told me 'those women' would never say anything against him—ever. Then he winked at me."

"Who is he referring to?"

"I don't know."

It didn't matter. I would find them.

"What happened after Brad slapped you?"

"I got the he...the heck out of there. I hid in the new barn until I saw the Uber turn in from the county road."

"Did Clarice see all the bruises? Any on the rest of your body?"

"No. Just my face."

"Did Harbin ask you anything about the bruises to your face when you met him?"

"No. Not one question, not one comment."

The photos were just what I needed to light a fire under Harbin.

9

"Hello girls!" Victoria strode through the front door of the Community Center in four-inch heels, her simple black dress just past her knees, something she picked up on her last trip to New York. She looked out of place in the white, concrete block building that had been converted from an old convenience store. Located in the middle of North Charleston, it had become a popular place after school, particularly with the girls.

A chorus of "Hi, Mrs. Marshall" bounced back at her from the room. Her after-school mentor sessions were in full swing. Each older girl was assigned a younger girl to help with homework, projects, or whatever the younger girl might need to succeed in school or life. Victoria set up the mentor system several years ago, now the pipeline for her auctions.

Early on, she realized that her son Brad's method of using the children at the ranch for his trafficking business was too risky and supplied them with very little income. His primary buyer, Theron Fish, had become a significant liability, given his rise to the king of trafficking in the Savannah area. Her system was much more lucrative.

Dropping her leather bag onto the nearest table, Victoria made herself a tea from the kitchen counter that ran along one wall and surveyed the center. Even though it initially took work, the center now ran efficiently, and she had more girls than she ever expected coming through its doors.

Victoria learned early in her marriage that Jack's vision of running a non-profit home for boys did not support her routine trips to New York and Europe, the clothes she liked to wear, or the expensive dinners to entertain those donors who had serious money to fork over to their charity. Her father would not let her starve but made it very clear once she got engaged that he would not support her and her husband and the expected two-point-five children. According to him, that was all on Jack, and Victoria would have to modify her spending habits.

So, for the first few years, Victoria worked hard to be the best traditional wife for her religious husband. Even though they were generous with money, her parents had raised her in a strict religious household. She knew what was expected of her in marriage, kept her and Jack's small farmhouse meticulously clean, made sure tempting meals were on the table, and kept her mouth shut when the farm expenses outstripped their meager donations. She did her duty in creating the expected children, attempting to be the perfect wife in and out of the bedroom.

Jack was consistently exhausted from farm work, trying to raise donations, and raising the dozen boys he had taken in. Even though there were farm hands to help and a new set of house parents to train, they could not keep the newcomers for long. Victoria's part of their marriage became a never-ending treadmill of laundry, meals, and cleaning.

While her husband was comfortable living like a pauper, she was not. Jack resisted when she suggested several ways to provide additional income to supplement the donations. She decided it would be best if she searched for income alone and let her husband think it was her parents who provided their additional support. After begging her mother for seed money and swearing her to secrecy, Victoria searched for a way to use the ever-increasing children to provide income. Then as the ranch expanded, and Jack began taking in girls, it gave her an idea.

Many of the girls that came to live at the farm left home because of sexual abuse, threatened or actual. When they arrived, the girls were bedraggled and starving. After living at the ranch for months under her tutelage, they blossomed into attractive young ladies. She initially attempted to sponsor her small-town Southern girls in New York for modeling contracts, acting as their agent. She knew Jack would think this idea was ludicrous, throwing the girls into un-Christian-like environments. Victoria was desperate to prove him wrong and never told him her plan.

But he wasn't wrong. She failed at enticing interest in her girls from the modeling agencies in New York, Los Angeles, or the smaller cities and lesser agencies. There was too much competition, and she was inexperienced. One night in midtown Manhattan at a bar in Murray Hill, she was exhausted from beating the streets and verbally unloaded on the unsuspecting bartender. After three martinis and a detailed rant to someone she thought she would never see again, the bartender surprised her.

"I may have someone to help you," he slid a business card across the bar. "This guy is always looking for models."

She called the number the next morning and arranged a meeting later that day. Hank Reed was not what she expected in an agency owner. In his mid-fifties, just over six feet, and in excellent shape, the man was an attractive, sandy-blond surfer type originally from California who modeled in his past. Now older with his own agency, he told Victoria he hired those routinely shunned by the larger agencies. He recounted his frustrations attempting to break into the modeling world that mimicked hers. They quickly devised an arrangement for Hank to interview girls with a video conferencing system. If the girl met the requirements he needed for a recent contract, Victoria would take the risk and send the girl to New York. If the girl was accepted, they would then negotiate the contract. To her relief, no girl was ever turned away.

For several years, Victoria kept her business quiet. While not as often or as lucrative as she had hoped, the contracts provided additional income and kept her from sponging off her mother. She had needed a more extensive portfolio of girls for Hank, and thus, the Community Center was born.

It wasn't until she ran into one of the girls who had successfully "made it" in New York that she learned the reality of Hank Reed's agency. After the initial modeling contract was completed, the girls were offered additional positions as "assistants" to executives, essentially a ruse for trafficking.

Victoria picked up her tea. Taking a long sip, she remembered her angry conversation with Hank.

"What are you doing to my girls?" Victoria had called from her car, far from the ranch or the Community Center, allowing her no reason to hide her outrage.

"Giving them the opportunity of a lifetime, Victoria." Hank's voice was incredulous. "Do you think they could live in New York and all these other places any other way?"

"I talked to Sheena, Hank. She said your so-called job position with a CFO of some company was no such thing. She was pretty much a prostitute."

"That was her choice, Victoria. She didn't have to accept the contract. I didn't hide from her what was expected. She made damn good money at that job. I bet she didn't tell you that part. And remember, you're part of this. There is no way that girl would have come to me except through you."

"This is not my fault. You entice them through me, then get them hooked, and then prostitute them out. I had no idea you were doing this. There is no way I'm responsible."

Her outrage was met with laughter. "Seriously?" he replied.

"These girls crossed state lines, and I'm sure no Fed will believe you didn't know what was happening. Especially when you accepted the money."

"I'm going to call the Solicitor in Charleston and get him involved."

"I wouldn't do that if I were you." Hank's voice took on a softer note, less threatening. "Look, Victoria, we have a good thing going here. What if I increase your percentage and throw you more contracts? That make you feel better?"

"What are you offering me?"

"A fifty-fifty partnership. I think we have the potential to make this into something big. Your girls are by far the ones who do the best."

"Send me the numbers, and I'll think about it."

"Don't think too long. And don't do anything either of us will regret."

Dani approached her. The girl's face was creased with anxiety, taking Victoria out of her past.

"Have you heard anything from NYU, Mrs. Marshall?" Dani had waited weeks for an acceptance from her number one choice of university, which Victoria knew would never come. After shredding Dani's paper application that the girl entrusted her for Fed Ex, a ludicrous act given that all college applications were now online, Victoria never called her contact at the NYU admissions office. Dani was slated to bring her the highest bid of any of her girls, and she and Hank already had several clients in negotiations.

"Dani, be patient. You know there are thousands of applications that have to be reviewed before any acceptances are released. Besides, we have quite a while before the date."

"But you said—" Dani's whine made Victoria put out her hand like a stop sign to force the girl to stop speaking.

"Trust me, Dani. Have I ever steered you wrong?"

"No, ma'am." Dani looked at the young girl she mentored,

who waited across the room. The girl waved, and Dani looked back at Victoria.

"I need to get back to Ariel. I didn't mean to bother you."

"It's no bother, Dani. Just don't get overanxious when there's no need," Victoria replied. "Don't try to make life go so fast. You'll be in New York before you know it."

Dani will definitely be in New York, but only for a day before she is flown for "a shoot" to either Singapore or Frankfurt, Germany, depending on which bidder is the highest. Intelligent and athletic, the young girl will be a handful for any man who purchases her. Victoria was thankful her clients appreciated strong-willed girls. She would be in trouble if she had to produce wilting flowers or submissives. The South didn't tend to breed those.

She caught Dani's arm before the girl could leave.

"How is Glenna? I haven't seen her for weeks," Victoria asked.

Glenna was the next prize on Victoria's list, but the girl would be more work than Dani. According to Dani, several schools were courting the track star, and Victoria knew bringing the girl into the fold would be difficult. Glenna was uninterested and openly suspicious of anything at the Community Center and rarely attended any of the events Victoria sponsored. If she were to get the girl into her auction system, Dani would have to be the one to bring her in.

"She's busy training for the next regional. I don't get to see her much myself," Dani replied, clearly happy to discuss a less stressful topic than NYU.

"I'd love to see her involved a bit more. If she doesn't get the track scholarship she wants, I'll happily help her find another university."

Dani beamed. "I'll tell her. I'm sure she'd appreciate your help. I know I do."

"It's nothing, my girl. Now go on to Ariel. Let me know if she says anything about how her parents are doing. I'd hate for her to show up one day at Timberline Farm. We need to do whatever we can to help them."

"Yes, ma'am," Dani replied. "I'll find out what's happening and let you know."

Victoria watched as Dani crossed the room and hugged the ten-year-old. She pulled her phone from her purse and dialed Hank's number. He picked up after the first ring.

"Hey. You know that guy in Sausalito who likes them pretty young?"

"Yes. What do you have in mind?"

Victoria realized how many girls were within listening distance, grabbed her bag, and took the call outside.

10

I plow through a nasty property title that is giving me fits. Leaning back in my desk chair, I need a break to work on something else while my subconscious works on Beth's case.

"Clarice, can you call Angus and Nikki?"

A chuckle floats from the other side of the wall. "They're on their way in. They're stopping by to pick up your grandfather. I thought you might need a powwow with them, given the hornet's nest you've just kicked over by taking this case when even our illustrious Solicitor wouldn't touch it. Do you want Lauren to meet with us as well?"

"Not for now," I reply, "unless you think she needs more to do?"

"She is chugging along. By the end of the week, we will need to review and evaluate."

"Sounds good."

My investigators, Angus and Nikki Garrett, are two of the best I've worked with, either from my time with the sheriff's office years ago or with the two most prominent law firms in the state after graduating from law school. In my practice, I do take other cases that, from time to time, require a more thorough investigation than I can do from my office. Our latest case together was a real estate fraud matter where I needed Angus and Nikki to handle the forensic accounting end and testify to their conclusions in court. Neither investigator has qualms about thinking outside the box, yet I have never known them, unlike me, to regularly bump against the line of legality.

Within minutes, Angus enters my office. A faded Atlanta Braves baseball hat covers his riot of dark blonde curls. He drops into a conference chair, slapping his hat on the table. His wife, Nikki, follows behind in a navy skirt and white blouse, his opposite in every way.

Angus began his career as an investigator for the Ninth Circuit Solicitor's office, where my grandfather was chief judge for twenty years. I was one of the first attorneys who hired him when he went out alone, and he hasn't forgotten. The couple is in their thirties and are experts at being nondescript and blending into any situation. Angus and I treat each other as siblings, having known each other most of our lives. When he and Nikki married, I was a bridesmaid.

"The Judge stopped at the courthouse for a bit. Said to tell you he'd be along shortly," Nikki says.

I dive right in. "Are either of you familiar with Timberline Farm?"

"Not much." Angus's brogue is similar to my grandfather's. "Some sort o' home for boys, maybe they take girls, I dunna. Never had much reason to be in that part of the state since I don't hunt."

I look at Nikki. She shrugs. "What I know is gossip."

She is a stickler for facts, which is one thing I admire about her. "Anything you can tell me will help, even if not yet vetted for accuracy."

"Rumblings of things changing," Nikki begins, "kids running

off yet never found by law enforcement, several sets of house parents leaving in the middle of the night."

"Have a time frame for this?" I ask.

Nikki taps her fingernails on the shiny oak conference table. "It's been going on for several years. The people I know, the wife anyway, was one of the house parents."

"Think she would tell us why they left?" Angus asks.

"I'll try to find her and see. She moved back to New Mexico with her parents. Whatever the problem was, it caused their divorce."

"Don't mean to be pushy," Angus interjects, "but do we get to know what's going on here? Or is it the type of case you'd rather us not know?"

I bring them up to speed on my meetings with Beth.

"Beth's allegations of trafficking raise serious red flags," Nikki says.

"I agree, if they are accurate," I reply.

Not that I don't trust Beth, but I know all clients have their version of a story. Before I specialized in various types of real property law, for several years, I handled almost anything that came through my door, whether it be civil or criminal cases. It was my job to delve in and get to the bottom of each case. The truth between the plaintiff and defendant usually met somewhere in the middle, almost always to neither party's satisfaction.

"I see several problems with this case. I'm looking for any input you wish to give me. First, I have a client who alleges rape against Brad Marshall, the son of Victoria and Jack Marshall, who now runs Timberline Farm. She has been to the Solicitor, who refuses to prosecute for reasons unknown. There are written journals from the time she was raped to the present, but to my knowledge, no other witnesses or evidence of the repeated rapes. Second, she has alleged that a trafficking ring exists at Timberline Farm, the same place where she was raped. She has provided no evidence other than her personal experience. These are things that need to be handled by the Solicitor's office. You have more experience with Harbin than I do. How do we pressure him to move forward?"

I look to Nikki, then to Angus.

Angus frowns. "If you want Brad in jail for criminal or sexual assault, that's definitely Harbin's job."

"When Beth went to file a complaint, he told her that his son, Dan, and Brad Marshall were college roommates and best buddies, and he wouldn't touch the case."

Angus's lips purse in irritation. "Well, he may have an ethical conflict, but he's still required to appoint someone to prosecute when he has evidence. There's a law on it, I'm sure."

"The statute requires the Attorney General to step in to prosecute the case and even prosecute the Solicitor if needed. But I don't want to threaten Harbin by going to the AG if there's any better way to use him to our advantage." I reply. "We might need Harbin for a future fishing expedition and I don't want to burn down that boat dock just yet."

"Do you think he is hiding something?" Nikki asks. "Just because his son and Brad are friends doesn't sound like much to me."

"I agree," I respond. "Until we know if or how he's implicated in this, we need to create a list of pressure points that might work to prod him forward."

Nikki looks up from her notes. "Well, we can get the newspaper involved. The farm is already in the news because of Jack Marshall's death. There are already rumors about what will happen to all those kids out there."

Angus stares at his tablet, speaking aloud as he makes notes. "What we really need is to catch Brad in the act. Or find out if there are other victims. Does Beth know if there are others? That way, Harbin would have to prosecute."

"Beth said she continued to let Brad force himself on her to protect the other girls. She thinks there are no other victims, but I doubt she truly knows. And I have no idea how you'd catch him in the act, Angus," I respond. "This is really outside my comfort zone. How do you guys feel? Unless the Judge can provide us with something creative, I must tell Beth that I can't help her."

"We can do anything you need," Nikki says, "but I agree we should hash everything out first and include the Judge, especially when we're all this uncomfortable. Pushing a Solicitor to do his job could backfire. Maybe there is already something in the works with local law enforcement that he doesn't want to hamper."

She looks at Angus, and he nods his agreement. "There are children involved. We canna sit by on this one, but I agree we need to have ourselves straight before we jump. I'll ask around and see if the Sheriff's office has anything going on at the farm without raising any eyebrows."

"I'll set up a whiteboard to start a list of plausible options for us to sort out with the Judge," I say. "Without proof of something happening and confirmation, I doubt the press would run anything. It's the same problem I have with the police. I have no proof of anything, just a young girl's statements about rape and trafficking and her journals, one of which I have only skimmed. As to the trafficking, she says she wasn't involved. Her testimony will demonstrate clear statutory rape, but she filed no report, told no one, and it started five years ago."

We look at each other until Angus breaks the silence.

"We have to figure out how to get into the ranch. You said this went on with Beth for a long time. I bet he already has her replacement by now."

"You and Nikki are the least religious couple I could find," I respond, "and you want to infiltrate a religious institution?"

Angus laughs.

"We can be anyone we need to be." Nikki turns to her husband with a sly smile, then shifts to face me again. "We always have. If we dig around a bit and get more information on how many house parents, office staff, and others are in the organization, we can do this more professionally. Do you have any information at all on the numbers?"

I shake my head. "Other than what Beth can tell us, my information is twenty years old."

Angus leans back in his chair, his eyes in a squint. "You have some personal connection with this place?"

"I worked there in high school as the ranch secretary for four years for Jack Marshall, Brad's father." This was as far as I would go concerning my relationship with Jack.

"He died of a heart attack?" Nikki asks.

"No. I've received evidence that he was murdered. That's another problem our Solicitor has. An anonymous caller's photo proves it." I pull up the photo and pass my phone to Nikki, who then passes it to Angus. "But I can't talk with him about it. He'll accuse me of desecration."

Angus hands me the phone, his face screwed up in confusion. "Desecration?"

"I got angry at Jack Marshall's funeral and spit on him in the coffin."

With his impeccable timing, my grandfather takes this opportunity to enter the conference room.

Both Nikki and Angus burst into laughter. "You didn't!" Nikki looks at me incredulously.

"I did." I can't hide my embarrassment.

"She did," confirms my grandfather as he sits beside me, "and the entire town knows about it. And if I know Victoria Marshall, she will not let this slide, my dear." He pats my hand and winks at Angus.

"If you are all finished making fun of me, we need to bring the Judge up to speed and work out what we plan to do."

11

———————

At seventy-six, Judge Thomas Augustus Rhineholdt is as sharp as he's ever been, even more possibly, given his health regimen since he retired from the bench. He runs five miles each morning in the sand and gave up meat. To my knowledge, his only vice is two fingers of twenty-five-year-old scotch each evening at sunset. Just under six feet and whippet lean, I expect him to live forever.

We take the next few minutes and bring my grandfather up to speed. He listens intently as I summarize, his hands folded in his lap.

Angus speaks, his eyes still laughing at me, "Is it possible to go after Brad in civil court?"

"I'm kicking around several ideas, but I don't have a conclusion yet. If you find any financial wrongdoing, I can sue for malfeasance. I'll need something unconventional. It won't put Brad in jail, but it might get the Board of Directors to kick him out."

Nikki pursed her lips. "You know this will be expensive."

Investigative work is always expensive. I use Angus and Nikki for the wealthiest clients, commercial banks, or big developers with money to spend. They work across the southeast, and I know the work I give them is small time.

"I have enough in the bank to cover approximately six months of hard-core investigation and research. After that, we'll need to see where we are."

Nikki's eyebrows raised. "You're doing this pro bono?"

"Yes." I am working for free on Beth's case. Technically, the client must pay for expenses, such as Angus and Nikki's fees and costs, but that isn't possible under her circumstances. Even though Clarice hates that we will be draining our slush account, we agree that something has to be done, even if I have to pay for it.

"We may be able to get someone else to pay your fees and expenses, Lee," my grandfather says. "You know it depends on what type of action we file."

"Of course, Judge. But I can't go into this without understanding that I might never be paid."

"We won't take payment if you don't," Nikki says as she looks at Angus.

"Agreed," Angus says.

"I can't let you—" I start.

"What is the best way to approach the ranch, then?" Nikki interrupts, ignoring my protest.

I tap my pen on the notepad. "I can call Morris, the Timberline manager. My first idea is that you should try to get on as employees, particularly you, Nikki. If you can get a job in the administration building, I bet you will find what we need."

"This manager," says Angus, "how well do you know him?"

The irritating voice in my head starts a retort of "too damn well," but I shut it down.

"He was the manager when I was there. He was a bit stern when I was a kid, but mellowed as he and I got older. When I call, I'll ask a favor as an old friend for some new folks in the community. If he balks, that will tell us something right off. He may no longer be there, but he was six months ago."

"Ok," the Judge says, "that's the first step. Then what?"

"We need to get more information from Beth on the trafficking she thinks is going on there. She told me kids were being sold—and I don't want to guess for what, although most likely for sex. But you guys will dig out for me who's buying."

Angus's lips purse in a straight line. "We can snoop around without getting the wrong attention. Can't we, babe?" He grins at his wife.

Nikki laughs, leaning over to poke her husband in the shoulder with her index finger.

"Oh, no, you don't. I'm the one that doesn't have immunity if the Sheriff gets wind of it. I don't have Judge Rhineholdt to bail me out like you. How are you going to keep me out of the big house?"

Their laughter breaks the stress I've been under since Jack's funeral.

"We'll work that out before you guys get in too deep," I respond. "What name do you want me to use if I can talk to Morris?"

Nikki looks at Angus, who rolls his eyes before cutting them away. "Williams. Mark and Mindy Williams. We have complete identification with those names. They will work." She laughs and slaps her husband's hand resting on the table, an apparent inside joke.

I look at them to explain.

"We're big Robin Williams fans. Don't worry about it. It's just a joke we took too far."

"Call Morris now," the Judge says to me, "and put him on speakerphone. It will be one thing less to do later."

I pull up the number on my cell and tap the phone to initiate the call.

"Jessup." Morris's voice is curt and irritated. The last time I'd heard that tone, I was fifteen and on the receiving end of his lecture on responsibility after I'd tried to hide out from Victoria in the barn, and he'd caught me.

"It's M. L. Danforth, Morris."

"Hey, Marjorie Lee." His voice softened. "It's been a while. I still can't get used to calling you M.L." In ten years, I had bumped into Morris once in the grocery store and another time in a movie theater ticket line. Amicable, both of us avoided the subject of Jack. The men had been friends for over thirty years, and Morris knew much of what had happened in my past.

"It has been a while. You know what it is like in this town. M. L. made me look a little more grown up." I shift the subject to him. "They promoted you, I see."

Morris brays like a donkey. "Only you would know it's the same job. Same old crap, different day. Like they say, just working for the Lord up here."

I laugh. "How many houses are there now?"

"We're up to twenty. Jack ran out of land, given that we have the big house on the hill for Victoria and the new administration building right at the entrance. That woman has some goals. Rather than try to squeeze in more houses on smaller plots, we opened a new girls' home in Berkeley County."

"Wow. That is a lot of kids. Aren't there six in each house with two house parents?"

"Yes, the same format as when you were here. We made the more recent houses a little bigger, but they all have four bedrooms and two bathrooms.

I wonder if it has the same convoluted financing arrangement with the Deacon, the commercial contractor Jack dealt with when I was in high school. The Deacon is Victoria's father's best friend. The man made a fortune from building houses for Timberline Farm and then turning around and financing them for years at an exorbitant interest rate. Given that Jack had no other income or ability to obtain a loan from a bank, he swallowed the unfavorable terms to move forward and make his wife happy.

"I heard that but didn't know the details. The Deacon part of the new facility as well?"

I hear the creak of his chair as Morris ignores my question. "More girls there than boys, but it works."

"I guess you're happy, or you'd have left long ago. How's Victoria since Jack's death?"

His laughter from the phone's speaker bounces off the conference room walls. "That's ripe coming from you. She has preached how sinful she thinks you are for a week now. I'd watch my back if I were you, Lee." His voice turns wistful. "I already miss Jack. He was good to me. I don't know anywhere else that would have given me the trust and responsibility Jack did."

Even though I desperately want to, I have no way to bring up Beth. I need to focus on the purpose of my call, yet all Southern conversations must include an unnecessarily detailed level of small talk.

"I'm glad he took care of you," I say.

"So, what have you been up to?" He asks. "I missed your stunt at the funeral. They had the pallbearers getting organized behind the curtain in the sanctuary. Other than that, anyone else you've spit on? You always were a handful here. Remember the time you took the horse in the lake? I thought Jack was going to tan your hide."

"Yeah, well, let's not reminisce, shall we?"

"Well, I—" He suddenly goes silent as if someone had entered his office. "I guess maybe that's a conversation for another day. How can I help you? Care to donate some of your ill-gotten attorney fees?"

He can still make me laugh. "No, Morris. No money today. But the last time we saw each other, you told me to let you know if I ever met anyone that might be a good addition to your staff."

I look at Nikki and Angus, then continue.

"Last week, I met a couple trying to move to the area and wondered if you had any openings."

"We have several right now. Do they have any group home experience? Or office experience?"

"Their last name is Williams—Mark and Mindy. They're just a pleasant couple in their thirties. They're looking to move to the area but want to find jobs first. I'll give them your number if that's okay. The man may have some farm or ranch experience, and she has been an administrative assistant. We didn't talk religion at all."

"Yeah, have them call me, and we'll see what happens. I appreciate you thinking of us stuck way out here. It's hard to find good people." His boots slam to the floor. "Sorry, but I've got to let you go. Thanks for the help."

Cutting the call, I look to the investigators. "Well, looks like you're in."

12

—————

After Angus and Nikki leave, my grandfather takes Beth's journals and heads for Sullivan's Island to read them all. Clarice stands in the office doorway, her arms crossed over her chest, one foot tapping against the floor. She has a look I can't identify between disgust and curiosity.

"What's up?" I shove away the file I am working on.

She points at the telephone on my desk. "You need to take this one."

The desk phone line blinks red with a caller on hold.

Her hands clench, then rest on her hips as her voice fills with sarcasm and a fake British accent. "It's the mighty right and not-so-honorable Solicitor, Mr. Clint Harbin. The one who threw Beth from his office?"

"He's still our Solicitor. Be respectful. Wait—why is he calling me?"

She shakes her head. "I don't know. I'll need to catch you up on the gossip once you finish, though."

Before punching the speaker's button so Clarice can listen, a cautionary twinge makes me set the phone to record.

"M. L. Danforth." Out of habit, I reach for a pad and pen, then shove it away. I'm recording and need to focus on Harbin.

"Hello, M.L. It's Clint Harbin."

Clint's Southern drawl stretches each word to its most extended possible length. The older he gets, the more distinctive his vernacular. Few people know he isn't from Charleston but is a transplant, the same as me. His parents divorced before his father became Solicitor, and Clint grew up with his mother in Rock Hill in the northern part of the state. After law school, he moved back to Charleston. Clint and I work on the same bar association committees and other charitable or social events, but we'd had no cases together. He is entirely criminal law, and I am civil—different worlds.

"Well, I'm not used to having calls from the distinguished Solicitor. How may I help you today?" Clarice rolls her eyes at my attempt at an easygoing manner.

A lighter snaps, air sucks in, then a long puff is all I hear for fifteen seconds. Harbin is notorious for his cigars, and I am glad we aren't in the same room. His tone is friendly, nothing different from all the years I've known him.

"Well, I'm not sure. Today, I got a call from a particular lady who insists you were inappropriate at a funeral service. Does any of this ring a bell?"

Clarice's face screws into a grimace. I stay silent, waiting to see the direction of the conversation. He wouldn't give me a courtesy call in advance if he plans to charge me or go before a grand jury.

A door slams on Clint's side of the conversation, and I can envision him sitting behind his mahogany desk, his feet kicked up on the corner as he leans backward in the cracked leather desk chair.

Are we having a prosecutor/defendant conversation regarding my spitting on Jack's body? If so, I need to shut him down as fast as he had Beth. Otherwise, I need a lawyer and fast.

Of course, my grandfather is always on speed dial.

"What are the allegations?"

"We're just having a friendly chat, M.L."

Every red flag in my body goes on alert. In the South, a friendly chat can mean anything from a verbal dressing down to an all-out war.

He continues. "There are no allegations at this point, at least from my office." Clint's chair creaks through the phone. "Did you or did you not spit on Jack's body?"

"If there are no allegations, there is no case. So why the questions?"

"I hate when people get testy with me when I'm trying to help them. M. L., Victoria Marshall wants me to do something. As you may or may not know, given your current practice in real estate, under the South Carolina Code, Section 16-17-600, and I quote: Subsection (a) *It is unlawful for a person willfully and knowingly, and without proper legal authority to: (3) desecrate human remains.* There are other parts, but they have nothing to do with our conversation. But there is the penalty section that says, and I quote: *A person violating the provisions of subsection (A) is guilty of a felony and, upon conviction, must be fined not more than five thousand dollars or imprisoned not less than one year nor more than ten years, or both.*"

I bite the insides of my cheeks to keep back a retort. But that doesn't stop the wiggle of fear that runs down my back. While jail time won't be pleasant, more importantly, I will lose my law license.

I respond as if am too busy to give this any time or consideration. "And what does this have to do with me?"

"If I take this before a grand jury, you fit the elements, and they'll be bound to issue the indictment. Help me out here."

I can't respond. This is far out of my comfort zone.

Harbin keeps talking, trying to get me to say anything. "She alleges you said ugly words and then spit on Jack's face. The family is most definitely offended and outraged, fulfilling the statutory requirements. They're pushing me to prosecute."

"They are contending I desecrated a body. With spit. You have a witness who will go on record to prove the actual desecration?"

"Not at this point. The woman insists she can round up ten witnesses of her friends and family members."

Clint most likely wants fodder for gossip, not a grand jury indictment. If I am really a possible defendant, we would not be having this conversation.

"They will say whatever she wants them to say. This is a pissing contest, Clint. Is there anything else you want to tell me? Like, what's really going on here?"

I keep my voice light and friendly as if we are two attorneys discussing a hypothetical case over a hypothetical beer at Buddy's, who, by the way, doesn't hold a hypothetical beer and wine license.

I keep going. "Anyone video this event?"

He takes another draw from his cigar. "Not to my knowledge, but that could change after we talk to the witnesses."

"And do you intend to do that?"

"Well, that depends, counselor, on what you tell me your answer is." Clarice has rounded my desk and is tapping on my keyboard. She points to the website she's pulled up on my over-sized second monitor.

"Clint, we've known each other for years since I graduated from law school." Harbin doesn't respond, so I continue. "I think my reputation in the community speaks for itself. You would look mighty silly next year when you run for re-election having to account for all the tax dollars you wasted on trying to prosecute something like this."

"I think my constituents know that I only send cases to the grand jury when I know they are truly worthy of prosecution."

"You think you can win this? Who do you think you're talking to?"

Clarice grips my shoulder and fiercely taps the computer screen. The statute that defines "desecration" is staring at me. I grin at her. She is always one step ahead.

I don't throttle my tone. Even though I am playing with fire, I let the contempt roll. The unwritten rules of Charleston require an attorney to not test the mettle of the local circuit solicitor. Well, to hell with that.

"Let me tell you how our state defines desecration since you read me the statute like I am a first-year law student. 'To desecrate is to treat a *sacred* place or thing with *violent* disrespect.' From my understanding of the facts and this definition, you can't prove your case. Do you have any proof the church building or anything sacred was affected? Or are you alleging that Jack Marshall was a sacred person? Come on, Clint, you'll send something like this up?"

"Whoa, missy. Don't get your dander up."

I sigh with exasperation. "Clint, I'm busy. Get to the point."

On his side, the lighter snaps once again. "Well, he was one of the most revered members of our community."

"That member of our community is not a sacred space or thing. Trust me, I know." While I have him on the phone, I want to push him a bit. I am dying to know what he knows about Brad, but I don't dare tip my hand. So I push. "Did you even investigate his death?"

"That's not this conversation."

"Have you looked into the death of Jack Marshall or not, Clint?"

"Cases of this office are not something I can discuss."

His officious tone makes me almost hang up on him. I stare across the room at the photo of my grandfather, always a sure fix to stop me from doing anything in the legal world I shouldn't.

"Look, Clint. I'm not admitting to anything. It's your burden of proof. You've already tipped your case by talking to me. I have better things to do, like the case file in front of me."

I almost toss out a statutory rape threat of my own. "Let's just say I have no comment. If the lady wants to accuse me of something, let her go right ahead and throw that first stone. There's been a lot of accusations in her part of the county. But I'll tell you, she and you might not like the ballistic missile fired in return."

I hope he hears me. He should, with Jack murdered and Beth raped. Harbin's inaction has a lot to account for. He responds. "What are the allegations on your end?"

I parroted his words back to him. "Cases of this office are not something I can discuss."

"Understood. I'll pass that comment along."

"Thanks, Clint. Been good talking to you."

I slam the receiver and lean back in my leather ergonomic office chair, cocking my own feet on the corner of my glass and steel desk as I scroll through the South Carolina criminal code section Clint cited.

Clarice steps back into the office with fresh cups of coffee. "Well, bless his heart. You were so loud I could hear your final salvo from the kitchen."

I point to the screen and look at her. "Damn. Spitting on Jack carries one to ten years if I'm found guilty. I thought maybe he'd made that up." I drop my feet to the floor and take the cup from Clarice. "But, like I said, he's got to prove it."

"You know what?" Clarice says, "Harbin wouldn't dare do anything like this if the Judge was still on the bench."

I mimic my grandfather's speech. "You are most likely correct, madam, but this Judge has retired, and in retirement, we shall let him remain."

"Well," Clarice leans back in the guest chair, a sly grin crossing her face. "It looks like we need to get moving faster. I sure would hate to see you in orange. I don't think that's a suitable color for you."

13

The following day, I am deep into the legal research needed to shove a square cause of action into a round body of case law. South Carolina passed a trafficking law in 2012 covering labor, sex, and other types of forced services. I know what happened to me at that farm, and every cell in my body shouted that those events were nothing compared to what was happening now, both with Beth and the other children and teenagers.

Clarice strolls into my office in her long green tulle skirt that floats about her like a ballet diva. Given that I need a break, I point to the couch along the wall. Grabbing us both a fresh coffee, I sit at the other end of the sofa and ease my feet out of my too-tight shoes as I scrutinize my friend.

It always amazes me how beautiful she is. Her skin has aged little even through two rambunctious, now grown, boys and the stress of being married to a power company lineman. Brooks was always close to danger. Now, however, he is retired and drives her to distraction, always needing something to do. Older than me, she is a role model, not just a friend. But today, something is eating at her.

"Don't be angry with Harbin," I say. "You know he won't send me before the grand jury. It's too small-time."

Clarice twists her mouth to one side, a habit when uncomfortable with something. She changes the subject. "I don't understand what's happening in the East End," she says, referring to a Black neighborhood in the northern end of town where her sister Darlene lives. "Harbin ignores what's happening there. It's not his neighborhood, so he doesn't care."

"What does Darlene say is happening? Clue me in here. I'm lost."

"Most of Harbin's 'clients,' as you called them on the phone, aren't from your world. They're from mine and Darlene's. And they aren't his clients." She uses air quotes around the last word. "They are the defendants charged by the police and prosecuted by his office." Clarice's eyes smolder with something akin to hatred. I lean toward her and take her hand. "Have I done something?"

"No," she continues. "It's just that this city has a long history of not dealing with its past. He's part of that problem, and it's time that changed."

Clarice pulled a sheet of paper from her gray sweater pocket. "I started this list for myself, thinking that my suspicions of Harbin were all in my head or just gripes of my neighborhood circle."

She reaches over and hands me the list. "But I was wrong. So very wrong. Charleston has a problem, and we—you and me—can no longer ignore it."

I take the piece of paper from her. "What is this list?"

"This is a list of all the people I personally know the Harbins, both Senior and Junior, have wronged. The longer it got, the angrier I got. After listening to his call to you where he treated you like a dang law student, I can't sit by any longer."

I pick up the paper and read it aloud. "Annie Lee Long. Age fourteen."

"Here," she says, reaching for the list. "Let me read it; otherwise, we'll be here all day." I hand the list back to her. "Annie Lee was the fourteen-year-old daughter of the secretary employed by Senior. She was raped in 1995 by Senior. Junior was in college, and he—

"Yes, I know," I interrupt. "He and Jack Marshall were roommates."

She cuts her eyes to the garden window, and I shudder. This is the second time this week *we* are discussing the word rape.

She continues, "Mr. Benson Ragsdale. Ran a roadhouse on Highway 17 near Ravenel. He was my grandfather. In 2000, he stopped a fight between a white man and a Black man and ran everybody out. The next day, the place burned to the ground. Glass bottles full of gasoline and lit rags were thrown through the windows in broad daylight. Senior was the Solicitor then; John Parsons was the Sheriff. There was no investigation, no prosecution, nothing. My granddaddy lost everything."

She lowers the paper to her lap, her eyes wet with tears. She takes a breath and continues for ten minutes, listing infractions, oversights, and injustices caused or overlooked by Clint Harbin or his father. A few incidents were things I vaguely remembered. Most were not.

The latest was her point—a string of missing girls from East End. Done, she looks at me, her face open, pleading. "This must stop. This isn't just a Beth problem. Someone's taking a lot of girls from the East End. After what Beth told us, I think this is connected to Timberline Farm. They're taking girls from the entire county, and Harbin is playing stupid."

Clarice blows out a large breath. She places both hands on the arms of the chair and then returns them to her lap in frustration. I start to speak, but she stops me.

"Look, I need to say something first. I've tried to do what I could about some of these things. But I've run repeatedly up against the wall of indifference. I need your help. But more than that, I need you to *see*. See what's happening around you. See what's happening in the community—including the Black community. Can you do that?"

"Yes." It is the least I can do for her. "I will do my best."

"Let me get organized with what I have," Clarice says as she gets to her feet, "and then you can tell me how it fits into your research."

Clarice and I meet at the end of the day, as is our habit. She is at the end of the couch, me in the overstuffed chair opposite, and my bare feet propped on the side table.

I speak first. "We've never had something like this come between us. Every time there's been a problem, we've tackled it head-on. Don't think I don't see you. I do and always have. Don't let there be an issue between us."

"I want to get something out of the way first," Clarice says. "Truth be told, I've heard stories of you and Jack for years. I expected that you'd tell me if you wanted me to know. But after over a dozen years, I wondered if you didn't trust me. Do you?"

"Clarice, you're like my sister. No, that's wrong. It's more than that. You are my best friend. I trust you with my life. It's just that with Jack..." I look away. "It's too damned embarrassing, that's all. One day, I'll tell you all the details, but not today."

Tears well in her eyes. "And you are the same to me. Our lives are different because of each other. But we need to do better at talking with each other." She leans forward, her elbows on her knees and a wistful look on her face.

I copy her position. "We will."

She leans back on the couch and smiles. "New rule. No more silence for us."

"Agree. Now, about East End?"

"Black girls have gone missing increasingly for the past few years. Girls run off, but that is not what this is. There are too many now. The most vulnerable ones get snatched first, but mostly in North Charleston. Until Darlene pointed it out to me, I hadn't realized the problem since I live downtown and not in the north where she lives. Over the last year, whoever oversees whatever this is has upped their game. Travis and Janelle's girl, Emily, was almost taken right off East Bay two weeks ago as she got into her car. That's what got my attention."

Tourists frequent the East Bay Street businesses in downtown Charleston the most. The district's "riffraff," as one of the prior police chiefs called them, were told to stay away from the tourist areas. To grab a girl there during business hours is a breach of too many unwritten rules and a few written ones. Whoever is taking the girls is under pressure, causing them to make mistakes.

"So you think these disappearances are related to the trafficking at the farm?" I ask.

"I'm not sure," Clarice responds, "but even if they aren't, we can't let Harbin get away with this. To me, it shows he isn't doing his job. It will be more ammunition if you have to contact the AG."

I write the girl's name on my pad to follow up.

"Why do you think they picked Emily?" I ask.

"Last year, she was on the homecoming court. She's a beautiful girl. I'm assuming that she would bring a higher price for whatever God-awful things they are doing with those girls."

"If trafficking is what this is," I reply. "We have to realize this might be a standard abduction for rape or murder, so let's back up. No assumptions. What months have girls gone missing?"

She pulls out a notepad. "Years, you mean. For the past five years, there have been fourteen Black girls missing and one white girl."

She was right. Fifteen girls are a definite cause for concern.

I made a note. "What did the investigations turn up?"

I look up as Clarice lets out a sarcastic laugh.

"My, you are naïve. What investigations?"

I can't hide my surprise. "No investigation at all? Not even for the one white girl?"

"Yes, that is what I'm telling you." She hands me her list. "Here are the names of the girls and the dates they went missing."

"Good. We'll need that information. I need to bounce a few ideas off the Judge about how we can best use this. Did the parents file missing persons' reports?"

"Every blessed one. The police did not search for any of these girls, no matter how much the parents hounded. And yes, I have those reports."

"*The Times* run stories?"

"Buried. One or two minor stories and no follow-up. I have clippings or screen prints in the file. There are only a few places that publicize missing Black girls. A California-based website called '*Our Black Girls*' lists them. There needs to be more people to pull their heads out of the sand and do something."

"I feel like a racist."

"That's not what this is about, Lee. I don't see you that way, so don't look at yourself like that. These blind spots are systemic, you're white, so you have the privilege not to see them. But now you do; where you take it from here is what determines the person you are."

Before either of us can continue, Clarice's cell phone rings in the other room. After finishing her conversation, she returns with an open bottle of wine from the fridge.

"That man," she laughs. "He thinks I can't remember that he plays cards every Thursday night?"

She holds up her glass in salute, and I do the same. I place my glass on the table and inspect my reading glasses while pulling the square from my dress pocket to clean the lenses. For some reason, this little habit helps me think.

"What one thing connects East End with Timberline Farm?" I ask, placing the glasses back on my head. "I don't see any real connection here."

Clarice leans back on the couch and crosses her legs. "Two of my church members work at Magnolia House, where Beth now lives. Their residents are girls leaving Timberline Farm, other girls leaving the state system, and women released from the county jail who need to get their lives straight before they try to start again."

"A decent place?"

"It is. Clean, colorful, and supported by the community, Magnolia House was greatly needed. Victoria Marshall is a large moral supporter but gives no money. The Magnolia House ladies have heard rumors from the Timberline girls for a while. The genuine fear ramped up close to two years ago."

"What kind of fear? What was happening?"

"The girls from Timberline Farm are paranoid to an extreme. Several refuse to talk inside the house, swearing the house is bugged. The ladies at Magnolia found a security office to sweep the place after the fifth girl refused to talk. They had the Timberline girls follow the process, hoping it would gain their trust."

"Anything found?"

"Nothing. It relieved the girls staying there somewhat, but not completely. When the women who live there, especially the former Timberline Farm residents, want to discuss anything important, they go to the backyard and turn on the radio. They still believe someone is listening to them in the house."

I take a sip of wine. "Beth said Brad Marshall had started running the home two years ago."

Talking about that place makes me cringe.

"So, according to Beth," I continue thinking aloud, "Jack was out raising money and rarely at the farm. Where was Victoria?"

"Other than public relations for their Christian school and checking in on the girls and boys facilities, she's been setting up her center in North Charleston."

"Christian school? Seriously? Does she teach? And what center?"

"Where have you been? Victoria has an outreach program in North Charleston, Timberline Community Center, and their

Christian school is located in one of the rehabilitated furniture stores downtown on the peninsula. Dani has been involved at the center. It's close to Darlene's neighborhood."

Every nerve in my body stands at attention.

Clarice continues. "She's used the community center at East End to get middle and high school girls focused on success whether they go to college or decide on a career after high school. Victoria helped Dani with college applications. That's when everything changed. Dani's excited about a trip to New York. I think Victoria Marshall set that up as well."

"What does Glenna think about New York?"

She and Dani have been joined at the hip since kindergarten.

"Glenna has said nothing to me, but I'm sure she's not happy since they planned to attend the same school. The last time we talked, NYU was not on Glenna's recruitment list."

I lean back and close my eyes, my brain digging as I return to my time at the Timberline Farm. After a few gut-twisting minutes, I open my eyes to Clarice's worried face.

Dani needs to stay away from that woman.

"I think you need to talk with Dani," I tell Clarice. "She needs to stay away from the farm and Victoria."

"You've said that," she replies, "but haven't told me why. Dani's too headstrong. Why don't you talk to her? She'll listen to you more than me."

"Probably. I'll get her to meet me for lunch. Add my two cents into her college selection list as an excuse."

Clarice's shoulders sag. "If something happens to that girl—"

"Don't, Clarice. You're borrowing trouble."

14

As Victoria studied the idiot her son called "Breaker," she drummed her fingernails on the table to calm her raging nerves. Without telling anyone, the idiot had snatched a girl off the street—one of hers. The man sat in her grandmother's antique Chippendale chair with one muddy boot atop the opposite knee, and the chair kicked back on two legs. His body dwarfed the delicate chair.

She kept her voice low and controlled as she bent to speak in his ear. "If you break that chair like you broke that girl, you'll have me to answer to."

He slammed the chair to all four legs and removed the dirty green John Deere cap, scrubbing his head. She shifted away from the man, his body odor so strong it made her gag. Breaker had a severe case of eczema, and while she knew he was treating it with creams and ointments, he needed a bath.

She glared at Breaker. "Tell me, did you target Glenna or just pick her up off the street?"

He scratched under his armpit. "She was a walkin' down Rhett Avenue as pretty as you please." His eyes slid toward hers for only a second before returning to watch Brad, who was making his daily phone calls, oblivious to their conversation.

"So, you just snatched her for fun without checking with me or Brad?" she asked.

Breaker sucked the inside of his cheeks while twisting his cap around and around in his hands. At least her scowl appeared to make him nervous. She spent months cultivating the outreach program and focusing on the East End girls. No one noticed when they slowly disappeared, as each girl appeared to her family to be a success. Individually, her girls brought in a minimum of ten thousand dollars. The more talented, intelligent, and, of course, the prettier they were, only increased the price. She trained her girls to be exceptional, like Glenna, the athlete, or Dani, the brain.

And now Glenna had been taken out of her control by Breaker, used for himself, and then beaten for fun. This man's recklessness had set her back, and he would pay. While Glenna was a girl she coveted for her system, it was Dani she would need to watch carefully going forward. That girl was too valuable to lose.

It would be weeks before Glenna would be in any condition to be auctioned, even with her runner's body. Formerly in perfect shape, she was now black and blue. Victoria did not want to sell the girl at a discount overseas. She would find an American client once the girl recuperated, hiding her until then. Since her friends and family would miss this girl; damage control was imperative.

Victoria had come too far with the auctions she had put so much time and effort into. She pulled up the photos she had snapped while the runner was asleep in the basement of House One. She compared the photo to the marks on Breaker's face. The girl was a fighter, a survivor. That meant trouble when not appropriately controlled.

Breaker's sausage fingers pawed at the weeping blisters on his skin. He swept his hand over his stubbled head, and she held back a gag as his smile revealed the gold front tooth he prided himself on, along with the rest of his cigarette-stained teeth and the hole created by a missing incisor.

This man had to go.

"That isn't going to happen." Brad's reply into the phone was testy. "We can deliver, but not on that timeline."

She assumed it was Theron Fish on the phone. Fish's contract rate only gave Brad a few thousand a head at best, for initially any girl. But now, the weasel of a man had become too picky. Brad was forced each month to cast a more expansive net. He raked his free hand through his hair as she rested her hand on his shoulder. He relaxed. She still had the touch to make a man do what she wanted. It was too bad that Jack had been immune after the first year.

Watching her son, Victoria was determined to separate them from Fish. Besides, her girls brought in a much higher profit. They no longer needed Fish's money—and the significant risk— even though Theron Fish was an impatient little ferret who could bite.

"You want how many?" Brad sat upright in his chair, suddenly staring at her, the phone pressed to his ear.

An increase in girls would break the routine—a problem in a small town. She wondered how much of a jump in numbers the man wanted. Brad leaned forward, placing both elbows on his desk. He closed his eyes and shook his head.

"Fish, man, this creates a big red flag that could raise attention here. It will wipe out—"

Victoria couldn't hear the other voice but was sure the man had given Brad an ultimatum: Either produce the number of girls he wanted or the man would take revenge.

When the call finished, Brad tossed his cell phone into the inbox on his desk and scowled at her.

"First, he expected us to provide fifteen girls a month; now, he's upped again and wants five a week. Every week. There is no way we can snatch that many. Too many eyes and ears here. And once that many go missing in a town of this size? Charleston may have grown, but it's still a small town. There is no way I can hide that. The man is crazy."

Brad wiped both hands down his face. Breaker leaned forward to jump into the conversation, uninvited as usual, and Victoria bit her tongue to stop herself from chastising him again. He technically was Brad's employee, not hers. She stayed away from facility employees and concentrated on her girls. However, this man was about to make her cross the line if Brad could not get him under control.

"We need to branch out into other towns." Breaker flipped his hand at Brad, unconcerned. "Make a run or two up around Georgetown. It's not that big a deal."

"Going north is ok, but Georgia's Theron's," Brad replied. "Stay away from that side of the state."

"Brad, when does Theron Fish's contract end?" Victoria asked.

"What contract?" Brad let out a laugh. "We are so far beyond that now. He'll never let us out. Never."

There was no way around it now. Victoria would have to phase out this portion of the business herself. It was too rough and way too risky. She didn't believe Fish had the balls to kill either of them because they wanted out, but she couldn't take that chance. She looked at first one man, then the other. Neither would dare eliminate Theron Fish. It had to be her.

Brad looked at Breaker. "Go poach other towns."

He leaned back in his chair, and Victoria wanted to make sure that idiot, Breaker, knew the risk of snatching another of her girls. She pointed her finger at the man.

"Head north and stay remote," she said. "If you pick up another girl in North Charleston, I'll take care of you myself. Monck's Corner and Summerville might work if you only take one or two far enough apart in time. Mt. Pleasant, Sullivan's Island, and Kiawah Island are off-limits. Too many rich white people in those areas. Maybe McClellanville. Or Orangeburg. Go to the North Carolina line if you have to, but damn it, stay away from North Charleston."

Brad refused to meet her gaze, staring at the wall across the room.

Breaker's eyes reduced to a squint as he glared at her. "Why don't you let me run this end? You don't want to know, anyway." He looked to Brad, as usual, for confirmation.

"Just do what she says, Breaker."

"I know what I'm doing," Breaker muttered. "I don't see ya'll out there gettin' these girls." He grabbed his green ball cap as he stood, slapping it against his leg. He headed out the door, scratching both arms through his shirt sleeves.

"Breaker!" Victoria shouted after him.

He turned and gave her a mock salute. "Absolutely. Yeah. No North Charleston girls. All under control."

Given the girl's condition in the basement, Victoria knew that nothing Breaker did was under control.

15

___

Glenna shivered in the dark, the scraps of her clothing draped haphazardly around her shoulders in a futile attempt to keep warm. With her back against the wall, she willed the room to stop spinning. She could only breathe through one open nostril, overwhelmed by the smell of mold and decay.

Her fingers touched the damp wall, and she recoiled as tiny toenails on concrete scurried around her and something furry brushed her leg. But it wasn't the room or its creatures that made her shiver, but the lingering odor of the monster who had grabbed her right off the street. Glenna took a long breath to slow her heart rate and stop the rising panic.

She would survive this.

Her abduction had taken only seconds. The van had rolled up on the sidewalk next to her, and two strong arms grabbed her around the waist, snatching her butt-first into the vehicle, a black bag wrenched over her head, and doors ramming shut behind her. With one more second's notice, she'd have run.

And they would never have caught her.

The man who smelled so terrible had, within seconds after

the van was underway, handcuffed her to rails that were welded onto the van wall, ripped off her shirt, yanked the jeans down her legs, cut off her underwear, and raped her. His taunts to her as he slammed into her over and over were joined by laughter from the driver at her angry retorts, only adding fuel to his fire. She fought him like a wildcat. Her fingernails broken from defensive moves had only served to make him more enraged, and after he had finished, he had beaten her unconscious.

Now in the dank room, disoriented, with pain radiating over her entire body but mostly between her legs, she realized he had raped her again while unconscious. She was covered in a sticky substance, and when she touched herself and then brought her fingers up to her face in the dark, she smelled the tang of blood and his rank semen. Vomit ejected with force, and on all fours, she heaved until she thought she would turn herself inside out. The shivers took over, and she sank back against the wall, the chains limiting her movement. As the bile rose again up her throat, Glenna lurched in a different direction to avoid putting her hands into the prior vomit. She didn't make it.

She needed to stop thinking of what he'd done, or the fear would never let her leave this place. She had learned from her mistake. To live, she had to comply. Her instinct was to fight back or run if given the chance. Glenna pictured the track at school, the circle she had run so many times for so many days. What she would give to see that orange surface one more time.

The chains attached to the heavy steel cuffs on her wrists clinked on the concrete floor. She gingerly reached to touch her nose and winced. Blood trickled down to her chin. While her nose seemed to be the only thing broken, the skin on her wrists was ripped from the cuffs.

Glenna leaned against the wall as the darkness threatened to take her under. Her head throbbed with what was probably a concussion. She took long, slow breaths to stay awake, shivering from the fear and the cold. But she would not cry. She had learned long ago to block out the pain from running and the resulting cramps and injuries. If she cried, she would give up breathing through her nose entirely once the other side was blocked, and to run, she needed to be able to breathe. Frustrated, she let out a blood-curdling scream.

"Won't do you no good." The male voice came from a few feet away. He snorted a laugh. "No one can hear you." She heard the rattle of keys as his feet shuffled closer to her. She could picture herself like an animal locked in a cage.

Him. That was why she could still smell him. Tremors engulfed her entire body. She rocked slightly back and forth, trying to calm herself, waiting for the sick monster to do whatever he wanted. She tensed, ready to use her feet to lash out.

He breathed and scratched in the dark.

She waited as the minutes dragged until his muffled laughter echoed from further away. Glenna waited, her body quaking in the silence. Then, with the shuffle of feet, the rattle of keys, and a slammed door, he was gone.

There had to be a way to escape. She needed to be prepared next time if he came into the room. Keys would be a significant weapon if she could grab them. So could a flashlight. Maybe he would bring one next time.

Carefully feeling around her wrists, she checked the gap between her arm and the cuff. Her legs were free. If she tried hard enough, she could use her feet to hold the cuffs and pull her hands through them. It might leave her thumbs dislocated, but it was a chance she was willing to take.

There was no light from any direction to give her a sense of time. She waited—with the damn scurrying noises—for the man to return. Suddenly, something furry brushed against her cheek, and a warm body landed on her head. Glenna violently shook her head and flailed her arms. Tiny feet pushed off the top of her head, dropping to her shoulder and down her arm. Glenna's screech echoed in the room, as much from the biting pain as her body inadvertently jerked from the rat as from her terror. Panting, she waited, praying nothing else would scamper over her in the dark, crawl up her bare leg, or, God forbid, bite her.

A rattling noise echoed down the hall sometime later, and she scooted as far from the door as the chains would allow. It was a different man, a plate in his hand that he wordlessly thrust at her, his cell phone flashlight blinding her so she could not see his face.

She didn't move.

"God, you stink. Don't know what Breaker was thinking when he took you."

When the light shifted, she saw it was the van driver with the same filthy orange baseball hat. He thrust the plate toward her again. She kicked at the man's knee but hit the plate. It clattered to the floor, and the smell of turnip greens wafted around her.

"Now you'll have to eat it off the floor with that upchuck. Be sure that floor's clean, or else you'll pay for it."

Glenna refused to look at the man. In the phone's light, she took in her surroundings. It was a simple basement storage room —the size of her bedroom at home—a concrete cell with an iron-barred door. There was nothing scary, nothing going to hurt her —except the man standing in front of her and the other monster who had put her here in the first place.

When she didn't respond, he leaned down and grabbed her face. With his face inches from hers, his feet trapped her legs so she couldn't kick at him again. She held her breath at the odor of rancid garlic, cigarettes, and whiskey. Glenna shifted her eyes to the cell phone in his other hand. It was too far for her to reach in the chains. She struggled to pull her face from his hand.

"Look, if you do what the man says, you'll live and maybe grow to enjoy what will happen to you. If you don't, he'll make you wish you had."

Glenna refused to answer and closed her eyes. Finally, as he released her, she struck, her foot aimed for his crotch, but she missed.

"Need to work on your aim there, girly," he said, then laughed.

Van Driver shuffled out of the room, slamming the iron door behind him, the lock slamming into place with a loud clank. She watched the phone's flashlight bounce down the hall until it disappeared out the door at the end of the hall. The door slammed shut, and then the key twisted in the lock.

She needed a better plan.

16

———

"Glad you could meet me for lunch. I want to hear about New York."

Dani and I are at the Pickled Palate, my favorite restaurant in the Charleston area. It is in Mt. Pleasant, a shack with a comfortable garden shaded by oak trees and umbrellas, a place my mother would have loved. It has the best pimento cheese sandwiches in the South.

"I'm so excited, I can't tell you." She points to her deep-purple NYU t-shirt. "It's a dream come true for me. I can't wait to start."

Even though Clarice warned me Dani was set on NYU, I am surprised she is considering a school without Glenna. The girls planned to room together in college the entire time I've known them.

"NYU really where you want to go? It's a long way from Charleston."

"Oh yes. I'm into augmented reality and artificial intelligence. MIT or Stanford might have better programs, but New York is the *City*, you know?" Her grin is infectious.

"You received your acceptance letter? Get a scholarship?" I ask, even though I know the answer is "no." Clarice would have shouted it across Charleston if Dani had received any scholarship. Since I supported every dance team, ball club, and car wash fund-raiser in which Dani had participated, there is no way I wouldn't have known something like this. Dani took a bite of her sandwich. She was a ball of energy, constantly looking at her phone, admiring her new nails, and touching up her makeup.

"They haven't sent out that information yet," she said, "but there's no doubt I'll get accepted."

This girl needs a reality check. For most students, gaining admission to NYU is challenging. But more than that, Victoria Marshall is involved, which means Dani is in for a big disappointment. I can feel it in my gut.

"I guess it's good to be confident," I say, hesitating to mention Victoria's name.

"Well, Mrs. Marshall has assured me that everything's in place. We're just waiting for the official date for NYU to send the notices."

Warning bells go off in my head, along with the standard twinge from my gut. Going to NYU will be great for Dani, but what purpose does that serve Victoria? At this point, I don't know.

"Where else did you apply?" I ask. "Any responses from those?"

"Mrs. Marshall said I just needed to apply to NYU." Dani's reply is nonchalant. A mental picture of Dani getting a declining letter from NYU and Victoria rushing in with whatever scheme she has cooked up causes a wave of panic so sharp I almost drop my sandwich. Casual, I force myself to eat some bread and butter pickles as the waitress stops by to refill our drinks. I take a swig of tea so sweet it makes my teeth hurt, waiting for the waitress to leave.

"How did you meet Victoria?"

She looks down at her plate, her fingers fiddling with a french fry. Then, she watches a butterfly alight on the flower of a purple bottle brush plant. I wait her out, finally lifting my eyebrows for an answer to my question.

"She has an outreach program close to our house and is there every week, meeting with anyone who wants to work on college applications or needs help with jobs."

My trepidation increases as I watch a group of kindergarteners pass by.

"I worked for the Marshalls when I was your age. I was their office assistant for four years."

Dani leans forward, suddenly very interested. "Oh man, I bet that was fun. Mrs. Marshall told me you were friends."

Friends. What garbage had Victoria told Dani about me? Her statement hangs as I listen to the chatter of the long line of children, then choke down another bite of my sandwich while I count to ten in my head. Dani checks her phone for the thousandth time, typing a response and setting it back down.

I can't just act like nothing is wrong with Victoria railroading Dani's life.

"Dani, did Victoria guarantee you entry into NYU?"

"She called some contact just after I applied. With my grades and my SAT scores, she said I'm a shoo-in. It sounded like they want me."

"But you didn't talk with anyone from NYU directly?" I ask.

Her eyes slide to the left as she responds. "Well...no."

I force myself to take another drink of tea.

"Clarice told me you have a straight four-point. Congratulations." I pin her with my gaze. Ever heard the expression that if 'something sounds too good to be true, then it probably is?'"

"But it's Mrs. Marshall. She wouldn't lie."

I have to change the subject before I lose my cool. "I haven't seen Glenna lately. I wasn't in the last time you guys stopped by the office. How is she? Still running track?"

Has Victoria promised Glenna a scholarship as well?

"Oh yeah, she just won the last invitational." Dani's response is enthusiastic. "She has some study group this afternoon that's going to last a while, otherwise you know I'd be dragging her here with me."

"So, where is she going to college?"

Dani is wistful as she picks at a torn place on her phone's cover.

"She hopes Notre Dame so we won't be so far apart, but Alabama will win. They've been recruiting her hard for months."

"You two seem to have it wrapped up. Victoria helping her, too?"

"Oh no, six schools scouted Glenna. Plus, she doesn't know Mrs. Marshall as well as I do." She pops a fry into her mouth. "I'm confident I'm going to New York. And if I don't, I'll take a gap year, be an assistant to Mrs. Marshall, and try again next year."

Here we go. I know what being Victoria's assistant means.

"Have you ever considered starting a year here and getting ahead? I did that before I went to college."

"Mrs. Marshall says she can line up a job for me with one of her friends, some CEO or something up there. He's been looking for an assistant, so I'm good. I don't think I want to go somewhere else and then transfer. I want to be in New York."

A job with one of Victoria's friends? That woman collects men for the sole purpose of getting their money. She has no friends. My brain hurts with the possibilities. Whatever Victoria is doing is more than cages in a basement.

I push at Dani again. "What type of job would it be? CEOs rarely hire without a college degree and a decent level of experience. Did she tell you what company? Maybe it's someone I know from when I worked there."

"No, she didn't tell me." Her eyes shift to the left again, then down to an errant thumb cuticle.

Why is Dani lying to me? It is all I can do to keep from growling in anger. Victoria is attempting to suck this girl into something, and I will not let that happen.

Dani blinks at me several times, then drops her arms and leans forward.

"What's happening here?" she asks. "You're never like this."

My jaws clench so hard that I may crack one of my teeth.

"Tell me the details of this job," I say quietly. "I need to know what she's up to."

"Okay." Dani begins to mumble. "Well..." She hesitates, then picks up her phone. I rest my hand on hers, then slide the phone across the table out of her reach. I lean forward, shifting into lawyer mode.

"Dani, tell me exactly about the job she offered you."

She picks at her fingernail. "She said she has an impressive track record of getting good jobs for her assistants. She trains them in high school and places them with excellent companies even before graduation."

"What types of jobs?"

"She's never told me. It depends on the available positions, and I haven't applied for anything yet. We decided to wait on NYU first."

"You haven't interviewed?"

"No. Just with her to help her at the Timberline Farm office. They're behind on technology. She wants me to set up something for her, but she didn't explain."

"Has she asked you to help with donors? Certain men, maybe?"

"No, not at all. What's happening here?"

"The job she offered you is some scam. You need to run—fast and far away."

Her body relaxes. "So that's why she told me not to tell you." A smirk crosses her face.

I lean forward, my hands flat on the table, not caring if my voice is too loud.

"Enough with the games, Dani." I never talk to her this way, and shock crosses the girl's face.

"I'm not playing any games. She knew Aunt Clarice worked for you and said you weren't her biggest fan. Told me you wouldn't have anything nice to say about the farm or anyone named Marshall."

"Did she tell you why?"

Dani shook her head. "No."

"She manipulates people, Dani." My voice is low enough this time that no one else can overhear. "She manipulated me for years. I worked for Jack for four years and was also her *assistant*." I made air quotes around the word. "She will force you to do things with men that make her money."

"What things?"

"Do I need to explain the word grooming? Or pimping? I'm sure there are more slang words I don't even know. You're one step away from dropping off a cliff."

Dani's mouth opens to say something, but nothing comes out. For several seconds, she sucks her cheeks in so hard she looks like a fish.

I continue. "Look, I just don't want you to get hurt. If it's not too late, you need to apply to other colleges, and don't rely on anything she tells you."

Dani shivers. "But the job working with her...it's good."

"Turn it down. If you need a job, I'll give you one. If you don't want to work with me, I'll help you find one elsewhere."

Her bubble burst, Dani lets out an enormous sigh. Her shoulders sag under the weight of reality as she squints to hold back tears. "What did she do to you?"

I shake my head. "I will not tell you that. It's too embarrassing." I feel the flush start in my chest and travel up my neck. Dani sees it, too.

"Bad things are happening at that farm. I know you don't want to give up whatever you have with Victoria at the outreach center, but from now on, I don't want you to go one step near her or Timberline Farm."

17

After finishing my morning appointments, the Timberline Farm file is open on my desk to research probable causes of action, even though I'd rather be doing anything else. I sip my fourth cup of coffee and watch the ebb and flow of tourists walking through the neighborhood. Downtown Charleston overflows with visitors now year-round. Tourism is more important to the city council than the residents' quality of life.

"Your latest client is here." Today, Clarice wears a flowing red silk caftan with a gold belt, always positive and professional. Only when Clarice wears black do I find I must stay closeted in my office, away from whomever her irritation targets.

"I got here as fast as I could." Beth's hair is in a single braid, and her side bangs are caught with glittery plastic butterfly pins. She wears the yellow and brown uniform of Buddy's Diner, several blocks over on Logan Street.

"What's the rush? Take a breath." I grab a bottle of water from the kitchen and hand it to her. "I see you got a job."

"There's another shipment." Beth pulls a long drink from the bottle. "I ran all the way here to tell you. I only have a few minutes."

I shift to lawyer mode. "Let's go to my office. I'll need you to tell me in as much detail as possible." Twisting the top of her water bottle back and forth, I see the scared child inside.

"Trish, the girl at the ranch, texted me. She's a little different, but you can trust her. The ladies at the safe house insisted I get a phone for safety, and boy, I am glad they did."

"Isn't it risky for Trish?" I can't imagine anyone from Timberline Farm buying cell phones for the kids.

"To use a hardline phone, you have to get permission. I have no idea whose cell phone she used. Ah, wait a minute." Recognition comes onto her face. "She used the house's computer. Man, I hope she wiped the history."

"Tell me about Trish, and let me see that message."

Beth hands me her phone. "Trish is a year behind me. The other kids make fun of her, because one of her arms is a little wonky. Her father broke it--actually he stepped on it--when she was a little kid, one of the reasons she was sent to the farm."

I scan the complete text, then reread it. "Do you trust her?" I squint at Beth.

"Trish may be a little weird, but she's got a big heart. She feels like it's her responsibility to take care of the little ones when they get sent to the farm." She hesitates. "Yeah, I trust Trish. She's probably one of the few kids there I do trust."

I look at the text again.

MORE GONNA GO. DON'T KNOW WHEN. MAYBE A WEEK? THEY TOOK JAN, ASHLEY, JACINDA AND BOBBY. DARLA'S NEXT, THEN ME. YOU KNOW IT. I'LL FIGHT IF THEY TRY TO TAKE ME. I'M SCARED.

I send it to myself to forward to Nikki. If it is a ruse, the person does a good job of being terrified.

"If this text is legit, Trish is taking a gigantic risk here." I look up.

Beth's eyes grow wide. "What are you typing? I shouldn't have shown you that text. Don't you dare send her a message. Trish will get in serious trouble, and if she gets beaten one more time, she won't make it through it. The last concussion made her a little off." Her body tenses. "Seriously, be careful." Her voice is anxious. "Breaker's running the house right now."

I grasp her upper arm to calm her. "I sent it to myself. Beth, we're in this together. I'm on your side, remember?" I re-read the text. "Four girls, one boy. A week?"

"Yeah, but that's never a sure thing," she replies. "I'm pretty sure this is just Trish's guess. Darla's my best friend, Ms. Danforth. You have to do something!" Her voice is shrill as she grabs my hand and squeezes hard, her knuckles white.

"Breathe." I squeeze back, standing tall and taking a breath. Beth mimics me, taking in a long, calming breath. "I can do this. I'm just scared, Miz Danforth."

"It won't help us if we can't stay calm. How do they decide which kids get picked?"

"Most of the time, it's the newest ones, and they pretend they've run. Easier that way. With a pretty girl, you can bet your a—they, um, take that one as soon as they can make up some realistic disappearing act. Right before I left, there were five girls."

"In the past years, how many?"

"Last year, I think there were three."

"Before that?"

"Seems there's two or three every year. Not a lot at one time. This time, they seem maybe like they're trying to ramp up, 'cause there's five. Now, five more."

Beth twists her bottle cap again. I place my hand on hers.

"Are they from the same family house?"

"Oh no. They are always from different houses, but mostly House One."

"How do they get away with so many missing?"

"The last time, the story was that the girls ran together."

"Do they follow through with the ruse? Call the Sheriff's office, I mean, and try to have the girls found?" Timberline is in the rural edge of the Charleston County Sheriff's jurisdiction.

"Every time. The sheriff's office doesn't do anything. A few kids are real runners. But there aren't many of those.

"The little kids are too scared to leave," she continues. "Some older ones think they're smart enough to return home, no matter how bad their parents were to them. They take off in the middle of the night. To them, being with their folks is better than taking orders from house parents who shove the Bible at them all day."

"Any come back on their own?" I ask.

"Sometimes. They will be crying and snotty, clothes ripped from the briars, scared of something in the woods. But some kids are downright mean, and nothing scares them. Those you never see again." Her words tumble out. "The mean girls go missing fast. One of Breaker's guys whistled at a girl in the barn one day. She'd smarted off to him, and he just laughed and got close to her face. He told her he had something she could do other than cleaning stalls. That girl disappeared pretty quick after that."

"When was she taken?"

"When I was sixteen." She twists the bottle cap.

I hope my confidence in her shows on my face. She meets my gaze, and her pale green eyes relax as her face softens.

My words are soft. "We can do this, you know. You have to be brave."

Her eyes return to the water bottle in her hand. She isn't where I need her yet, but she will be.

"Tell me again," I ask, "how they use that basement."

"At night, a van comes with women dressed up. I've never seen that. I've just been told that by Trish. She's the house snoop, not me."

I wish I could talk to Trish, but can think of no ruse that will get me in the same room with her at the farm.

"What goes on in the basement?"

"Don't know." She shakes her head, wisps of hair escaping her tight ponytail. "After a few hours, according to Trish, the kids, the women, and Breaker's guys leave in the van."

"See any of the missing kids again?"

"Never." She looks down at her watch. "Crap! I've got to go!"

Beth grabs her purse and runs out the door. I watch her run down the block from the front window and text Angus my concerns about the girl's safety.

How do we protect Beth? We aren't the FBI with witness protection. How can I protect those children in Trish's text? Court processes take years, and even obtaining a restraining order is useless, given my client is not subject to the harm about to occur, even if I could prove it. Stepping into serious allegations of criminal law is way beyond my real property expertise. I need hard proof.

I forward Beth's text to Nikki. She and Angus are interviewing at the farm soon, and I expect them to get hired. If anyone can determine a safe way to communicate with Trish while she is out there, it is Nikki.

18

———————

Victoria watched Clint Harbin as he stood over his desk looking at an open file folder, his readers perched on the end of his nose. He had gotten old. He was developing jowls, and a gut was starting to protrude over his belt. He was far from the handsome man he had been when they met in college. His nose crinkled at the smell of her perfume, and she waited, knowing her signature scent would register with him soon.

Harbin looked up from a looming stack of case files. As the Ninth Circuit Solicitor, he handled the rapidly growing counties of Charleston and Berkeley on the coast. Close to fifty people per day moved to the Charleston area, and he and his staff prosecuted the criminal cases.

Working downtown at the Four Corners of Law, Harbin had told Victoria on the day he first took the position that he was proud to follow in his father's footsteps and carry on the family prosecutorial tradition. It was why she had selected him as her paramour all those years ago. He had power. It also did not hurt that he was Jack's college roommate and one of her husband's best friends. He had been easy to seduce, and the resulting affair gave just enough of a reminder to her husband that she would never forget his relationship with Marjorie Lee Danforth.

"Hello, Victoria." Harbin screwed on the top of his Mont Blanc pen she had given him last Christmas and placed it on the desk. Rubbing his eyes, he collapsed into a scarred maroon leather chair behind the desk.

"You're failing at your job."

Victoria posed seductively as she leaned against the door frame, the height of her gym-enhanced thin body accentuated by four-inch heels. She had selected her thick, round sunglasses and a red wrap sleeveless dress. From the admiration in Harbin's eyes, she had succeeded.

She gave him a seductive smile. Rather than the return sexy smile she had anticipated—he bellowed. Not quite the response she desired.

"Marie!" He shouted past her to his secretary.

Victoria chuckled, and he bellowed again.

"Marie!"

Clacking footsteps, accompanied by a grunt and a huff, hurried from down the hall.

"Yes, sir. So sorry, Mr. Harbin. I was on the telephone." Marie fiddled with a pencil as she stood in the doorway. Busty and plump, she dropped her eyes and retied the cloth belt around her flowered summer dress. The air conditioning in the courthouse struggled in mid-summer, and the woman's hair was an exploded frizzy bun.

"Please be certain I have no interruptions after you see Mrs. Marshall out."

"Yes, sir." Marie turned, expecting Victoria to follow her as she returned to her office. "Right this way, ma'am."

Victoria remained firmly planted against the door frame, inspecting her manicure from the day before. She needed to find a different manicurist. The girl had failed to color the ends of her nails.

Marie's voice called out to her. "Mrs. Marshall?"

Victoria ignored the frumpy woman and spoke to Harbin. "I'm not leaving until I get an explanation why nothing has happened against that Danforth woman."

Pinching his lips together, Harbin waved Marie back to her desk. He rose and went to stand next to Victoria.

"I'll see her out, Marie, thank you. Just tell anyone else I'm not to be disturbed. Please close the door."

With the click of the lock, Harbin gave her a stony gaze. "You've worn out your welcome around here."

Victoria removed her sunglasses, wanting him to see the dark circles under her eyes. They weren't real, but with her expert hand, he wouldn't know that. As planned, Harbin scanned her face, noting the artful changes she had made to gain his sympathy. She would never mourn Jack, but he didn't need to know that. She ignored his motion for her to sit opposite him as he shoved the papers on his desk in a neat pile.

"If you'd do your job, one that your voters pay you to do, you'd be rid of me." Still standing, she smiled at him again, this time victorious over being able to dominate him in his own office.

"I very much doubt that. With Jack dead and gone, you're here trying to weasel your way back into my life. As I told you the last time, I'm not interested. You've put those claws of yours into me one time too many. You need to leave."

She gave a pointed look and a flick of a fingernail toward his crotch. "Your body says otherwise."

Harbin slammed into the back of his chair with a grimace.

Their relationship crossed the line the first year she and Jack married. Infatuated with her early on, Harbin regretted their relationship and had told her so. Lately, he did everything he could to escape her. Yet once entwined, she made it too difficult for him to separate himself from her—just like with Jack.

Victoria sat, crossing her long legs in a way she knew would catch his eye. "What did the grand jury say about our little friend?"

Harbin's voice was flat. "I didn't put that matter on the docket. In fact, I never opened a case file. Even if it occurred, proof of which you've not provided, there's not been one case on the record using that statute for spitting on a corpse."

Victoria laughed. "Why are you afraid of her?"

The forced smile on her face remained as the twitch in her left eye grew stronger. She wanted that woman humiliated before a grand jury. Marjorie Lee Danforth had spent seven years embarrassing her with Jack. It was time she received payment in kind.

"Afraid?" Harbin laughed. "Not afraid of her, or you either. I won't ruin a decent member of the community's reputation who may have lost her head in a moment of anguish. I might have done more than spit on Jack if it was me. You know better than me what he did to her."

"She broke the law." Victoria looked out the window to hide the twitch. "All of Charleston saw her do it."

"Stop wasting my time. I have a lot to do." Harbin rose from his desk, and she had to admit, he still cut a striking figure. She had misjudged. Despite the jowls and new paunch, middle age suited him well. It was irritating how men seemed to age better than women.

He continued. "Unless you can prove to me that she desecrated the church or Jack's body, and I mean with serious photographic or video proof, or solid witness testimony to that desecration—excuse me, *alleged* desecration—proof that is not from your best girlfriend or paid relative, or someone else you have under your pointy little thumb, then I'll consider this matter closed."

Walking around the end of his desk, he grabbed her arm and pulled her out of her chair toward the door. She shoved away from him.

"Get your hands off me," Victoria hissed at him. "I'm not done with you. We'll see what happens to you in the next election."

"Oh, I'm sure you'll do your best." He dropped his hand from her arm and grasped the doorknob. He turned toward her. "By the way, Victoria, just remember. Given our history, any mud you throw my way will splash back on you. I'd hate to ruin that pretty dress of yours."

With a *hummpf*, Victoria shoved her way past him and out the door. She turned back to Harbin, and Marie watched them from her desk.

Victoria pantomimed a whisper, intentionally loud enough for Marie to hear, "There are a lot of things you don't want your constituents to know, aren't there?"

His eyes squinted with the reaction she expected as he followed her into the hall, closing the main office door behind him. Her smile turned to a sneer. "I thought so."

Harbin took a step toward her. "Like I said—"

"I have photographs. And videos." Her voice grew louder as it echoed down the hall.

His face red as he glanced down the courthouse hallway behind him. He took a step toward her as she tossed out another taunt.

"Quite a few videos, in fact."

Harbin stopped. She knew he was silently counting to twenty-five, something he did to reign in his temper. Did he think those perverted things he made her do in that bed would go unanswered? She reached into her purse for lipstick, liner, and mirror and checked her face while letting him stew a little longer. Finishing, she closed the compact with a loud snap.

Harbin was still steaming as she waved her fingers at him. "Too-da-loo."

"By the way." The malice in his voice stopped her. Harbin always wanted to have the last word, but this tone was one he had —before now—reserved for others. She thought of ignoring him, but at the elevator, after punching the down button, she turned, her eyebrows raised in question. After all, it was the polite thing to do in Charleston.

"Rein in that son of yours. I'm hearing things that I will soon no longer ignore."

Harbin stood in the brightly lit hall, hands on his hips, as if he had just completed a convincing closing argument in front of a jury. Victoria spun and waited until the ancient elevator door screeched open. As it closed, she threw out a casual reminder.

"I think you've forgotten—he's your son, too."

19

"They took Glenna!" Clarice's voice screams across the office. "Lee! They took Glenna! My sister says her parents can't find her anywhere. They are all at my sister Darlene's house, trying to figure out what to do."

I bolt from my office to reach a sobbing Clarice and hold her up as she sags in my arms. My first thought was my lunch with Dani a few hours earlier. Had she broken her promise and immediately confided in Victoria? Had she slipped up and made a sarcastic comment, her usual means of conversation? I freeze. "Was Dani with her?"

"No. Glenna was walking on Rhett Avenue when they grabbed her right off the street." Clarice's voice sounds as if she has run a mile. "A man in the gas station at the corner saw them kidnap her. He called 911. She was going to a calculus study group at another girl's house. When she never arrived, Glenna's study partner texted her mother. Glenna's mother called everyone she knew. When she called my sister, Darlene texted Dani to come home immediately. The police are at Glenna's house."

"I need to go." Clarice pushes away from me and grabs the large carryall she uses as a purse.

I put a hand on her arm. "Why don't I drive you? It will be safer that way. I can help."

Clarice shakes her head in defiance. "You have too much to do here. I can make it. But I'll call you if I need your help."

When she reaches the back door, Clarice looks at me with a fierce expression. "If the police do not take this seriously, I'll need you and the Judge quickly. Keep your cell phone handy."

I stride across the room, grabbing Clarice in a bear hug. "Call me and let me know. You know I will be there."

I kiss her soft cheek and hug her once more. "Don't be frantic when you drive. Your getting hurt won't help."

I watch out the back door as she runs to her car. Grabbing a coffee pod, I slam it into the kitchen machine, then go to my office and close the door while it brews. I immediately call my grandfather. Luckily, he is already downtown, and within ten minutes, the Judge strides through the garden, and I sink into his outstretched arms. Neither of us speak for several minutes. I shift to observe the details of his face.

A curl of soft white hair rests on his shoulder. When he left the bench, he surprised me and let his hair grow long, wearing it in a ponytail at home or when he was active. I always reached for his curls as a child. His Scottish heritage is evident from his bushy eyebrows, which always need a trim, and his sparkling blue eyes underneath. Even though he usually chides me about something, those eyes always look at me with love.

"Hear from Clarice yet?" he asks.

I shake my head. His eyes narrow at me. "Let's see what you've collected on your case while we wait."

"I'll print the usual agreement."

Whenever he consults for me, he signs non-disclosure and confidentiality agreements, essentially making him a firm member for that particular transaction. We move into the conference room to review the scant information collected on Timberline Farm. I bring him up to date on the missing fifteen girls.

"What I need most, other than our usual organization discussion, is legal research," I say.

He retrieves a laptop from his worn leather messenger bag, opens it, and logs in. His eyebrows raise in question, and I begin with the legal theories we can use, and he counters with his own. With a running idea list, we settle on the strongest arguments. I then bring him up to date with Harbin. We toss around ideas after I answer his questions.

After some time, his brow furrows. "Should we go assist Clarice?"

"I think the entire community is at her sister Darlene's house," I respond. "She instructed me to wait for her call. You know how she is. I don't butt in unless she says so."

"If she contacts you, my driver can take us there." He shifts back to his laptop.

"Yes, sir." While I'd rather have my vehicle, I don't argue, but instead, round the table to wrap my arms around him and kiss the top of his head.

His voice softens. "Now, let us get on with this." He focuses on the computer screen.

"Sorry, last interruption. You have a driver?"

The Judge does not look up. "Ah, well, yes. While I can still drive myself, I don't want to. I'd rather ride in the back and order someone else around."

I snort a laugh. "I need to meet this guy. Anyone who can put up with you has armadillo hide for skin."

"That, my dear, he does." He closes the laptop. "Should we break for lunch? I skipped breakfast."

"Sure, where do you want—"

My response is interrupted by the pounding on the front door. Since Beth's last visit, I started locking the doors. Clients must buzz the doorbell when arriving for an appointment. It is all the security I have. Pulling back the curtains, I see Beth waiting outside.

"Hi, Beth," I say as I open the door. "What's happened?"

Out of breath, Beth shoves a sheet of paper at me. "A new message from Trish."

I take the paper from her. "I can't read this. Is it in code?"

"Fifteen girls for Friday." Beth is still breathing hard. "The basement's going to be packed."

I can't believe the number has increased to fifteen almost overnight. "How does Trish know this?"

"I don't know," Beth answers. She bends in half, still trying to catch her breath. "Looks like whoever is sending the lists is afraid of the safe house. The list was faxed to *me* at work."

Hoping to hide my concern, I let her go ahead of me into the office as I close the door.

"I wish you could tell Trish to send them directly to me from now on. We don't want people in this town to learn something is happening."

I need to call Nikki immediately.

"Agreed." The Judge's voice interrupts us from the conference room. Beth flinches at the unknown voice. She is probably concerned about being locked in with a strange man.

"Let me introduce you to someone."

When we reach the conference room, my grandfather is standing. "Please allow me to introduce Judge Rhineholdt, my grandfather."

The Judge comes forward to meet her. "Aren't you the young lady I met at the farm last year? You've grown, I see. Are you out on your own now?"

Beth's arm is outstretched, and she freezes, her face in shock. I stare at the two of them and wait for Beth to speak. She takes two steps backward and looks like she will flee through the front door at any second.

I take her arm before she can escape and rub her shoulder.

"Beth, it's ok. He scares everyone like this. I promise he won't hurt you."

"He knows them." Beth points her index finger at the Judge.

"Yes, he does. I also know the Marshalls, as does almost everyone else in the state." I place both hands on her shoulders, forcing her to look at me.

"Beth, he's on our side. I promise. He's my grandfather."

"But Miz Victoria has talked about him, gloats about her power over him. Says he will do anything she says."

Her hands grip my arms, squeezing hard, and I look at my grandfather. He returns Beth's gaze with a soft smile and a dismissive wave.

"I will do everything I can to help bring Timberline Farm down. And as for Victoria, her ego will be her downfall. She believes she rules the world but is about to learn otherwise."

My cell phone rings.

"I need you here, by God, right now." The exasperation in Clarice's voice comes through loud and clear. "They've given Glenna's mama the run around the entire time I've been here, saying Glenna was a runaway, she was trouble in high school, blah, blah, blah. That girl is none of those things. She's even more trustworthy than Dani!"

I put the cell on speaker. "Who are the officers present? What department?"

"Dorchester Sheriff's Office. Don't know their names."

"Do they know you're talking to me?"

"No, I'm out in the front yard. They can't hear me. There are only two of them, and they're inside. If you don't get here soon, girl, you'll have to bail me out for assaulting an officer."

"On the way. I'll bring a surprise or two," I respond.

I smile at my grandfather. Victoria has me itching for a good fight. "Beth, we can drop you back at work."

The Judge removes his reading glasses and looks toward the kitchen. "Do you have something I can take with us to eat?"

I turn around. "Beth, can you call Buddy and see what he can have ready for us when we drop you?"

Beth is already on her phone. I like this girl. She stands up for herself, has no qualms about saying what she thinks, and takes instruction well in the thick of things. My grandfather calmed her, showing she could listen to reason.

"Let's get going." The Judge scoots his chair under the table and closes his laptop.

I hold up a finger. "I have one call to make before we go." I grab my purse and keys and select a number in my phone's contacts.

"Hey, I got a hot one for you," I tell Vince Whittingham, a local journalist. "Meet me on Jacobs Avenue in East End. You'll know which house. Look for the cop cars."

Not waiting for a response, I follow the Judge and Beth out the door to my grandfather's running Mercedes sedan.

20

———

There was a drip, drip of water in the darkness and the scurry of another mouse in the corner. At least Glenna hoped it was a mouse and not a New York-sized rat, which Dani had told her was in photos of the subway tunnels. She listened for other sounds, desperate to return home with her mother and brother, eating pizza and laughing at Dani's stories. She closed her eyes and filled her head with her friend's ecstatic energy.

She would get through this.

The stink of vomit and the cold turnip greens on the floor filled the concrete room. A faint light seeped into the room from under the hallway door. She studied the jail cell where she was held. Even with basic physical therapy training from her athletic director for minor injuries, Glenna had nothing to fix her broken nose. She used what was left of her blouse to stop the trickle of oozing blood between her legs. She needed to stop the blood loss and gain her strength. When he returned, she needed to be ready.

She tensed as the lock rattled at the other end of the basement. The door clicked, and she heard soft steps down the hall.

The shoes stopped every few feet and then continued until finally, they stopped in front of her barred door.

"Don't make any noise." The soft voice was female with a thick Southern accent, but Glenna could tell little else.

"They don't know I'm down here." The girl said. "I don't have much time."

What if this was a setup? Glenna's mind had more questions than answers. "Who are you?" she asked the girl.

"Shhhh! My name is Trish. I live here. I heard them laughing about what Breaker done to you. I had to see how bad off you are."

Another shiver shook Glenna so hard it made her dizzy. Could she trust this girl? She shifted as far as possible toward the door, the cuffs cutting into her wrists once again.

"Can you get me out of here?" Glenna tried to focus on the girl in the dark. She could only see the tips of the girl's white running shoes.

"Not yet. I can't find the other keys, just the one to the main door. It must be in Nelbert's pocket. I'll keep looking and try again. I'm sorry. It's good to know that I don't have to call 911. I'd get beaten for that."

The girl's shoes disappeared. Glenna stretched toward the door, the pain in her arms at the breaking point.

"Wait, don't leave me!" Glenna shouted a hoarse whisper. "How else can I get out?"

The shoes re-appeared. "There isn't any other way. I'm not trying to be mean. I'll do my best, I promise. I know you're hurt, and I'll try again as fast as I can. If they catch me, I'll be there with you, and we'll both be stuck, understand? Oh, what's your name?"

"Glenna."

The girl's words grew softer as she moved away from the cell. "You're in a basement at the farm. Look, I've got to go. I've been down here too long. They're going to miss me."

"Farm? What farm?"

It was all Glenna could do not to scream, to beg and plead for the girl to come back and not leave her in the dark with whatever was gnawing on the other side of the room. Two words floated into the cinderblock cell from midway down the hall.

"Timberline Farm."

Glenna's stomach plummeted to the cold concrete floor. It could not possibly be true. Dani was an active part of the youth center Mrs. Marshall had set up near East End. Dani's dream of NYU would be a reality solely because of the woman.

Glenna's grew frantic. "Why did they take me here? What are they going to do with me?"

The last sentence was so soft Glenna could barely hear. Just before the door lock snapped, she heard the girl's final words.

"Whore you out."

21

The Judge begins once Beth is dropped at Buddy's.

"Harbin's telephone conversation with you has me concerned."

I nod my head toward his driver. The Judge smiles and buzzes up the privacy screen. I relax, but only somewhat.

"I don't know what's up with Harbin. His telephone call is out of character. I'm trying to figure out whether he will even put something so silly as me spitting on Jack's body before a grand jury. We have time—at least I hope we do—before I must deal with it."

"We will plan accordingly." The Judge pats my hand. "The statute only requires three days' notice if you are subpoenaed. They may force us to have a quick trial. If so, I will represent you and insist on a continuance. Maybe we can use his prejudices and peccadilloes against him."

"You know him very well, then. Much better than me."

"Yes. He's a slimy one. He hires several less reputable police officers in their off-duty hours to do his bidding and takes great glee in stirring up our lower-income neighborhoods. Once, an officer visited a local bar in North Charleston and roughed up several patrons for no reason. Harbin likes throwing his weight around. He likes it when others fear him. I've thwarted him several times, but rarely enough."

"Remind me to give you Clarice's list of grievances against Harbin and his father. Given their tendency to ignore half the city, we need a decent solicitor in Charleston. It's time you threw your weight behind a better candidate this next election."

Entering East End, the Mercedes turns onto Jacobs Avenue, a cookie-cutter neighborhood where Clarice's sister, Darlene, lives. The Judge's driver parks behind a sheriff's vehicle in front of a pale blue house with white trim. The boxwoods are carefully trimmed in front, and a new chain-link fence extends toward the back. Darlene's home is well maintained. Her neighbors have knee-high grass, several houses with curling paint and others missing roof shingles.

Clarice stands in the front yard, her hands fisted on her hips as she leans toward a uniformed police officer. I can't remember the last time I've been here. I look around, remembering what used to be a clean street, with children playing hoops and impressing each other on skateboards in the cul-de-sac. Now, garbage overflows the bins in front of each house, and the last boarded-up house on the right has a rusted junker of a car up on blocks.

A beaten gray Chevrolet Caprice with a rusted hood cruises in behind the Judge's Mercedes. Vince Whittingham, the local journalist I called, is in the driver's seat. I ask the Judge to head off Clarice before they arrest her for saying something ridiculous to the officer.

Vince rolls down the driver's side window as I walk up. His newspaper, part of a state consortium, works to fend off the information desert caused by the collapse of smaller newspapers nationwide. Because funds are tight, Vince only chases big stories.

"Hey," Vince says as cigarette smoke floats out the driver's side window. "What have you got for me?"

I lean over and rest my arms on the car door, ignoring the smoke. "Right now, missing girls."

Vince shakes his head as he reaches out the window and flicks his cigarette over my shoulder. "That's not new, M. L. You called me over here for that? I was way over in West Ashley."

"You made good time."

He taps the top of an unopened cigarette pack on the steering wheel. I watch him unwrap the plastic and light another cigarette with a pink Bic. When he finishes, he tosses the lighter into the overflowing change compartment above the gear shift.

His rattletrap of a car looks like a tornado has raged through. Ankle-deep fast-food wrappers are piled in the floorboard. Clothes, books, and file folders are scattered across the back seat. Vince needs a shave, and I catch a whiff of body odor combined with stale alcohol. Barely forty, his face looks sixty, showing his hard life as a journalist enhanced by alcohol and nicotine. I've known and trusted him since elementary school.

"It needs a little deeper dive than your paper's been giving it."

"Yeah? How deep?"

I lower my voice. "Corrupt county higher-up, dishonest charity bigwig, a questionable death, and a sudden increase of missing teenagers, you know—the typical run-of-the-mill trafficking ring."

Vince's eyes squint as if he is trying to reach into the depths of my mind and pull out the details without having to fight me for them.

"You going to give me any names?"

"Why don't you just hop out? We'll start at the bottom and work our way up. Let's call this an exclusive."

At the last word, Vince snatches the sports jacket folded in the front seat of the Caprice as he rolls up the window.

"I'll bite this once, M. L., just because we're friends. If this wastes my time, you'll owe me a big steak dinner at Halls downtown as reparations."

He looks at the people standing in the yard, and the hand with the cigarette freezes halfway to his mouth as his curiosity piques.

"That Judge Rhineholdt?"

"The parade of stars begins."

Not waiting on Vince, I stride toward Clarice, now ten feet away from the deputy. Her arms are crossed in front of her, and one foot is thrust out in front with a hip cocked to one side. Her mouth is in an angry twist with enough seething energy to make an electrical storm.

The Judge stands leisurely next to the sheriff's deputy; the men engaged in what appears to be a pleasant conversation.

"I'm sure you understand our predicament, Deputy Farnsworth." The judge is using his bench voice. "As you've learned from your interviews, our young lass, Glenna, is not your typical runaway. We would appreciate a report being filed and initiating an immediate search."

I don't dare smile. The entire county knows that the Judge's suggestions are politely couched demands. The deputy's face screws up in a frown.

"Yes, Judge, I understand, and I've already started a report. But you know how kids are, especially these girls out here." The deputy concludes the sentence with a sneer.

"Deputy, keep your personal biases out of this conversation." The Judge leans forward, and his voice lowers. "I won't stand for it."

The officer shifts backward, his body ramrod straight, as if berated by a drill sergeant.

"Yes, sir. The investigation will be up to the Sheriff after I file the initial report."

"Then I will converse with Sheriff Nims. May I have his direct cell number, please?"

The Judge has his cell phone ready and waits for the number.

"Judge, please. You're putting me in a serious bind here."

My grandfather gives him a frosty expression.

"Deputy, it is simply a telephone number. There will be no reason for me to indicate where I obtained this number."

Farnsworth gives in and rattles off the number.

"Thank you, kind sir. Now, if you and your partner finish your report quickly, you may begin your search."

The deputy doesn't move but looks toward the house at his partner. He turns back to the Judge, who taps the face of his watch.

"Tick Tock. Glenna has been missing for four hours. You and I know the first twenty-four are critical."

Farnsworth shuffles toward the house in search, I assume, of his partner. The Judge begins a conversation on his cell, walking away from us across the front yard. I turn to Clarice.

"What happened that made you light up like an electrical storm?" I ask.

"Who is that man over there?" Clarice points to Vince, leaning against the half-rusted sedan.

"A reporter from *The Times*."

"What does he want?"

"I called him. He needs to hear everything you can tell him about Glenna, any other missing girls, and any additional information you learned from neighborhood gossip. Do not tell him anything from our office about the case. Can you tread that line?"

"I can, and I will. I was already sick of this in my community, and now with Glenna it's affecting my family. What if it was Dani that disappeared?" She looks at me with anger, fear, and determination, all rolled into those deep brown irises.

"Where's Dani?"

"Inside." She looks at me, her shoulders relaxing, then at Vince again. "Is this another waste of time?"

"Not if you make him see it. Call over anyone affected and get them in on this. You go first, get others over here, and then have Darlene follow suit. We have one shot at this, so convince him. I'll need you at the office when you finish your part. We have a long forty-eight hours ahead of us."

Clarice grabs me and hugs me so hard it forces my breath out. She lets go, her eyes locked on to mine.

"His paper has ignored this the entire time. He's probably going to do it again."

"Then make sure he doesn't." I wave Vince over.

"This is my best friend, Clarice. She works with me. You're here because girls have been missing from East End regularly, and law enforcement is ignoring the problem."

"Missing girls—" Vince says, and I cut him off.

"Let me finish. Today's missing girl is Glenna Stockbridge. She is a top-recruited athlete, not a runaway. You need to help us find her by putting this in front of the entire city. Her family and friends can give you the background."

I look at Clarice. "You guys should chat in the backyard until the deputies leave."

"This is just the beginning." I catch Vince's eye and lower my voice. "Remember what I told you at the car."

As Vince and Clarice head to the back of the house, I feel the Judge's hand loop my arm through his.

"Sheriff Nims will open an investigation and appreciates my hurrying his deputies along."

"You have something on him, don't you?"

"Nothing bad. The good Sheriff used to work patrol in Charleston. And I've known him since he was a boy who always seemed to be in trouble."

"Must be nice being all-powerful."

"It's a burden. You tee up your reporter?"

"Yep. When he finishes, we should double-team him with information on Brad and Victoria. Then I'll give him Jack's photo and Harbin's audio. Do you have any other aces up your sleeve?"

"Possibly." The Judge wipes his brow with a linen handkerchief before folding it and returning it to his jacket pocket.

"Judge, we're running out of time. What else can we do to find Glenna? And stop the next group at the farm that Beth told us about from being taken?"

"Patience," he replies. "With the way radio chatter is being monitored these days, I'm sure someone has already placed a call to our boy Brad. We only need to ramp up the heat."

"You think he'll release her?"

"If he even has her, you mean. No. I don't. He might hurt her, but he won't kill her." He faces me. "To handle this situation correctly, we need the dominoes to fall at the right time and pace. Please tell Vince we will need him to meet us at Circa for dinner one night soon. Today, we need him to file a detailed news report, preferably on page one, nothing further back than page three."

He gives me a wink. "Tell him I'm paying for dinner and remind our journalist he will need to be appropriately dressed—I won't dine with someone in his current state—and he'll need a jacket, unwrinkled."

I laugh as I text Vince. In my bubble for so long, I had forgotten how delightful and resourceful my grandfather could be.

22

"What in God's name were you thinking?" Victoria stood as close as she dared to Breaker, given the sickly odor. She raised her voice. "Didn't you understand what I told you before? Stay. Away. From. Mt. Pleasant."

The man was a slave to his physical desires and had no discipline. He'd killed the little boy. Billy? Bart? Brent. That was it, Brent. Then he had snatched Glenna. Now another girl, in broad daylight from the popular outdoor shopping area, Towne Centre.

Brad joined in, yet his tone remained unconcerned. "Breaker, seriously, man, what's up with you? Can't you do what we tell you?"

Victoria clenched her teeth, willing the angry twitch in her left eye to stop. Brad's description of Glenna's injuries had been grossly inadequate. The second time she had checked on the girl, a ten-thousand-dollar asset now worth nearly nothing, she still needed serious medical attention. It would take weeks of treatment before she was ready for a sale, not just rest and recuperation.

Breaker removed his ball cap in a half-hearted attempt at respect as he responded—to Brad.

"Your client wants more girls. I brought you one."

Brad shook his head. "There are limits, Breaker. We gave you those limits. Stop snatching girls from the wealthier areas like Mt. Pleasant. We need to take our time and plan. These girls must disappear for a reason."

Breaker's voice whined. "We don't have time for all that crap. Besides, how am I supposed to follow them, huh? There aren't enough girls at the farm. I have to get them from somewhere."

Victoria shifted in front of him, forcing him to look at her. "Get out of my sight. Take no more girls for any reason until I have given you specific instructions. Do you understand?"

Not responding, Breaker turned and headed out the door of Brad's office, slamming it so hard the mirror on the wall rattled.

Victoria turned to Brad. "Get rid of that man. He will be the end of us both."

Brad wiped his face with both hands. "Mother, I can't. You know Theron is upping the quota. There's no time to pull a new manager into this mess."

She perched a hip on the edge of Brad's desk and pointed an index finger at him. "We need to get away from Theron. I don't know what you thought when you partnered with him."

"When *you* came up with this idea, you knew Theron Fish controlled the entire southeast. And no, we can't get out," he responded, his face puffed out like a petulant child.

Victoria kept her face expressionless, hiding her irritation. "We can, with a little creativity."

Brad spit out his response. "Well, sure, if we both want to die. Have you ever seen what he does to someone who crosses him? I have. It wasn't pretty."

Victoria shrugged. "You'll find a way."

"Right now, we need to deliver fifteen girls this month," he retorted. "Fish wants twenty more next month." Brad's right index finger slammed into the palm of his left hand with each number. "Not three, not five, not however many we can find."

He stood from behind his desk and leaned toward her, his face inches from hers as he spit out the word once more.

"Fifteen."

"Then get the man what he wants. But stay away from my girls, and for God's sake, stay away from the wealthy neighborhoods. They aren't part of this."

23

Her stomach grumbled, but at least her head had stopped hurting. Glenna forced herself to be fully awake, focusing on the scratching sound in the far corner and then on the dripping sound to her right. Even with her eyes wide, she could not see a tiny difference between the solid wall and the open barred cell door.

Earlier, someone had been brought into the cell next door, but Glenna had heard no movement since the jailers had left. Her questions received no response, even though she could sense someone was there. With no window, she could not calculate how much time had passed. The smell of the spoiled food and her vomit on the concrete floor continued to make her gag, her body ignoring the three-minute rule where her nose should have been used to the smell.

This was a dungeon just like in the books she loved, only there was no fire-breathing dragon to save her.

Glenna began to make lists, saying them aloud. It was something she did while running to keep herself mentally occupied. The list of the things she loved most helped with the fear—her mother's sweet potato fries, her border collie Max, the enormous live oak tree in the backyard of their home with the family of bluebirds, her math teacher's bright red hair, her friend Dani's sarcasm, the way the muscles in her boyfriend Marcus's arm flexed whenever he reached for her hand.

If she could not escape, there would be no college, new friends, or new boyfriends (sorry, Marcus). Her hope drained at the thought of never being allowed to have the life she'd dreamed of.

"Why me?" she asked aloud.

Her scream of frustration echoed down the hall, but it didn't motivate anyone to bring her food or water. Would they leave her here until she died?

No. She would not die. She would fight.

Glenna forced herself to stand but was prohibited by the too-short chain. The blood had stopped its ooze both from her nose and her body. She did a slow squat to determine if anything else was damaged enough to prevent mobility. At some point, she would need to run. Fighting was useless; she had already learned that rule. She was sore down her thighs, and the area around her buttocks and between her legs was excruciating. She could feel multiple bruises, but her arms and legs seemed to work, other than a wrist that appeared sprained or broken from the chain. No broken fingers, no broken toes.

Interesting. She still wore her running shoes.

She didn't dare touch her face. She could tell from the continuing pain that her nose was definitely broken. He had hit her hard enough to see stars several times and slammed her face-first against the side of the van. She didn't want to know what damage he had done to the rest of her face, especially when there was nothing she could do about it.

When the pain was too much from her prodding and stretching, she returned to the floor. Again, she made the lists, adding new things to each section and new subjects, talking mentally to herself, Dani, and her mother.

The quiet closed around her like a heavy wool blanket as she studied the familiar images in her mind. There was only one thing that mattered. Family. Her mother. Her brother. Dani. The more she thought, the more the surface anger drilled deep into her core, causing the fury to rage within her.

She had a life, a future, and a family who loved her. No one, especially not that horrible monster, would take them from her or her from them. If she was smart enough, she could escape.

24

———

My cell phone buzzes across the nightstand. I bat it silent, desperate to return to sleep. The call stops, and I roll on my side. It begins again. Snatching up the phone, the caller ID's "Unknown" increases my irritation. It is three forty-five a.m. The call stops, and the voicemail dings just before I toss the phone in the drawer.

My habit of never shutting off my cell started the day I passed the bar exam. As my general law practice shifted to real property matters through the years, the after-hours calls became less frequent. There isn't much in real estate that is urgent during the middle of the night, but I still leave my phone ringer on out of habit.

Given yesterday's circumstances, I listen to the voicemail.

"Good morning." An unfamiliar male voice begins talking, different from the synthesized voice I talked with on the day of Jack's funeral.

"Sorry for the early wake-up call, but it's a two-hour drive to Georgia. That should tell you where you're going. Information is waiting for you on the dining table. Do not tell a soul. Don't get followed."

Huh. At least there are no gruesome images. Yet. I wonder what this has to do with me and whether there is a connection to Timberline Farm

I listen once more to the message as I prepare a strong pot of coffee. Then it hits me. A two-hour long familiar drive to Georgia. *That* dining table. Willow House. Morris is the only person besides Jack who knows the house exists and its significance, yet the voice isn't Morris unless electronically masked. Who else can this call be from? Was it Morris who sent me the earlier photos of a very murdered Jack? Did Morris murder him? Shivers rattle my body as I tug the belt of my bathrobe.

Throwing on jeans and a t-shirt, I pull my hair in a messy bun. I grab clothes for the office and my briefcase and fill two thermoses of coffee for the drive. Before heading out the door, I leave a message for Clarice at the office to delay the next investigation meeting.

A half-hour later, my brain, soaked in an entire thermos of coffee, finally focuses. I slide into a deserted gas station on the Ace Basin Parkway. Why am I doing this? Upon receiving a cryptic message in the middle of the night, would a normal person jump in their car and drive for two hours?

I lower the window and feel the breeze. I close my eyes and hear the calming sound of the marsh reeds rustling across the road. An early morning fishing boat chugs on the Intercostal Waterway headed for the Atlantic Ocean.

I should turn back, go home, and forget the stupid farm. Yet I know I will never be able to forget that place. It, and Jack, was too large a part of my life for too long. Whatever awaits me at Willow House has something to do with the farm. If it can help me stop the sale of children, it's worth a few hours.

When I open my eyes, an egret lands in the marsh. Its head turns toward me as the bird takes slow, measured steps in the tall grass. Listening to the Audi's engine ticking, I reach for the ignition, start the car, and continue toward Savannah. I want—no, I need—to see Willow House. I had to rid myself of everything related to Jack and Victoria, including the cottage I used to love so much.

Just before dawn, a bright blue convertible swerves in my lane to miss a turtle crawling across the road. As I slam on the brakes to let the car correct, I remember the day I had bought my car—a gray conservative sedan—something a Charleston attorney would drive. I wanted that same sky-blue convertible zipping by me. The salesman had badgered me to test drive it, and I had. But I didn't buy it. It was too flashy.

This is the story of my life. Don't stand out. Don't say the wrong thing. Don't do anything stupid. Don't do anything to make people talk. Somewhere between fifteen and twenty-one, I had left the real me behind, thanks to the Marshalls.

Then I spit on Jack, and the universe responds by setting chaos in motion.

I slow at the speed limit sign for Barton Springs. Now a bedroom neighborhood for Savannah, the town limits are closer to the little house that holds so much of my history. At the end of the winding driveway, I turn off the engine. Lowering both front windows, I listen to the quiet, taking in the house and garden. The willow tree still drapes over the pond, its whispy fronds high-lighted by the rising sun in the distance. The house looks well-tended, and the gardens burst with blooming flowers.

I spent so many hours here with Jack. After his nasty call during my senior year in college, I drove from school the next day, dropping the keys and garage door opener in the ceramic bowl on the kitchen table and bidding farewell to that part of my life. Now, here I was, two decades later. Why? Who wanted me involved to clean up Jack's—or Victoria's—mess?

Locking the car, I walk to a new potting shed across the back-yard. Bags of tulip bulbs, my favorite flower, wait on the counters for planting in the fall. Pots wait for herbs; new tools hang on the pegboard—a gardener's dream.

Yet this place, this house—Jack—had burdened my entire life. I am the woman who is unloved, unwanted, and in Jack's last words—a whore. Grabbing a clay pot, I slam it into the back wall, and shards explode. A second, then a third pot, shatter against the wall. Yet they give me no satisfaction. Tears explode with a wail as I collapse to the cold stone floor. On my knees, I cry and rage, throwing pieces of pottery until there is nothing left to throw, no tears left to cry.

I force myself to stand. I am not here for an exorcism. Sniffling, I retrieve my purse from the car and find a tissue. Cleaning my face, I glare at the small stone craftsman house. It is a building, nothing more. It is time to move on. I pull out the old gun I keep in a safe under my car seat. The Judge insisted I carry it after a messy divorce case in my first year of practice. I've never needed it—until now.

I focus on finding the hiding spot for a key, yet when I grab the antique front door handle and push the lever, it is unlocked. Inside, the house is sparkling clean, with a tiny whiff of fresh-baked muffins in the air. I wait in the foyer, listening. After a full minute, I step into the living room.

The furniture is new except for a few antiques. The hardwood floors are varnished with a glossy sheen. I avoid the memories behind the master bedroom door to the left and turn in the opposite direction. I'm surprised at the new chef's kitchen with marble countertops and commercial appliances. I stop, catching a whiff of Jack's cologne. Grabbing the counter, I steady myself. Is this real? Or am I imagining him?

Who lives in my damn house?

But it was never really mine, even though Jack said it was. He rented it from Morris after the manager's mother died. Did Morris live here when not at the farm? Why not meet closer to

Charleston? Was driving two hours and putting me through this emotional upheaval necessary?

Yes.

I enter the dining room.

A rustic table holds stacks of documents, photos, and file folders. A pile of leather notebooks in various sizes and thicknesses is at the far end. A single sheet with a typed note in ultra-large font jumps out at me: START HERE.

The first document under the note is a copy of a gift deed. I am the grantee, and an unknown trust is the grantor. I scan the property description and match it to the surveyor's plat.

Willow House.

Well, apparently, it is my damn house.

With nervous fingers, I flip to the signature page. An unfamiliar Georgia attorney's name is listed on behalf of the trust. My heart thumps against my throat. This is getting weird. I need to find out who gave me this house. I dial the office and wait through Clarice's voicemail message.

"Hey. After you get caffeinated, please call the guy who runs our titles in Savannah for Chatham County and tell him I need a rush on a property." I give her the address for Willow House. "Have him focus on the grantor in the last deed and see if that trust owns other properties. Thanks, bye." There is no need for more details. Clarice will call the minute she listens to my message.

A small leather bag holds the house keys, garage door openers, and other keys I will identify later, most likely to the outbuildings. The rest of the pile deals with the house. The insurance is paid for the year, the taxes are current, and utilities are in order.

Why did Morris give me his mother's house? I grab my cell to call him, then change my mind. I *assume* the house came from Morris. It could have changed hands many times over the past twenty years. After I sort through the table of documents and get the updated title work, I will be able to confront him properly at a decent hour.

Shifting to the next pile, I find photos in a sealed manila envelope marked with my name on the front. Someone took professional surveillance photos of Brad in various compromising positions with young girls, others of a van, its license plate, and girls getting in that van. The back of each photo has names and a date. More images show an unfamiliar strip motel, grass sprouting in its parking lot, and the entire building ready to collapse. A dozen photos show men going in and out of two rooms at the end.

The photos support Brad's sexual assault proclivities and Beth's trafficking story, but I need the photographer to use them in court.

I pull out a folded page, a screenshot of an email sent to Clint Harbin with detailed allegations against Brad. The email has the date and time but no name or other identifying information. The sender's Gmail address only contains numbers. Dated two weeks prior, before Beth visits him, it is proof Harbin knew Brad was a rapist. Yet Harbin cannot chase an anonymous email. He needs an actual witness, just as I do. Nikki can run the address, but I am pretty sure it will be a dead end.

And this doesn't feel like Morris. He isn't this smart.

The next pile is Timberline Farm's financial and legal records from the beginning through the previous month. Another contains personal and financial information for Jack and Victoria. There is enough financial data for me to trace any funds received by Brad or Victoria for the trafficking.

I remove my readers to clean them. Once I confirm the deed is recorded, I will change the locks to the house. Even with new locks, this information has to be protected. I will need to take it to Charleston.

In the sunny kitchen, I drain my second thermos of coffee. Wishing I had breakfast, I open the refrigerator. Empty. Whoever lives here cleaned the fridge before they left. I down the last dregs of the coffee and head back to the dining room.

This is all too easy. I've been handed an entire house on a silver platter, financial information to scrutinize Victoria, and conclusive proof of Brad's guilt. Something tells me that what remains in the dining table stacks cannot be good.

25

I stand at the end of the dining table in front of the two stacks of ten leather-bound notebooks—Jack's journals. Each date is written in Sharpie on the front, from the year he dumped me until now. Picking up the latest journal, Jack's sprawling handwriting covers the first page, and I drop it like it is covered in fire ants.

I need two weeks of fortification with the Judge's scotch to read these. I leave them.

Behind me, on a sideboard, lays a zipped black portfolio. Inside are charcoal drawings, watercolors, and acrylic paintings, all varying subjects in Jack's style. Marketing flyers from an art dealer open to paintings of Jack's for sale, a hobby, it appears, that progressed to a business. The business card for the same art dealer in New York is taped to the front, the address in the West Village. I place Jack's art back in the folder and zip it tight and wonder how successful he has become.

Picking up a second sealed envelope of photos, the words "only for Lee" are scribbled on the front. Pictures of Jack and me are interspersed with photos he used for the drawings. One of me napping in the daffodils behind the willow tree takes my breath.

I'd had the memory of this at the funeral. Collapsing into one of the dining chairs, my exhaustion is beginning to take over. I drop each photo, one by one, back in the envelope and re-seal it for later. Much later.

I look across the table at the leather bag of keys. A shiver of fear runs across my shoulders. The thought of Morris—or anyone else—seeing these photographs makes me flush with embarrassment. Whoever left me this table full of information kept access to the house. And has most likely seen the photos, regardless of the sealed envelope.

The gun tucked into my back waistband provides little comfort. There is nothing it can do to stop the dissemination of nude photos of me sprawling in the sun to give Jack inspiration to paint, pictures of me and Jack together *in flagrante delicto*, and others I took of a distinctly unreligious Jack that no one should ever see. Just one leaked photo will ruin my career and my life.

Yet, I long to see Victoria squirm.

I began ethically walking a fine line by taking the Timberline Farm case, one I'm not truly competent to handle and one with a definite conflict of interest. Hiring the Judge as co-counsel, I've stepped back from that cliff. But I keep pushing, like my conversation with Harbin, as if I no longer care about my twenty-year practice and my reputation in the community. Something deep within me desires to throw my life to the wind, to send one of these photos to the local newspapers and see what happens. Let chaos reign.

These desperate thoughts of self-destruction have only one goal: I want to be free.

At only eight in the morning, I feel like I've run a full marathon. Resting my head on the wooden table, I close my eyes momentarily. I do not dare sleep. The caller this morning is correct. Tick Tock, as my grandfather says. I need to get this information back to the office.

The last item on the table is a white standard-sized envelope with my full name typed on the front. In it is a single sheet of paper. I drop my eyes to the name sprawled across the bottom.

Shaking, I read.

My dearest Lee,

If you are reading this letter, I am dead. I thought about making a video but spent most of it in tears when I tried. I wasted both our lives and the possibility of a relationship with our child by being afraid. Even though we were apart, you were always with me. I talked to you daily, wrote to you in my journals, and planned for us to be together one day soon.

While it is too late for me, it is not for you. You were always the fearless one as a teenager and a young woman, so fearless at times that you terrified me. You must be that brave woman now.

The personal information was gathered only for you. Given how I treated you when we last talked, I am sure you will build a bonfire out back and torch it. Lee, no one has seen the photographs and art but me. Only one painting has your face. I could not bear to destroy it. I am sorry if this is painful.

As to the rest of the information, truth is the only goal. Victoria and Brad must be exposed for the vile people they are, and there is enough information here to destroy what they have built. I trust you to carry on what I could not and what they most likely killed me for. Please protect the children. They are my life's work.

Given Brad's associates, you must leave the Timberline Farm information here. The office has a safe. The combination is a date only you will know, one of the most important dates of our lives. There is enough financial information for you to track the flow of the money, photos to prove the trafficking, and more evidence to put Brad in prison for the rest of his life.

I advise you to make even your private notes secure and offline. You'll know better than me how to handle that. The documents on the table are copies, the originals of which are in a bank vault. The local attorney and you have the only keys. Hire security, especially when you are here alone. Be careful. I am confident they will kill you if they learn you have everything I know.

Do what I could not, Lee. Victoria and Brad must be stopped. They have not only destroyed our lives but so many others. For twenty years, I turned a blind eye to her damage to you and everyone else she touched, hoping that if I stayed away from her, her anger and hatred against you would subside. Instead, her anger has fueled something much, much worse.

I beg your forgiveness.

All my love,

Jack

26

———

Dropping the letter on the table, I head for the bathroom. I splash cold water on my face and take several minutes to breathe deeply. My head is spinning. Dropping to sit on the edge of the bathtub, I expect to be sick, but it, for once, doesn't come.

All these years, he knew about our baby. *But, of course he did,* my legal brain replies. As the father, he had to give up his parental rights for the adoption.

Looking for the office Jack mentioned, I head for the bedroom where he used to keep his art supplies. It is now the office and library. The shelves on one side of the room hold books on French poetry, world politics, and mystic religions. Other shelves hold fiction, non-fiction, textbooks, and reference manuals. I run my fingers over the leather edges of several old texts.

The faint trace of leather and cinnamon slaps at me. The room smells like Jack, and the cologne I smelled earlier in the kitchen is definitely his. The entire house looks, feels, and smells like Jack.

A wave of confusion washes over me. He left me abruptly with no contact for twenty years until now. Yet, as a gift, he transferred to me the place where we lived together for four years, the place of love and safety that I believed would be mine forever, the place he lived for twenty years without me--and a letter of love and regret.

And everything I need to bury his wife in an avalanche of litigation and cause his son to spend years, if not his life, in prison.

I cannot think about Jack now. There is too much at stake.

Ignoring the trembling in my hands, I spin to locate the safe in the office, only to come face to face with myself—a life-sized nude portrait of me sleeping in the flowers in the field behind the house. The memory of that day and the sex that occurred after Jack had completed the painting whirls around me. Grabbing the edge of the painting to rip it from the wall, I tug hard—only to find the frame bolted to the wall.

I collapse to the floor and cover my face with my hands as the room spins. Is a duplicate of this painting in an art gallery in New York? Has he sold my nude body, even without my face, to entertain others? Mortification takes hold, and I gasp for breath. From his cologne, the perfect smell of baking muffins in the house, the arrangement of the words on the instruction pages to the books on the shelves. Everything is precisely as Jack would have left it.

Everything molded by him.

Even me.

I stand and head to the room he and I shared. The walls are dove gray, complemented with dark gray sheets on the bed perfectly tucked. The wilted vase of flowers on the nightstand stops me cold. Narcissus. Jack's favorite. I force myself to look to the opposite side of the bed. A vase of wilted tulips, orange with yellow edges, graces my side table. The hair lifts on my arms. I hug my body, trying to stop the shaking. There is a small card next to the tulips on the table. It is the rangy, oh-so-familiar sprawling handwriting that finally does me in.

"Mon coeur."

Bolting to the adjoining bathroom, I make it to the toilet just in time. When the dry heaves finish, I sit on the floor, leaning against the clawfoot tub. New candles decorate a small shelf near the tub—waiting just for me, like the tulip bulbs and tools in the gardening shed. He was waiting for me to come back. But why?

Another round of dry heaves later, I force myself to breathe. Jack was recently murdered. Had his planning to reunite us been the reason for his death? Had it been Victoria who killed him?

I cannot make myself feel empathy—only confusion.

My cell phone rings, and I sigh in relief to see Clarice's number.

"Hey, you got my message." I try to keep my voice calm and reassuring even though neither is what I feel.

Clarice's voice is worried. "Where are you? What in God's name are you doing?"

"Everything is okay, I promise. I'm at a house in Georgia. There's no one here but me and stacks of documents. Were you able to order the abstract?" I run water in the bathroom sink and clean the mascara from my face.

"Yes. Savannah Abstracts will have it for you later today. Is that water running?"

"I'm in the bathroom, if you must know." I hope my attempt at levity will calm her. "Hang on a minute. I need you to do something else." I run back into the dining room to grab the deed.

"Can you call this attorney for me? I need an appointment as soon as he can see me. I'm too shaken up right now to talk to him myself."

I spell Hayward Kendrick's name.

Clarice is quick with another question. "Who is this? And why are you shaken up?"

"An attorney that signed some deeds here. I'll explain later."

"You won't tell me exactly where you are or what you're doing? Lee, this is risky, given what has happened lately."

"I'm in Barton Springs. I have a gun, and I'm alone. I locked the house. There is too much to talk about now," I pause, "and I don't want to discuss it over a cell phone. We will talk when I get back to the office."

"You promise you're okay?"

"I promise. I need to go now. There's a lot to do."

In the office, I search for the safe. Instead, I find liquor. Jack only drank cognac. I stare at the familiar half-full bulbous bottle. Taking another calming breath, I shove the memories of Jack back into my mental box.

I look around the room. Other than the bolted painting, the four walls are covered by floor-to-ceiling bookshelves and cabinets. I don't have time today to pull every book and inspect the inside of every cabinet. I re-examined the picture frame inset into the library shelves. Touching the painting, I feel a hard, unforgiving surface rather than a typical springing canvas. I knock on the canvas and am rewarded with a dull leaden sound. The canvas has been glued to the front of the safe itself, the edges wrapping around the safe door as if on a wrapped frame. I am in that tourist movie where the main character is dead, and his wife is given clues to find him in Venice. Only Jack can't come back and save me from this. And Barton Springs isn't Venice.

This detail is ingenious in hiding the safe. I step back, searching for the keypad. Feeling the edges of the "frame," I find a slight bump under the bottom right-hand corner. Pushing it, three books on an adjoining shelf fall forward, and a hidden keypad pops out.

Jack must have had too much time and won the lottery to pay for all this. The code is a date important only to us. I fidget, wishing he had just given me the code in the stupid letter. Yet this was Jack. What would Jack think would be essential to us?

The day we had come to Willow House. It was the day he had first made love to me, the day I had given him my virginity, the day he promised to love me forever. It is also the day I've tried to forget for over twenty years. Stepping to the keypad, I enter the date with the entire year and wait, sweat beading on my upper lip. With a whirr and a loud click, the front of the safe pops open a half inch.

Pulling the heavy door, I expect it to be an empty box waiting for me to fill with the stacks from the dining room. Instead, the top shelf has stacks of various currencies and a thick leather passport folder. I reach for the leather folder first. Inside are passports in Jack's name for the United States, St. Kitts & Nevis, and Portugal.

Another passport slides and hits the floor. My website photo peers back at me when I open the Portuguese passport. And there is another for the Caribbean island. There is no doubt now that Jack was planning for us to be together, even if it meant leaving the U.S.

Several shotguns are in the large bottom section of the safe, and I slide them carefully to one side and begin loading the documents from the dining table. This takes repeated back-and-forth trips between the dining room and the office. Fifteen minutes later, the chore is complete. I close the safe and grab the leather bag with the keys.

I have a two-hour trip to mentally organize this information and decide how to best use it with my team. But first, I need to talk to attorney Heyward Kendrick. I stuff the START instruction page and Jack's letters into my bag when anger washes over me. The presumptuousness is just like Jack. Dump me, watch me live alone for twenty years, and then assume I want to start over again with him.

I check all windows and doors, close the blinds, and leave on lights for my return. I make a list of what the house needs for security. I almost take the flowers from the bedroom and toss them in the garbage. But I don't. Their significance no longer matters.

Jack is dead.

27

———

My phone rings over the car's speakers. Distracted by the voluminous information from Willow House and the full-sized nude painting I cannot get out of my head, I answer the call using the steering wheel button, ignoring the caller ID.

"You never responded to my letter. I would have thought your reputation more important to you than that."

Victoria's voice causes me to jerk the wheel, and I almost run off the road. I mentally kick myself. What good is caller ID if I don't use it?

"Hello, Victoria." I reach toward the phone to swipe the call away. "I'm hanging up now."

"Oh, I wouldn't do that if I were you." The soft southern accent contains a threatening edge, one I've been on the receiving end of many times.

I can't keep the challenge from my voice. No longer a teenager, I refuse to allow this woman to intimidate me.

"What, more threats? Like that silly letter?"

"There's something stronger coming your way."

I can't suppress a laugh.

"Your lapdog, Harbin? I already talked with him. I did nothing wrong. If you have proof otherwise, go for it. I'll be happy to defend myself to the likes of you and throw a few stones at you myself. You've done nothing your entire life but make everyone around you miserable. I will not play your little game, Victoria."

"These aren't games, Marjorie Lee."

I bite my lip rather than correct my name. She won't get to me.

"You're wasting your time, you, and your bogus Christianity. What would our little town think if I told them the truth about your marriage to Jack?"

"You have far more to lose."

I don't respond, letting her think her threat has hit home. Any ammunition she has against me is locked in the Willow House safe, while the financial information I have sets her seriously within my sights.

"What do you want from me, Victoria?"

Her voice screams through the car's speaker. "I want you out of our lives!"

She never lost control before. Not with me. I wait silently, watching the marsh grass and egrets to my left as I start over a bridge. The *ka-thump, ka-thump* of my car's wheels over the Ace Basin causeway is the only sound. After several miles of quiet, I poke the bear.

"You know the exact day he left me, Victoria," I say, keeping my courtroom voice calm and level. "I know you were in the room with him that day. And you know good and well that I have had no connection to you or your dead husband since that phone call."

"You've forgotten about your love child? Jack tried to protect you so many times, but he must have forgotten this little thing." Her voice suddenly grows vicious. "Your child and I are attached at the hip now that Jack is dead."

I pull the car over to the side of the road. Maybe I am just tired, but the woman isn't making sense. Jack and I gave up all rights to our child years ago.

"I have no idea what you're talking about." I grip the steering wheel.

"Oh yes, you do. You thought you kept her from the entire world. Only my overprotective husband made it his business— and then upon his death, our family's business. I know all there is to know about your little mistake. Or did you two intentionally get you pregnant just to torture me?"

My hands are shaking as I jam the car into park. I force my voice to counter Victoria's bluff.

"Victoria, you have lost your mind. Unless you have something serious to discuss, I have a lot to do today."

"You can't fool me, Marjorie Lee. You're coming home from that disgusting place where you and my husband lived out your perverted fantasies. I know everything there is to know about all that."

She is following me, or more likely, given no cars behind me for miles, has bugged my car. Willow House likely has cameras that I missed. Then her sentence hits me. Aside from the stalking, my child is her weapon. Yet it will do no damage to me. It will only hurt the child. Doesn't she see this?

Grasping the steering wheel, I hold my ground and play stupid. I need to see if she will tell me what she knows.

"What child are you talking about? I don't have any children."

"The one who inherited everything from Jack. The one I'm having tracked down." Victoria's laughter bounces around the car. I picture the gift deed for Willow House in my mind. Has Jack done more than gift me the house? Has he given something to our child?

"You're not making any sense."

"My attorney needs your signature on several documents regarding Jack's estate."

"I have nothing to do with your family, and I'm not signing anything."

"It's her future you're toying with, you know. Whoever she is, wherever she is. I'll find her, and both of you will regret it. I will not allow for that bastard child to inherit one dime."

The sun burns through the car window and onto the left side of my face. I breathe slowly, willing myself to say the right thing that will not set off this crazy woman. I am positive that Jack gave up all rights to the child, as did I, when we signed the adoption paperwork. I keep my voice steady.

"I won't be within two miles of you again, Victoria, much less talk to you in person. This is harassment. Never contact me again."

I hit the red button on my iPhone so hard it flips out of its holder and onto the floor. Shaking from head to toe, my anxiety escalates. My daughter. I've never seen her. My grandfather handled the adoption paperwork. The process was clean, and she is with her new parents in a faraway state. I don't know which state, and it isn't my place to find out. Victoria's manipulation is vicious. That is the only word for it.

But still, I need to talk with the Judge.

Still on the side of Highway 17, my breathing finally under control, I call my grandfather. The traffic flying by shakes the car, but I don't care. He picks up on the first ring as if he is sitting next to the phone.

"Well, if it isn't the long-lost granddaughter. Where are you today, my child? We're all here working, and you're sleeping the morning away?" His Scottish accent fills the car and I hear laughter. He has me on speaker.

"Good morning, you guys. I've been working, I promise. I'll tell you when I get back to the office." I hope my voice is polite, calm, and southern-correct. I don't want any of them to know how badly Victoria rattles me. The fear isn't for me, though—it is for the child. The girl may not even know she is adopted.

My hands shake against the steering wheel. This conversation is a bad idea. I need to see his face, feel his strength. If Victoria wants me to sign something, I will need a lawyer. My grandfather taught me the adage that "a fool for a lawyer has himself as a client" or something along those lines.

"I'm going to need your help and, most likely, your representation on a new matter."

He takes me off speaker.

"Want to give me a hint?"

"We need to discuss this subject outside the office, and I'd rather not talk in front of the others. Do you have time for later?"

"Always for you, my girl. Always."

"Good. Consider yourself on retainer."

28

I make it to Charleston quickly, with the speedometer too far past one hundred more than once. Nikki's laughter and the smell of Chinese food greet me. This small group—my team, The Judge—is my family. Plowing through the emotions of the past two hours, I see my life for what it truly is. I have fiddled away the last twenty years. It is time for me to pay closer attention, especially to those who matter.

I drop my purse and briefcase in the office and join them.

"You've had a lovely sleep, I gather?" Angus's familiar brogue floats out of the conference room before I enter. He looks at his watch, his eyebrows up in exaggeration, an exact copy of my grandfather.

"Nope, been working, and I'm starving. Is this breakfast? Or lunch? It doesn't matter. Give me some food, and I'll fill you guys in."

Eating Chinese food for breakfast is a long-standing tradition of my investigators. I have no idea where it began, but now the morning tradition is part of my office routine when they are around.

I glance over at Clarice. "Everything else ok?"

"The church ladies called to update me on Beth," she replies. "I asked them to call immediately if they see or hear anything important or unusual. Your title abstract for Willow House is complete. The information on that attorney in Barton Springs is on your desk. Your closings are on track; your inbox is full, but nothing is a problem."

From her irritated look, she is ticked at me for not telling her the details over the phone. I stand behind her, wrapping my arms around her in a big hug.

"Don't be upset with me," I whisper in her ear. "I'm running on fumes."

Clarice passes me a plate and silverware, her irritation relenting somewhat. "You need to eat a little and rest. I think you've had a long morning."

"Where is my grandfather?"

"He said he had a few things to do and would see you later," Clarice responds. "Your one o'clock reservation is at 82 Queen. That gives you a few hours, so eat at least a little."

I add a small pile of noodles, lo mein, and pork dumplings onto my plate and sit next to Lauren. Working directly with Clarice, this is the first time I've seen the law clerk since hiring her. I am used to my summer clerks hounding me for face-time, lunches and advice. They are waiting for me at the coffee station and pounce on me every time I step out to go to the ladies room. This girl, so far, is the opposite. I'm not sure how I feel about that. I'm hoping her work speaks for itself.

"I've been getting the closing packages ready for tomorrow's closings," the law clerk says, excited that I am finally in the room for her to get coveted face time with the senior attorney. She is dressed as if going to court in a navy power suit jacket and skirt with a light pink blouse, even though our dress code is business casual.

"If you don't mind," she continues, "I'd like to input the summary the Judge dictated of Beth's journals."

I look at Clarice. She frowns and shakes her head ever so slightly, clarifying that the journal entries are Lauren's idea, not hers.

Before being given any other work, all clerks work on real estate titles and closing. I need to know they understand the basics before they can advance. I also do not want Beth's case to be discussed before Lauren until we all know she can be trusted. This is our standard office procedure, and Lauren is already giving me a cautionary vibe.

"Have you finished with the research I requested yesterday?" I ask her.

Lauren scoots back her chair as she straightens her part of the conference table.

"I'm not quite done," she says nonchalantly, her eyes avoiding mine. "I wasn't sure you meant you needed all that today."

"Lauren, the due date was first thing this morning. I said so in the memo." I keep my voice low, my eyes on my plate. "I could have played it in the car on my way back and been ready for this afternoon if you'd sent it timely. Now I'm behind."

Nikki stands, and grabs her plate and glass, motioning with her elbow for Lauren to get moving.

"Oh, shit." Lauren mutters under her breath.

I follow the clerk with my eyes as she scurries out of the room. The others hold it in until the soundproof double doors close behind the poor girl, and they break out in raucous laughter.

Angus looks from me to his wife.

"Ok, now you've both got her outside the room," he says. "What is it you dunna want the lass to hear? And you look like a lorry hit you this mornin' with that hair disaster, so spill it, please."

I give him a look at the hair comment and keep my voice low. "Got a nice little wake-up call at three-thirty."

"Like that divorce case where we handled splitting all the real estate?" Nikki asks. The case in question involved a dispute at two in the morning. Rather than calling 911 or her divorce attorney, the wife had called me for help. She hid under a church pew while the husband fought the minister to locate her.

"Not that level of crazy."

"Going to miss that silence," Clarice responds. "Thought those crazy days where you took anything were over." She puts her open palm on her chest. "Oh, my bad. I forgot we just took the Timberline Farm case."

"Who called you in the wee hours of the morning?" Angus's concern is evident.

I look at him, then at Nikki. "I don't know who it was. Another of those electronic calls—I think. I'll send you the voicemail to analyze."

Clarice drops her fork on her plate. "Seriously?"

Angus pauses over his chopsticks and leans back in his chair. "What did he—or it—say?"

"You can listen for yourself." I play the cryptic message.

Angus breaks the silence after the voice on my phone finishes.

"So, a voice in the middle of the night gives you an order, and you get up and go? Have you lost your feckin' mind? Where is this place?"

"Only me, Jack, Morris, and Jack's lawyer know about this place. It's a secret hideaway in a little town called Barton Springs northeast of Savannah." I take another bite of food. "Well, that's not true. Victoria also knows, which means Brad probably knows."

I rest my fork on my plate and cast my eyes to the ceiling, realizing how stupid I sound.

Angus resumes eating, scooping up an enormous mound of rice with his chopsticks.

"Brad and Victoria have others who work for them. That means they will also know where this location is." His sarcasm sums it up. "Enough of the cryptic mess with this house. Let's have what you're about then."

"This needs to stay between us." I look at Angus. "Have we swept this room? And take a gander at my car. I received a call from Victoria on my way back; she knew where I'd been. Either they followed me down and back, or I'm being electronically tracked."

I toss him my phone.

Angus leaves through the front door, returning with a hand-held electronic bug sweeper. I follow as he goes into each room with the gadget in his hand, watching the length of the red bars. There is no reaction from the gadget until he's in my office. Then, the bars flash rapidly.

Bending under the heavy glass top, he runs his fingers along one of the welded stainless-steel legs and removes something black, round, and tiny, blinking a soft blue. Holding it so I can see the microphone, he puts his index finger to his lips, takes the bug to the front unoccupied office desk, sets it there and closes the door.

"To be certain, we have no other eavesdroppers I've missed, let's use this." Angus sets a black box in the middle of the conference room table and switches it on, filling the room with white noise.

"We can talk with just this?" I look skeptically at the box, shaken that someone has planted a microphone under my desk.

"There is another layer of distortion you cannot hear from this box, but let's all move outside to finish our discussion." He stands, patting my shoulder. "No worries, love. I'll make a few calls. We'll get this sorted."

The office's back garden explodes with flowers. I stare at the same orange and yellow tulips I planted at Willow House every spring.

"What's wrong, Lee?" Clarice asks, standing next to me.

"Nothing. I'll tell you later."

"I think I'm missing information," Nikki says as we sit around the wrought iron table. "Can we start at the beginning?"

Clarice and I discuss Glenna, the missing girls, and the activities at Darlene's house. Next, I detail my entire morning, including the past that still haunts me, the documents left for me on the dining table, the painting attached to the safe, and the safe's contents.

I retrieve the letter from Jack from my bag and slide it across the table. The three lean in to read it. Clarice breaks the silence after they finish.

"Well," she says, "So Jack was definitely murdered. You think Victoria did it?"

"Probably," I reply. "Victoria is behind everything, including Glenna being at the farm, but I can't prove it."

"On the security aspect," Angus says, "I have a friend who can finish checking for listening or video devices here and in the car and then go to Barton Springs."

Some of the fear in my neck and shoulders releases.

"For security," I respond, "I'd prefer someone out of the area."

Of the few private security services in Charleston, most are filled with retired police. They are all part of the same small-town network. I cannot risk it should one of them talk.

"Atlanta ok?" Angus asks.

"That should do it."

"I trust Mac with my own life," he continues. "We served in the military together, and we've kept in touch over the years. I'll see what he recommends and get back to you."

"See if he has anyone that will be a good fit as a bodyguard." I point to the warning letter from Jack.

"Let me think about it, talk to Mac, and I'll get something rolling for you. It's going to be pricey."

"I think it's necessary." I look at Clarice, who blinks her agreement, the two of us back in sync.

"Nikki, I'll need your help with the documents, photos, and

everything I found at Willow House. I don't want to take the documents from the safe at Willow House, but we need working copies available here that cannot be hacked and are searchable."

"I'll make calls from our house until Angus gets Mac here," Nikki responds. My face must have reacted somehow.

"Sorry, Lee, your office isn't bug-free until Mac says it is. And we all can't work out here in the heat." She looks at Angus.

Angus smiles at his wife, then looks at me. "She's right, Lee. It's an appropriate protocol. No worries."

"Ok, now that I've spilled my guts, fill me in on what's been happening on your end." I looked between Clarice and Angus, then to Nikki. "Talk to Morris?"

"We had an interview with Morris this morning at the farm. We start tomorrow."

I think of Glenna. It is a giant leap to assume she is at that farm, but my gut tells me it is no leap at all. I hope Dani has stayed away from Victoria.

"Morris seems in genuine need of staff," Nikki continues. "More than a few people quit. I need more information on this place. I don't enjoy walking into a minefield without knowing where to step."

"My information is old, but I'll tell you what I know. Clarice can give you the rumor side. You'll be essentially on your own, though."

"It won't be a problem," Angus interjects. He looks at his wife and smiles. "We've had a lot worse experiences than this overseas, haven't we, love?" Nikki smiles in return, her look conveying absolute trust.

"Let's set the conference room up as a war room," I say. "We can reconvene after I meet with the Judge."

I look at Angus, then Nikki. "We'll need a plan before you start at the farm tomorrow. Our priority is to find Glenna as fast as possible. But we will need Brad and Victoria's routine, copies of their calendars, the routine of the farm and the workers, and any current financial information you can find. We need to get a handle on the money flow and identify any trafficking income."

"Clarice," I shift to her, "let's change the code for the conference room and keep it locked. Only the four of us, my grandfather, plus Angus's security guy, get the code. And follow up on Lauren, will you? Until we are sure about her, I don't think she should have access to Beth. We need to know how she got access to her journals."

"I know she hasn't seen them," Clarice replies. "Your grandfather still has them."

I instantly relax. "That's it, then," I say to the group. "Let's get going. Let's check in again at three."

29

———

"I am so pleased you could visit me this afternoon."

Victoria hugged Dani at the front door. The girl was blessed with glossy hair, coffee-colored skin, and an athletic shape with curves in the right places. Dress her up, and she would be stunning in front of the camera. Victoria could not wait to see the furor Dani would bring to the auction website.

She led Dani into the living room, decorated in a cream monochrome. Since Victoria could not live in New York, she brought the city to herself, here in hicksville Charleston. It also impressed the girls and gave them a hint of their fictitious future. And, of course, the client needed to see a girl up close occasionally. It helped to have the proper environment for those introductions.

"I hope I can help." Dani interrupted her thoughts. "You mentioned technology. Anything I can learn in the technological arena will help when I get to NYU."

Anxious and ready to please, Dani's pliability was a plus.

Dani continued, "I'm considering integrated design and media. Do you have anything I can do with augmented reality?"

Victoria thought of a particular client who would pay a bonus for this girl and almost laughed. Dani's intelligence would serve to ramp up her bank balance once more.

Her clients were at the top of their fields and demanded beautiful and intelligent women. They had no time to use dating apps or hunt for single women. Her girls were hired as employees, treated well, and paid accordingly. Yes, sex was required, but there was more to their service than sex. She was not a call girl madam providing prostitutes. She provided talent and built a reputation for delivering the best.

Several clients had inquired as to available women who spoke multiple languages. She could build this service at the Community Center. Dani's desire for advanced technological proficiency might also benefit others at the Center—anything to increase the bids.

"I'll look into that, but let's cover the basics first. I need our website freshened as soon as you can get to it. It is too basic and needs to be more interactive. We should build a significant social media presence that extends across the country, not just in Charleston."

"I agree. You need a following." The girl's face wrinkled in thought.

"Certainly. We run on donations. Without all the ways to contact people, we won't increase the level of funding we need to progress. Funding must begin to come from the younger generation. While I do not believe a significant social media presence will increase our funds, it will increase our name recognition for future donation marketing efforts."

"Oh, sure," Dani replies. "It will help if I can see the entire marketing picture when you have time."

Victoria hoped she would remain this agreeable. "Dani, if you have any ideas, let me know. I'm open to almost anything you'd like to suggest. I consider you the expert regarding technology and your generation."

"Where would you like me to start?" Dani asks.

"Let me show you our technology room where you will work." Victoria rose and pointed to the hallway. "We shoot video and sound from there."

She ushered Dani ahead of her down the hallway. They entered a large bedroom converted into a recording studio with a small, windowless recording booth in one corner.

Dani's face lit up. "What do you do here?"

"The girls looking for jobs outside Charleston come here for private interviews. We have been doing this for several years now." Victoria made sure she was upbeat. "I've set up quite a few girls with fantastic jobs in New York and Chicago. With unemployment so low, many companies are searching outside their areas. I worked hard to create such benefits for the girls in Charleston to have better lives."

Victoria turned to face Dani, dropping her voice. "This is a secret that I guard. Please remember the confidentiality agreement you signed."

The non-disclosure agreement drafted for every girl to sign had no wiggle room. They needed to believe everything happening in this room was confidential, professional, and kept within these walls.

The truth—and the illegality—was irrelevant.

"Yes, I remember." Dani dropped her head, then clenched her fists, stuffing them in her jeans pockets. Victoria considered the sudden change. Was she nervous? She should be. This was a new job. Dani surely knew she needed to impress.

Victoria motioned toward the desk. "You will work here most of the time." She pointed to a computer attached to a camera and an audio mixer. "At some point, we will upgrade this equipment."

"You must keep a backup of all interviews." She pointed to a neat row of external hard drives lining the credenza. "We use an individual file for each client. They are arranged alphabetically. Put the employer's name under the copy you make. Don't worry; I will show you what needs to be done, the first time or two."

Dani replied, "When do you need me to start?"

"It would be helpful if you could stay the remainder of the day. Review some of the tapes and see the process. Work on the website and social media. Think about how you will update our charity website. Get familiar with the equipment. You can come for a few hours each afternoon after school beginning tomorrow. I would prefer you work here rather than at home. When we have our first taping, I'll walk you through it. Then you can do it without me. I usually know about those several days in advance."

"All right."

"Let me show you the kitchen and the bathroom." Victoria extended an arm to guide Dani toward the other side of the house. "Then you can get comfortable. I'll be out this afternoon, so make yourself at home. Please give me your ideas by the end of the day. Leave a detailed memo on your desk."

Once the girl was settled, Victoria gathered her purse and keys, smiling as she started her car and headed toward Charleston. Dani's technical abilities were a bonus, and she needed a better way to keep watch over the girl so she would not end up like Glenna.

It didn't hurt that someone close to Marjorie Lee Danforth was at her disposal.

30

I walk from my office to the popular tourist restaurant, 82 Queen. My grandfather moved to Charleston for work forty years ago and stayed for the food, the ocean, and the southern woman he nicknamed Pearl—my long-widowed grandmother. The restaurant serving Lowcountry cuisine was one of their regular haunts and remains one of the Judge's favorite places. The restaurant counts him as a regular, serving him in one of their small private dining rooms.

Angus's arm is looped through mine. He leans closer, his voice conspiratorially low.

"Just to let you know, my security friend, Mac, is single."

"And if you weren't practically my brother," I reply, "I'd make you regret that pool you three always have on my dating life."

Angus snorts as he drops me at the front of the restaurant where my grandfather waits. I suddenly feel like a five-year-old who can't go to the bathroom alone rather than a woman who prides herself on being able to take care of herself.

We go upstairs to an empty dining room with six tables and a window overlooking Queen Street. After the required polite conversation with the server, our order is taken, and a wine is selected from the Judge's private stock in the restaurant's cellar. My grandfather waits until the door to our section closes behind the waiter. We listen to the loud floor creaks as the man shuffles down the stairs of the old house. I bring the Judge up to speed on my trip to Willow House, Angus's plans for a security team, and the investigators' new job at Timberline Farm.

Up since three and worn to a frazzle, I drop my chin to my chest. He lifts my face with his fingers, scrutinizing me. "Why are we away from the office?"

"I hate to drag you into this, but I received a call this morning from Victoria Marshall."

"And?"

"She alluded to something I needed to sign that had to do with Jack's estate—and our child we gave up for adoption. I told her never to contact me again and that I would have my attorney contact her directly." I tip my head toward him. "And that would be you."

My leg bounces hard under the tablecloth.

"Did she give you any indication what paperwork?"

"Not specifically. She alluded to the adoption, Judge. She says the girl still stands to inherit from Jack."

The Judge shows no surprise, even though I thought he would have. My heart's pounding ramps up another notch.

"Victoria insists she will find the girl."

I grasp the glass of water and drink half, hoping the coldness of the water will calm my nerves.

The Judge takes my hand and kisses my index knuckle. "Would you like a glass of wine or something stronger? Maybe a scotch before this conversation?"

"No." I shake my head. "I trust you. I just don't trust her."

"Yes, *mo ghradh,* you did trust me. And I promise you, I did nothing except what was in the best interest of you and that child." His forehead wrinkles in concern as he leans toward me.

"Lee Danforth. That witch is playing you. The adoption

severed all relations between the child and you and Jack Marshall. I have paperwork to prove the adoption was clean and aboveboard."

The Judge rose and went to the door, calling down the stairs for the waiter to bring a bottle of Caymus from his private stock instead of the white he had selected. The waiter promptly returned with the requested bottle.

"Please hold our lunch order. We have a bit of attending business before we dine." The Judge remains silent as the waiter uncorks the wine. He waits until the waiter leaves again, and even though this is my grandfather's normal behavior, the delay in getting to the point might shove me over the edge.

"Judge…" He picks up his glass, and I perform the obligatory clink. He knows me too well.

I rarely drink, a rule I made after law school. I have been breaking it consistently since the Timberline Farm case started. I have alcohol only for special occasions or a very special bottle. This bottle is over a hundred dollars. And for whatever reason, he is making this a special occasion.

"I arranged for the adoption of your daughter by a couple in Boston. I selected them myself. They agreed to a closed adoption, but that you could have a relationship with your child if she consented. She is beautiful, as beautiful now as she was when born."

"What…?" I almost drop my wine glass. I set it on the table, staring at the tablecloth for several seconds until I can look at him again.

"Let me finish, please. Enjoy your wine." He motions for me to take up my glass. "It is time to clear the air. You have been old enough for years, and I shirked my responsibility."

I dare not interrupt.

"Even though I am technically not your blood relative, I made a promise to your grandmother and then later, after her death, to your parents. Given the untimely death of your father and given your mother's cancer afterward, your welfare was imperative."

He releases my hand, takes a sip of the dark cabernet, and wraps his wrinkled fingers through mine again.

"Your mother asked me to be your guardian should the need arise. Just before her death, I reminded her you were an adult but promised I would always be at the ready should you ever need me."

He hesitates, taking a long breath.

"I first learned of your relationship with young Jack when you were in college, long before you told me. I suspected things weren't right before then." He looks at me. "We have discussed this."

The memories of those years flood over me.

"You were such a firebrand. That man attempting to kidnap you and abscond to Las Vegas...." The Judge shakes his head.

"But then—in your last year at the university..." The Judge sits back, his demeanor changing with the next sentence. "Jack's wife, a 'viper' as I believe you have referred to her most aptly, came to visit me asking for assistance. Victoria wanted you to leave her husband alone. She referred to you in very unsavory terms. I showed her the door, telling her I did not know what she described."

He finished the last fourth of his wine, and I see this is as stressful for him as it is for me.

"I then called your paramour. We met the next evening. To Jack's credit, he laid everything on the table. Jack admitted to legally being a pedophile only because he was in desperate love with you. It was all I could do not to have the Solicitor at the time file charges against him for statutory rape. I have regretted not doing that for years, but the damage to you and your reputation would have been significant. I chose the lesser of two evils, essentially."

I can't speak. The Judge never said a word to me. I am not sure whether I feel betrayed or grateful. He poured more of the burgundy liquid into his glass and continued.

"I also knew the retribution I wanted from him for ruining you was already underway. His wife had him so entwined in the non-profit that he would have needed a significant amount for attorney's fees to disentangle himself from the farm and Victoria. There are penalties in all the documents for early payoffs and refinances.

"And, according to Jack, there was an element of blackmail, he admitted, that he needed to avoid. In reviewing the recorded documents, the scoundrel of a church deacon providing private financing structured each tract of real estate to be cross-collater-alized with high interest rates. What a thief. The real estate trans-actions were tied together in such an intricate mess that it was like one of your grandmother's crocheted blankets. One pull of the yarn and the entire place would unravel. Jack insisted he could not do that to the children he undertook to care for at the farm."

He twirled his wine glass. "But it was neither here nor there. Victoria and her family had trapped him. He could not sell the ranch, transfer it to anyone else, or divorce his wife without several penalty clauses kicking in. He was imprisoned in his own personal hell. So, I left him to it."

I don't try to hide my embarrassment but stare at the thin stem of my glass until I can find the words to speak.

"Why didn't you tell me before?"

"Because Jack asked me not to. He said you already knew everything he told me, so there was nothing to do. You needed to enjoy your final days in college. He wanted your lives to continue, even as ridiculous as it sounded, until he could figure out his predicament. I feared his wife might take legal action against him and you, but no suit was ever filed on her behalf. I would have heard almost instantly at the courthouse during those years if there had been."

"Then I called you."

"Yes, you called me that same day, distraught. He had viciously dumped you, as I remember, which I found hard to believe given my conversation with the man."

His concern radiates over me, distress reflected on his face.

"So, I assisted you. Not just out of duty, mind you, but out of love. You are my granddaughter; you always have been. I fell in love with you when you were a mite and love you still."

My napkin is useless in stopping the tears. "You've always been there for me. Especially when I was so lost after my senior year in college. Then you helped me with law school. I know you've always wanted me to do other things than real estate. I know it's not the most glamorous of attorney jobs, but I'm okay with it. Yet, I've consistently ignored your advice, and for that I'm sorry."

"And I have continued to goad you. I take full responsibility. I attempted repeatedly to get you over that man and to live your life. You have so much life to live, and you're wasting away in this town doing real estate closings and odd little things for do-nothing clients."

"And here I go again." He stops himself and rests back in his chair. "It is your life to live. I love you and will let you live as you see fit."

My throat closes, rendering me unable to speak. Only Daddy had shown me this level of love and affection, and I can only remember his face now by looking at the worn photo in a frame on my mantel. Mama had released me into the wild that sixth-grade year after Daddy died, letting me live unfettered, unsupervised, and unloved.

I stare lovingly at my grandfather's wrinkled face, the age spots scattered across his forehead, and the lovely white hair that curls on his shoulders. He has protected and loved me more than anyone else. Ever.

He interrupts my thoughts. "You need to eat. Let me get our waiter."

I know he is right. The Chinese noodles from the office are long gone. I drain my wine glass and pour another. Yet once the food is served, I have no appetite and pick at the sea bass. Wistfully, I watch the Judge enjoy his shrimp and grits.

"I didn't want to give her away," I say softly.

He rests his fork on his plate, his blue eyes locked on mine. "Yes, I know you didn't, but as you know, we discussed every possibility, and you decided on your own. I think it was the right decision. Neither of you were harmed. You both have had a good and decent life."

I still have more questions.

"Is she still my daughter?"

"No, you know this from law school. You are the birth mother only and retain no parental rights. You signed those away at her birth."

"Does she know this?"

"Yes. Her parents and I decided honesty was best. Of course, I insisted I be allowed to check on her routinely. I sealed the adoption file so that the viper of your paramour could not gain access."

"How are you so sure?"

"Because I still have the original file in my possession. I retrieved it from the clerk once logged. It is correctly recorded. However, if the clerk should need to pull the file, he or she would find nothing."

"But it's a court record."

"And we are discussing the child of my grandchild."

He swirls the wine and watches the colors change in the sunlight.

"I believe Jack never told Victoria of the child. I am estimating that it wasn't until she visited his estate attorney, most likely recently, that the subject came up. The estate attorney, finding the birth record but no adoption file, believed the daughter could inherit, and since he could find only a docket entry, but no actual adoption records…" His voice trailed off for a few seconds. "He was doing his job, though inadvertently setting off a war between you and Victoria."

"Does she know about me?"

"The child? She knows of the adoption. She does not know your name. The adoptive parents would only agree to open access after the child reached thirty."

She is twenty-one. Her birthday is a repeating entry on my personal calendar.

"What is her name?"

"Alexandra. She goes by Alex. I did not believe until now that you knowing any details was in your best interest."

Since I gave up this child at birth, other than the birthday remembrance, it had been a subject kept closed in my mental box and locked away. I think of all the years I've missed.

"What do I do about her now?"

"There is nothing to do until she reaches thirty and you wish to be identified to her, or the adoptive parents request otherwise."

"What if, now as an adult, she wants to meet me?"

"Let's cross that problem if it arrives."

"What do I do about Victoria?"

"Do nothing. Rest assured, Victoria is bluffing. Hold your cards when you deal with her and refer her to me. There is no reason you should deal with that woman."

"Judge, why was Jack so mean on that last call? Why?"

"I do not know, my child, but I'm certain that wretched woman is most likely to blame."

My phone buzzes in my pocket. It is a text from Angus.

"We need to head to the office. The security guy Angus called is on his way."

31

Sifting through the real estate files and the overflowing inbox proves that this day will be the longest of my life. With the Judge working with Clarice in the conference room, I look up as Angus enters my office, followed by another man. "M. L., meet my mate, McCabe Lawrence. He's the security from Atlanta." Tall and athletic, the man is in his forties, has receding dark brown hair cut high and tight, and a salt-and-pepper two-day beard. Angus takes a step back, a sly grin on his face capped off with a wink. Lawrence moves forward with his hand extended.

I have to give it to Angus. The man is attractive. He, Nikki, and Clarice have an ongoing conspiracy to get me dating again. While I appreciate their efforts, I will strangle Angus later for the wink.

I shake the security man's hand, and he reciprocates with what I expect—a firm handshake he keeps in moderation that otherwise would crush my joints. He is at least six inches taller than me, his bearing professional, and the creases in his pants are sharp. His energy strikes something inside me, and immediately, I shut it down.

No time for that.

"Great to meet you," I say. "I hope I'm not wasting your time. I'm sure this is small potatoes for you, but I appreciate you coming this fast. And how did you get here so quickly?"

"There's no job too small." Mac's demeanor is pleasant, his voice folksy. "Angus's call was good timing. I just finished a job in Columbia."

Angus motions for us to go outside to talk as before. Seated around the patio table, I look to Angus and then Mac. Someone, Clarice, most likely, has placed a table fan nearby to blow away the summer flies and mosquitos with a much-needed breeze. Too bad it can't get rid of the distinct excrement smell from the horse carriages that roll past the front door hour after hour.

"I looked at what Angus found in your office," Mac says. "It's a basic listening device, not high on sophistication, not military grade, and nothing close to high-level spyware. It's easy to buy online and small enough to hide."

"We're talking small-town criminals here, then," I respond.

"Most likely, but it never pays to shrug them aside," Angus interjects. "These southern boys can be as mean as they come."

I can't argue with that. In Charleston, the thoughts and actions of the fathers have passed to the sons for generations. Several boys in my high school, I suspect, have parents and most definitely grandparents who were or had been members of various local right-wing groups.

Mac continues. "I looked at your neighborhood with Angus and rode past the farm for a quick drive-by. I'll need more time to ensure someone isn't watching your office. There's another man coming tomorrow, and given your plans for Angus and Nikki at the farm, an additional one is available if needed. We will sweep your building on an erratic schedule as Angus says you have some reservations regarding one of your employees."

"Yes, it's my new law clerk. I don't think she's a problem, but she's only been here a week. Right now, she is not performing to my expectations and wanted to insert herself into a particular case this morning rather than do the work I'd assigned her. We're keeping her out of the loop except for basic research and work on other closing files. As a local, she's the primary suspect for the bug planted under my desk. No one else has been in the office except for me and Clarice."

"Of course," Mac says. "I've met Clarice, and I'll get with her to be certain about any clients, office cleaners, food delivery, express mail, or other outside people and their schedules. If I have questions, I'll let you know.

"It will be a good idea," he continues, "if you move into the apartment over the office. It will cut down on the places that need surveillance. Angus has only authorized three additional men. I do not want us to be spread too thin."

Whether it is the lack of privacy or my need for freedom, I relish my space away from the office. My condo is a fifteen-minute drive and the first place I'd entirely chosen for myself after Mama's death when I finally left home. The second-floor apartment in my office building has remained empty for years. The walls are unpainted sheetrock, there are no window treatments, and the appliances have never been turned on. I planned to use it for additional rental income but never had. Something about having a tenant living over a law office with all its confidential files and information never sat right with me.

Before I can catch myself, I let out a dissatisfied huff. This entire Timberline Farm mess needs to be finished. My routine is off track, and I am already tired of it.

I consider Mac's idea as I tap the desk with my fountain pen.

"My first thought is a hard no," I say, "but it won't kill me to camp out in the apartment."

"It's temporary," Mac says. "Maybe consider it an extra workspace? It's only so we can sufficiently monitor you."

Besides the butterflies in my stomach that started when Mac walked through the door, he—and Angus's confidence in him—gives me a calm feeling. I decide to trust him, and let myself relax.

"Who will be my bodyguard when I'm off the premises?" I look at Angus.

His eyes flick to Mac, and I catch his slight nod for Angus to proceed. Interesting. I'll have to quiz Angus on his relationship with Mac. An apparent rank between them extends outside their prior military positions. I don't want Angus deferring to a prior commander when he works for me, even if Mac works well in providing security.

Mac responds, "If you have no objections, I'll take that role on myself."

The low-level butterflies are now a hard flutter. Apparently Jack's death has released more in me than I anticipated. I'm not sure how I feel about that.

He continues. "We'll need to come up with how we met…"

I shove down sudden, unprofessional thoughts. At least my body still functions in that area. I give Angus the side eye, hoping he knows I will wipe that silly grin off his face at the first opportunity.

"Let's work on that tonight," Mac continues. "Give the town something to talk about." His smile shifts him from military warrior to eighth-grade imp.

This is trouble. The cheering down below has turned into a full-blown party. I return his smile, knowing that his presence is about to upend my life. I don't want my life to change.

"Tonight, I have other—"

Angus interrupts me. "This is in your best interest, Lee."

"It's important, M.L.," Mac adds. "From what Angus has told me, it is imperative we move as quickly as possible."

After an organizational staff meeting between my office and Mac's team and a detailed discussion between Mac and me over the cost, he and I head to 167 Raw on King Street for oysters. The hostess leads us outside in the back garden area, and Mac selects a private booth in the corner.

After we get settled and order drinks and appetizers, I learn about his office in Atlanta, a little about his military career, and details of his relationship with Angus. He is interested in my childhood in Charleston and how I became a lawyer. I stay away from the subject of Jack and Timberline Farm. There will be enough time for that later.

"Your favorite restaurant?" Mac asks, looking around.

"Honestly, I liked the tiny original location better over on East Bay Street. A friend and I regularly met there to catch up and have oysters. She moved away last year, and neither Clarice nor my grandfather like oysters, so I haven't been in a while."

I am nervous, and my rambling shows it. Sipping the delicate white wine from New Zealand, I stay silent, and after a minute, Mac fills the awkward silence between us.

"Angus says you don't date much," Mac says, sipping his beer. "Says you're a workaholic that only takes a vacation for a weekend to stand on the beach at your grandfather's house on Sullivan's Island and brood."

"Yeah, well, Angus talks too much," I respond. He might practically be my sibling, but he needs to learn to keep my personal life to himself.

"It's my fault," says Mac. "I purposefully prodded him to get information about you after we met."

"Do you do this with every client?" I ask.

"No, I don't. This is the first time I've done this." Mac sets his beer on the table and pushes it to the side. "Look, I'll be straight with you. Without going into my past relationships, it's been a long time since I've found a woman attractive."

"Mac, I—" Flustered, I don't know what to say.

"No, hear me out," Mac responds. "We are in a professional relationship, and I think this is important enough to put out there. We will work closely together, and I will act as your private security. If you feel uncomfortable with it being me, then Mike and I can swap assignments."

"I'm not sure what to say." I take a sip of my wine as we look at each other. This is most definitely a first.

I am used to being wined and dined, but in Charleston, there is a lot of wordplay, what I refer to as "Charleston nice." I am used to unnecessary flattery, tall Southern tales regaled at dinner, invitations to hunt or fish, glasses of wine on docks, and walks on the beach. I don't do anything fast when it comes to relationships, and for the most part, after several dates, the men here don't like the effort it takes to break through my walls.

I'm embarrassed to turn down someone so obviously suited to me. Even in the fifteen minutes we've been here, Mac and I have talked about things at a level I'm not used to. But I am his client, which is a line I am not willing to cross, even if he is.

"Mac, I'm not looking for a personal relationship," I say, unsure where to go in the conversation.

"And I'm not offering you one." He gives me a smile that I return with a quizzical look.

"Then what are you saying?"

"That I'm physically attracted to you, and you need to be aware of it. I think you feel the same. I thought so, at least when we met in your office. Maybe I'm wrong." He takes a long draw from his beer. "We will be in stressful situations that can amplify even the smallest of attractions."

"So, how have you dealt with this in the past?"

"Hasn't happened. This is new ground for me," he replies, clearly flustered now that he's opened this Pandora's Box. "I need us to come to some comfortable agreement to move forward. An understanding, if you will."

"That's not hard. I've never met a man who says exactly what he thinks other than Angus. This will be refreshing. I'll treat you exactly like I treat him."

Mac's mouth is downturned in evident disappointment.

"Like I'm your brother," he says. "I don't believe I thought this through well enough. Can I try again?"

"No, apparently not." I can't help but laugh. "You started this."

"Ok, seriously, I'm trying to stay professional here, but what a blow to the ego." He laughs, and it breaks the tension between us.

"Mac," I turn serious. "I know the people at Timberline Farm. I had an affair with Jack Marshall when I was in high school and college. Victoria, his wife, continues to hate me to this day. As you know, Jack Marshall is now dead, and his son, Brad, has taken over the farm. I lost it at Jack's funeral, and Victoria is threatening some action against me."

"I know a lot of this, and I'm sure I'll have questions," Mac responds, "that is if you want to tell me."

"And you know that now I have a client who alleges Brad raped her. She also asserts that the Solicitor here in Charleston won't prosecute. On top of that, she swears Brad is running a trafficking ring out of the farm."

"Yes," he says, "Angus filled me in."

"So this is my warning to you. We won't simply be in stressful situations together. By the time we finish, I assure you we will both be fighting for our lives."

32

Mac's easy driving toward Georgia the following day lulls me into introspection. Sitting in the low-slung Porsche 911 Targa, the car hugs every corner as Mac does his best to keep to the speed limit, his decision, not mine. If I were driving, the speedometer number would double to complete this chore faster.

Last night, after I approved the expenditure of his three-person team, Mac had a technical crew immediately sweep the house. They found nothing. Still, Jack's presence in that house hangs over me like a cloud of dread, as does the thought of Victoria attempting to drag an adopted child into this mess. I can't fault my grandfather for trying to stop her, but I want him to stay away from her.

After dinner with Mac last night, I returned to my office and pulled my copies of the adoption documents. Neither Jack nor I have any rights remaining, and Alex has no legal inheritance rights from us. Victoria's attempt to harass Alex is a ruse.

I should listen to the Judge and not allow Victoria to push my buttons. She has to be after money. With her, it is always about money.

Mac parks the car in the garage at Willow House using the openers in the leather bag. Punching in the code to the new security system, we enter through the kitchen back door. Feeling as if I'm assaulted by a tornado, the world suddenly spins so fast that I wobble and grab the kitchen counter for support.

"Everything ok with you?" McCabe's words are soft as he stands behind me, holding both my shoulders. "You look like you could sleep for a week."

He is right. Sleep has been my nemesis lately, and its lack takes a toll. It is all I can do each evening not to plunder the credenza in my office for the latest wine Clarice stocked to knock me out. "I'm fine. I'm more exhausted mentally than physically, although being in constant motion with little sleep hasn't helped."

He gives me a knowing smile. "I felt the same way in the military, but I promise we will make all this as easy as possible."

"No, I know." Holding up my hands in surrender, I continue, "I'm not complaining."

We lug Nikki's equipment into Jack's library and begin to set it up. The rapid scanner feeds copies of the pages into a hard drive sitting next to it on the table. Mac and I will return the drive to Nikki, where we will upload the data into air-gapped computers at my office in Charleston.

"Tell me about Victoria and Brad," Mac says. "I had some background pulled, but I need to know how you and she got to where you are now. It seems she was a bit of a princess in high school and college, a rich daddy, and a socialite mother. That square with what you know?"

"Yes, her parents are well off, and their friends have a lot of political pull in South Carolina. She graduated college, married Jack, and started taking in children at the farm long before I met her. And yes, she is a bit of a diva."

"How did you two meet?"

"Victoria was a good friend of one of my ninth-grade teachers.

She was very pretty and married to a popular guy from her university, who was not bad-looking himself. They were the perfect local power couple from the day they married. He sponsored my school's Fellowship of Christian Athletes and participated in several other high schools' sports activities."

"Active otherwise?"

"Religious—very. Both were leaders in a small country church when they started the facility at the farm. Once the donations started, they moved to a more affluent one. They sponsored a religious-based academy, another foster facility in a different county, and others, but those came long after I worked with them."

"We'll get to the money. Did he preach?"

"He didn't consider himself a preacher. The only talks he gave were to donors for the fundraising." I hesitate as the memories of Jack and our private "teaching" sessions almost strangle me. "And Bible studies for teenagers at my high school."

We are quiet for a few minutes, organizing the documents to feed into Nikki's sophisticated scanning system. I focus on the paperwork before me, ensuring each set of mortgage documents is ready.

"It's interesting," Mac says. "Jack was the President and CEO of Timberline Farm from the beginning until fifteen years ago. Then there was an abrupt internal election of the board, and those positions shifted to his wife."

I squint at him. "How did you get that information?"

Mac only smiles. "Let's just say a confidential source. I have a verbal summary—documents will be here tomorrow."

He continued, "The story from the family, coroner, and funeral home are consistent that he had a heart attack. Jack's letter says otherwise, though. Angus said you have a photo?"

I retrieve the photo from the day of his funeral and hand my phone to Mac.

"Clarice said she was told the same thing by anyone she talked with," I respond. "This proves otherwise."

His fingers enlarge the photo. "Doesn't look like a heart attack to me. Who sent it to you?"

"I don't know. Can you discuss with Angus if there is someone at the federal level we can partner with? Or act as an advisor? I think the locals are hiding something because of Clint Harbin, the local solicitor's unwillingness to act. I don't know if that extends to the state level. Jack's death, honestly, is the least of my concerns. There are children my client says are being trafficked that are of more importance. Finding Jack's killer won't bring him back."

And I don't want him back.

I shift the conversation. "Other than Jack's removal from the board, what else did you learn?"

"Their children. The girl seems to have no involvement in the farm. She attended UC Berkeley and works in San Francisco. Once she left Charleston, my sources tell me she visits infrequently for a day or two at Thanksgiving or Christmas, never both. She's not close to her mother and only somewhat close to her father. This surprises me since most girls are the apples of their father's eye."

"And Brad?"

"That's a different story. Total terror. His first arrest was at age fourteen when he was caught joyriding in a stolen car with some other guys. According to my source, his father let him sit in jail and refused to bail him out. I pulled that criminal file myself. The bail form dated the next day had Victoria's signature."

"Sounds like Jack. He always was big on lessons and responsibility." Yet only for others, never for himself.

"According to my guy, there were a few more alcohol incidents. They also caught him in the football dorm at the university with his sock drawer full of marijuana. The school made him sit out only one game when the rules required him to be expelled. My guy found no arrest record for that incident."

"Why did the school protect him? Because of Jack? Or Victoria?"

"It could have been either of them, but my money is on the grandparents. I'm working on that; I don't have information yet. Victoria has been protective of both children, but particularly the son. Brad sat most games on the sidelines because of his temper. The coach kept him, but Brad saw little field time. He was hot-headed, creating way too many penalties per game."

"Anything recent such as bar fights, drunk and disorderly charges, assaults—sexual or otherwise—that type of thing?"

"There are several sexual assault charges, but none came to trial. The witnesses all retracted their statements, and the charges were dropped. My source says the consensus in the community is negative. Brad was a brat as a child and is now an even worse adult. Only a few people talked. Most absolutely refused to discuss Timberline Farm or anything dealing with Brad. That's a serious level of fear."

Shifting to sit behind the scanner, I feed stacks of documents into the high-speed machine, pondering Mac's information. He organizes more papers and slides them next to my elbow. We will electronically sort and name them back at the office as a group. Having searchable electronic documents at trial has proved invaluable in the past.

I need to bounce my ideas off Mac. I start talking. "The information we are gathering against Timberline Farm has multiple purposes. I need any information you can find, but definitely for these things." I stop scanning and begin to tick off the points on my fingers.

"First, based on the testimony and written diaries of the person he raped, I want to build a criminal case that forces Clint Harbin to prosecute Brad for rape. I have one girl, but I believe there will be others. Find me those names. Second, my client says he has some basement set up like a prison as an area for punishment and part of a trafficking system. I need clear proof to support this trafficking to get it stopped. I have some names and photos. We need to run down those people and places.

I think for several seconds, then continue. "Once Nikki, Clarice, and I go through the financial data, I anticipate some suit for mismanagement of funds, but that's down the road. Depending on what I find, I forsee the state's Attorney General or the Department of Justice getting involved and possibly the IRS for fraud."

I resume scanning. Mac is quiet as we feed in stacks of documents.

"Getting Angus and Nikki on as employees at that farm was a good idea," he says. "If there's anything there, they'll hear it."

"Lucky for us, they got hired. Or is it?"

Mac stops his paper shuffling. "What do you mean?"

"I don't know. It was just too easy. My brain is so fried that maybe I can only create crazy-person theories."

"Sometimes the crazy things are true. Usually, though, it's the ones that are the simplest and the most logical. Maybe Morris simply needs the help."

"What did you find on Victoria?" My fingernails bite into the palms of my hands at the mention of her name.

"Community sentiment is neutral. Some believe she is the paragon of virtue; others have no opinion. There is something just under the surface I've not yet identified. It won't be long before they know they're being watched and investigated."

"It's a small town, so I'm not surprised. How are your guys handling the questions?"

"They are posing as journalists looking for human interest stories involving Timberline Farm. Since the deceased was a public figure, it was an easy cover."

"I'm going to need some dirt on Clint Harbin, the Solicitor. He and Jack—"

"Were roommates in college." He stops looking at the documents and turns to me. "There's something I don't understand.

Why did this client come to you? How would she know you were connected with the farm? And why didn't you send her somewhere else? You're not a criminal attorney."

I look out the kitchen window to the meadow beyond the willow tree.

"She says her employer, the guy who runs the diner down the street, referred me. I think there's someone else behind it, but I haven't pushed it. Maybe it's time to do that. I tried to refer her to other attorneys, but she refused."

Resolved to let it out, I continue.

"Mac, I just couldn't tell her no. Parts of her story were too similar to mine."

"What do you mean?"

"Jack and I had a relationship when I worked as the ranch office manager as a freshman in high school. While he wanted a lover, Victoria had something else in mind. She kept throwing me in front of older men, teaching me what to do to—in her words—get more money from them in donations."

I stand up and stretch. "Let's take a break." I find a more comfortable chair in the living room, and Mac drops himself into the chair beside me.

"Was she grooming you?"

"Yes. It's only now I see how malicious she was. Back then, no one used the word 'grooming.' I thought she was just a jealous wife. I had just turned fifteen and didn't know much about these things. Every time she tried a new avenue, Jack would shut her down. He knew she was up to no good, or maybe I just hoped he knew."

I sigh and force myself to meet Mac's gaze. "By seventeen, Jack and I were in a full-blown relationship. He protected me even though he took advantage of me. To sound cliché, it's complicated."

I pull my feet up on the chair, resting my head against my

knees. Wrapping my arms around my legs, I feel emotionally naked.

His eyes hold mine. "You're not responsible for what Jack did to you, just as you're not responsible for what Brad did to your client."

"You ask why I'm representing Beth even though I shouldn't. It's because I'm pretty sure I was the first girl taken advantage of out there. I'm the one Victoria test-drove all her ideas on." I put my head back on my knees. "I could have said something then."

"Still doesn't make you responsible," he says. "Even at seventeen. In the relationship, it appears Jack was more patient than Victoria. He's responsible for his actions; she's responsible for hers. Still don't see where your responsibility comes into this."

His hand is suddenly on my knee, and he leans forward. His softly worded response is an inch from my face. "And it's a damn good thing he's dead."

I sit up and drop my legs to the floor, staring at him, blinking. How can he see this so easily?

He leans back into the chair. "I need to confess something. You probably won't like it."

"What?"

"I already know some of this."

My face flushes with embarrassment. "I didn't know it was common knowledge."

"It isn't. I have a good investigator. She can dig out things others can't. Also, I looked at your grandfather. I needed to be sure he wasn't part of the problem or connected to the farm. Honestly, I didn't find much other than social interaction. I couldn't find that he's ever been a donor. He's a cagey old man. Most of his information is locked down tight. I caught the connection to you. It appears that it's not a blood connection, yet you've remained close. Is there anything else I should know?"

"He's my grandfather. I love him more than anyone, and I'm

glad you didn't find anything. I would have been floored if you had."

"Come on," Mac responds. "We don't have much left to do. Then we can leave this depressing place and get you home."

We scan the remaining stack of documents and then the items in the safe other than the currency. We make copies on additional hard drives: One for Nikki, another in a bank safe deposit box, and a third into the fireproof safe. Mac agreed I should take the artwork, journals, copies of the essential property documents, and all the keys for Willow House.

I stare at the leather journals in my hands. I can only imagine the details Jack has included in them of our lives, sexual and otherwise. I remember how terrified he was of anyone ever finding out about us and how many times Victoria threatened to ruin his reputation if he didn't leave me. So why did he keep journals?

A shiver of fear suddenly travels up my spine.

"Hey, where are you in there?" Mac's fingers snap in front of my face.

"The entire town saw me spit on Jack at the funeral. My anger was evident. It is only a matter of time before Victoria uses her version of the information I am guessing is in these journals and accuses me of murder."

33

M y appointment with Hayward in Barton Springs, Georgia, is at noon. Arriving fifteen minutes early, Mac and I stroll down Adams Street, taking in the small, friendly town. Kendrick's office is like mine, old brick with a large tree in the back. Ancient oaks across the street cover the park, the center of the small town. Multiple businesses have outdoor tables, chairs, benches, and even swings, using the significant shade as protection from the Georgia sun. As if in New Orleans, the upper balcony of Kendrick's office extends over the front door of the building, shading a colored bench with pots of deep red geraniums on either side of the entrance.

Inside, a tidy receptionist's desk greets us. The person behind it is a man of approximately thirty with oversized ears that balance thin, wire-framed glasses on the end of a beaked nose.

"May I help you?" The man pushes the glasses up his nose.

"You must be Greg. I'm M. L. Danforth, and this is McCabe Lawrence. We're here for my appointment."

"Certainly. Please follow me to the conference room."

An overweight man in his sixties steps out of an open doorway. "That won't be necessary, Greg. She's a lawyer."

He speaks to me. "I'll meet with you in here." He motions toward the office behind him.

"Hayward Kendrick." He shakes my hand and then Mac's. The large room holds worn leather furniture and a massive desk stacked with files, reams of paper, and used coffee cups. Law books line one wall, and another holds framed diplomas and certificates, the typical lawyer "wall of glory." The small windows and large furniture in the room make me feel claustrophobic. His desk chair groans under the pressure of holding up a man his size. With a spare comb-over and wrinkled brown suit, the lawyer looks exhausted.

Kendrick sits, then slides a file across the table to me, along with a key. "I see you had no problem finding me. I apologize for not contacting you first. After Jack's death, I have decided to retire and have been focusing on that. And a few other things. I was waiting on a death certificate before I contacted you, but I still haven't received one from Charleston County."

The man rubs the back of his neck. He straightens his tie, clearly uncomfortable.

He extends his hand toward Mac. "Out of an abundance of caution, may I see both your driver's licenses?"

The man is stalling, but we comply. He looks at Mac's PI licenses carefully before handing back our information. My patience has run out.

"A trust conveyed the house in Barton Springs. Your name is on the deed. You also seem to have some relationship with Jack Marshall."

"Yes." Kendrick fidgets as he reaches over to punch a button on his phone. "Greg, do you mind bringing us all coffee? Use the portable carafe, please." The lawyer smiles at me as he releases the call button. "Need my afternoon fix."

As the coffee is being served, Kendrick says to Greg, "Take off early. Turn out the lights in front and lock up. I'll see you in the morning."

Greg gives his boss a slight rise of his eyebrows. He leaves the room with a shove of his glasses up his nose. They hear the front door close, and the deadbolt turns a few seconds later. Kendrick relaxes.

"Sorry, this case has me spooked. For his protection, I don't want him to overhear anything. I don't trust that damn Marshall woman."

He pulls out a large folder from a desk drawer, dons reading glasses, and finally begins the meeting.

"As the Personal Representative of the Estate of John "Jack" Carter Marshall, Victoria Marshall sued me. She is unhappy with the terms of Mr. Marshall's will. More significantly, she is very angry with you, Ms. Danforth."

He looks at Mac. "There are things in this will that only Ms. Danforth should hear. If you don't mind, please sit out in the reception area." He points toward the door. "Given Mrs. Marshall's volatility of late, I prefer you stay close, but I need to talk to Ms. Danforth alone."

Mac doesn't move.

"She will be fine with me, I promise." Kendrick stares at McCabe, and his voice becomes testy. "I'll have her along soon."

Mac protests. "I don't think—"

"If I were in your shoes," Kendrick responds. "I'd do the same. But my client's will requires this."

Mac's face is rigid. I squeeze his arm.

"I'll be fine. I know you'll be close enough to hear me whisper, much less scream."

He leans toward me, saying under his breath, "But not close enough to do anything. I don't like this, but I won't be far."

Kendrick waits until the door closes. "I understand you have a strong constitution."

I meet the other attorney's gaze with my own. His face is ashen, tired. Either his career or Victoria has worn him to a nub.

Since I don't truly enjoy my practice, I expect to look the same in a few years. When I do not respond he continues.

"Jack has been my client since you both gave up your child some twenty-odd years ago. He hired me to review the paperwork drafted by your grandfather. We, Jack and I, grew to be friends over the years. When he asked me to arrange the house in case of his death, I couldn't refuse. He was my friend. I thought his concerns regarding his wife were overblown, even when he hired a private detective to investigate his wife and son. The stress of all those conspiracies in his head must have gotten to his heart."

"Then you don't know," I say.

"What?" His face wrinkles with concern.

"That someone murdered him," I respond.

His mouth opens like a wide-mouth bass.

I show him the photos on my phone. "Look at these."

He swipes through the photos and then hands me the phone. "Who did this?"

I hesitate, but the pain on his face when looking at Jack's murder photos pushes me forward.

"I don't know. That isn't why I'm here. Do you have the name of that private investigator Jack hired?"

"No. He never told me who that was." Kendrick shakes his head and continues. "The police never mentioned a criminal case to me."

"There isn't one that I'm aware of."

I pull out the title abstract from my briefcase. "Was Morris Jessup involved in the trust that deeded the house to me?"

"No. Jessup wanted no part of anything. You know how persuasive Jack could be, but Jessup was firm. He wanted nothing to do with the house. He sold it to Jack long ago and considered the matter closed."

He retrieves a blue-backed document from his file, the standard form for a will. "I need to read you Jack's will."

"That's unnecessary. I don't need to know what he left his family."

"He left nothing to the family. That's the issue. Victoria Marshall wants to declare this will invalid because of your alleged undue influence."

"Has she seen the will?"

"No. I didn't let her read it. She only knows what I've told her verbally, that neither she nor her children are listed as beneficiaries under the will."

"How can I have had any undue influence? Was Jack incapacitated in some manner? This is wrong in so many ways. I haven't seen Jack since college. You know that. I can't imagine that Jack would let anyone tell him what to do."

"Yes, but she doesn't. She insists you two have been carrying on behind her back the entire time."

I snort. I am amazed at the fiction Victoria can create. My concern is that the people who matter, such as a judge or a solicitor, might believe her.

"Who inherits?" I know before Kendrick opens his mouth.

"You do. Assets only, no liabilities. All liabilities are Victoria's responsibility. That's another reason she's so mad."

I squint at him. "Did you draft his will?"

"Oh, no. I'm just the Personal Representative. Our friendship was too legally conflicting. I sent him to Columbia, South Carolina, to have it done by that law school professor who wrote all Estates and Wills textbooks up there. I can't remember his name, but I'm sure it's in my file. I tried to get him to hire the professor to be the PR, but Jack wouldn't hear of it."

Victoria will most likely add me as a party to the estate lawsuit. Great. One more thing.

"What are the assets?"

"The house that has already been deeded to you. A little cash, a few stocks. All his artwork, including the original of that piece that is in the house's library. They are in the New York gallery."

"Is his art a lucrative business?"

"The smaller pieces—and I do mean small—go for around five thousand. The gallery owner will provide the prices for the large pieces. I taped the card to Jack's portfolio on the dining table."

I sit, stunned. Everything in the house was from Heyward Kendrick.

"I found all that. Anything else? Bank accounts, insurance policies?"

"No. He felt Victoria could contest those, even with their estrangement."

"Estrangement?"

Jack never left Victoria. I twist the ring on my middle finger so hard that my finger is about to fall off. Kendrick stares at me, surprised by my lack of knowledge.

"He left her the day after he signed the adoption paperwork. I didn't read any of the journals he wrote, but I'm sure everything's in there. He said writing to you was the only way to keep his sanity. He wanted to contact you but couldn't bring himself to do it. Said he'd ruined enough of your life."

It is my turn to gape like a fish.

"I apologize for the flowers and note by the bed. I promise I didn't look at all the private photos." His voice breaks. "It's just that..." Kendrick hesitates. "...he instructed me even to the color of the tulips. I couldn't ignore his wishes and dishonor my friend like that. I just couldn't. I'm sorry."

He drops his head in his hands. I let him have time to get himself together. He looks up with red-rimmed eyes and a weary smile, pulling a small square of cloth from his pocket. He removes his glasses as he cleans the lens, and I smile at our familiar habit.

I cannot be angry with a man who was only doing his job.

"Is there anything else I need to know?"

"Don't turn your back on Victoria. I'm betting she will either expose your relationship with Jack to the press or have you charged with his murder."

34

"We didn't have to meet over a trifle like this document, Judge." Victoria waved her right hand at the city view, her left on the paperwork spread before Judge Rhineholdt, her fingernail tapping the signature line. "Although you did select a lovely place."

They were seated in the Citrus Club, the rooftop bar at The Dewberry Hotel. A light fruit and cheese snack sat untouched on one side of the table. She had ordered it only to be polite. The stuffy old windbag thought he was king in Charleston, dressed in a blue seersucker suit, robin's egg bowtie, and a summer straw hat, which he adjusted to protect his face from the sun.

"I thought it best we meet in person," the Judge replied, "since you refused to believe me when we discussed this matter by phone. Ms. Danforth will sign nothing for you relating to the estate of Jack Marshall. Even if she agreed, which she does not, as her grandfather—and her legal counsel—I would not allow it."

Victoria looked over the man's shoulder toward the Ravenel Bridge and Sullivan's Island, where the old coot lived. He should have stayed out there, old, retired, and away from her business. She pushed the file folder toward him.

"Just give these relinquishment documents to your client and have her sign them immediately. She is not entitled to any of Jack's estate, of course. And neither is their child. My attorney is simply being cautious. Marjorie Lee is being obstinate, and it's causing me a problem. I need to get it off my plate."

Her shiny red fingernails glinted in the sun as she baked in her new sundress from Gwynn's. She hated the sunlight and should have insisted they eat indoors. Regardless of the thick makeup and fake eyelashes, she could not hide the heavy wrinkles and layers of skin on her neck that seemingly replicated overnight. She opened her compact to check her lipstick, and the harsh sunlight caught the difference in skin tone where she had missed a spot with her foundation on the side of her face. She hated getting old.

He picked up his wine glass and swirled the pale red wine. She preferred white. Why couldn't he have ordered something light and refreshing? He was so set in his ways and always had been.

"Victoria." The Judge leaned forward to get her attention. "You are not listening. My client will sign nothing."

"And why not?" He could protect that little whore all he wanted, but it wouldn't do any good. Victoria had already consulted an ambulance-chasing attorney she had found through a friend. That lawyer was ready to sue for what happened both at the funeral and for the original emotional distress caused by their affair. All attorneys were the same as Marjorie Lee, ready to sue to make a buck. It was time she used one or two.

The wine was going to her head. She attempted to focus on the Judge's words, although watching his lips move between that wooly beard and mustache nauseated her.

"Because nothing requires it," he responded. "Your husband signed the adoption paperwork years ago, and none of that involved you. You were not a party to that transaction then and are not now."

"This bastard child will inherit from Jack, and I won't have it. It will open the door to Marjorie Lee attempting to take a share. I want their signatures on these documents to prove that neither she nor her child wishes to inherit. If I'm not mistaken, you drafted those poorly written adoption documents. They left too many loopholes, and my lawyer wants to close them all."

"I drafted them in my client's best interest. I am sure you have never seen these documents, or you would know this yourself. If you were as concerned when the adoption occurred as you appear now, you should have hired counsel to review them before you allowed Jack to sign them."

"I didn't know about them until now, or I would have. It took Jack's death for it all to come out. My lawyer found the child's birth certificate when he was checking Jack's assets. He's considering whether to sue you as well as Marjorie Lee."

Her threat did not affect Rhineholdt. If she had been aware of the bastard child at her birth, she would have indeed hired an attorney, but Jack, and this moron Judge, had kept it a secret.

The old man eased back in his chair. "Victoria, can you not see how ridiculous these threats are?" After drinking one more sip of wine, the Judge wiped his lips with his napkin and prepared to rise. He carefully folded the napkin and placed it on the table, then stood, tugging at his jacket and adjusting his hat.

"Where are you going?" Victoria gathered the papers on the table, her hands shaking with anger.

"This meeting was a waste of my time. If you require anything further, please have your counsel contact me directly. I do not believe it will benefit you or my client, and most definitely not me, by further direct contact."

Victoria stood, the blood-red nail of her index finger shaking in the Judge's face. She didn't bother to keep her voice down. The entire town could know for all she cared.

"You tell Marjorie Lee that neither she nor her bastard child will inherit one penny from Jack. I'll make damn sure the sham adoption is nullified and Jack's will is declared void. And don't think you can stop me, you old fool."

The Judge looked at her with a blank stare. "Enough, Victoria. You are making a spectacle of yourself. Good day." Tipping his hat to her, he left the restaurant.

Victoria remained rigid in her seat as she reined in her anger. The old coot didn't even pay. Southern etiquette required that the person inviting pay the bill. Victoria opened her patent leather purse, scrambling for a good enough excuse to provide to the waiter when her credit card was declined.

35

Heading back to Charleston with my computer open in my lap, the car suddenly swerves, and a splash of coffee hits my knee, barely missing the keypad. I close the thermos as Mac's fingers shift his Porsche into a lower gear, tossing us forward like a rocket.

His body tenses. The force of the car leaning into the next curve causes my internal alarm to kick into overdrive.

"What's happening?" I slam the computer and look over my shoulder.

"We have a tail." He shifts again, his hands and feet working in tandem. Glancing at the rear-view mirror, he mutters. "Too bad. I like this car."

I look in the side mirror. Mac's head shifts from side to side, his eyes flicking to catch mine.

"It's one of those trucks with huge tires and a serious lift kit. He's sitting four feet above us. There's a bright yellow winch on the front that will do serious damage if he rams us. Unless he's made some changes under the hood, I can lose him in the straightaway, but we need to get off this two-lane and on the freeway."

"That's miles away, Mac."

I look behind us. Much of the truck's body is covered in large spots of unpainted Bondo. Like a giant clown nose, the large yellow winch is mounted on the front. I wedge my computer into its case on the floor behind my calves and against the seat. I double-check my seatbelt and then test Mac's. Seeing there's no service on my phone, I jam it into the waistband of my pants.

"How many people are in the truck?" I ask, unable to see through the glare of the truck's windshield.

"Three, I think." His voice is curt. "Driver, passenger, and a third behind."

"Guns?"

"I'm sure they have a few, but I haven't seen one yet."

The roar of the truck's diesel engine suddenly surrounds us, and I turn again to look. The truck grill blocks the entire back of the car.

"How is that truck able to keep up with this Porsche?"

"He's modified his engine. There's no telling what is under that hood. Hold on. He's about to hit us."

Before I can prepare, the winch hook crashes into the Porche's back window, and glass explodes toward me. I snap my head forward and close my eyes. The truck bumper hits the Porsche, and my head slams forward toward the dashboard. I scream, covering my head as the wind roars and pieces of glass rain down my arms.

"Are you okay?" Mac yells. The car shoots forward again like a cannon under his experienced hands. He can't look at me and drive.

"Lee?" His shout competes with the wind.

"I'm fine." My voice is sucked out of the car by the wind. "Drive." I point toward the road and brush glass from my body, trying to stay below the seat back. Tiny cuts bleed as I pull out my cell.

An open marsh surrounds us. The cellular service icon on my

phone shows one bar. I punch in 911. The call won't go through. I grit my teeth and force myself to concentrate.

Text. It might go through even if a call won't.

I text 911 and hold on to the door handle as Mac swerves to the right, the centrifugal force thrusting me toward him as he tries to widen the gap between us and the truck.

The truck engine's gears grind close again. I turn to look. My heart races, and sparks fly in the wind as the truck's undercarriage grinds the Porsche's metal trunk.

I check my phone.

A text appears.

This is 911. Please state your emergency.

Steadying my elbows on my knees, I type, twisting to take rapid photos through the shattered window, hoping to get one clear shot of the truck. I send the best one, praying for it to load.

Rounding the next curve, the Porsche takes to the air, bottoming on the pavement when it lands as Mac swerves to avoid an oncoming sedan. I twist again to look at the truck. On its surface, the truck is a lumbering piece of junk, but it has kept pace mile for mile with Mac's sports car.

The wind noise screeches through the small car. I look at my phone.

No response.

Frantic, I type another text to 911.

"Get ready!" Mac's shout carries over the noise.

With one last look, I see the huge yellow winch fill the entire rear window. With a goose of the gas, the winch comes for me. The truck roars, preparing to climb up and over the Porsche like a tank. I scream when it crashed into the rear of the car. I cannot believe the engine is still running.

"Sit up. We're going to fly." Mac shouts.

As he floors the gas, I throw my body backward, clinging to the armrest as we finally reach the straight, flat portion of the road before us. The speedometer is over one hundred twenty, and we fly from the marsh, passing Woods Seafood in a blur. With only one quick turn on Highway 21 a mile ahead, we will reach Interstate 95 within a minute.

"Mac, look!" I point at what's ahead.

At the turn for Augusta Road, two Georgia State Patrol vehicles block the intersection, the cars nose to nose in a V, the officers standing in front. I glance back at the truck. It takes the last turn and races toward us again. The officers dash to their cars, ready to pull away if the rockets flying toward them fail to stop.

The screech of tires behind us makes me duck again, my arms over my head, ready for a crash. The contents of my stomach rise, waiting for the impact.

Instead, I hear a loud screech of rubber tires against the pavement.

Behind me, the tires smoke, leaving snaking black tracks as the driver attempts to maneuver a three-point turn without flipping. Successful, a cloud of smoke billows from the exhaust as it blasts away from us.

Wind rocks the Porsche with an ear-splitting *whoop* as one of the Trooper vehicles roars past. The remaining police car is waiting for us at the end of the valley.

"I think you should stay in the car. Since I was driving, they'll want to talk to me." Coming to a stop, Mac is out, wallet in his up-stretched hand, the other out to his side, making it clear to the officer that he is unarmed. "Thank God you guys arrived." Mac's voice is so loud I can hear him even though the roaring sound of the wind is still in my head. "Whatever that guy has under his hood is unbelievable."

Unable to hear the Trooper's response, his hand movements signal Mac to stop walking and explain. McCabe's voice is now too low. I watch as he pulls things from his wallet. The Trooper holds a white card up as he reads, looks at Mac, then at me, and then uses his shoulder microphone.

My face drops to my hands as I try to get my thoughts

together. I open my door, waiting for the inevitable vomit to hit the grass. But it doesn't. Jittery, my head is splitting, but I'm still in one piece. I can thank Mac for that.

Any movement causes shards of glass to bite through my clothing. Without Mac, I would be floating out in the marsh or flipped upside down in my car, injured or dead. I hold back the tears as the adrenaline rush crashes and my exhaustion takes over.

"Ma'am, are you all right?" A male voice asks. "Are you hurt?" A hand rests on my shoulder. I wipe my eyes with my hands, not wanting to use my sleeve for fear of all the broken glass. I focus on kind gray eyes under a large brown trooper hat.

"I'm fine," I respond. "That's a lie. I'm still terrified. I can't tell you how much I appreciate you showing up. My security head is a fine driver. I'm not sure what would have happened if you hadn't arrived,"

I stop, realizing I'm babbling.

"You're the one who contacted 911 dispatch?"

"Yes, sir." I hold up my iPhone so the officer can see the texts and photos.

"May I see your license, please? And I could use that photo. Can you send it to me?" He hands me a business card. "Send me all the photos, ma'am, you have if you don't mind."

I pull my purse from the floorboard and place it in my lap in full view of the officer. Finding my wallet, I hand him my license and a business card.

"They are pretty blurry, but I'll send them all."

"At the station, I'll need an accurate report. We'll also need to get your statements since this doesn't appear to be a simple hit-and-run."

The officer strides away from the Porsche, my license in his hand. He returns Mac's to him as he passes.

I step out of the car, and glass pieces scatter the ground. Taking off my jacket, I shake it and wipe glass out of my seat, then

Mac's. Mac uses a handkerchief from his pocket to wipe tiny bits of shattered glass from around the gearshift and off the dashboard.

The trooper comes back to the Porche.

"Follow me to the station, please." He hands me my license, and Mac buckles himself back into the car. I wait for him to start the engine. When nothing happens, I glance over at him, then see steam coming from the engine in the rear.

"Will it start?"

McCabe's face is laced with concern, then shifts to fear. He doesn't respond. He blinks, and his steel-gray eyes lock onto mine. I watch as he pulls himself together, his face returning to a professional mask.

"Mac, I'm sorry I got you into this. But if I had been driving, they would have killed me."

"It's not your fault—just part of the job." He punches the ignition button, and after a wheeze, the engine turns over. "We'll need to give our statements. Are you up for that?"

I give him what I hope is a confident look. "That's what the officer told me. I'm sure I can handle whatever he asks me. He was nice when he checked on me."

Mac snorts a laugh. "He wasn't checking on you. He was, but he also needed to ensure I hadn't kidnapped you. Just because I gave him a story didn't make it true. He's still making sure our little fun ride is the truth." He looks at me and shrugs, his face softening with a smile. "It's what I would do, anyway."

After the trip to the Georgia trooper's office, we continue our journey back to Charleston, even though the Porche engine is running roughly. Nikki and Angus are at the farm. Mac begins to search for the truck's owner. With his team ensuring the safety of everyone at the office, he finally crashes upstairs in the apartment, and I sleep on my office couch. Two hours later, I am thrown into a panic by Clarice's quick triple knocks on the door. Realizing who it is, I calm my breathing as she comes in with two mugs. I sit up, hoping I'm over the exhaustion from the adrenaline crash.

"Is everything all right? Mac just said you had a run in with some guys in big truck."

"Man, that coffee smells so good. Thank you." I take a sip and let the caffeine magic flow through my body. "We had a little runover, rather a run-in. I'm sure it was Victoria's thugs."

Wrapping both hands around the mug, I take another long, slow sip of the coffee. Rotating my neck in a circle, I hope the pain is from sleeping on the couch and not whiplash. Clarice rests her mug on the coffee table and collapses into one of the chairs.

"What happened exactly?"

"We got rammed from behind by a giant truck. They tried to kill us." I take another sip and set my cup on the table. My hands are shaking. "The back of Mac's Porche is crushed, and the rear window is trashed."

"Were either of you hurt?"

"I don't think so, but sometimes whiplash takes time to show up. It scared us both. Even the big bad military guy was alarmed."

"They're trying to scare you off."

"Well, I'm frightened. This tells me I've touched a nerve, though, and I'm on the right track." I lean against the back of the couch and take in a breath.

Clarice stares at me with concern. "What's wrong?"

"I haven't tossed my cookies yet. I should have been sick when the Trooper came to get my license." I stand, fold the couch blanket, and place it in the credenza.

"Maybe someone should have run me off the road long ago."

36

———

With the excitement and adrenaline from the Barton Springs trip over, I open the cabinet in my office and stare at Jack's journals hiding inside.

No. Not today.

I slowly close the door to the cabinet. I can't face anything related to Jack—not yet, anyway. I am still blown away knowing that his artwork, possibly nudes of me, is hanging in others' living rooms and bedrooms.

I check my cell phone for voicemail messages from Angus or Nikki about Glenna. There's nothing. It feels like they have worked there for a week, even though they have been at the farm less than one day. The incident with the truck has scrambled my brain.

At my desk, I get organized. My most pressing issue today is my law clerk. I still have no research from Lauren. I admit researching the Rule Against Perpetuities is boring, but I need the most recent case citations for my oral argument scheduled next week at the Court of Appeals. I search again to be sure. There is no research memo in either my electronic or physical inbox.

Never one to wait when I can act, I pour myself another cup of coffee, add oat milk, and step down the hall to the clerk's office. The girl needs to do her job, or I need a new law clerk. I hear Lauren's angry tone as I raise my hand to knock.

I lean closer to the door.

"I did what you asked, you asshole." Lauren is shouting now. "I'm not doing anything else for you. She's done nothing to me besides providing me with a desperately needed job. You can take your threats and shove them!"

The slam of the desk phone makes me jump. Grasping the doorknob, I stop myself. I wait and listen through the door.

Lauren's office is silent for almost a minute. Then I hear a drawer open and then close. After hearing more shuffling and a nose being blown, I hear the familiar boot-up sound of the computer. Stepping backward, I walk around the corner to the office where Mac and another of his team are setting up equipment for the office.

As I open the door, Mac is already rising from his chair.

"Just caught a call from your clerk on an outside line. Want to hear it?" Mac's face is angry as he folds his arms across his chest. "She planted the device in your office."

He returns to his chair, as I stand beside him. Clicking the keyboard, I'm caught off guard by the amount of hatred in the male voice blasting from his computer. I grab the back of Mac's chair.

Brad Marshall. I listen to the recording, then have Mac play it again.

"Hey, baby doll."

Brad's voice is sickeningly sweet.

"I told you not to call me here."

"I just wanted to hear your voice."

"I doubt that. What do you want?"

"You did great. I can hear everything loud and clear. Or at least I could. Got quiet, though. I need you to check it and be sure it's still

working. I don't think your dumbass attorney can find her ass without help, but you never know."

Lauren doesn't respond. Mac and I wait through the silence."

"I'm not going back to her office. What do you want, Brad?"

"Thought you might want to have dinner tonight. I have a few things we need to talk about face-to-face. Plus, there's a bonus for this next thing.

"Brad, I'm not doing anything else for you. Putting that bug in her office was enough, especially for what little you paid me."

Lauren's voice on the tape wavers, and her fear is palpable.

"Look bitch. You need to do what you're told. It was an easy job. And you didn't get caught, did you?"

"Not yet. But she already suspects me. They threw me out of the conference room. I'm so nervous I can't get my regular work done."

"Not my problem."

"It is if I get caught. You don't think I'll tell them who put me up to this?"

"No, you won't if you know what's good for you. I need this next thing by tonight. Bring me whatever files she has on Timberline Farm. Shred the paper ones and bring everything digital to me on a thumb drive."

"You have lost your mind. The entire office is working on that case. There is no way I can do that."

"Sure you can unless you want me to go to the police about your little drug problem. I'm sure the law school would love to know they have a dealer in their midst."

"I did what you asked, you asshole." Lauren is shouting. *"I'm not doing anything else for you. She's done nothing to me besides providing me with a desperately needed job. You can take your threats and shove them!"*

The call ends.

"That call compromised your clerk, Lee," Mac says. "The prudent strategy would be to remove her immediately from the office. However, since this affects the Timberline Farm matter, another move would be to play her and use her for disinformation. But it is up to you."

I grip the insides of my cheeks with my teeth, a habit formed in law school to make me think before I speak. The pain makes me focus.

Without prior consent, recording either video or audio calls in South Carolina without permission of at least one party to the call is illegal. Yet Lauren signed such a consent as a condition of her employment. She also signed a statement that there is no expectation of privacy for any calls made in the office or when using office equipment.

Had she wanted to be recorded? Possibly, if only to get Brad off her back.

"Mac," I say, "Angus and Nikki need to listen to this. Leave them a message saying that we need an update about Glenna and that they need to come by here first before going home."

"Agreed," he responds. "Who is the caller?"

I sit in the extra guest chair.

"It's Brad Marshall, which means Lauren can't work here," I say, continuing to think aloud. "I'm sure the girl cannot access our electronic files as she is a probationary contractor and not yet an employee, but you never know. We need to be sure she hasn't taken anything related to the Timberline Farm case electronically from this office."

"I can do that." Mac reaches for the desk phone. He punches the button for Clarice's line and hands me the phone.

"Clarice, can you meet me and Mac in the front office?"

"Coming," Clarice responds. I return the phone to Mac.

"Why are you in such a tizzy?" Clarice comes into the office and slides fresh coffee in front of me and Mac. I drink half of it in one gulp, even though I don't need an additional layer of jitters. "The new girl is toast. She's a plant from Timberline Farm. Brad sent her to plant that microphone in my office."

"You're kidding me." Clarice's eyebrows rise toward the ceiling as she lets out an exasperated huff. "This is on me, Lee. I'm the one who found her. Well, she found me."

"No, actually, this might be just what we need."

"In what way?"

"It's another way to incriminate Brad. As long as Lauren cooperates."

"We hired her the week before Beth first met with you. I bet he cooked this up with Harbin right after Beth visited the Solicitor's office."

"Yeah," I respond, "I need to find out whose idea it was for her to work here, hers or Brad's. If hers, I need to know her connection to him." I start for the door. "Come on. I need you guys as witnesses. Clarice, bring her to my office, please."

37

Lauren follows Clarice into my office, Mac closing the door behind them. Clarice points silently to one of the chairs in front of my desk, and Lauren sits.

"We have a tape of your conversation with Brad Marshall," I begin. "Don't think about disputing it. We found the microphone you placed under my desk."

"Ms. Danforth, please let me explain." Lauren clutches her purse tightly against her stomach. Her face is a study in abject fear. As a law student, she knows this is more than just a termination. There is possible jail time if I press charges.

"Clarice will go over the termination paperwork with you. We have a standard exit interview that usually occurs, but at this point, I'm trying to decide whether just to terminate you or call the police."

"Please," Lauren begs, "it wasn't my idea. It was Brad's." Her tears begin, and neither Clarice nor I move to hand her a tissue. Right now, I don't have it in me to be decent. I sit silently until she stops crying.

"Okay, you have two minutes. Tell me about your relationship with Brad."

"It isn't a relationship. Well, it isn't now. Right now, it's black-mail." Lauren's face is sullen as she wipes ruined makeup from under her eyes. She takes a long breath and lets it out slowly.

"I met him in college, about a year ago," she continues. "We dated a few times, and he introduced me to a few of his friends. At first, he was charming. He took me to dinner and introduced me to his mother. Quite the gentleman. Then things began to change."

"I'm listening." I place my elbows on the desk, my fingers steepled under my chin.

"We started going to parties, drinking too much, that sort of thing. Until then, I'd not taken any drugs." She tried a light-hearted smile. "A little weed, but no pills or anything else. I'm in law school and these type things don't look good on a back-ground check for the bar.

"As the months went by, the parties got sleazier, and the drugs got worse. I begged off several times, but it didn't go as expected. The harder I tried to escape him, the worse he got. Finally, on our last date, I told him I never wanted to see him again. He slapped me and told me to get in the car. That was the worst night of my life. Since then, he's stalked me and showed up everywhere I go. About a month ago, he left some photos in my mailbox."

"Photos?" I guessed at how bad that last night was. Probably worse than Beth's.

"Ones showing me in compromising positions—doing disgusting things, if you want to know—with lots of different men, doing a lot of drugs. At first, I couldn't figure out how those could have been taken until I realized they had photoshopped another girl's body with my face."

"What did you do?"

"I wanted to go to the police but had no proof. Brad showed up that afternoon at my apartment. Said he had a job for me, and if I didn't do it, he would drop copies of the photos in an envelope and make sure they were delivered to the dean at the law school."

"And the job was working here?"

"Yeah. At first, I said no. You weren't hiring, and I'd have to talk my way into a job that didn't exist. But then, as I thought about it, I figured it might be just what I needed to escape him completely. If I did whatever he wanted, I could make him hand over the photos."

"Seriously?" I asked.

"I know it wasn't realistic. He could have kept digital copies forever. But I just thought he would want simple things. I had no idea I would be bugging your office and stealing files."

Lauren hangs her head, staring at her feet. "I was desperate. I still am. I can't get away from him."

I look first to Clarice, then to Mac. They both nod their agreement. "Lauren, look at me," I command. Ringed in pink, Lauren's gray eyes hold nothing but despair. "You cannot work here again. But we can do something about Brad if you cooperate."

"I'll do anything. Otherwise, I'm trapped forever. I'm assuming you'll want me to testify against him."

"Yes. We may need you for other things, but I'm not going into that now. You have to make me trust you again first because I don't. Don't make me regret this."

"Will I be able to return to law school in the fall?"

"Yes, if you do what we say. And otherwise, keep your mouth shut."

"Then I'll do whatever you want."

"Go home for the day. Say nothing to Brad, and if he calls, don't answer. Just show up here tomorrow like normal, and I'll have Clarice keep you busy. The work won't be much fun, but that's the price you pay. If you don't show up tomorrow, the deal is off, and I'll go to the police with the tape of you and Brad."

As Lauren leaves, Nikki strides into my office with the hard drives from the day's trip to Barton Springs.

"Any damage to the drives?"

"Surprisingly enough, no. Everything was in the front trunk, so other than being thrown around a bit, I don't see any problems. We will check everything out in a second. Let me put all this in the extra office. I'll be right back."

She returned within a minute.

"I need you to listen to an audio file Mac has. And do you have any information on Glenna?"

"Heard it on the way in, and no. Was that ugly crap coming from Brad?"

"Yes."

"I heard some of what Lauren told you," Nikki says. "I do feel for her a little, but there's no way we can trust her after this."

"No, she can't work here," I reply, "but Brad can't know she's been terminated. I'll use her as a witness against Brad." I lean toward her. "What is happening at the farm?"

She shifts in her chair. "How well do you know Morris Jessup? I guess what I want to know is how close are you as friends?"

"Well, we're not friends. He was the farm's manager when I worked there as a teenager. He punished me once when I was at the barn when I shouldn't have been. I've seen him only a few times in twenty years. What happened today?"

"He is one of the most stressed human beings I have ever encountered. He is quite different from the folksy manager I expected to meet. Your pleasant, laid-back phone call on speaker with him isn't reality."

"What happened?"

"He needs house parents just as you thought, but he needs an office manager worse. He asked about my experience in accounting systems and paper record keeping. He is shifting from a paper system to a decent automated one but is getting pushback, I guess, from Brad. I got the impression his record-keeping methods were a mess."

"Did you meet Brad?"

"No. It seems we do that later."

A quick two raps at the door, and Angus steps inside, throwing up a hand in a quick wave.

"Hey, M. L." He looks at his wife. "Nikki, Morris called me. I've got to go back out there tonight as security. The guy he suspected would eventually leave just quit."

"Angus, what's your take on Morris?" I ask.

"Well, he was very positive about you in the interview. He said you two went way back." Angus picked a cuticle on his thumb as if he was reluctant to continue. "It's the energy of the place and the people," he said. "I don't know how to explain it otherwise. His is chaotic. The energy of the farm is depressing and forlorn. The children look cared for, but I can tell there are not enough adults in supervisory positions. Tonight, I will go into every building and house as part of the standard security check, and when I find Glenna, I'll call. He had both of us trapped with him all day, getting us oriented.

"There is only a receptionist and an office clerk in the office," Nikki says. "Morris is acting as manager but is pulled in too many directions. The farm work is sliding. There is theft and property damage—genuine issues. I see already why Brad needs the money. The place is falling apart."

"You two should trust no one at that farm." I say. "Victoria is a slithering snake; she always has been. Morris is in this up to his neck, trying to keep the orphanage afloat with all this chaos, and even if he acts like a friend, he probably isn't. There's too much I've heard about Brad, and none of it is good.

They both stand to leave, and I walk with them to the door. "Whatever happens, our priority is Glenna."

38

A fter Angus and Nikki leave, Clarice ushers Beth into my office. Dressed in jeans and a bright yellow T-shirt with Buddy's restaurant logo and her hair in a messy bun, her smile doesn't reach her eyes. Clarice places a bottle of water on the side table and discreetly leaves us, closing the door softly behind her.

"I got a call last night." Wringing her hands, she shoves them into her jean pockets. "I'm worried."

I motion for her to sit as I shove a stack of files to one side. "Tell me."

"Trish heard Brad and Breaker talking in his office while she was cleaning. The next shipment is Monday."

"In three days? You're certain?"

"Yes." Her voice chokes with emotion. "You have to do something, M.L. And I remembered something else. On the night I saw the women go into the basement with Breaker, the police were involved."

She takes a drink of the water. Her shoulders sag with despair.

"Which department? The City of Charleston? Or the county sheriff?" I ask.

"The sheriff's office, I think. They turned their top lights on when they hit the county road. It looked like a sheriff's car." She drinks the rest of the water. "Unless you can work miracles, you won't be able to stop them."

"We're working to get hard evidence. Trust me, Beth."

Beth looks out the window. A bluebird preens itself on a branch a foot from the glass. "I do trust you, but you need to be careful." When she looks at me, her eyes are laced with fear.

I don't tell her I already know how nasty these men can be.

"Breaker carries a handgun with him everywhere he goes. He says it's because of the snakes on the property. I know better. That man scares the everlivin' shit out of me. No one can stop him."

She stands, her nervous hands sliding down the front of her jeans. "Look, I gotta go. Buddy is by himself today."

"Can I ask you one thing before you go?"

"Sure," Beth says.

"I know you said Buddy gave you my name, but did someone else tell you to come see me?"

Beth squirms a little and looks at her feet, giving me the answer I expected.

"Ok, so who is it?"

"Charlotte O'Neill. She's the senator's wife, the man who died recently." Beth stuffs her hands in her jean pockets. "She said she would cover any legal fees as long as I used you as the attorney."

"Ok, thanks. I thought it would be something like that. If you talk with her, can you have her call me?"

"I will. There's no problem?"

"No, Beth. I think I should talk with Mrs. O'Neill and ensure we are on the same page. Remember, everything needs to be confidential."

"I haven't talked with her since I came here."

"Still," I reply, "she might be expecting you to. Let me talk with her. Don't worry."

I escort her out and then find Mac in the conference room. I convey the abbreviated timeline, the involvement of the police, and that yet another person might be involved in this mess.

"Mac, I need to assure Beth that she can trust us. I intend to keep her updated as much as possible, but she needs more than that. And we need a plan. I can't let Glenna and those kids get taken."

His expression is stern. "I wouldn't tell her too much. You must know the expression 'need to know.' Telling her anything could blow our cover, get Trish hurt..." he tilts his head toward me as his voice lowers, "or harm those children. Keep her out of this."

"She thinks it's just me. She's scared I'm going to confront Breaker on my own."

"We need to keep it that way. Let her think what she wants."

I reluctantly acquiesce. Mac and I discuss the beginnings of a plan using what I know of the farm and Beth's statements. Phase one is to gather evidence surrounding the children being taken. We have Beth's testimony to prove their disappearance, but not enough to identify the actual traffickers. If Glenna and Trish can be rescued, assuming that Glenna is at the farm, our proof will be complete, even though I don't relish having to put either on the stand. There will be no testimony if we cannot find her. It is amazing to me that a girl has been missing for days and no one seems to care.

I plan litigation against Brad, Victoria, and Timberline Farm for phase two. News articles from Vince will ramp Victoria to a fever pitch. Dani and Clarice can accelerate social media with help from the East End crowd. With Victoria's reputation as her most valued commodity in the community, dribbling out the facts is the best way to throw her off balance. And, of course, the

Judge is always my wild card. I know he will throw in a thing or two once we get further along.

"But I am concerned with this new information about police involvement," Mac says.

"Maybe Beth is mistaken," I say. "She saw all this in the dark. There's no reason two vans of kids need a police escort."

"It's not the kids that need an escort, Lee. It's the women."

I squint at him. "Explain."

Mac continues, "The women are most likely prisoners from the jail, reducing their sentences by watching the children. Brad and Victoria are short on staff, and their buddy at the police department, for a fee, helps them out. Remember that they are trafficking children. These female prisoners ensure the kids won't scream or run and are handy with the pitstops, getting the kids ready for the transfer, and those kinds of things.

"These women are vested in ensuring the kids get delivered," he continues. "They do their jobs, and their time in the county lockup gets reduced or eliminated. With some, I bet there's a ready job at the farm when they get out of jail."

He lets out a long breath, and the exhaustion shows on his face.

"You know how this is done." I feel his painful memories as his eyes meet mine.

"I do. At my last job, I took part in several trafficking stings. Kills the soul. I had to leave—struck out on my own."

"You were with a police department?"

"No, a private service for the wealthy. We had several kidnappings associated with trafficking. It's a rough world, even at that level of money. What's more difficult is the young girls are not snatched or coerced. Maybe it is similar to kids at the farm—the ones they have groomed. They are talked into running away by someone they think they love or who they think loves them, which makes them believe it's a good thing."

I can tell the look on my face conveys embarrassment. This is not my world, and I'm embarrassed that I know so little.

"Look, Lee, this isn't about you." Mac's face squints with concern. "I know you feel responsible for these children, but it's been years. Even though Victoria—and Jack—did things they should not have, it wasn't your fault then and isn't your fault now. You didn't cause any of this."

"You'll never be able to convince me of that."

Mac stands and walks over, placing his hand on my shoulder. "Lee, we may never see those children after Monday." His expression is stern. "We may never see Glenna, if she's there, ever again. We'll do our best to track where they go, but you should be prepared to face reality."

My right knee bounces with machine gun precision. "I know. We are here to build evidence against Brad for Beth's case. But every day seems to tip over a rock with another slimy thing inching out. Shouldn't we tip someone off? We can't just let the kids disappear."

"I have a friend at the state who I can call." He scrolls on his phone and then shows me a contact. "He worked with my former security service on several cases, and I trust him. But I need your permission to make the call. It's your case."

"So this will be our last phase, then. Pulling in your guy at the state to help."

"He's actually in the South Carolina Office of Homeland Security."

"Those guys won't help us. Of if they do, they'll kick us out and take over. We're just private citizens."

"He's short-handed, and we've worked together before. Just let me do my thing, Lee. Do I have your permission to call him?"

I grit my teeth, my knee still in machine gun mode, my anger at a dangerous level. If Clint Harbin had been standing in front of me at that moment, I would have strangled him.

"You have it."

39

The crescendo of Barber's Adagio rips through the darkness as my cell phone vibrates on the bedside table. Fighting the exhaustion, my hand slaps the table in the dark. The ringing stops, and I settle back into sleep. The phone rings again, blasting me awake. Three forty-five. I snatch the phone and swipe the green button across the bottom.

"What?" Static sizzles in the background.

"You are being watched." The electronic voice is male this time with a German accent. The wonders of technology.

I swipe up on the screen and set the call to record. "How do you know?"

The voice grows softer. "Because I'm observing them. You should keep your blinds closed tighter."

Disgust rolls through me. I rarely wear clothes to bed, but now I wear PJs since Mac's guys are always in the building. Looking down, I realize how skimpy they are.

"Who is this? Why are you watching me?" I watch the seconds tick on my bedside clock as I wait for a reply.

"To keep you safe." Even through the electronic voice, I can hear the sarcasm.

"If you are watching me, you know I have security." I am too tired to converse with a machine.

"He's qualified. If he hadn't been, I'd have warned you."

"Who's watching me besides you? And where are they now?"

"Two men across the street. They are on the roof of the old furniture store."

Rolling out of bed, I crawl to the window and slide up the wall. With one eye past the window frame, I peek through the blinds. Nothing moves except a lone car on the street. As it passes, a reflection flashes on the dilapidated roof of Stiles Furniture.

Binoculars. Or a scope. I swallow hard and shift my position.

"So, where are you?" If the voice can see me, I can see them.

"Quit wasting time. You keep screwing around, and he's going to get away with it. Things are about to get serious. Watch your back."

The hissing stops as the call ends. Dropping to the floor next to the window, I call Mac.

"Lee? What's wrong?" Mac's voice says he is fully awake. Just hearing him so alert helps with the creeped-out feeling.

"I just received another call."

"From your mysterious caller?"

"The same. Creepy. Says I am being watched, and we are wasting time, that things are about to get real."

Mac's sigh shows his exasperation. "Everything's under control. A man has camped on the roof of the Canterbury House across Market Street for the past two nights. I'm pretty sure your caller is in one of the apartments in that building. We've seen binoculars in one apartment used several times on both nights."

"Remember me telling you about the woman who really referred Beth?"

"Yeah. That it wasn't her boss but some senator's wife."

"Yeah. I think it's time the senator's wife and I had a chat. See if this is her idea."

.   .   .

THE NEXT MORNING, Charlotte O'Neill arrives ten minutes after Clarice's call, and I escort her into my office. The older woman folds her hands in her lap and raises her chin in my direction.

"While you may not remember me, you may be familiar with my deceased husband, Lamar." Senator O'Neill was a regular at bar association events, but I never remembered seeing Charlotte. The man had been a bore at the dinner table after multiple drinks. His hands roamed when seated next to women, and I had given him a wide berth at the few events I attended, avoiding even an introduction.

"I'm sorry for your loss. I know it was some time ago, but our entire state misses Senator O'Neill. We lost a good man when he died."

What a lie. Practicing law in the South forces niceties. Even though God knows most of the time, I don't want to be pleasant. I force myself to focus on Mrs. O'Neill, zeroing in on the intricate brooch in the shape of a chameleon she wears on her lapel. It certainly fits her changing personality. She doesn't realize that I remember her.

I cut straight to the point. "You want to tell me of your relationship with Beth Swindle?" The rapid pink coloring sliding up the woman's neck gives me the answer I expect.

"Mrs. O'Neill, your face just told me the answer. What is your relationship with Timberline Farm or the owners, Brad and Victoria Marshall?"

"I've only been a charitable donor, nothing else." She looks away from me, then to the carpet. She would make a piss-poor poker player.

"Please refrain from ever contacting Beth Swindle again. I'll be happy to show you the way out." I rise and motion for Mrs. O'Neill to follow.

"Well, I never..." She remains seated. I walk around to stand before her.

"I remember you well, Charlotte, and your little competition with Pricilla Conroy." My voice is low and controlled. "Jack knew, you know," I continue. "We used to laugh about you two betting to see which one of you got to have sex with Jack. Didn't happen, did it?"

I wait for an answer. She slowly shakes her head.

"Did you have another competition over Brad? Did you win that one?" I lean down, my face only inches from hers. "Oooh, and did he tie you up," I ask, "do things one only finds in those dark erotic books you kept hidden from your lecherous husband?"

"I have no idea what you are talking about."

Her face flushes bright red, and her eyes blink rapidly until she finally closes them and lets out a long sigh. Trying to speak, Charlotte sputters as a violent shudder jerks her body. I wonder if she is about to have a stroke right in my office. Whatever Brad did, it was terrible. Her body is telling me everything.

Brad is the reason she referred Beth and the reason she is here now.

"Let's get back to the case at hand. I assume you will be Beth's economic support. Is that correct?" I tap the end of my fountain pen rapidly on my desk, not wanting to give her one second to weasel out of what I have planned.

Charlotte's eyes pop open. "Well, I'll need to know more about what your case will involve before I can commit to that."

"And that is a confidentiality I have with Beth, not you. Do you want Brad dealt with? Money will do that. Here are the things I will expect from you to continue with this matter."

I hold up my hand, all fingers extended, dropping each point by point.

"First, Clarice will have forms for you to complete for automatic payments of our invoices by either a credit card or bank draft. Those bills might be substantial. For Beth's case, you will not be given details, only the balance due. A complete set of the invoices will remain on file here for Beth to review, but those details will remain confidential. You will sign a statement agreeing to this procedure."

The woman's mouth drops open for several seconds. I wait for her to close it.

"Second, you will not need to come to this office for any reason. I don't deal well with liars. You can talk with Clarice or leave voicemails. We'll respond when we have answers for you that do not violate Beth's right to confidentiality."

O'Neill slouches in her chair with her arms crossed over her chest. Her hands are closed so tightly that her fingernails cut into the palms of her hands.

"Third, I expect Beth needs monetary living support, food, and possibly a place to live until she takes care of these things herself. You will need to plan accordingly.

"Fourth, you will not question Beth or any other person in this universe regarding this case or anything relating to Timberline Farm until this case is fully settled, which could take years. Along these lines, you will refrain from going to Timberline Farm until this entire matter concludes. If your actions jeopardize this case, I will not hesitate to take action against you."

Dropping her arms in defeat, Mrs. O'Neill still has her jaws clenched tightly, her lips twisting from side to side as I continue.

"Fifth, you, or anyone you've hired, will refrain from ever calling me in the middle of the night or any other time by using electronic means to disguise your voice."

Bingo. The woman looks away, her face chagrined from being caught. Once she regains her composure, her expression is cold and calculating.

"If I agree to all this, can you one hundred percent guarantee that Brad will be in jail?"

"I cannot guarantee the outcome of any case. It's unethical."

Charlotte doesn't need to know that half of what I had just demanded skirted or outright violated the bar's rules of ethics.

"Then what can you assure me will happen with Brad?"

"Look, Mrs. O'Neill—Charlotte—my goal is not just to put Brad in jail, but to have him permanently buried under it. However, should he leave the state or country also works for me. Even though I'd prefer it, I'm not Clint Harbin nor the police. I can't put him in jail. I'm a civil attorney, not a criminal prosecutor. I'll try my best to get him criminally prosecuted and in jail for life. But to get there, no one must know what we're doing. If you or Beth talk, the entire case will be over before it begins. I need your absolute promise to stay quiet."

Charlotte stands, facing me. "You have it."

"Is there anything else you wish to tell me about Timberline Farm?" I ask.

"No. What happened to me at that farm stays with me to the grave. Just get that bastard."

40

Victoria was on her way to Berlin's on King Street in Charleston Friday morning to pick up a dress that had been altered, but the closest parking space she could find was three blocks away. She was late. Her breakfast meeting with the Charleston County Sheriff had run entirely too long. She had meant to drop off his monthly payment and head back downtown, but he had insisted on "breaking bread."

And one didn't want to piss off the sheriff who gave your son's trafficking business its protection.

At the traffic light, the ugly gray truck sat on oversized rims and tires, the suspension at its highest. Victoria covered her mouth with her hand as she crossed the street from her parked car, holding her breath to avoid the cloud surrounding the vehicle. The diesel engine spewed out its heavy exhaust with a loud rattle. It had to have been modified to be the loudest truck possible.

The skinny girl crossing the intersection on the other side of the street paid it no mind. Mud track events were common in the South, and Victoria was sure that the two rednecks in the truck looked just like most of the high school kids that made up the local population. The men in this county were daily farm work-ers, mechanics, and blue-collar workers, all stupid, useless, and lazy with the effects of their constant use of weed and beer.

Something familiar made Victoria stop when she reached the corner. She looked closely at the skinny girl, then glanced again at the two men sitting in the gray truck. She had seen all three at Timberline Farm, just not recently. The two men worked for Brad. The girl lived there in the past, but Victoria remembered little about her.

"What are they up to now?" Victoria mumbled to herself, shifting to stand under the awning of a dress boutique. She pulled out her phone as if she needed to take a call.

Even with her warnings to Breaker, Victoria had a good idea of what the men were doing. She could not believe that idiot would snatch another girl right in the middle of downtown Charleston, but here they were. Pretending to talk on her phone, she walked down the street, then ducked under another awning to watch.

Strolling toward the restaurant, the girl wore her purse strapped across her body so both hands could carry two large paper bags of groceries. The closest grocery store was across town, at least a dozen blocks away. The girl stopped for a second, setting the bags on the sidewalk to give her sore arms a shake and her body a rest, a lot of physical labor when the girl was as skinny as a mosquito. She was not one of her Center girls. Mosquito Girl was not the type to wear a homecoming crown.

What was the girl's name? Brandi? No. Bethany? No, it was Beth. The girl flexed her hands to regain the feeling and re-twisted her long blonde ponytail into a bun on the top of her head. Victoria watched as she hefted the two grocery sacks off the ground, shaking her head as if talking to herself. She walked faster, leaning forward to propel herself into a running skip.

Taking a step off the curb at the corner across from Buddy's Diner, where it looked like she was headed, the gray truck from the intersection suddenly screeched to a halt in front of her. The passenger's side door swung open high, and Beth jerked backward to avoid being struck.

"Git her in here. Stop wasting time!" The driver glared at the passenger, a scrawny forty-ish man with dirty blond hair stuffed under an orange trucker's cap.

"Hold your horses. I'm a-goin'," Orange Hat twisted his body with one leg thrown into the air, wasting time to hunt the metal step to climb from the cab rather than jump directly onto the street.

"Hurry!" Driver's voice sounded louder. "Get her in this damn truck!"

Beth froze. Victoria saw from her body language she knew who the men were and that she was their next target.

Dropping both bags, she sprinted around the nose of the truck and headed for the deli's front door. Driver wrenched open his door and jumped straight to the pavement, catching Beth by the wrist and jerking her toward him. The girl sank to her knees in pain. Driver struggled to get Beth back to her feet and in the truck.

"Stop right there." A tall man in a white dress shirt and gray slacks had his forearm around Orange Hat's neck in a chokehold. Over six feet, skinny Orange Hat was eight inches shorter and weighed at least a hundred pounds less. Victoria watched as Tall Man flipped off Orange Hat's cap and rested the end of the pistol's barrel against the scrawny man's temple.

"Let the girl go, and your friend here will stay alive." Tall Man's voice was calm and professional. "I've already called the police.

"Man, you don't know who you're a dealin' with now." Driver grinned, exposing gray drug-damaged teeth with a missing incisor. His grin lowered a bit at the sound of sirens in the distance. Victoria was too close. She moved into the next alley and hid behind the building as she continued to watch, trying to remain out of sight.

"Oh, I know who you are and who you work for." Tall Man sneered at Driver, his chin pointing toward the truck's cab. "Let her go, and reach in your truck and toss me the keys."

The sound of police sirens grew louder.

"I ain't a gonna do that. When the boss man learns I gave her up and lost the truck to boot, there'll be a lot more hell to pay than a hit with your little pea shooter there. Besides, that boy there ain't worth much. Go on and shoot him. I got what I came for."

Today, Victoria could not get involved, even with the idiocy these men exhibited. They were worse than Breaker if that was possible, and precisely the type of men Breaker would hire. She had been putting off taking a more prominent role. It was absolutely necessary now.

Driver twisted Beth's arm as he pulled her toward the truck.

"Stop it. You're hurting me!"

Her curdling scream made everyone on the street stop and turn to the commotion. She used her free hand to scratch Driver's face, trying to gouge his eyes and escape his grasp. With Driver focused on her, Tall Man slammed Orange Hat's head into the hood of the truck, leaving the skinny man in a heap. Rounding the vehicle, Tall Man's gun was aimed the entire time at Driver's face.

He stopped three feet in front of Beth and Driver.

"Not going to tell you again. Let her go. Give me the keys to your truck."

Two Charleston Police Department cars slid in then, one behind the truck on Logan Street, the other in front of it on Queen Street, the sirens off, the red and blue lights bouncing blasts of color along the white brick wall of Buddy's Diner.

"Drop your weapon. Everyone to the ground. Let go of the

girl." Four police weapons were pointed at the men. The driver continued to hold Beth's arm and waited.

"Let the girl go." The police officer's warning was louder and more insistent this time. Looking at the guns pointed at him, the driver let Beth go. Her arm was finally free; Beth cradled it to her chest and crawled toward the curb, immediately gathered by a man from the diner and rushed inside.

Victoria watched as Tall Man lowered his gun and tossed it toward the police car. "My information is in my front left pants pocket. I'm private security in town on a job. I saw this happening and couldn't stop myself."

Driver looked up in surprise. "Security? Some ole country bumpkin girl has her own security?"

The tittering from the crowd gathering told Victoria something she already knew—gossip in this town ran like a river to the ocean—rapidly. This little incident would be talked about for the rest of the day. She had to get Brad on the phone, and now.

Tall Man responded with a laugh. "I didn't say it was her. You are stupid, aren't you? I feel sorry for your boss."

Victoria felt a tremor of fear in her gut. This was no yokel. She would have to get this man eliminated without revealing her involvement.

Driver lunged. His hands grabbed Tall Man's neck. Two police officers tackled Driver from the rear, breaking his grip. The officers pushed Driver face forward, then cuffed his hands behind him. Miranda rights were recited as two of the officers hauled him into the police car. One officer approached Tall Man.

Victoria leaned forward, hoping to hear who this man was.

"Slowly, hand me your identification." The officer trained his gun on Tall Man, watching as he pulled a wallet from his front pocket for his information.

"I'd be happy to discuss everything at the station with you. I don't enjoy having my client's information common knowledge."

Tall Man cocked his head toward the growing crowd across the street, his eyes stopping abruptly when he saw Victoria.

She refused to return his gaze. Instead, she casually shifted, turning away from him to look at clothing in the store window beside her, raising her phone back to her ear.

"Any need to cuff you?" Victoria heard the officer say behind her.

"For a statement?" Tall Man responded, then laughed.

Victoria glanced over her shoulder. The officer straightened, sliding his gun into his holster but leaving it unsnapped, his hands remaining at his side. "You pulled a gun in the middle of town."

Tall Man shook his head as he grinned at the officer, his voice carrying to everyone around him.

"You know I'm allowed to do that when threatened under your state's open carry law. Besides, you're holding my PI license." The man's gaze snapped toward Victoria again. He knew who she was.

"Come along then. We'll work this out at the station."

The officer tilted his head toward his cruiser, and Tall Man got into the passenger seat rather than the back. Victoria watched them drive away, leaving her with a nervous tick in her eyelid at the anger forming in her chest.

Breaker would pay for this.

An ambulance arrived, and Beth was loaded in the back, accompanied by another police officer. Orange Hat, in the back seat of the second police car, was slowly driven away in the opposite direction.

What a catastrophe. She raised her cell phone to call Brad, then changed her mind. This was her responsibility now.

41

My lawyer armor is a comfortable navy suit, reasonable heels, and a conservative blouse with the standard string of white pearls. The firetruck red Chanel suit is my favorite, but it isn't a firetruck type of day. I need to work with the police, not pummel them into submission. On the red suit days, I enjoy my work. Too bad today isn't one of those days.

Mac is waiting for me on the front steps of the police station on Lockwood Drive. He jumps in the passenger seat before I can park.

"Why are you outside?" Ready to let off steam inside the police department, I am disappointed.

"They only took a quick statement." Mac grins. "Since we'd already given the Georgia Troopers detailed information two days ago, these boys felt this was round two of the same thing. Not much for me to do."

"Now they're trying to be efficient? Small town South Carolina isn't usually that way."

Mac resumes his professional mask. "We talked shop, played

Who You Know, talked military assignments, and now we're all good buddies."

I expel an irritated *pffffft*. I'd be locked up for a week if I had given my statement.

"Well, pooh. I got dressed, and there's no dance." Not even a little pummeling today.

"No, ma'am, but there will be a grand ball next week. Oh, and Victoria was there watching from across the street."

"What?" Driving to the hospital to check on Beth, a garbage truck stops my progress. I glance over at Mac. "What did you do?" I tap my fingers on the steering wheel, impatient for the garbage guys to move faster.

"Let her know I knew who she was. As for the event, the police do not know when or where, only that it is next week. No one knows the details, but the rumors are flying."

"Who gave them the information?"

"The guy they took into custody isn't as bulletproof as I bet Brad, or maybe this Breaker character, thinks he is. Sang like a bird once they put a little pressure on him, even though he doesn't know much."

"Not surprised."

"Your grandfather is larger than life to those cops." He shifts to face my profile. "They told me some interesting things."

"Like what?" Finally, in the parking lot for Roper Hospital, I watch as a sailboat heads toward the bridge just before Charleston Marina. It will have to anchor in the middle of the river since tomorrow morning is the next time the bridge will open. I feel the captain's frustration. This is precisely how I think this case is going.

"You're his untouchable protégé." Mac forces me back into the conversation. "Most of them wonder why you aren't taking advantage of that."

"Something my illustrious grandfather has said to me quite a few times."

So much for trying to stay under the radar.

He motions toward the hospital. "Let's check on Beth. With both guys in custody, the police think she's safe and probably has no guard. I'm sure Brad has more thugs where those two came from. We need to get her back to the office."

Getting through the front desk at the downtown Roper St. Francis Hospital is easy, but finding Beth in the emergency room bed maze is more complicated. With the help of an ER nurse, we locate Beth in a corner bed, surrounded by blue curtains on three sides, and as expected, no guards. She brightens when she sees us, her arm in a short cast.

"It's broken right above the wrist. I thought that bas—idiot would twist my arm off."

I envelope her in a tight hug. "Ok, M.L., you can let go now." Her voice is muffled against my jacket. "I can't breathe."

I laugh and let go. "Glad it was just your arm. Those guys tried to—"

"You were great out there, Beth." Mac interrupts. "Mike was tracking the truck, so I was right behind you. He got the police coming in as backup. You did great. Didn't lose your head."

He pats her shoulder as he looks at me with a wink and a cautionary glance.

His attempt to protect her is admirable but useless. Beth's face tells me she knows how close she came to being kidnapped. She survived years of Brad's rape and life at the farm without being shipped off. I imagine she would turn into an angry lioness to stop the two men from dragging her into that truck.

"Beth, from now on," Mac continues, "my guy Mike will be with you the entire time. I didn't want you to think we weren't there, but we didn't stick as closely as we should have. With the two men caught at the scene by the police, the kidnapping charges should stick."

"I wish Breaker had been one of them," Beth responds. "He's the one you need." She looks at her cast. "But if Breaker had been in that truck, I wouldn't be here. Either he'd have snatched me as the truck was moving, or he'd have killed me once he saw you." She looks from Mac back to me. "I don't think either of you understands how violent he is."

I don't mention the little joy ride Mac and I had when returning from Barton Springs.

"Mac," I say, "Beth needs to move in with me until this mess ends. What do you think?"

"I can't put you out like that," Beth protests. "The women's safe house is just fine for me."

I shake my head. "I'm not trying to curtail your freedom, and as long as Mike is with you, nothing will happen, but it would make me feel a lot better."

"It's not my freedom," Beth insists, "it's your safety. They're already coming after me. I don't want them coming after you, too."

Mac breaks his own rule and tells Beth the truth. "Those two guys already tried to run Lee and me down on the road on the way back from Georgia. While we couldn't identify the men, it was the same truck. Paint from my car is on the truck registered to the man who hurt you."

Beth's face crumples. "It's all my fault." Her unbroken hand squeezes mine.

"Come live with me for a while. We'll get this settled as soon as we can. Besides, Mike will be with you at all times."

A flush rises from Beth's neck to her cheeks. "A bodyguard. I don't know how I feel about that."

"Trust me, Beth," Mac replies. "Mike will be happy to be your security. Let me get him over here, and you can get to know him."

Mac picks up his phone, and we hear the start of his conversation with Mike as he walks away.

"Hey man, Beth is in the emergency room. When you finish your statement, we're only a few blocks from you…"

Beth's blue eyes are wide with concern. "Mac left you to look after me."

I squeeze her good arm. "You're the star witness, Beth, not me. You're more important."

"But someone could have..."

"We're prepared for all of that. I'll stay with you until Mike gets here. Do nothing that will cause you to be out of his sight. He'll bring you to the apartment upstairs over my office and we'll get you situated."

"Thank you for letting me stay with you, Lee. I feel safer already. I sat here before you arrived and worried about returning to Magnolia House. It's safe and all, but..." Her voice trails off at the end.

"No need to worry. You're safe now."

"Yeah, well, I don't know how to repay you. I guess I lost my job." She holds up her cast. "Can't work for Buddy with one hand."

"Well, I'm short a staff person. How would you like to be my new paralegal?"

42

———

Victoria leaned over Brad's shoulder. They were in the farm office, going over the books. As usual, there was not enough income to meet expenses. She could not hide her irritation.

"We can't meet Fish's demand for higher numbers, Brad," Victoria kept her voice low so the other workers in the office could not hear how angry she was. Even though the door was closed, the walls were thin. And the new girl Morris hired the day before seemed a bit too nosy. "It is simply too risky. We can meet the five on Monday, but twenty next week? What happened to fifteen? He keeps changing the numbers, but it doesn't matter. There aren't enough girls in the area to fulfill his demand."

"Then we'll have to move toward Myrtle Beach to meet the quota," Brad replied. "I don't have a choice, Mother. You know what happens if I don't meet Fish's deadline."

Victoria remembered the last time they had balked at Fish's request. He had taken one of their girls and beaten her to death as an example.

"What will you do about the two guys sitting in jail?" Victoria asked.

"Nothing until I hear Breaker's version of the story."

"You're kidding me. Why? I was there. I saw it myself."

"Maybe he had a good reason for grabbing the girl." Brad shrugged his shoulders.

"He's not worth the risk, Brad. You need to get rid of him."

Jack had paid her back for trapping him at Timberline Farm. Insisting that Brad would thrive in a business for which he could take responsibility, he convinced the board of directors to give their son full operational control. Instead of thriving, Brad treated the farm as if it was a tremendous burden. His decisions were poor, the boy never took her advice, and the farm operations and finances suffered significantly.

Brad reached for the glass of amber liquid on the desk, and Victoria snatched it away. The office door crashed open, slamming into the wall causing her to jump. The glass slipped from Victoria's hand, and whisky and glass shards exploded across the floor.

Breaker strode into the room, almost wrenching the door from its frame as he slammed it behind him. He strode to the bar and began preparing himself a drink.

"What the hell do you think you're doing?" Victoria shouted. She reached for a roll of paper towels in the bar cabinet, then snatched the bottle of bourbon from Breaker's hand.

"Dammit, I just need a drink. Gimme that bottle." He wrenched the bottle from Victoria's hand, sloshing the alcohol on her dress.

"Stupid Nelbert got himself arrested in town trying to swipe another girl." Breaker declared. "Why in the world would he do it during broad daylight?" He looked to Brad.

"Because you told him to do it." Victoria retorted. The two glared at each other, each ready to strike. Victoria looked at the roll of paper towels in her hand, a useless weapon against Breaker's bottle of liquor.

"Come on, guys. Enough." Brad rose and walked across the room, taking the bottle from Breaker. "Just calm down."

Breaker's immense body collapsed into his favorite antique chair that strained to hold him. The scratching began the next minute as both hands roamed his body.

Brad returned to his desk chair and sat. "Talk to me, man."

"Well, he wanted that skinny girl that just left the farm, the one named Beth." Breaker directed his comments to Brad and, as usual, ignored Victoria. He took out his pocket knife and cleaned the dirt from his fingernails while he talked.

"I think he's got a thing for her. She's not bad looking, with long blonde hair and tiny tits. Whatever floats your boat, you know? She was always useless to me, but some of our clients go for that skinny type. Nelbert promised some guy from Dothan, Alabama, that he'd get Beth for him."

Victoria pictured Beth. The girl was all sinewy muscle and hard edges, with pale green eyes like the shallow waters of the Caribbean. She was her son's last indiscretion or the last that Victoria knew of. Why did everyone want this cantankerous girl?

"Where is Nelbert now?" Brad pulled out a silver flask and added two fingers to another glass on his desk, flinching as Victoria snatched both glass and flask from him.

Victoria's voice was low as she bent to reply in Brad's ear. "You need to keep a clear head."

She placed the glass and flask inside the bar cabinet. Brad leaned back in his chair, focusing now on Breaker, who continued with his fingernails and scratching, never making eye contact as he responded.

"Locked up in the hoosegow in town. He knows to keep his mouth shut. I'm not worried. He's part of the brotherhood." Breaker pointed to the blue prison tattoo on his left arm.

"He was alone?" Brad asked.

"Well, no." Breaker huffed. "Larry Jenkins was with him." At Brad's inquisitive look, Breaker continued. "You know the short, skinny guy who always wears an orange ball cap?" Victoria looked out the window, remembering what she had seen. She knew exactly who Jenkins was. That runt of a man was even more useless than the others.

"So where is this Jenkins now?" Victoria snapped at Breaker.

The man waited for Brad to look at him before he spoke. That constant lack of authority was beginning to crawl under her skin.

"Well, they knocked him out cold. Some guy stopped them from grabbing the girl in the middle of town—with a pistol, no less." Breaker smiled, his missing canine tooth highlighted by a black hole, his hands exaggerating his story. "What's the world coming to? Anyway, they took Larry to the hospital, and I'm concerned. He hasn't got the sense God gave an amoeba. He didn't even call me. He used his one phone call at the station to contact his mama."

Breaker pantomimed rubbing pretend tears from his eyes.

Victoria walked to the credenza and leaned against it, her arms and legs crossed, one high heel kicked up on its toe. She glared at Breaker. It was all his fault the CPD was involved. It was bad enough with the Charleston County Sheriff on the payroll. Enough was enough. She walked to stand in front of the nasty man, leaning inches from his face, wishing she had a bat to beat him with.

"Ok, Breaker, how will you fix this mess? The shipment's due out tomorrow night."

"It's all under control." Breaker looked at Victoria like an indignant ten-year-old, then turned to Brad for help.

"Bullshit!" Victoria screamed at the man, her spit hitting him between the eyes. "You are not in control of one thing, you mongrel! Your reckless and inept behavior has caused us to lose one more girl and two employees. You'll do nothing but make this worse. You've got to stop grabbing girls in broad daylight." She grabbed a fistful of T-shirt in her hand. "Pack your shit and go see a doctor for that nasty itch."

The man had the decency to cower, his eyes bulging as he wiped his face with his sleeve.

Victoria turned to Brad. "Take care of this problem," she said, "or I will."

Leaving the office, she slammed the door with the same force as Breaker. In her car, the rear tires spun gravel as she headed up the hill for home.

"W ELL?" Brad looked at Breaker. "What's your plan?"

"I'll have your mouthpiece—you know that attorney you use —spring them from the jail."

"Uh, no," Brad replied. "That will directly connect me to them. Find someone else."

The burly man continued, "Ok. I guess Jenkins will have to lie low until his arraignment, then I'm cuttin' him loose. If he needs bail, we'll have to spring for that."

"No, man," Brad replied again. "That's on you."

Breaker shrugged.

"Whatever. I plan to send him to Florida with a one-way bus ticket. I don't care if he's charged or misses his court date. I can't trust his mouth and don't want him around."

Brad stood, his arms crossed over his chest as he leaned against the desk. "Just take care of your Jenkins problem— permanently. A one-way bus ticket won't do it."

Breaker headed for the door.

"And for God's sake," Brad said, "would you stop pissing off my mother?"

N OW THAT J ACK WAS DEAD, Victoria knew Brad would report to neither the Board of Directors or her. He would do whatever he wanted, regardless of how it affected her or the farm. If she was patient enough, however, Theron Fish would solve the Breaker problem for her.

Victoria remembered the look of shock on Jack's face when he'd discovered Brad had been selling children to Fish. She relished Jack's blustering, angry reaction. Brad had proudly pulled one over on his father. She had stood by, listening as Jack continually berated his son, waiting to step in.

But her son didn't need her help. Brad pulled a pistol from his desk drawer and unloaded five shots in the center of Jack's chest, the sixth a stray shot right at the hairline.

It had taken cash—a lot of it—and even more persuasion to get the coroner and funeral director to swear Jack had died of a heart attack.

The look Brad had given her just now? It was the same hateful expression he'd had the day he had killed Jack. And now he meant to kill her too. Waiting on Fish might not be an option. She would have to take care of him herself.

43

Glenna shivered at the sound of footsteps. She didn't know how long she had been trapped in this cell, but enough time for two more beatings. The monster was perpetually angry and took it out on her. She didn't know if she would live through another.

"This won't call out. I can only text." Glenna jerked. Struggling to focus, she looked at the direction of the sound. A cell phone lit up in the hallway.

It was the girl. Trish. She approached the iron door and poked her face through the bars.

"Give me a number I can text," Trish whispered. "Somebody you know that can get us out of here."

"Where have you been? I'm going to die if I stay in here much longer." Glenna felt the anger deep in her stomach rising. The girl had left her here to rot instead of helping Glenna escape.

The shadows from the phone's screen bobbled in the dark as if the girl was shifting from one foot to another.

"Come on! I don't have but a minute!"

Glenna hesitated, unsure whose side the girl was on. At this point, however, she had no alternative. She spit out her mother's number, then Dani's. "Text at the same time. Tell them where I am, but to be careful. You tell them everything—this place, that monster."

"I will. What's your full name?" Glenna could hear the tapping sounds from the phone as the girl rapidly typed.

"Glenna Robertson."

"You from around here?"

"North Charleston"

"What's something only they would know about you? I have to say something like that; otherwise, they'll think it's spam."

"Just say we're first going to LA, then Brisbane. They'll know it's me."

Glenna's dreams were not of college but the Olympics. The first possibility was in LA in 2028 when she was a junior in college, but the real target was the 2032 Summer Olympics in Brisbane, Australia. Only her family and Dani knew her dream. They were sworn to secrecy to avoid the expected taunts and ridicule from the kids in the neighborhood and school. No one from North Charleston would believe she would ever make it.

It didn't matter. She knew she would.

But she had to get out of this cage.

"Done." The girl started shuffling down the hall. "I'll come back when I can. Things are starting to move fast."

"Wait!" Glenna shouted. "You need to find my friend Dani. She was supposed to start working here with Mrs. Marshall."

"OK, I'll see what I can find out. If I see her, I'll tell her. But I need to go. It's time for your food, and they'll be coming."

The basement went silent.

Glenna didn't care about food. Her only thought was an open door to freedom and the speed her feet would take her.

44

As Mac and I arrived with Beth and Mike through my office's back door, Clarice was waiting outside the conference room, her hands fisted on her hips, her face screwed up with mock indignation.

"Where have you guys been? Nikki, the Judge, and I have been working here."

Beth hugged Clarice. "Some men from the farm tried to kidnap me, but Mac took care of things."

Clarice squints her eyes at me. "You mean to tell me there's been this trouble going on, and you didn't call, didn't text one word?"

She peruses me from toe to head, taking in the navy suit and three-inch heels.

"Were you ready for an insurrection? You never wear a suit unless it's serious." Clarice has no idea how much her concern means to me.

The Judge laughs. "She thought she might do real lawyer work today." He smiles at me. "But the boys over at the police station weren't very concerned."

"Yes, I was ready for anything." I point to Mac and shrug. "He seems to get me into all kinds of trouble. I don't think hiring him was a good idea."

Mac snorts a laugh. After I kiss my grandfather's cheek, I plant myself in one of the conference room chairs.

"Come on in, guys. Get to work. We're behind on Clarice's schedule, and unless you want to lose dinner from Buddy's, you'd better get started."

A visibly exhausted Nikki slogs away at the conference room table. "Hi, Nikki." I squeeze her shoulder. "Where's Angus? Did you work all night?"

I turn to Mac. "Wasn't another guy on your team to work with us today?"

"Yeah," Mac replied. "But Angus took him to the farm. There was hay to be cut, giving them a chance to get close to the house Beth described and know the exact layout. He was hoping to get inside and see that basement. We couldn't miss this opportunity."

"Yeah, yeah," Nikki said, her comments directed to Mac. "You guys hate paperwork. You forget that most cases are made with details. And yes, I've been at it for a while. Once I eat and have another coffee, I'll be good."

Mac gives her shoulder a sisterly pat. "Show me what you want us to do."

"I'm here to help too," Beth said. "Lee said I could be a paralegal. Could you tell me what that is? I want to get started."

Mac sits beside Nikki, with Beth on the other side. The Judge and I are across the table. As Nikki describes the various types of documents to Beth, the young woman takes notes, making herself a cheat sheet. Clarice lists every document chronologically on a spreadsheet, and each document is labeled and scanned with her specific naming convention. It is tedious work. For documents that identify significant events, Mac adds them to the whiteboard. The Judge and I quietly discuss which legal arguments we will keep and which to discard.

The "Shipment Team" suspect list on the whiteboard includes people with legitimate pay records and names of the daily workers taken from the cash journals. Nikki prints a list for Mac to review and have Mike investigate, although, with a Monday deadline, we have little time for a proper investigation. All I can hope for are accurate names and decent photos, maybe recent addresses. With the physical surveillance I had in mind for the farm, we need to know who we are watching.

The sound of breaking glass echoes in the room.

Beth gasps. "I'm so sorry. This stupid cast bumped it. I'll clean it up." Everyone shifts toward her as she drops to her knees to collect the shards. Clarice is immediately at her side with a kitchen towel.

"You will do no such thing. Sit yourself down, and Lee and I will clean up this." I reach for the towel, and everyone settles back into their chairs and returns to work.

"Beth..." I wait until she looks at me. "Don't be nervous. This job is common sense. Look at each page and give Clarice your summary in a sentence or two. Say something if you don't understand. If you have a question, ask. You may see something relating to the farm that sticks out that we wouldn't catch."

Beth returns to her stack of paper, checking her notes as she goes. I would take ten Beths over one law clerk like Lauren any day.

Nikki bumps my elbow, handing me a spreadsheet. The bottom line: Timberline Farm is in massive debt. Twenty houses were mortgaged and refinanced as the property values increased. The older houses were mortgaged multiple times during the early 2000s real estate craze. Nikki's research is a gold mine. With each refinance, the equity of each house was taken from the closing as cash.

Jack signed the original mortgages. The refinances were signed by Victoria. I grab the laptop from my office and pull up the foreclosure site I use most frequently. The house payments would not have been made with the farm finances so upside down. Sure enough, three of the twenty houses were scheduled to be foreclosed. The others would be close behind.

This had to be Jack's plan—to reduce donations over time, knowing Victoria's greed would destroy Timberline Farm and take her with it. Increased mortgage payments with reduced income always spelled disaster. I pull the box of Timberline Farm abstracts toward me.

"Judge, help me find the cross-collateralization language in the title work for each house. You told me earlier each house was tied to the others. I looked quickly in the abstract summary when they all came in, but it wasn't noted, and there was no separate collateralization document."

I give him ten abstracts, and I take the other ten. Two other abstracts included the tract of land for the farm buildings, pasture, and original farmhouse, as well as a separate tract with Victoria's home at the rear of the property. I will look at those last.

He and I both knew that the language most likely would be hidden in the fine print of the note and mortgage, with a requirement that if one house were foreclosed, all other houses would also be foreclosed, thus bringing down the entire non-profit. To be sure, we needed to read each promissory note and any collateralization documents.

Had Jack begun the downfall, knowing it was his only way out? That might explain the motive behind his murder. Who had the most to lose? Victoria, Brad, and possibly Morris. My cards were on Victoria. She would lose her home and her status in the community. And the profits from the trafficking.

"Nikki, were you able to find the latest donation count? Were there any donations at all?"

"I downloaded everything I could find. Give me a second." Nikki looks like she has run a marathon.

I hold out my hand to stop her. "Let's break and have dinner.

We're tired. I can't ask any of you to work longer today. Nikki, you need to head home. You're exhausted."

Yet, after dinner, no one leaves. Mac works his computer and phone, attempting to pull background on the non-payroll list of people working at the farm. Beth is a troubleshooter with Mac and Nikki. Clarice tracks the post-refinance cash while I unravel the real estate records for the original tract of land containing the farm buildings. The Judge is in my office having a private off-the-record call with the Equity Court judge to discuss any additional foreclosures expected from Timberline Farm.

Nikki shoves back her chair and breaks the silence. "They're broke. Not just barely surviving, but dead broke."

Beth and I look at each other. One hundred twenty kids will be thrust back into a bogged-down state system. I stand at Nikki's shoulder as she points to the screen.

"Here is last year's donations list created by Timberline Farm. As you can see, it's a short list." She opens another list and slides it next to the first. "I can find some expenses from last year, but they are far more than the income, and I may not have all of them. I found no evidence of any trafficking money." She looks over the table at Mac. "I will need your help if we think it's offshore."

"No wonder Morris is scrambling to get things paid," I reply. "This explains why he's so stressed and why people are quitting." I return to my seat. "Did you find the same in previous years?"

"Yes, but I'm not sure Morris is involved in this. He doesn't sign the expense checks. Brad does."

"I might feel the same way if Morris wasn't the ranch manager," Mac says, "but he is, and I bet he's up to his neck in all this."

"I agree," I say. "Even though Brad signs the checks now, Morris can't simply turn a blind eye. These last two years especially show financial malfeasance at its highest form. I don't think Morris can say he doesn't know how bad the finances are. Even though it won't pay for Brad's criminal actions, this evidence will give us a very tight malfeasance case against Brad and the legal entity for Timberline Farm. I can't ignore Morris as a party at this point."

"The farm was solvent when Jack was there," Nikki says. "At that point, Morris did the office management and signed the checks. The books were audited by a CPA firm in Charleston. I didn't find any issues during that time. They broke even most years and always had enough to pay the mortgages. Fifteen years ago, Jack relinquished control of the farm, giving it to Victoria. Morris continued to handle paying the expenses until two years ago. His authority was revoked then, and Victoria and Brad signed everything. From the records, Brad was financially in charge the last two years, and appears to be the cause of the steep decline."

My computer dings with a spreadsheet from Clarice.

"Open that file. I think you'll be happy." She gives me a wink.

Clarice's spreadsheet confirms with dates, amounts, and references to the relevant closing documents that Victoria's signature is on every refinance document for every house. The cash she collected after refinancing those twenty houses totals just under a million dollars.

I look away from my computer. "Honestly, that's a lot more money than I expected."

"The older houses' original value and mortgage balances were very low. Once the real estate boom hit, six houses went through two significant increases, and the equity balance was substantial. She refinanced just before each surge. It was as if she planned it."

"I see that. We need to trace those funds." I look at the others.

"Nikki, you or Mac will have to help me with that." Clarice smiles her Cheshire Cat smile and returns to her computer.

"Nikki, we need to find that money. That's our civil misman-agement suit against Victoria."

The Judge walks into the room.

"What did you find out, Judge?" I ask.

"Judge Carwell believes everything associated with Timber-line Farm will foreclose. Or at least everything that was mortgaged."

I bring him up to date on Clarice's refinance information and the cash Victoria accumulated.

"I'm assuming the original funds used to make the house down payment and any mortgage payments were from donors' funds," I tell the Judge.

"That is an assumption, though," he replies. "If she and Jack personally paid for those houses, depending on the non-profit agreements, she may be entitled to the cash."

"Yes, but I was there at the beginning, remember? As the office secretary, I made the monthly mortgage payments on the original five or six houses for the first four years. I prepared the checks from the farm account, and Jack signed them. Then I mailed them."

"You are sure Victoria had no personal funds involved in those payments?" he asked.

"No. I'm positive."

"Then come over here," said Nikki, "and let's compare. I need to be sure I'm tracking the right funds."

"What are these?" I ask, pointing to accounting ledgers.

Nikki holds up a thumb drive. "I downloaded everything I could find yesterday at the farm. We can't use them in court, but it will at least let us build the case correctly."

"You know that is theft of corporate property," the Judge says, his arms crossed over his chest. He squints at me, then at Nikki.

"Yes, and I'll destroy the information when the case is over," I retort. "Only we will know about this. If you're uncomfortable, go do something else for a while."

"Well, it's a bit late, my dear." Exasperated, the Judge sits before his laptop. "Guess it is time to pull the cases for mismanagement. I cannot imagine Victoria putting her own funds into the farm account."

"You think they are in the Cayman Islands or somewhere similar, don't you?" I ask.

"Absolutely."

45

Nikki pulls up the farm's account ledgers and the personal bank account information Jack provided at Willow House. I shift seats, with Clarice's summary on my computer screen.

I point to the screen. "Find the date of every refinance. The funds received at closing will be in the form of a wire transfer or certified funds check. Find the deposit into either her account or the farm account. From that deposit, follow the money. If you find the funds deposited back into the farm account, she's clear."

"Not going to happen," the Judge says under his breath.

"If it goes somewhere else, or she uses it for personal expenses, we can prove the mismanagement." I look over at Mac. "But I think the Judge is correct. The funds are offshore."

"When we find that slush account," Mac says, "we need to see what she used it for—or if she invested it."

I lean back and stretch, trying to get the kink out of my neck.

"We're on the right track, guys, for me to sue in civil court—"

Nikki interrupts me. "Wait. I'm pretty sure there's a second set of books. None of this is matching up." She points to her computer screen. "For example, Victoria's house at the back of the place should have expenses. It's a Timberline Farm property, yet I found no expense record relating to that house. There is no mortgage payment, no utilities, nothing. Same with Brad's house."

"There is no mortgage on Victoria's house tract or the original farmhouse where Brad lives," the Judge interjects. "I finished reviewing the abstracts when in your office."

He points to the pile of title documents. "Only the homes for the children have mortgages. Check behind me, Lee. I anticipate that Victoria has a developer under her thumb, and Timberline Farm will eventually be a subdivision with the houses updated or replaced."

I quickly check the abstracts.

"You're right, Judge. There is no mortgage on her house, Brad's, or any of the original farm buildings. They are free and clear."

"Maybe those are personal expenses since they are private residences?" Clarice suggests.

Nikki shakes her head. "Not according to Jack and Victoria's checkbooks."

I drop my head in my hands to think.

"She can't pay the bills with cash," Clarice says. "Well, she could, but it would be hard. Once we sue, we'll need to send subpoenas to the banks in town."

"I agree," says Nikki. "There are more accounts somewhere."

"Let's do as much as we can tonight," I say.

The most essential thing in the next twenty-four hours, besides stopping the trafficking, is getting Glenna back. I look at Mac as he stares at his watch. I know he is counting the hours until, as Beth had said, we have to "do something."

Clarice gasps. She holds up her phone. "Glenna just texted Dani. It's hard to read, garbled, but from what I think it says, it's her." She hands me the phone, Mac reading over my shoulder. I read it aloud, as best I can, for the rest of the group.

"bring h*%elp at farm base#&%ment monster hurt me. no text back phone broke no call so%dine sad fatejhkawt dont forget LA and Brizbane."

I read it again. "What do LA and Brisbane have to do with this?"

Clarice reaches for her phone. "Glenna dreams of going to the Olympics. It's code so we would know it was her."

"Send me that text," Nikki says, "and the number it came from. Let me see what I can do." She wipes her hand across her face.

Clarice looks at me. "We need to get Dani here now, don't you think?"

Before Clarice can call her, pounding begins. Mac heads for the front door, Mike on his heels.

"It's Dani. She's texting me," said Clarice.

When Mac opens the door, Dani shoves past him and bursts into the conference room, out of breath.

"I know where Glenna is. We need to get there now." Stopping in front of Clarice, she pulls at her aunt's shoulder. "Get up! What are you guys waiting for? Let's get her. Have you called the police?"

I shake my head. When no one in the room budges, Dani steps back, her arms crossed over her chest, her face screwed up in anger.

"Didn't you guys get my text?"

"We got the text," I tell her. "Sit down, Dani. It was time you were part of this discussion."

Mac frowns, but I give him an overruling glance.

Huffing into the chair next to her aunt, Dani glares at me. "We're wasting time. She's hurt, and we need to get there. Trish told me, but I didn't understand."

"How do you know Trish?" Beth asks.

Dani looks at her with skepticism. "Who are you?"

Before Beth responds, I get Dani to focus back on me. "We

have a plan formed, and we're going through with it. You'll blow the entire thing if you do anything outside that plan. You have to be patient and do what I say."

"Why didn't you call the police?" Dani slams into the back of her chair like a five-year-old about to explode into a tantrum.

"Dani!" Clarice cautions her niece.

"It's okay, Clarice. I understand she's angry." I keep my eyes on Dani. "The police are involved, just not on our side. We don't want any of the departments tipped off."

"What?" Dani asks, confused.

"They bribed the cops, Dani," Clarice says.

"It's worse than that," I reply.

Beth interrupts, staring at Dani. "You don't know me, but I can tell you, I saw a Sheriff's car myself."

"Then you know we need to get Glenna." Dani pleads with Beth.

"That would be a hard 'no.'" Mac could no longer keep silent. "You must stay here with your aunt and Beth and help us from this end."

"Do what?" Dani snaps at Mac. "And who are you, anyway?"

Clarice slaps her hand over the girl's mouth. "Stop this, Dani. You are out of control."

Unfazed, Mac continues, "Because the men at Timberline have guns. We don't need a stray bullet catching you. And I don't want to—"

"I need you to do something else," I interrupt before Mac can say, "babysit."

Dani narrows her eyes at me, her voice contentious. "What?"

I look at her with caution. "You ignored me the first time. Don't do it again."

She looks away, telling me I am correct. "What do you mean?"

"You've been working at the farm. How else would you have talked to Trish?"

Dani opens her mouth to object when Nikki pipes up. "Yeah,

Angus saw you there yesterday. He told me he watched you walk into Victoria's house. You were there several hours because he also saw you leave."

Dani winces and covers her face with her hands. Then, after looking sheepishly at Nikki, she turns to me, her eyes pleading.

"The opportunity she gave me was something I couldn't turn down. I didn't know Glenna was there. I wouldn't believe it if I hadn't received that text myself. But it's Glenna; I know it. I wish I'd just listened to Trish. She tried to tell me." She starts rocking back and forth in her chair.

I lean over and put my hand on her shoulder until I feel her relax. "Back to the farm for a minute. What does Victoria have you doing?"

"I'm handling technology for Timberline Farm. I've cleaned up their website, set up social media accounts, and will start on several auctions for fundraising. They have a pretty cool video system. Has to do with job recruitment."

Now, it was my turn to squint at her. "Auctions? Job recruitment?" I worked their charity auctions in high school and knew exactly what was involved—from a young girl's perspective, nothing good. "Do other girls work there? Or just you?"

"Victoria has several girls she refers to as her assistants. I'm her T.A., short for technology assistant."

Clarice grabs my arm as I close my eyes and sink into the chair behind me. Surely, I am not too late in stopping Dani from getting sucked into whatever Victoria is doing. Opening them, I look at Clarice, but my words are for Dani.

"I need the full names of every girl who works as an assistant. Then call them. Find out what Victoria has promised each one of those girls."

"I don't have their full names," Dani replies, "but I can get them. Their goal is to get jobs after graduating from high school. These girls live in North Charleston with no hope of going to college. They're interviewing for assistant positions for Victoria's friends."

Friends. Right. Who would hire a high school graduate with zero experience as their right hand? How could any high school girl believe this? I look at the ceiling, trying to rein in my temper—the same way Victoria tricked me into doing things I didn't want to—because I didn't know any better.

I lean toward Dani, my hands flat on the table. "How do they interview?"

"That's where I come in," Dani says. "Part of my job is to set up a professional interview using the recording booth. The girls have complete privacy in this booth. The employer can see their entire body, not just their face on a Zoom call."

"See their full bodies?" Nikki asks.

Dani simply blinks.

"Are they in there alone, Dani? Can you see the girls as they interview? Are they wearing clothes?" I have so many questions.

"What?" Dani's face squints in shock. "It's private. No clothes? What do you mean? I just started and haven't done an interview yet. That's supposed to be tomorrow."

"Think, Dani. Are they auditioning for Hollywood? Why would they need a full-length viewing? If your resume shows you can type 80 words per minute and dress professionally on the Zoom call, what else would an employer need to see? Most applicants have follow-ups in person unless these are online jobs. Does that ever happen?"

"Victoria told me that there are no in-person interviews. All are through the video system. Victoria says it's the best way to get economically disadvantaged girls to the bigger cities with better jobs."

This is becoming less and less logical. What is Victoria offering them? "Do you know anyone who has accepted these positions?"

Dani's brow furrows. "Well, no."

I tap my pen on the pad before me as I continue to think, daring myself to use Dani as bait. I look at Mac, then at Clarice. Both must have guessed where I am going because both shake their heads. Outnumbered, I turn back to Dani. "I need you to call in sick tomorrow."

Clarice doesn't hesitate. "I agree."

"Wait. I can be an inside source and testify if you need. That is..."

Silently, I dare the girl to continue.

Dani looks at the table. Resigned, her hand goes up in a scout's salute. "Okay, okay. I'll be a good little girl."

Clarice pats the girl's hand. "I know you don't like this, but it's for the best. You need to be home, safe and sound."

"Glenna's my best friend. I can't believe I have to sit here and wait." Dani stands, her fists clenched at her sides.

Clarice stands beside Dani, wrapping her arms around the girl as if she were still a small child. "You don't know how dangerous they are."

I join in, "I know Victoria is involved with what happened to Glenna, but I must prove it. Just give Clarice any information you have. Are there tapes of interviews?"

"Yeah, there are a lot of backup discs and drives. I've not looked at them, though."

I would have to get those tapes myself. Or use Dani as bait and have Clarice kill me later.

Dani's face screws up in thought. "I guess my ticket to NYU is toast."

"We'll discuss college once all this is over," Clarice says. "Give me a list of anyone who might have interviewed through Victoria. We'll call your friends together and ask around."

"You need to warn them not to talk to Victoria or anyone else," I remind them. "If it's all legitimate, Dani, I'll move on. Leave you and Victoria alone. But..."

Dani's eyes lock on mine. "...nothing Victoria does is legitimate."

46

─────

The next morning, everyone is gathered in the conference room to work out the details for what we were calling the evening's "surveillance run." Mac's remote IT staff were tracing Victoria's money. We had confirmation of Glenna's location, and we needed concrete proof to support Beth's allegations of trafficking. We wanted to find Glenna and, if possible, save any other children at risk.

But Mac kept telling me not to get my hopes up.

"Give me a few minutes, guys," I tell my team. "I need to make a phone call."

My gut says I have to try talking with Morris one last time. If he knows anything about Glenna, my call is worth a shot. When alone in my office, I dial the number for the farm office. Given this was the weekend, my call was a long shot. Yet, instead of the receptionist or voicemail, Morris answers.

"Hey, Morris. How is the couple I sent you working out?" For a split second I almost used Nikki's and Angus's real names.

My ridiculous hope is that he will cave and tell me about the shipment to happen that night, Willow House, or anything else.

"They're doing well." His voice is friendly, just as always.

"Mark pitched in to get the hay cut, even though he knew we couldn't pay overtime. It's nice having a crew that works for a living."

"I'm happy they worked out for you." I keep the conversation light.

"I think Mindy will work out fine with Brad," he responds. "She seems to understand she needs to..." Morris stops.

"What is it, Morris?" I hope my voice conveys a lack of concern.

"Nothing." He goes silent for a long moment. "I forgot you don't work here anymore." He laughs nervously, then coughs. "There's no need for me to air our dirty laundry."

He is ready to talk, but something is stopping him. Maybe he thinks his call is being recorded. Given that Brad planted a device in my office, that thought isn't farfetched. To learn what I want, I'll have to tread lightly.

"Look, Morris. I called because I have a question."

It takes him several seconds to respond. "Fire away."

"About your mother's house in Willow Springs."

Another silence. Then, a long breath out.

"Morris?"

"I sold that property years ago." Morris hesitates. "I have nothing to do with it now, M.L."

"Can I ask who you sold it to?" Will he tell me the truth about anything?

"Some trust bought it." I hear him opening and closing desk drawers. "Would have thought you'd never want to see it again." Chair wheels squeak, and then a door slams. "Then I think they sold it."

Had Jack forced him to sell his mother's house?

He takes another long breath. "M. L., look. I did what I was told. That's all I do around here, even when..." His voice trails off.

"Are we still talking about Willow House?"

"I can't tell you that," he replies. "I can't tell you anything. I've already said too much. Tried to do too much."

"Morris, let me help you." I hesitate to say anything further. I don't want him to tip anyone off. But I have to try. "I know Glenna is there, damn it. Help me get her out. Your being on the right side of this will go a long way when this thing blows up. Let me help you get out of this before it's too late."

He chokes, coughing into the receiver. "No one can help me now, M.L. That ship sailed a long time ago. I'm sorry."

He cuts the call, and it is all I can do not to throw the phone across the room.

I thought he might give me Glenna without a fight. Instead, I got nothing. Less than nothing. Now he knows I know. Even if Morris had not been involved with the trafficking, he is now an accessory. But will he say anything to Brad or Victoria?

I join my team in the conference room. Mac stands at the whiteboard, reviewing the farm map with his men. My notes are details from memory, and Angus added more items based on what he had seen.

Mac begins. "Ok, let's start. I've talked with the local office of Homeland Security on this, and they want our surveillance before they step in. They are skeptical that anything is being run out of this particular children's home, so we must do whatever it takes to convince them."

He points to the map on the whiteboard.

"Let's start with phase one. Mike, You're team three. Park on the west side and come through the trees to watch House One." He points to another spot. "Set up here. You will have the best view of the entrance to the farm and the driveway up to the house."

House One is easy to identify. The first house built on the farm is the only one built on a slope with a walk-out basement. With the other nineteen, Jack believed the basement was unnecessary and only an added expense, eliminating it from the plans in the future.

Mac points to the map again. "Stay behind this tree line, as the property line is not far beyond it. Do not cross into the property for any reason."

Mac shifts his gaze to my investigators. "Team two, Angus, you and Nikki will come from the opposite side. Park here." He points to a dirt logging road running along the eastern side of the property. "We're lucky their shipment date landed on a night with only a quarter moon. It should be dark enough for the infrared equipment to get clear photos. You will have the best view of the back of the house. Nikki, I assigned you here because you are most experienced with the equipment, and whatever you film will be critical. Again, do not cross into the property, even if you need a closer vantage point. Don't risk your lives."

My entire case—and Glenna's life—rests on the shoulders of the people in this room. I look around the table.

Mac continues, "I'm team one, the wild card. I'll move where needed. M. L, you're zero. Hide your car here." He points to a place three-fourths of a mile from Victoria's new house, a farm track branching from the county road. "Park in this pull-off and stay hidden. As discussed, you will track the incoming vehicles and confirm the direction they take when leaving."

He shifts to Beth and Clarice. "Office, you need to man the phones. We may need 911 calls or other help if this gets out of hand."

"We need to avoid this guy, Breaker, if possible," Mac tells the group. "He has been arrested for a multitude of offenses, including prior sexual assaults and multiple weapons offenses. The man likes his guns. Because of this, I'll be the only one to enter the property and find Glenna."

"This is risky," I interject. I don't like Mac being the one who takes all the risk, but I won't undermine his authority in front of the others.

"You all know," I continue, "that even though we aren't trespassing, except for Mac, they may shoot on sight to defend the property if they see us. They won't check to see if we're over the property line. South Carolina adopted the Stand Your Ground defense, and there is no longer a requirement for anyone in that house to retreat or hide and wait for help. Our only excuse is that we're there for information. That won't help if one or more of us are dead."

I tap the end of my fountain pen on the pad until Clarice places her hand on mine to make me stop.

"Mac, his guys, me, and Nikki have all been in situations worse than this, Lee," Angus responds. He places his hand on Nikki's. "There's a lot at stake, but we know what to do."

The night shipment had to be recorded for HSI to get involved. Even though we all would be live witnesses, we need video and audio with night vision cameras and high-level recording instruments. While Beth can testify at any trial about the basement and the cages, she has not seen the faces running the show. Glenna's testimony will be invaluable—if we find her alive—but she might not even know the man at the top or be in any condition to testify.

"Does anyone have any questions?" Mac asks the group.

No one speaks.

"Ok then," I say. "Our goals are to rescue Glenna, witness the full process of a shipment, and photograph or record everything for HSI to use going forward. We need to know who is running the end game before we can get them involved. Much of what we're doing may not be useable evidence in court, so don't worry about specifics. Film anything and everything. We're just using it to get the higher authorities involved."

My eyes travel to each person at the table. "Be safe."

47

A t eleven that night, I am parked in the dirt logging road, listening through the single comms earbud Mac gave to everyone on the team. My job is to notify the team should any vehicles arrive at the farm and the direction they are heading when they leave. Except for Mac's whispered checks every fifteen minutes, there is silence.

The plan for tonight has changed, at least where I am concerned. Mac's focus is on the children and the trafficking. He is prepared to follow the children wherever they are being taken. I am determined to find Glenna, especially if she is not in the van. I refuse to leave her behind.

He insists that if Glenna is locked into a cage in the basement, I will not be able to get her out and that I am unable to defend myself should someone pull out a gun. He might be correct, but I have to try. I cannot leave Dani's best friend behind.

Even though we argued—heatedly—I won by default as the client. I know my way around Timberline Farm better than anyone, and I refuse to endanger the others who are there only to watch and film. I snuck in and out of that farm in high school. I can do it again.

Fifty yards past Timberline Farm's front gate is the dirt road where I turned in, hiding the rental car I'd picked up at the airport. This car won't be immediately identifiable as mine if someone spots it. The farm is dark and quiet, a small light burning in several houses, nothing glowing in House One. Beth could not pinpoint the time each prior shipment had occurred, but she believes it has always been past midnight. We all settle down to wait.

At one o'clock, Mac's soft voice in my earbud brings me to attention.

"Lights on."

Each team responds in the affirmative with clicks of their handsets. I parked sideways to keep the car's headlights from reflecting toward oncoming traffic. The windows are down, and the cicadas buzz in the summer darkness as I wait for the pickup vehicles. Within ten minutes, I hear an engine. A white van appears two minutes after that.

"Van," I whisper into the tiny microphone. "White Econoline —no windows, sides, or back."

I receive clicks from each team.

As the van recedes, I call Clarice on my cell.

"Texted you only a partial plate. They covered part of it with mud. The last letter is Z, followed by 530. Georgia plates on an older model white Ford Econoline van. My guess is sometime mid-2000s. We'll get the rest of it when we follow."

At the office, Clarice is ready. "Beth has the GPS map up. I have a flat map ready for the back roads. Let me know when you need routing."

"Will do. I'll keep the line open, so hold the noise down on your end. If Glenna is in the group, I'll let you know."

I roll my neck to relieve the stress while I wait in the darkness for instructions from Mac. The van slows at the Timberline Farm entrance and then turns in. The sound of wheels on gravel fades as it moves away from me. "Incoming," Mac says.

Angus's soft voice follows. "Good vision here. Recording."

I wait.

No sounds bounce back through the trees to tell me what is happening. A dozen people are moving around in the middle of the night, yet I hear nothing. Switching the overhead light off, I remove the key to cut the alarm. Opening the door, I tiptoe to the front of the car, squinting in the darkness.

I mentally count to one hundred. Then again.

After the tenth round of counting, I give up and return to the driver's seat. I check my phone. It has only been twenty minutes.

"Glenna is not—repeat—is not with the group. Zero, you're up." Mac's voice jolts me upright.

I whisper my response in the microphone. "On it."

I can hear Clarice's frantic voice coming through the cell. "What does he mean "You're up?"

"I'm not leaving her behind, Clarice. Just chill."

Leaving the car, I shift into the woods, heading for the fence line. I wait until the van leaves, then hop the board fence at the perimeter. I plan to head for Victoria's house at the back of the farm. I assume Breaker moved her since Glenna was not with the other children. The only place feasible to hide Glenna is with Victoria.

"Clarice," My words are as quiet as I can make them. "I'm going. Text only now." I lower the screen brightness on my phone.

"Find Glenna, Lee." Her voice is tense. "But watch out for yourself."

"Target leaving." Mac is breathless. I hear the clicks in response.

I watch the van from the woods as it rounds the gentle curve in front of the two horse barns. Behind me, another vehicle approaches. Squatting on my haunches, I stuff my cell phone in my front jeans pocket. A patrol car comes into view. As the van exits the farm, its headlights span the side of the waiting vehicle, the Charleston County Sheriff's office banner on its side.

"Charleston County SO escort arrived," I convey into my mic. "Met van on the county road."

Clicks sounded, then Mac's response, "Van tagged. We'll follow."

Relieved that the van has a tracker, I watch as both vehicles leave, then freeze as they turn in the opposite direction we expected. I wrench my cell from my pocket and text Clarice with a copy to Mac, then put the phone on mute.

On back roads. Headed west to Georgia, not east to Myrtle Beach.

The farm is quiet again. Staying at the tree line, I skirt around the edge of the property to avoid crossing another fence until I reach the back of the original house. It is dark, so I head toward the barn. I halt at the sight of Dani's battered Prius behind the barn, my heart slamming to my feet.

In my head, I mutter a multitude of curses at the girl.

She is parked in the same place I'd parked twenty years ago, hiding from Victoria. I take three long breaths, calming my heart rate. Now, I have two people to rescue. I jump when a head pops up in the driver's seat of Dani's car. Looking around to ensure the farm is still quiet, I tiptoe to the vehicle and tap my fingernails on the driver's window.

Dani freezes. Her head slowly turns toward me. She buzzes down her window, her eyes round with fear until she recognizes me. The silly girl grins, and it's all I can do to check my anger.

Whispering, I lean within an inch of her face, "What in hell's name are you doing here?"

Dani keeps her voice low. "Same as you. Finding Glenna. Trish texted me again. She says she has somebody named Nelbert's keys. I'm to meet her at House One at one-thirty."

"Get out of here." I fling my arm toward the front gate. "Go slow so your engine doesn't kick on."

"No," she hisses. "I'm not leaving without Glenna."

Dani reaches into the passenger seat and pulls out a shoebox packed with thumb drives. "Besides, you owe me. Look what I got. You were right. These aren't interviews. They had to strip in that recording booth. Now I know why it has no windows."

I squelch a smile. "Trish is sure where Glenna is?"

Dani's braids bounce as she nods. "She texted me a half hour ago that Glenna's still in that basement. I'm positive she isn't at Victoria's. I looked everywhere. We need to get over there." She points to House One.

"My team says Glenna is not there."

I stop. That isn't right.

Mac's exact words were that she 'wasn't in the van.' There is no way to confirm Glenna was in the basement without going inside.

"Trish says she is, and I believe her. She's waiting for us, so let's go."

"I'll go." I point to the front gate. "You get out of here."

Ignoring me, Dani opens the car door and, without a word, jogs toward House One, avoiding the circle of light from the single bulb over the barn door.

"Damn it." I curse under my breath and follow her. Clarice will pull every hair from that girl's head and start with mine when she finds out.

As we approach the house, a shadow steps from behind the garage. Dani and I freeze, waiting. I grasp Dani's trembling arm and pull her behind a tree. The shadow moves again, taking a cautious step toward us. I push Dani behind me, stepping forward until the shadow waves.

Dani shoves me out of the way. "It's Trish. Come on."

We run toward the side of the garage. My elbow slams into the concrete wall when I misjudge the shadow from the wall. I suck in a scream as the electric pain zips down my arm.

Trish is barely audible. "She's still here. She's too beat up, so they wouldn't take her. They have a van full, anyway. I heard Breaker say he'd keep her for the next week, that he wasn't finished with her yet."

"How do we get her out?" Dani asks.

Trish holds up her right hand to reveal a large key ring with a dozen keys. "Stole Nelbert's keys before he left. Breaker gave him a bus ticket at the police station, so I don't think he'll be back. No one's missed them yet." She motions for us to follow her.

Trish's left arm hangs at a strange angle. At some point it had been broken and incorrectly reset. She walks to the basement door. Trying key after key on the ring, she holds the rest so as not to make noise. Finally, the steel door pops open, and I take a breath.

We follow her inside. The stench of vomit, spoiled food, perfume, and cigarette smoke almost make me lose what little dinner I'd had. We step into the building, and I hesitate to continue in the dark. Unfazed, Trish walks down the hallway until I can no longer see her.

"The men are all gone," she tells us, "and all the kids down here, but there are kids upstairs asleep. Be as quiet as you can." Dani and I tiptoe behind Trish, my eyes slowly getting accustomed to the dark. Reaching the last door on the right, Trish pulls out the key ring and again tries them all until, finally, the cage door swings open.

"Glenna!" Dani's frantic whisper explodes in the concrete room. She rushes in, her phone's flashlight revealing a dank prison cell with Glenna chained to the floor. The girl's face is scratched, her nose bloody, her eyebrow split open, and the other eye swollen. Her hair and part of her face are matted with blood.

Trish drops next to Glenna and, using one of the many keys, opens the cuffs of the chains, first one wrist, then the other. Bruises and dried blood cover Glenna's arms. Most of her clothes are in tatters.

Dani's tears run down her face. With a body hug, she pulls

Glenna upward to stand. "I've got you." Taking off her jacket, Dani covers her friend as best she can.

Glenna croak's a response. "You came. I knew you would." She turns to me and reaches for my hand. "That man is dangerous. You don't know what he will do if he finds you."

"We know," I say. "Where is he now?"

Glenna shakes her head as her entire body trembles. "I don't know."

"Dani, run. Get your car. I'll stay here with Trish and Glenna. Tell Clarice you will take Glenna to the Emergency Room at Roper Mt. Pleasant. It's the closest hospital. I'll make sure you get out of here without trouble." Dani freezes when I pull my gun from its sticky holster in my right jeans pocket. I shove her out the cell door as I pull Glenna into my arms, trying to determine if putting her in a fireman's carry would be faster.

"Go on. Run." I flick one hand at Dani. "You wanted to be part of this. Just don't get caught."

48

The minutes feel like a year. Trish and I walk Glenna to the basement door until Dani returns, her electric car silent on the grass beside the door. Glenna lays in the back seat, and Dani jumps into the driver's seat.

Glenna grabs my hand before I close the rear door. "Get that bastard."

I lean over and kiss her forehead. "We will. Don't worry."

Dani puts the car in gear. I place my hand on the hood to stop her.

"Trish, what are you waiting for?"

"What?" She looks at me, eyes wide.

"Get in. Give me the keys. We're not leaving you here." The girl tosses me the keys and sprints for the passenger seat.

I watch the car leave through the front gate. Using my cell phone flashlight, I steel myself and return to the basement. I take photos of every inch of the basement as quickly as possible, terrified that Breaker will suddenly appear. Finished, I head straight for the trees rather than the circular way I'd come in, even though it means climbing fences.

As I reach the last fence, a limb snaps behind me. Paralyzed, I wait, my breaths shallow in the darkness, until I hear another footstep behind me.

Then another.

Something bumps me from behind, and I stifle a scream.

The soft muzzle of a horse comes over my shoulder. It snorts and gives me a soft nicker. I sink to the ground in relief, the horse bumping me several times, asking for a scratch. Standing again, I rub the soft nose, leaning my head into its side as I pull myself together.

I talk into the radio once I clear the last fence. "Target recovered. ETA twenty."

Clicks respond. I meet Mac at the Whole Foods parking lot in Mount Pleasant. Once I am in his Jeep rental, he takes off toward Georgia, his eyes on the road, flicking back and forth to the tracking map and the blinking blue light of the van's tracker still heading toward Savannah.

"Dani was waiting for me. Trish had contacted her. Somehow, she got the keys that used to belong to one of the guys who tried to run over us, and they planned to get Glenna out. Anyway, Glenna's on the way to the hospital. She's in pretty bad shape."

"Gutsy kids."

"Either that or exceptionally stupid." I shake my head, still unable to process the danger Dani put herself in.

Mac smiles. "We almost got caught. The dog Angus locked in the kennel got loose. When Angus installed the tracker on the car, the dog never barked but followed him. It made enough noise bouncing around to raise the dead. Caught the interest of one trafficker. I had to distract them while Nikki dealt with the dog. It's my bad. Should have included a tranquilizer gun in the pack."

"How many children?" I ask.

"I counted four girls and one small boy. The van arrived with two women and two men. Their cover presents as couples with children."

"What do they want with a small boy?" My brain catches how stupid my question is one second too late.

Mac doesn't respond. He glances out the window, his mouth in a grim line.

"Most likely he will be used to turn tricks. Or sold outright to an individual buyer."

"Sold?"

I cannot wrap my head around a child being sold for sex slavery. I stay silent for the next hour, not wanting to know more. At the merge of Highway 17 to I-95, the van stays straight, then takes the first exit at State Road 462. Moving parallel to the interstate at Ridgeland, the van stops.

We are the last in the chase line. Angus's vehicle and Mac's team's vehicle are ahead of us without tracking information. Mac grabs his mic. "Ridgeland exit."

Zooming in on the map, I see the van parked at a truck stop. Mac keeps his Jeep at the speed limit as we continue past. The van is at the pumps, and the driver is still inside. Mac continues through Ridgeland and another half mile down State Road 336 before pulling behind a rundown farmer's market stand, empty and collapsed on one side.

"You'd think they would have filled the van before they started this." Mac's comment is to himself, but I have to agree. We watch the stationary blue dot on the map.

Mac thumbs his radio again. "When you return to this exit, Mike, pull into the Exxon station. It's next door to the BP, where the van is stopped at the outermost set of pumps. You can't miss it. Pull in, head to the left, and maybe take a spot to the side. Use your judgment and let me know what you see."

Mac looks at me, then at the map, thumbing the mic again. "Angus, stay as close to the interstate entrance as possible and wait. They are too exposed for this to be the last stop."

The Jeep idling, we wait. Being blind is difficult. I want to get out of the car and run back to the children in that van. Used to having all parts of things planned and under control, sitting in a car with nothing more than an earbud while we wait is unnerving.

"Not a bathroom or fuel stop." Mike's voice breaks the silence. "Stand by."

I shove the cuticles back on all my fingernails and, when finished, start again.

Mike's voice comes over the speaker. "Text." Mac reaches for his phone as a text beeps.

Transaction in process. Woman selling older girl. Trucker paying in cash. Filming. Trying to move closer for audio. Truck stop interference.

"Call Clarice. Have her call HSI and Jasper County Sheriff's Office," Mac says to me. "JCSO needs to put out an amber alert for a child abduction."

He texts Mike.

Transaction complete?

Mike responds verbally this time. "Affirmative. A trucker took the girl. She's in his cab."

"Convey truck identification to the office," he responds. "Mike, stay with the girl in the truck. Coordinate any movements with us and Clarice. Handoff your video to Nikki to upload any video or audio to Clarice. Nikki, forward to the locals."

One after the other, Mike and Angus respond, "Affirmative."

"What will happen to that girl, Mac?" I ask. It is all moving too quickly.

"The police units will find her. Mike's with her until they do. Don't worry. He's done this before."

"What do we do?"

"Keep following."

49

Mac and I follow the van. At any moment, I know it will stop and sell the other children, like offering watermelons at a roadside stand. If they sell each child one by one, our surveillance will be useless. At least three of the children will be lost.

Fifteen minutes later, the blip on our map becomes stationary in Hardeeville, South Carolina. We wait out of sight across the street.

"Now what?" I ask Mac.

"Tell Clarice to update HSI. They can monitor our tracker, but only if close by."

As I call Clarice and give her the van's location, I watch Mac run his fingers through his hair. His eyes are red-rimmed from a lack of sleep. Exhausted, he is alert at three in the morning. Now I understand why Angus wanted him involved.

"You following?" He talks to someone on his cell. His shoulders relax with the answer that I can't hear. Seeing my concern, he punches the button for the speakerphone. An unfamiliar male voice blares inside the Jeep.

"Our vehicle is ten miles behind you, monitoring radio traffic.

The tracker should be within our range shortly. Local law enforcement notified us of the trucker, and Jasper County has units en route. Your guys at the law office are on top of things. As discussed, keep tracking the van as planned. We will take over if they cross the Georgia state line, as our Savannah team is waiting. Good work, Mac."

After he tosses his cell into the center console of the Jeep, Mac grabs his radio.

"Guys, the target has stopped again south of Interstate 95 at the Hardeeville, South Carolina exit, just past the welcome station. The van parked away from the pumps to the north. Angus, I will park at the rear of the QuikTrip station across the street. Mike, stay with the first trucker. Per HSI, Jasper County units en route. You should see them shortly."

When parked at the rear of the QuikTrip, I head for the bathroom and coffee. With the pump activity on the opposite side of the store, our vehicles are the only ones on this side. I make sure my hat is pulled low to hide my face as I round the corner to the front. I see no activity from the van. Backed into the space, its nose points away from the interstate. It is too far away to hear if the engine is running, but they are obviously waiting for someone.

Five minutes later, Angus and Nikki park beside us. I hand out coffees and lean against the Jeep, my eyes on the tracking map of the iPad resting on the hood.

"I wonder just how far they'll go with this next leg," Mac says.

"No clue," Angus responds. "My turn to check them." He walks away from our vehicles and around the QuikTrip toward the gas pumps. Five minutes later, Nikki follows him on her reconnaissance trip.

When Angus returns, he gestures with his thumb over his shoulder in the van's direction. "They're just sitting. Still no activity."

"I wish we knew the destination," I say. "We could get into place early."

"With luck, we will be okay," Angus replies. "Mac brought cameras with telephoto lenses that can shoot extremely long distances."

Mac looks over my shoulder as I swipe my cell phone's screen to look for drop sites. "One of these is where they will meet." I point to the map. An abandoned motel is on one side of the highway, and another newer motel is across the freeway interchange. "Both have rear access. At least, they appear to from the map."

Angus comes to stand with us. Mac points as he looks at Angus. "Go scout now around the Madison Motor Inn parking lot and that abandoned motel. Tell me what you think."

Angus starts his truck just as Nikki returns from her surveillance walk. She shakes her head. Mac sits in the Jeep as I watch the tracker. Using street view on my maps app, I see that The Madison Motor Inn has two levels, with all doors accessed from the outside and a staircase at either end of the building. The van might stop in the front or back or at the tiny office building to one side.

"There are at least a dozen rooms per floor facing the highway and another dozen facing the rear." I look at Mac. "Hard to stay out of sight, plus pick the correct side, especially with a duplicate setup on the back. Too many possibilities."

Mac points to another building. "There's a church on the corner for..."

"Guess we're leaving," I interrupt. The tracking dot moves and I watch the blip.

Mac starts the Jeep and radios Angus. We follow several cars behind the van as it heads from the interstate.

Angus's voice interrupts in my ear, calm but irritated. "They pulled into the dead motel across from the Madison. We're shifting locations a bit. Will advise."

"Affirmative," Mac replies. "We're three vehicles back."

I hear Angus's microphone click in my ear.

Mac looks at me, then at the tracking screen with the blip at the abandoned hotel, slowly looping around to the back. The Jeep lurches as Mac floors the gas.

"Head for the dirt road behind the dead hotel," Angus says quietly. "Gives us eyes on both sides. We're good on our end. You'll see the van through the trees. Make it quick."

Mac turns down the gravel road, flipping off the Jeep's headlights and continuing in the gloom. A hundred yards down, he slams the vehicle into park. On foot, we pause in a copse of trees and bushes that hide us from view. The bushes are thick and green in the middle of summer. Our only concern might be mosquitos, but I'll have to tough it out. With a one-handed maneuver, Mac sets up video and audio equipment in five seconds, directing it toward the van parked in front of the last unit. Crouched low, we are entirely too close to the building for my comfort, even in pitch-black darkness. The moon has set, and while I can see the buildings, I won't see anyone's face. And I don't dare sneeze or slap a mosquito. Mac quietly adjusts his audio and video equipment, and I'm unsure how anything will be recorded in this darkness. I quietly sit on the ground. This might take a while.

Built from wood, the old motel is from the 1930s, the roof collapsed at the opposite end of the L-shaped building. Scattered graffiti adorns the few remaining upright walls. The building is the same one from the photos Jack left at Willow House. Squatters used the doors and windows as fuel in the makeshift fire pit in the parking lot.

A black Cadillac Escalade pulls next to the battered white van. I sink lower behind the brush. Mac leans close to me, his face next to mine.

"I need to get a tracker on that vehicle," he says directly in my ear. "Stay here. The equipment will be fine."

Mac hands me night-vision binoculars, and I focus on the

vehicle, watching as he creeps from the brush and dashes behind the Escalade. The binoculars allow me to see clearly. Everything is in detail and not as dark or grainy as I expected. With my increased vision, however, my fear increases tenfold as Mac crouches behind the SUV, his arm reaching under the back bumper.

Before the two men can exit the Escalade, Mac is beside me again, and I let out the breath I'd been holding. The driver, about forty, wears a baseball cap and has a heavy dark beard. The man stepping out of the passenger side is in his late twenties with a stringy ponytail. As they reach the motel room door, it opens, and two women appear. Each thrusts a sleeping girl into a man's arms.

One girl looks about ten, the other a little older, maybe thirteen, and they each are shoeless, wearing T-shirts and shorts for sleeping. As the men carry the girls and roughly place them inside the vehicle's back compartment, I realize they aren't sleeping but heavily drugged. My fear rises, and sweat begins to roll down my back.

A scream pierces the night from inside the motel room. I swing the binoculars back toward the building. A struggling, crying four-year-old boy in footie pajamas is hefted into Bearded Man's arms. My heart breaks watching the child as he struggles to be free, his arms flailing, feet kicking, a Tasmanian Devil in shorts and a T-shirt.

"No wanna," the boy screams. "Don't like you. Lemme go. Wanna go home."

He opens his mouth to scream again, but instead, wraps his mouth around Bearded Man's arm and clamps down.

"Ouch, you little shit." Bearded Man rips his arm from the boy's mouth as he looks at someone inside the motel room. "You should have given it to him before we got here like the girls. Do it now." He flips the boy over so that he's upside down, still struggling to get away from the man. An arm from inside the motel appears and grabs the boy's leg. A needle is pushed into his thigh. Within seconds, the child goes limp.

"Just get him out of here. He's been a real pain," a female voice says loud enough for me to hear even though I am fifty feet away.

"Where's the other one?" Ponytail asks. Through the binoculars, I can see too much detail. The man looks as if he hasn't bathed in weeks. Tufts of hair grow sporadically on his face like he is fifteen and unable to grow a full beard. His clothes are torn, as if he's lived on the street for months.

After the last two children are placed in the back, both men get into the Escalade, and the vehicle begins to back away from the hotel. A backpack is tossed from the SUV driver's window to one of the men standing in the parking lot next to the white van.

"Tell Breaker," yells Bearded Man, "we'll have a moving truck next time. It'll need to be full."

Mac and I look at each other in the dark, and I know what he is thinking. Trish told us they wanted twenty kids in the next shipment. A moving truck holds a lot more than twenty.

50

The exchange concluded, after a spin of gravel, the Escalade loops around the motel and is gone. Mac and I watch the two men and two women return to the van, laughing and discussing their plans when they return to Charleston. Their gaiety quenches the burning anger that lives deep down inside me. The doors banging on the rusty white van, they leave, and silence returns to the abandoned building. They cannot get away with this. I cannot let them.

Since Angus and Nikki have to be at work at the farm in several hours, we have planned to split up if necessary.

"Let's go," Mac says. He looks at me. "This may still be a long night. You can head back with Angus and Nikki if you want."

"No. I'm staying with you. We need to know where they are going."

"You know we won't get those children, Lee. They will head toward Savannah. That's the only place near here, and once we cross into Georgia in fifteen or twenty minutes, the Feds will take over."

"I don't care. I need to see this through."

Mac and I stay with the children, following the Escalade

using the tracking app on the iPad. Angus and Nikki follow the white van back to Charleston, giving us detailed information over the radio and, at one point, getting clear photos of the driver and front passenger.

Mac calls Mike for an update on the girl in the semi-truck. According to Mike, neither the kidnapped girl nor the truck driver appeared from the sleeper cab for the first half hour. When the truck pulled out, Mike followed it as it headed north toward the Interstate highway. The South Carolina Highway Patrol stopped the long-haul truck within the first mile, forcing it to the next exit south of Walterboro. From a 24-hour Waffle House across the street, Mike watched as the troopers took the girl into custody in one car and the driver into another.

"Head toward Savannah," Mac says to Mike, "and I'll keep you posted. We're following a black Escalade now. Angus and Nikki are following the van back to Charleston. We will be available in case HSI needs assistance like last time. Otherwise, we'll stand down once we have the final location."

I call an old law school friend, apologizing profusely for the early hour, and beg her to meet the girl taken by the truck driver at the Jasper County Sheriff's Office. Updating Clarice by phone, I ask her to provide me with regular text updates until the girl is released into my friend's custody.

"I'm trying to get permission for her to use Beth's old room in Magnolia House," Clarice says.

"That's a good idea. What's the status on Glenna?"

"She's in bad condition. The physical, even as significant as it is, will heal, but the trauma, according to the doctor, will take time." Clarice pauses. "But she's a strong girl. And we will be there for her."

"We will. Keep me updated. I'll do the same."

The black SUV never stops. Mac now talks frequently with HSI, and we follow until the SUV crosses the line into Georgia. We ease back, always keeping several vehicles between us and the Escalade as we travel down the Interstate. Mike and Derrick are a few car lengths behind us, waiting for directions.

In Pooler, Georgia, the SUV leaves the freeway, and winds through neighborhoods. It pulls into the garage of a small ranch-style house, the garage door closing behind it as we turn the corner into the neighborhood. Mac drives past the house, turns left, and pulls to a stop, relaying the address to Mike over the mic and HSI by cell phone. A lengthy discussion ensues with HSI.

Mac's responses are curt, consisting of "affirmative," "will do," and "copy" until the call finally ends.

"We are to hold a few streets over. They want us out of the way until they can set up. Once they are fully in control, we'll head back to Charleston."

"This is ridiculous." I am ready to walk up to the house with the Escalade and snatch them myself. "Will HSI not go in and get these children?"

"There is a plan in place, and you must be patient. It does no good to get just the minnows at the bottom, Lee. We need everyone involved in the food chain, including the marlin at the top."

I hated fish and didn't appreciate his metaphor.

"Will they just sit and watch?" I ask.

"Probably. They have a good team here in Savannah. You have what you need for your case, so we're out. We'll have to testify if their sting is successful as to our part."

"We just leave them here?" My head pounds, and I rub my temples with my fingers. "They're kids, Mac. Little kids." The memory of the screaming little boy being held upside down by Bearded Man as the woman gives him a needle with drugs haunts me.

"That's all we can do right now, Lee. Let the process work. You know I've worked with them before. They feel the same way you do."

I slam my fist on the Jeep dashboard.

Mac's voice is soft, his eyes boring into mine. "We've done all we can. Remember, we're only at phase one of our plan. We have two more phases to go, and regardless of what HSI does, we will make sure Brad, Victoria, and this Breaker guy are stopped. These guys on this end are just the beginning for HSI. We need to help them see this through."

While we wait, Mac's two team members watch the front and back of the house to ensure no one from the Escalade house leaves. HSI rouses a local realtor out of bed. They gain access to several vacant homes in the neighborhood and quietly shift inside each using only the back doors. With their surveillance set and Mac released, we have nothing to do but head back to Charleston.

With the picture of the little boy in my head, it is time to start phase two.

51

Grabbing another coffee, I sit across from my grandfather. Even my bones are tired after the three-hour trip from Savannah that only took Mac two—and then two hours of sleep. Phase one is a success, especially now that Glenna is home, although bittersweet given the children trapped in a house under surveillance outside Savannah.

The Judge arrives at the office at nine and helps me gather information and photos for Vince.

"Exactly what do we want Vince to do, Judge?" I ask.

"We need him to produce an article sufficient to catch Brad, Victoria, the Sheriff, and especially Clint Harbin off guard," he replies.

"The entire time," I say, "these children have been trafficked, it has been in plain sight, right under our noses. I want the whole town to know what they've been doing."

"But first, we have to persuade Vince—and the editors at his newspapers. Don't put the cart before the horse, dear."

"We will load Vince up at dinner," I respond. "I think he needs something to get him going again."

"Yes," the Judge says, "Given his appearance and lack of

concern in the past, I am somewhat concerned that the paper's editor-in-chief may reject the story. We must help Vince by including photos of Glenna's prison and promise an exclusive interview with the track star once she is able. It will be up to Glenna whether she will follow through, of course."

The Judge wears a smug smile as he makes notes. I finish dictating the complaint and several motions for the Court of Common Pleas against Timberline Farms, Victoria, Brad, the board of directors for the farm, and any fictitious entities—people to be added later. My goal is to hit them hard and fast. First, I will file lawsuits against the farm and the Marshalls personally, then the news articles and social media that I hope will go viral, and then the raid of the last shipment from the farm. Quickly, I needed the headlines to broadcast Brad's and Victoria's arrests in big, bold typeface. Social media will take care of the rest.

After I schedule the electronic filing of the lawsuits, we head to the restaurant.

Circa 1886, the restaurant on Wentworth Street is the original carriage house of the Wentworth Mansion, built in the late 1800s by a wealthy magnate, and now a boutique hotel. To say it is the Judge's favorite is an understatement. He knows the owner, who reserves a table for him whenever he asks. The Mansion is his second home when he is not on Sullivan's Island. With twenty-one rooms, the glamour of the boutique hotel fits the Judge. My grandfather is most suited to its gilded age.

Vince is waiting outside when we arrive. Shaved and combed, he sports a light gray suit with a white shirt and coordinating tie. The only time I've seen Vince this spiffy was when he won a national journalism award ten years ago.

We sit, order the wine and dinner, and Vince relaxes as he leans back in the alcove booth. We, as usual, are away from the rest of the guests.

"Thanks for the exclusive on this, M.L.," Vince says. "I need a boost at the paper. Been a little slow."

He spreads the newspaper across the table, using his finger to point to the article about East End on page two. I don't speak the snark in my head of his slacking journalism. Plenty has been happening in North Charleston that he could have reported before now.

The Judge leans forward. "We need you to help us again."

"I'm listening."

I sit back, waiting for my grandfather to proceed. He is fresh; I am not. I don't want to say the wrong thing because I am exhausted.

"For this meeting and any other meetings or conversations we might have, you will treat me and Ms. Danforth as confidential sources. Our names will not be in print at any point. You will not reveal us as your sources of this information or any information we may provide you in the future. You will not reveal us to your Editorial Board or your Editor-in-Chief. It is imperative for the good of the city, as well as our reputation."

"I have no problem with either of you being a confidential source. And just so you know, my editor has already approved a story supplement for tomorrow's paper. We'll dig deeper into what's happening at East End. Interview the girl who was almost taken downtown, that sort of thing."

The Judge tilts his head, scrutinizing Vince. The reporter lifts his water glass and takes a sip. For him, not drinking alcohol is a significant uptick in professionalism.

"So—Lee alluded to kids being kidnapped? Trafficked?"

The silence makes Vince uncomfortable, but my grandfather will not be rushed. The Judge lifts his glass and inspects the wine before swirling it in his glass and taking a sip. I see the concern my grandfather has with Vince. He's too eager. We need him to be controlled and disciplined.

"We have information," my grandfather begins, "regarding

Timberline Farm and its principals and their connection with the incident at East End. Witnesses know of a trafficking ring at the farm. This operation is being run, we've been told, by Brad Marshall, the son of the founders, one of whom, as you know, is now deceased."

"Murdered." My involuntary response pops out before I can stop it.

Vince's face is skeptical. "I heard it was just a heart attack."

I silently offer the photo on my phone as proof.

"While there may or may not have been a murder," the Judge continues, "that is not our focus. I am sure you can follow up that line of questioning as you see fit."

"What is your focus?"

"The traffickers. They do not confine the ring to the orphaned children from the farm. When there are insufficient children to pilfer from Timberline Farm, the men running this operation have been roaming the streets of the Charleston metro area and beyond, scooping up unsuspecting young girls and children. Thus, the issues that have overwhelmed East End."

"You have proof of this?"

"Yes, eyewitnesses, participants."

"Then why aren't you going to Harbin?"

"One witness has already approached our solicitor about one particular sexual assault on behalf of Brad Marshall. Harbin refused to discuss the matter or authorize an investigation. Given this refusal, we hesitate to discuss additional criminal activity. We are concerned he may be involved somehow."

"I find that hard to believe if there is concrete proof," Vince says, removing a new pack of cigarettes from his inside jacket pocket and placing them on the table. He does not move to open them since smoking is not permitted inside the restaurant.

"The witnesses are young girls and the strongest has already been to him. He refused to talk with her." My grandfather takes another sip of wine. "If that is not enough for you, we have proof of at least one local police force also involved."

Vince begins tapping his pen on the table.

"Maybe you need to be the one to talk to Harbin," he says directly to my grandfather. "Talk about re-election shoo-in. And police corruption? How sure are your witnesses?"

The Vince I know is too slow tonight, especially concerning Harbin. I squint at him when he shifts his gaze to me. He needs to make some connections without us spelling everything out for him.

"I'm one of the witnesses to the police involvement and the trafficking, Vince," I say. "And all of this occurred at Timberline Farm."

"Wait. Wasn't there some scuttlebutt not long ago on Harbin and Victoria Marshall? Some affair?"

Ah. The lightbulb finally switches on.

"You may make of gossip what you will," the Judge continues. "Our witnesses, however, are solid. But it isn't only their stories. We have a recent video and audio of the holding cell where they keep the children. We have a young woman, recently released from the hospital, who resided in that holding cell for several days. Her injuries are significant. We have video and audio of actual trafficking."

"I'll need that for the online addition." Vince furiously scribbles notes.

"We rescued one child early this morning, assisted by law enforcement in Jasper County. Another two were rescued by Lee last night. Others are in Chatham County, Georgia, and are under surveillance by HSI. We hope to have them rescued within the next forty-eight hours and those abductors caught."

My grandfather leans forward, his face set in a grimace. "Do not let that last bit out. If you leak this, those children will disappear into the wind."

Vince sits back, stunned. "Video and audio of actual trafficking?" He scribbles more notes. "Can I have the witnesses' names?"

"One step at a time." The Judge shakes his head. "There is more that we require for this initial story. Print this information as part of your East End expose."

Vince continues to make notes.

"Look at me, Vince," the Judge says, and Vince stops writing to look at him. "It must be above the fold in tomorrow's evening edition. No exceptions. We would appreciate an exciting banner. Clickbait will be useful in this exercise."

"Judge Rhineholdt, you know I can't guarantee that. My editor must sign off on this. He'll want to run it by legal."

"Then contact him now while we have dinner and begin working this out."

"Why the quick deadline?"

The Judge looks at me, and I silently mouth "no."

"I am not at liberty to divulge our strategy." The Judge leans forward again. "I cannot stress this enough. The specifics remain confidential. Tomorrow evening, there will be an event where we will gain more evidence. Brad will expose himself with your forceful nudge, becoming part of the evidence we need to force Harbin's hand."

"I want in on tomorrow night. You can't keep me out." Vince picks up his glass and drains the water.

"Get your story on the front page," the Judge responds, "above the fold, with full headlines, and you can cover the entire explosive matter. You can watch the entire story unfold and report in real time. As for now, you get no more specifics until you have received your paper's approval."

Vince scrambles from the table, his cell to his ear before he reaches the front door.

The waiter approaches. "May I serve now, Judge?"

"Yes, Martin, please do. I don't think our friend will be long, but you might keep it warmed, just in case."

As the waiter walks away, I smile at my grandfather, patting him on the leg under the table.

"After his story," I say, "the entire area will go into lockdown, parents chaining their daughters to their beds. Brad will have no product tomorrow night unless Breaker has already snatched them from the street. Every law enforcement agency for all three surrounding counties, the City of Charleston, and other cities will respond, yada, yada, yada. And Brad will run."

"Yes, he may," the Judge responds, patting my hand. "Or he may stay. If Brad runs, he will be out of our area, and it is the responsibility of law enforcement to locate him."

"Victoria is the wild card."

"Oh, I think not. Your wild card is Breaker and her hold over him. The man is dangerous. Besides, Victoria will blame her son for everything and insist she has nothing to do with trafficking."

"Thanks to Dani, we have proof of Victoria's auction scheme. I wonder if she's missed the hard drives yet."

I sip my wine, savoring the deep cherry and smoky aftertaste. The videos Dani stole are more than explicit. Victoria is on camera, parading each girl in front of individual buyers. Nikki is now tracking the players and the money to give the Feds a starting point. "What do you think of Vince's idea of you talking to Harbin?" I ask.

The Judge smiles, and an eyebrow quirks upward. "You should invite him to go with us tomorrow night."

I place my glass on the table to avoid dropping it. "What? Go with us? What if he's in on this?"

The Judge gives me a sly smile. "Let us take care of that tomorrow after Vince does his part."

"You're going to suggest he be part of the solution rather than part of the problem. Help him save face, even escape prosecution."

"Something like that," he replies.

A waitress arrives with a bread basket and butter and refills our water glasses. The Judge is quiet until she leaves. He leans closer to me, his voice low.

"Harbin really should be dealt with the same as the rest. But this way…" The Judge winks at me, "… he will owe us. Owe you, actually."

The waiter serves our food as Vince returns to the table. Grabbing his water, he drains another entire glass.

"I got the approval," Vince says, "but my job is on the line. They're skeptical and said I needed actual skin in the game for them to approve. This better not be a wild goose chase. My job is all I have."

The Judge sets his fork on the edge of his plate, adjusts the napkin in his lap, and then looks directly at Vince, his face stern.

"As it should be, Vince. All journalists need a personal incentive in their reporting and not putting garbage on the page. That is not the case as of late. But no worries. Your editor will be pleased. Once you finish your dinner, we will give you as much information as you can write."

"I can't tape?"

The Judge shakes his head. "Our voices are distinctive. Notes only."

After an hour, with dinner completed, the issues outlined, and Vince on his way to *The Times* offices, I walk with the Judge to his Mercedes. In the back of the vehicle, he closes the privacy shield.

"I think filing a civil suit will be a waste of time," I say.

"As to any civil action you file on behalf of your client, I believe the feasibility of attempting to retrieve funds from Timberline Farm at this point is low, blood from a turnip and all that." He waves his hand in the air. "Besides, your client, Beth, came to you to do anything to put Brad in jail. Our current course of action will do that. Harbin will have no choice but to prosecute Brad."

The image of Beth flashes through my mind. "She will want

to proceed, no matter the cost. But we should wait on the criminal conviction. Once Brad and Victoria are in jail, and we see where they have hidden the funds, we can then decide if a civil action is in order."

The Judge smiles silently in agreement. "Any offshore funds may be frozen," he says, "and will be difficult to obtain. Sad, since your client could use the funds."

Looking at his watch, he buzzes down the privacy shield and speaks to the driver.

"Timothy, please park in the spaces reserved for Ms. Danfield's office when we arrive. We will be another minute or two.

"I've done one other thing," he says, raising the screen again.

"You don't trust Timothy?" I point to the screen.

"He's still new. There is a trust factor that must be earned." He continues. "I am concerned there may be an impact on Alex from tomorrow's events. Victoria may surprise me and do something unexpected. While I have done everything possible to ensure that Victoria cannot reach Alex, we cannot trust her. I hired counsel in Boston to advise her tomorrow night if needed, once we have proof. He will be her counsel *pro hac vice* here in Charleston, along with me, if needed."

"Does Alex know you?" I ask.

"Yes. She has not seen me since childhood, but we have exchanged Christmas cards for the past two years."

"You are such a surprise." I lean over and kiss his cheek. He smells of sandalwood and soap.

"Why is that?" He asks.

"You have protected not only me for all these years but also looked after her." I suddenly have a lot of questions. I want the details of Alex's life, about her parents, if she is happy and if they seemed to love her how I think she needs to be loved. I'm dying to know the details of her personality and whether she looks like me or Jack, or a mixture of us both.

He squeezes my hand. "It is my duty but also my pleasure." His eyes meet mine. "I know you have questions, but now is not the time. I will answer them all, I promise you."

I focus on the garden I love so much, the flowers highlighted by the lights in the tree and around the brick wall, and return to the problem at hand. "Since the adoption ended our rights, what impact could there be?"

"None unless Victoria attempts something untoward." My grandfather's smile reaches his eyes. "I would rather be prepared, like that action character in those books you love."

He is right. *Hope for the best, prepare for the worst.*

I need to get into that office and update everyone. Things, as Dani says, "are about to get real."

52

Vince's headline was the front page of the next morning's banner of *The Times*:

TIMBERLINE FARM AND MARSHALLS IMPLICATED IN TRAFFICKING RING

The primary story is above the fold with a Timberline Farm publicity photo. The East End stories about the kidnapped girls are below. On page three, an interview with an HSI agent appears under a different reporter's byline. According to the articles, no one from Timberline Farm's office, Brad or Victoria, would answer calls or interview requests.

I had no misgivings that this would stop the next shipment of children. However, the article did put the community on notice of the problem.

"Is this the calm before the storm?" I grin at my grandfather and walk into the conference room with two coffees. We met at the office at five this morning to get a jump on the day, stopping at the corner to grab several newspapers from the corner box to compare them to the online version.

The Judge clicks his computer mouse, and the printer spits

out cases he wants me to review. We are old school; we read our cases on paper with a pen to take notes in the margins.

"Sheriff Nims in Dorchester County will assist," my grandfather begins. "We talked a few minutes ago before he got to the station. I updated McCabe."

"And Nims agreed to help us because you know what buttons to push?" I ask. "Or because we have HSI involved?"

"A little of both. You should get ready for your meeting." The Judge's head is bent over a stack of cases. "I'll get through as many of these as I can. Here is your section to read on the way."

I shove the printouts into my briefcase for the two-hour drive to Barton Springs. Heyward Kendrick had insisted on a meeting at his office. I don't relish hours of traffic on South Carolina's coast nor the stress of making it back on time for tonight's event.

"You sure Nims can be trusted?" I ask.

The Judge closes his laptop when the printer stops.

"Nims assured me there will be no problems," he says. "At the last minute, he will line up his trustworthy contacts inside the Berkeley County Sheriff's Office and those in Charleston County. He insists there are only a few bad apples at both agencies. Unfortunately, the Charleston County Sheriff happens to be the most rotten."

The Judge and I stop talking as Mac steps into the conference room.

"Everything is underway. HSI will take the lead on tonight's sting. Everything is to proceed as usual as far as the traffickers are concerned. The Feds also want to see the process before making arrests to make the charges stick. There's less chance of an evidentiary problem in their eyes."

"As long as Brad, Breaker, and everyone else that works for them goes to jail, I'll do what I'm told," I reply.

I have to trust the Judge's years of working with the local offices and Mac's in working with the Feds. Real estate law rarely intersects with law enforcement, and I am out of my element. With Mac getting HSI involved, I am less stressed about the criminal prosecutions. Handing Harbin one of the largest stings in the state for prosecution, wrapped up and tied with a large black bow, did not mean he would prosecute. However, with the Feds involved, I am comfortable that Brad and his cohorts will end up in jail.

Harbin is prosecutorially aggressive, and the community might see his obliviousness to the double-digit numbers of missing girls in his area as a law enforcement issue, not a Solicitor problem. I suspect his relationship with Victoria, whatever that is, causes him to look the other way. With this beginning salvo, I am sure Vince will dig until the city knows the details.

The Department of Social Services will have to be called. There has to be a solution for the one hundred twenty children who live at Timberline Farm. But first, we—or rather the Judge—must call Harbin. We want the Solicitor to agree to meet with us at the farm this evening. The Judge believes Harbin should be part of the operational aspect of the sting, not a victim of it. Accomplishing his attendance is something only my grandfather can do.

"Are you ready?" he asks me.

I point to the desktop phone in the middle of the conference table. The Judge punches the phone number from memory.

Harbin's assistant answers. Marie has been an institution at the county courthouse for thirty years. With no age cap for her position, the Judge expects Marie to work until they find her slumped over one day in her chair. According to him, Harbin thought of asking her to retire early once he took office but stepped back from that position when the Judge reminded him she knew the location of—literally and figuratively—not only the bodies but the graves.

"Solicitor's Office."

"Good morning, Marie. This is Judge Rhineholdt."

"Well, hello, sir!" Marie begins with her routine tittering. "We miss you here, Judge. It's not the same without you. I was telling..." She stops talking. "I'm rattling on. How may I help you?"

"So gracious of you," the Judge replies. "I am enjoying my retirement. It was a long time in coming." The age rules forced the Judge into retirement. Because he was not ready to stop working, we had agreed he would work for me when needed until J. Henry Sturh, the funeral home established just after the Civil War, carried him out in a box.

He continued, "Is our good Solicitor in the office today?"

"Yes, sir, Judge. I'll put you through."

"Before you do, I'd like to give you advance notice of something."

"Certainly, Judge."

"If the Solicitor has plans this evening, you will need to move them to another time. I will require his undivided attention."

"Thank you, Judge. I'll do that now."

The Judge winks at me as we wait through the annoying "elevator music," one of the technological additions to the court he protested. He believes those funds would have been better used to upgrade the courthouse technology.

Harbin picks up, silencing the cloying flute. "Judge. I didn't expect to hear from you. Thought you'd be in Bora Bora or somewhere exotic."

"I've not been to Southeast Asia just yet. On my list, though."

The Judge rolls his eyes at me and I stifle a giggle. Harbin makes puffing noises with one of his perpetual cigars. We hear his lighter click and a creak from his office chair.

"How can I help you today?" Harbin asks.

"In full disclosure, I have you on speaker, and my granddaughter is here with me."

"Hello, M.L.," Harbin says.

"Hello, Clint."

"So what are you two cooking up?" Harbin asks.

"We need you to attend an event tonight," I say. "It's something you won't want to miss."

"With all due respect, I don't have time for charity events. You'll have to talk with Marie about that sort of thing. She keeps my calendar."

"This isn't charity, Clint. We've already spoken to Marie," I respond, "and requested she clear your calendar for this evening."

"Now, M.L.," Harbin's voice is condescending. "I'm sure whatever you're doing isn't proper. I'd be careful doing things that might get your license pulled."

When I don't respond, he shifts tactics. "Judge, you're retired. With all due respect, sir, you have no control—"

"You," the Judge interrupts, his voice cold, "have ignored this issue for too long, even when brought to your attention."

"What issue? What are we talking about?" Harbin's voice increases in volume. We can hear the rat-a-tat-tat of his fingers as they drum the desktop.

"Clint, my boy, you know very well to what I am referring."

We had decided earlier to be vague and assumed he would read the newspaper. If he didn't? Well, that is his problem. The newspaper article is all the advance notice we are prepared to give.

Harbin's volume increases. "Look, if you can't tell me what this is about, there's no way I'm going."

I cannot squelch a laugh.

"What?" I respond. "And have the great Charleston County Solicitor look bad in front of law enforcement? Or the reporter who has been running the series in *The Times* these last few days?"

Harbin is quiet. "What are you doing, M.L.?"

"You'll see tonight. Be outside your house tonight at nine," I say. "No need to dress up."

"Judge Rhineholdt—"

"Just be there, Clint," I interrupt, "unless you prefer the Feds to be the ones who knock on your door."

53

After the call to Harbin, Mac and I prepare to leave the office and head toward Savannah. My grandfather reminds us on the way out the door to be ready for our nine o'clock rendezvous that evening.

As if I can forget.

"Heyward Kendrick is insistent that I come in person today to sign documents for Probate Court at his office as quickly as possible," I say to Mac, pouring coffee for both of us from the thermos Clarice handed me on my way out. "His voice was a little strange, and he was abrupt. Would not take no for an answer."

"What do you think Kendrick wants?" Mac glances at me, then back to the road ahead. We are in my Audi with Mac driving because I don't trust myself to keep to the speed limit. In the passenger seat, I twist the ring around my third finger, spinning the center section that is supposed to relieve my anxiety. It's not working.

"Something to do with Victoria. He insists I need to sign probate documents in front of him."

"He could have mailed those to your office."

"Yeah, I know. That's what's bothering me." My fingers

continue to twist my anxiety ring. "Could Victoria have filed another lawsuit? There are so many possibilities that I don't know where to start."

I begin making a list of those possibilities in my head, with Alex at the top of my concerns followed by my grandfather, then down the line until I am almost frantic worrying about what will happen to the children at the farm after tonight's arrests.

"Lee, chill. I can practically see steam coming off your brain. We'll see soon enough," Mac says.

Reaching the parking lot beside Hayward Kendrick's law office I reach for the door handle.

"Hey." Mac's hand squeezes my left shoulder. "Protocol. Me first."

After a cautious scan of the neighborhood, opening his door, he comes to my side of the car. Walking to Kendrick's office, he stops again, his head cocked at a slant as if waiting or listening.

"Something's not right, Lee," he says softly. "I can feel it."

I look across the street at the park, but nothing seems out of place. Still, I unzip the hidden pocket of my purse that holds my Glock. Mac's prior safety warnings are slamming around in my head. I am thankful he took me to the shooting range to practice.

"We need to be sure," I say. "I'd hate to call the police on a hunch and be wrong."

He opens the front door to Kendrick's office and enters the reception area. No one is behind the front desk, and the office is deathly quiet. I follow him in, letting the door softly close behind me with a click.

Rapping the surface of the receptionist's desk, he calls out. "Kendrick?"

"In here." The man sounds like he is talking through a paper bag.

I nudge Mac's elbow. An overturned side table and spilled books scatter the waiting area. Mac eases his gun from his shoulder holster. He checks its readiness, then takes several steps toward Kendrick's office.

As I follow him, Mac stops. He reaches for his phone in his pocket and motions for me to text 911. I fire off a text and wait until the operator has received it and tells me someone is on the way.

I pull out my gun and toss my purse to the couch in the waiting area, stuffing my phone in my back pocket. Chambering the first round as quietly as possible, I stuff the Glock in the front waistband of my jeans and cover it with my shirt.

Mac's gun in his right hand is out in front of him, ready. He motions for me to follow. Silently, he pushes Kendrick's office door with his left hand. With a loud squeak, it swings open.

I gasp as Kendrick comes into view. The lawyer is seated behind his desk, duct-taped to his office chair. The tape is wrapped around his head, behind the chair, and across his mouth. His arms and legs are immobilized. His throat bulges from the tie that is wrapped around his throat.

When he sees us, his face turns bright pink with alarm. Kendrick begins to struggle, his screams muffled by the tape. I start to shove around Mac to free Kendrick, but Mac's arm reaches out to block me, pushing me behind him again. He shifts to my right.

Smiling at us, Victoria steps from the side of the room next to Kendrick. With her left hand, she jerks the ends of the tie, cutting off the man's air. Kendrick's hands are unable to reach his throat, and his prior muffled screams are now silent from the lack of air.

In her right hand, she waves a large antique pistol.

Jack's. It was part of a set that hung over the mantle in the ranch cottage.

"Damn, it took you long enough to get here." Victoria's voice is cold. "This blob of a lawyer won't do what's right. Marjorie Lee, you'll need to help him." Her eyes are wild, like those of a rabid fox. "He needs to declare Jack's will void. He refuses to do it. Says you have to relinquish everything because the will is valid.

"So get in here." Victoria motions for me to come into the room. "Sign these papers right now." Her arm extends, and the pistol points at me. Nothing prepares me for the zap of terror as I stare at the black hole of the gun's muzzle.

"Get in here right now, Marjorie Lee. You will sign these papers that release all your claims on that stupid house in this town, all of Jack's art, and anything else he gave you. It belongs to me, not you."

I don't move. Mac's left arm is still outstretched, keeping me from entering the room even if I wanted to.

"Victoria put the gun down," I say.

"You had your chance. And I tried to play nice with your grandfather, but he was his typical rude self. And then you had to go and put all those lies in the newspaper. You'll be nothing after I finish with you. Taking those two poor girls from the farm. Who said you could trespass on our property, anyway?"

"Victoria, I—"

"Don't deny it," Victoria interrupts. "I know you put Vince up to that stunt in *The Times*. You're trying to get rid of me, and I won't have it. I have nothing to do with what Brad is doing. Those girls you took can tell you that themselves. I was never there, never a part of it. He's been trafficking for almost two years, not me." She waggles the pistol at me. "Before all this is over, you'll be the one who is sorry."

"Sorry for what, Victoria? I've done nothing to you. My life with Jack ended twenty years ago. I haven't seen him since my senior year in college."

My voice has no effect. She pulls the ends of Kendrick's tie tighter and extends her arm, pointing the heavy old pistol at my face.

"Seriously, Victoria," I demand. "The police are on the way. Put down the gun and let him go. You're going to kill him."

Kendrick is beginning to turn blue.

I calculate the distance from me to her across the large office. Unless she is an excellent shot, she will miss, especially with the heaviness of that pistol.

"Come here!" Victoria flails at me with her gun. ""If you don't get in here, I'll most definitely kill him. I've had enough of all of you."

I look at Victoria's eyes. She is trapped in the past. Nothing I say to her will free the man struggling to breathe in front of me. I have to do something, or he will die. Hidden behind Mac's large body, I pull out my handgun, my left foot sliding shoulder width apart from behind Mac's body. I push the gun into his back so he knows what's happening.

With a slight shift to his left, he agrees.

When I see Mac's shoulder tense to fire, I aim at Victoria and pull the trigger.

Mac drops his large body to the ground, pulling me with him into the hallway as Victoria fires two shots in return. My ears are ringing from the explosions of the old revolver, which are like bombs. Two more shots explode above me, and Mac returns fire. The window behind the desk shatters in response.

I scramble backward into the hall.

Another shot from Victoria hits the hallway wall behind me. Mac's return shot blasts into the office. Scrambling to my knees, I aim around the corner at Victoria, her silhouette framed by the rear doorway now open to the outside.

"She's going out the back," I yell to Mac.

I pull the trigger multiple times as the window to the left of the door shatters.

Victoria screams.

Mac is suddenly on his feet across the office and out the back door. I hurry toward Kendrick, now lying on his side. With the ringing in my head, I can't hear a thing. I rip the duct tape from around his head and mouth and begin working on his hands and feet. His unfocused eyes stare at me from the floor.

Just as I think he is dead, he blinks.

A hand grasps my shoulder from behind, and in a split second, I wrench it away, pulling my gun up, ready to fire. Mac's familiar cologne reaches me, and I place my gun on the desk. "She's gone," he yells at me. "I wounded her again. She won't get far."

Or at least that's what I think he said.

I turn back to Kendrick and roll him flat on his back. A gunshot wound is in his chest just over his heart. Blood pours from the hole, which I probably made worse when trying to remove the tape from his hands. Pulling an old sweater from the back of Kendrick's chair, I push it as hard as I can against his shoulder, but blood still flows through my fingers.

"Call 911 again," I say to Mac. I can't hear his response, but see him dip his head in agreement.

I push with all my strength, but Kendrick is fading, his skin losing color. The bullet must have hit an artery.

Mac's hand grabs my chin, forcing me to watch him speak. "They're on their way. Push harder on his shoulder. I'll work on the leg."

He lets go of my face and straddles the heavy man, removing Kendrick's tie, then scooting back to use it as a tourniquet around the wounded leg.

The blood is coming too fast. I know nothing about first aid. Kendrick's mouth is moving, but I can't hear him even though the buzz in my ears is lessening. I lower my ear over his lips.

"Don't let her get away with Jack's death. Her son..."

Before he finishes, I feel the change in his body under my hands. I sit up to see his face. Kendrick's eyes, sightless, stare back at me. I close them, letting him go.

Hands push me away from Kendrick. The paramedics

attempt to revive him, continuing until the coroner arrives from across the square to pronounce him dead.

I sit on the floor against the wall, drained.

With the arrival of the police, chaos ensues. An officer cuffs me and Mac, ties us to the bench outside Kendrick's office, and reads us our Miranda rights. A young officer tries to take our statements.

I vehemently shake my head. "Nope. We need lawyers."

"A good substitute would be your police chief," Mac says to the officer.

The chief arrives about fifteen minutes later. After giving us both a once-over, he cuts the zip ties that attach us to the bench and unlocks the handcuffs.

"Sorry about that," he says to me. "The new guy's a bit over-eager. Kendrick warned me yesterday, expecting this Marshall woman to make good on her constant threats."

He looks at Mac as he bends over and releases his handcuffs. "We've reviewed the security tape from today. It matches what you've told us. If Kendrick hadn't given me some past tapes and a threatening audio message from Victoria Marshall yesterday, you both would be in the town jail charged with murder until we sorted this out."

He straightens and continues. "We have an alert across the southeast for Victoria Marshall, but as of now, she's avoided capture. Wish you'd kept this mess in your neighborhood rather than bringing it to our nice little town."

He fishes a pack of cigarettes from his pocket and taps them against his hand.

"Other than the security footage from today, she's on previous tapes from Kendrick's security system, raising hell. There are also telephone calls and some pretty hateful emails. I'm going to hand them over to GBI."

The Georgia Bureau of Investigation assists the local areas with criminal investigations and forensic services. "I'd like to get a copy of everything you have," I say. "I'll need it for several cases I'm filing against the woman in Charleston."

The chief purses his lips.

"Mrs. Marshall," I continue, "her son and their non-profit in Charleston have been running a trafficking business for several years. I need whatever you have against her, and so will Homeland Security. They are also involved in this."

"Yeah, I saw that on the news," the chief is suddenly interested. "Looks like that story has gone nationwide."

"Then I'm sure HSI would appreciate your assistance with their operation tonight. Let me give you his number. You can tell him what you have because we need to be on our way."

54

Brad sat at his desk, the office lamp casting a yellowed circle of light across the pages. He bent forward as he examined something on his desk. As he heard the door open, he looked up, his face shifting from surprise to concern.

"What are you doing here? Fish's men will be here any minute." He looked back down at his desk. "Seriously, Mother, go on now. I don't have time to talk."

Victoria sauntered to the antique hutch against the wall Brad used for his liquor cabinet. She grabbed his favorite scotch, and poured herself two fingers, downing half in one gulp. She grabbed the bottle again and filled her glass, then walked to a chair. Collapsing, she removed her shoes and kicked back in the chair, her heels on the corner of his desk.

Brad continued to ignore her.

She should be used to it. He had done it his entire life. Jack had done the same. Now Clint had cast her aside, her aging body having outlived its usefulness. She was so tired. But more than that, she recognized she was bitter. Everything always came down to her, and this time would be no different. One more mess to clean up.

Only this time, they were done. Timberline Farm was finished. With the news article from *The Times* hitting the national news wire and every girl in the nation on lockdown, there was no place to hide from Theron Fish when Brad did not meet the quota. Then with Glenna being secreted away in the middle of the night, combined with whatever that snoopy little Trish would tell the world, her Community Center would be an empty building. No one, not even Clint Harbin, could save them from the anticipated investigations. And jail time.

Damnation. All because of the careless manchild sitting in front of her. Victoria glared at the top of his head, wishing she could turn back time. The decision she'd made when faced with the pregnancy had been the wrong one. She'd known it for years, even as well-hidden as his parentage had been. As Brad grew from a toddler, to a child, then to a young boy and now a man, absolutely nothing had made a difference. He was a selfish, egotistical bastard.

And she hated him to the depth of her soul.

God help her.

Dropping her feet to the floor, Victoria slammed down her drink on Brad's blotter, sloshing the liquor on her hand and down the side of the desk. Brad let out an exasperated sigh, holding the spot where he was reading with his right index finger.

"Mama," he said, "you've never drunk alcohol a day in your life. I'm not sure why you're starting now. You're in a foul mood and I don't have time to deal with you. Go on home." He went back to reading.

She would not be cast aside again. It was time. She had thought of this day, dreaming of it even. But she never thought she would have the gumption to pull it off.

Victoria stood, ignoring the throb radiating from her right arm. The pain pills she had taken weren't working. The bullet had passed through her right deltoid, and she could not give herself stitches left-handed. To stop the bleeding, she bandaged the wound as best she could, changed into clean clothes to hide it and washed the ruined makeup from her face.

When he didn't look up, she rapped on the corner of his desk with her uninjured hand.

"We have a problem," she sneered at him, "and I want to know what you've done to fix it."

"What problem?" Brad took his pen and put a blue check-mark where he was reading. "What is this all about." He glared at her, waiting.

"Two girls from the farm escaped from Breaker last night. And your little trafficking crew is all over the front page of *The Times*. I need to know what you're going to do about it."

Brad's mouth turned down in a pout as he shoved his chair away from his desk. "Wait just one minute. You gave Breaker the authority to do his job. Deniability, remember? Why is this my fault?" He gave her an indignant glare.

Her ridiculing laugh sounded strange even to her.

"Brad, with every problem during your entire life, you've always tried to blame someone else. You brag, you flaunt, you insult, and you lie. But it's never your fault. That's your way. Well, now you've bragged your way onto the national news, and Breaker is going to land you in jail, buddy boy."

Brad scoffed, as he leaned back in his chair, his hands laced behind his head, elbows wide. "*The Times*? You're showing your age, Mother. I don't read the newspaper, and few people do these days. Now, it may be a problem if it's on social media." He flipped his hand at her in dismissal. "And if there was anybody missing from the farm, I'd know about it."

She pointed to his computer. "Why don't you check your feed, then?" Her anger was just about to erupt. She shoved her hands in her pockets to keep from flinging the glass of scotch across the room. "Then call Breaker."

Brad rolled his eyes toward the ceiling before returning to

scrutinize her face. "I think you should be the one concerned. You look like hell. Did you forget to put on makeup?"

She ignored his comment. "This will all be on you. I refuse to be responsible this time."

"What will? Look, you know I have another shipment due tonight, a big one. Go clean yourself up. Things need to be done before they arrive. This venture is about to hit the big time."

"Venture? Is that what you call this?"

Brad reached for his computer. "What do you want me to call it, Mother? A charity auction? You see things how you want them to be. Why don't we call it like it is? We are trafficking in children with a side deal in pornography. As part of that, we have a significant client base and various contacts who are unsavory. And that doesn't include your little side business."

Victoria's voice turned haughty as she drew out each word. "We are saving this farm."

He snorted a laugh. "We are doing no such thing. We're making money for ourselves. The farm be damned. It's a means to an end. Has been for a very long time. Time you went to the Caymans and spent some of it."

Someone had told him about her auctions. But her dreams about moving to the Caribbean? The only way he could know is by hacking her computer. She moved to Brad's side. She could feel the volcanic flush of anger as it rose up her spine.

Flashing advertisements of the Charleston newspaper appeared on the computer screen. Brad scanned the article, his face growing incredulous. She had already read every story, with the allegations of their alleged mismanagement of Timberline Farm and alleged connections to trafficking. The accuracy of it had incensed her.

"Who did you talk to?" Brad's spit flew at her with his accusation.

Her retort was quick. "Your idiot, Breaker did this. You know it. Own up to it. The paper got too many things correct."

He continued reading, scrolling down the pages, then clicking on the next. Brad picked up his cell phone and then stopped.

Victoria waited, glaring at him. "Go on. Call him."

Brad jabbed his index finger at her. "This is all your fault; the trafficking idea was yours from the get-go. That's your way. You make the plans and expect me to implement them, no matter how ridiculous."

She twisted her lips to one side. "You never could do anything right." She looked toward his computer. "I give you jobs to do, and you can't handle any of them without making a mess. The most important job you screwed up."

Brad squinted at her. "What important job? Do you mean Dad? We just buried him. Are you crazy? You saw him lying in the pasture."

"Dad? You idiot. Jack wasn't your father."

The confused look on his face twisted into a mix of anger and fear. "I could swear you have lost your mind. What do you mean he wasn't my father?"

She couldn't resist a sneer. "Clint Harbin is your father."

Victoria watched Brad's face as the revelation of his real father hit home.

"Didn't you ever wonder why he spent so much time with you? Took you to your baseball games? Was there for everything you ever did?"

Brad's mouth gaped. For a minute, he simply looked at her, the expression on his face confused.

"He was Dad's friend," Brad finally replied. "When Dad traveled, he was there. A good friend, that's all." Brad ran his hand over his face. "He's not my father. It's not possible. What's gotten into you?"

Victoria leaned over his desk, her face inches from his, her voice venomous. "Forget Clint Harbin. I need you to tell me why you couldn't finish the most important job I gave you."

"What job?"

"I asked you to get rid of Marjorie Lee Danforth." Victoria whirled around, almost losing her balance, grabbing the edge of the desk for support. She snatched up the glass of whiskey and drained it, then slammed it back down on the desk. "You chased her, watched her, even tried to kidnap that little Beth girl to scare her. Nothing you did worked."

Brad said nothing for a minute, then shook his head. "Now you've lost it. Get out of here with your stupid accusations, and leave me alone."

He refocused on his computer, his hand flipping as if to shoo her out the door. Victoria waited. When he heard her shift in her impatience, he glanced up--and stared directly down the barrel of Jack's pistol, the same gun Brad had used to kill him.

He scrambled backward, knocking over his chair. Rising to his feet, he inched around the desk. Reaching to take the gun away from her with one hand, he wiped away a bead of sweat on his face with the other.

Victoria took a step backward, keeping the gun beyond his reach.

Brad shifted toward her with his arms open, palms wide. "Don't do this. You're my mother. I admit we've had a few problems here and there, but..."

Moving to a shooter's stance, she raised the gun, aiming at his chest.

"Mother, wait...!"

Gunshots rang out one after another as Brad staggered backward, his knees giving way. Crashing against the wall behind him, he slid to the floor. The gaping hole in his stomach gushed blood that pooled around him on the carpet.

Placing the gun on the desk, Victoria leaned over him, waiting for him to die.

Brads eyes stared back at her in shock. "Why?"

"Because you never should have been born."

55

I spend the entire drive back to Charleston, anxious that I will face a murder charge for a man I didn't kill, regardless of what the police chief says. I can only guess where my bullets went, but how do you prove that? Forensics is not part of my world. I will have to wait for the GBI's determination.

Mac gives me a lengthy explanation regarding bullet trajectories. I finally suggest that, while I appreciate the information, he stop trying to make me feel better.

An innocent man is dead, Victoria is on the run, and at least twenty kids are about to be shipped off to only God knows where, and subject to despicable things. I'm not sure I'll make it through the rest of this day.

Back in Charleston, I have a shot of scotch after a shower and new clothes to calm my nerves. It doesn't help.

We pull up at Harbin's brick colonial mansion on Wappoo Creek. His neighborhood is a wealthy enclave of homes under hundred-year-old plus oaks. My grandfather's judicial retirement party was here, but I spent most of the evening on the dock, enjoying my wine and avoiding lawyers.

Timothy, the driver, ushers Harbin into the front passenger's seat.

"Good evening, Judge." He makes only a perfunctory nod to me. "M. L., nice to see you. Want to give me an idea of where we're going?" He doesn't look either of us in the eye.

"You've figured that out by now," I reply, "unless you don't read."

He faces the front as the driver pulls onto Folly Road.

"What does Timberline Farm have to do with me?" he asks.

"At a minimum, a bit of selfish blindness, which is unacceptable in a solicitor," the Judge responds. "We intend to rectify that for you."

"I can't prosecute without proof, Your Honor, and there's been no arrests to my knowledge."

"Be patient," I say.

Harbin twists around in his seat to face me. "What circus have you two planned?"

"There's no circus," I say. "You will see what's been happening at Timberline Farm." I reach over the seat with my hand. "I need your cell phone."

"You're not getting it." Harbin twists back toward the front, his face screwed up in distaste like a petulant child. "I don't want to be involved in this."

I laugh. "Well, that's too bad, Mr. Solicitor. The head of Homeland Security Investigations has requested your presence. Please hand me your phone voluntarily, or they'll take it from you when we arrive."

Harbin releases an exasperated breath, reaches into his coat pocket, and pulls out an unlit cigar with his phone. He hands me the phone, then unwraps the cigar.

"Homeland Security? Why?" He stuffs the end of the cigar in his mouth. I wait for the ubiquitous click of the lighter, planning to throw both cigar and lighter out the window if he lights it. I ignore his question. He'll find out soon enough.

He lets out a huff. "Just give me the details and what you're looking for on my phone. I didn't call anyone about tonight, if that's what you want to know."

Scrolling through his calls, I don't recognize any numbers. The government acronyms will have to do the leg work.

"It won't do any good to pester us the entire way," I reply. "You can ask the big dogs when we get there."

56

It's nearly midnight when most of us wish to be home with our families or significant others. We gather further up the logging road I used on the last shipment to hide my car. HSI wants to approach with stealth, of course, and not trigger a response at Timberline Farm.

Within minutes, Harbin acts as if the entire plan was his idea, attempting to interject his recommendations at every opportunity. I ignore him. If he is involved in the nastiness at the farm, it will surface—and he will pay.

We surround House One in the dark. The plan is for me to ring the front doorbell as a diversion for the men storming the back. If children are inside, I need to get them out. They will cover me, but because of the proximity of the children, they warn me they will not shoot unless there is no other option.

The HSI team is in tactical black, and the lead looks like the rest except for his piercing blue eyes

"Given the late hour," he says to me, "Breaker will be busy in the basement, and we anticipate that a house parent will open the door. If this does not happen, Lee, as we discussed, you must improvise. Remember, we are here and will come for you. We can monitor your movement with your heat signature." He reaches into his pocket and retrieves a tiny black disk. He hands it to me. "Put this in your pocket, just in case. If Breaker answers the door, do whatever is necessary to keep him away from the basement. The more time you can buy us, the better."

"She is not trained for this," Mac protests to the HSI lead. "Let me go."

"Then we'll have an immediate gun battle with a significant portion of the one hundred twenty children as collaterals. You know this, Mac. We cannot risk shooting through paper-thin walls, especially when we don't know where the children are. While we have heat signatures, they don't point out who the bad guys are."

The lead turns to me. "If you are not willing—"

"No, I'm going." I look at Mac. "I know you don't understand, but this is something that I *need* to do. I'm assuming the tracker is in case they take me off the property?" I direct my question to the HSI lead.

"That's not going to happen," Mac interjects.

I'm not sure I believe either man, but I'm hell-bent to get this over with. I am the person who gave Victoria the idea to traffic children. I will be the one to rid her of that ability forever.

"Just keep my grandfather away from all this. If something happens to him..."

"Will do," he responds curtly to Mac, rather than to me, and heads back to his team.

I swallow my fear. My newly purchased second gun is wedged in the top of my jeans at the small of my back. The GBI still has my first.

"Go back to the car with your grandfather if no one answers," Mac says. "Screw HSI. I want you out of the way. I don't know why I let you agree to this."

I glance over at Mac. His jaw is clenched as if wired shut.

"What if Victoria answers?" I ask him, trying for a bit of levity. "You'll all have a front-row seat to that catfight."

"Lee, this is not the time." Mac rolls his eyes, and my attempt to relax him falls flat. Mac and the Judge wanted HSI to handle the entire sting, but Homeland's team lead asked that I act as a diversion. I was not about to turn him down. I started this. I intend to finish it.

I rest my hand on his arm. "I can handle this."

The Judge's Mercedes is parked in the hidden space behind the barn. As I enter the farm property alone and on foot, I check on the Judge in the back seat. His driver has instructions to flee without me, if necessary, for my grandfather's safety. The Judge gives me the thumbs up, and I continue around the barn and head toward House One.

Knowing how many people are involved and hearing nothing but regular night sounds surprises me. I hear only the buzz of cicadas. A horse nickers softly in the pasture to my left. My running shoes make no sound in the grass. I pause at the sound of a fish flopping in the lake and wait thirty seconds. Hearing no other noises, I continue in the dark.

Taking the front porch steps one by one, goosebumps crawl my arms as if a sudden fall breeze has come early. I stand on the front door mat, reaching for the doorbell, then chickening out. My intuition says that whatever is in this house is evil. My body wants no part of it.

I look into the darkness toward the Judge and feel his strength. Pushing the doorbell button, the "ding dong" rings through the door.

I wait.

No one comes to the door, even though I hear footsteps inside. I push the doorbell a second time. Where are the children? Someone is definitely inside, and it's a large person. I can feel the vibrations of their steps through the wooden porch floor. I push the bell a third time.

Stomps come toward me, and a door bangs inside.

"Hold your horses, will ya?" A rough male voice yells through the front door. "I'm comin' as fast as I can."

A porch light flicks on.

The door opens, and the smell hits me. I gag. Even with Beth's description, the shock of Breaker takes me by surprise. Wearing a T-shirt with the arms cut out, his fingertips to his shoulders reveal scabs and chunks of flaky peeling skin the color of fresh sunburn, all covered in a rancid-smelling cream.

"Well, looky who it is—the woman who can't keep her nose out of other people's business. What are you doing here this time of night?"

"I know it's late, so sorry, but my niece is here somewhere. I'm here to pick her up, but I'm obviously at the wrong house. Can you tell me where Victoria lives?" His response is a glare.

"Ok, I'll go," I say. "Sorry, I bothered you." I turn to leave.

Breaker steps out onto the front porch. He grabs my upper arm just as I start down the porch steps. His substantial paw wraps around my bicep and squeezes.

"How'd you get here?" he asks.

"My car's down—"

Five or six shots explode from the office building across the road. I jerk my arm from his grip and bound down the steps, tripping on the last one and falling, twisting my ankle. My hands are bloody from catching myself on the gravel road, and there's a rip in my jeans. I curse under my breath.

Hopping on one foot, I am too slow. Breaker manhandles me up the steps and onto the porch, then grabs me around the waist from behind with one arm. My ankle is now a hot throb. I can't walk.

Undeterred, he drags me backward into the house, using his free hand to slam the door and lock the deadbolt, the other holding my body upright. I struggle to free myself, squirming until he slaps me hard enough to make my brain jiggle.

Something is wrong. The office was to be searched last, not first. And everyone's "oh, this is the safest place for you" plan has now gone to hell.

"I don't know what you're up to, missy, but it won't work with me. Who's out there?"

"Who fired those shots? Aren't you even going to go look? This is an orphanage, for God's sake. Who has a gun here?" I'm rambling, but I need to distract him, get him outside and away from me.

He yanks me toward the front window, but beyond the porch light, it is so dark neither of us can see anything. Turning off the lights inside and out, Breaker forces me to a different window across the living room, hiding behind me as he watches for shadows in the yard. He closes all the curtains behind us as we go.

I push at him, trying to get away from his grasp. "I'm hurt, can't you see? Stop dragging me everywhere."

"It's your fault you're hurt, not mine." Using both hands to turn me, his face is inches from mine. "Now, damn it, who is out there?"

The rancid smell of his skin, combined with his whiskey and onion breath, makes the nausea rise.

"I'm going to throw up. Let me go," I shout. He lets go of my wrists and grabs my upper arms with both hands, squeezing them so hard I almost faint from the pain.

"Go ahead and throw up, then." He shakes me like a rag doll and then releases me as the vomit from his smell and my fear explodes onto the living room floor. Leaving me, he strides across the floor into the kitchen and returns with a roll of paper towels.

"Clean yourself up and tell me what the plan is."

"Nothing. I swear it." My right arm is screaming at me from the pain. He has either broken a bone or ripped something. "I'm hunting for my niece."

I pray for children to wake up and at least be witnesses.

Where is everyone? Beth said there should be ten to twelve children here.

"Yeah, not likely." He glares at me. "Don't move. If you do, I'll strangle you."

Breaker marches to the front door and wrenches it open. He doesn't allow anyone outside a clear view, hiding behind the wall next to the door. He cups his hands around his mouth.

"You want her back?" His voice booms into the darkness. "Come and get her."

When he comes back into the house, I'm waiting, the Glock pointing at him, my right arm barely able to hold its weight. Yeah, I should have pulled the trigger.

57

———————

My arms shake as I wait for the entire Homeland Security team to blast open the front door and save me from this man. I track him with my gun as he closes the front door.

Then, before I can react, Breaker is in front of me in two strides. The weapon is batted out of my hand like he is swatting a mosquito, and I'm sprawled across the floor.

"Stupid bitch," he says under his breath, "bringing a pea shooter to a war."

Ignoring me on the floor, he starts for the kitchen, then changes his mind. Grabbing my right wrist, he jerks me to my feet. Pain shoots through my arm from whatever damage he did previously. Breaker is oblivious to my yelps as he hurries us to the kitchen with me hopping on one foot.

Reaching for his cell in his back pocket, my imbalance jerks us both, causing him to drop the phone. He lets go of my arm to retrieve it. Just as I shift to run, the slap across my face whips my head in one direction, then the second spins me in the other. I grab onto a kitchen chair to keep from falling, blood flowing down my lips and off my chin as he swipes the phone from the floor.

"Stop being stupid." He thumbs the cell phone as I crumple to the kitchen floor, my ears ringing and my head pounding. "I've been in this business a long time," he says. "There is nothing you can do that some kid hasn't tried before you. I anticipate everything."

I look for something to use as a weapon, but the counters are bare. No knives, no appliances, no nothing. The entire house has been stripped.

Now I'm very concerned that all the children who live here are in the basement.

His call connects through the phone's speaker. "Fish."

"Something's happened," Breaker says into the phone, shifting it to his ear. "We need to move it up. Yeah, I know we said two a.m., but we need to go now." He squints at me. "And I have an extra package I'll toss in for free." He interrupted the apparent protests on the other end. "Now. I need you here right now. Fifteen minutes or the deal is off."

Shoving his phone into his front pocket, he opens a door on the side wall of the kitchen, revealing a dark staircase. He leans close, and the smell causes me to struggle not to heave again.

"Some nasty folks are coming to pick up our girls downstairs. Since I only need five minutes to prepare them for pickup, that leaves ten minutes of my time just for you." He drags his finger down my throat. "After that, you belong to them. Even though I won't charge them, I'm sure they'll pay a nice little bonus for you."

Jerking me to my feet, he shoves me in front of him. I stumble in the dark, teetering on the edge of the first step of a gaping dark hole. Using the walls as support, I hop down the first step.

"Just get down there, or I'll shove you."

I scoot down the flight of stairs on my backside. Breaker kicks me in the back, step by step, as I go. I don't care. The slower I move, the less time he will have to hurt me before the vans arrive.

Too soon, I feel the concrete floor underneath my feet. He flicks on the overhead lights. Grabbing my right arm again, he pulls me down the hall toward the back room. Each cell is packed with young girls and children, both boys and girls. Like before, only ten times as many.

I almost pass out from what I know is about to happen to them.

He stops when we reach the cell. He pushes me inside, and I stop and take it all in. I'm in the same cell where we found Glenna. Chains and handcuffs still rest on the floor where we left them. The overhead light exposes a dead rat in one corner. An oozing black slime covers the far wall.

"I won't lock you up if you behave." Breaker kicks at a chain. "Of course, maybe you'd like that."

Shoving me further inside the room, he slams the door. The lock clicks. He turns on other lights, striding up and down the hallway, rattling the cages with a three-foot piece of lead pipe, the clanging so loud I cover my ears with my hands.

I look at my watch. Only four minutes have elapsed since his call upstairs. I need to make it through the next eleven minutes. And pray the pick-up party isn't late.

"Wake up." Breaker yells at the rest of the occupants. "Get yourselves up and get ready. We're going on a road trip."

Unlocking the room next to mine, he orders two girls out, impatient when they move like zombies, their half-lidded eyes unfocused, tripping over themselves into the hallway. He zip-ties one girl's wrists to the girl next to her. With each girl he rouses from bed, he zip-ties her to the next girl in line, making a human chain.

Vehicle doors slam outside. My knees go weak at the thought of these girls being taken—along with myself. HSI let the last shipment continue to Savannah. From the tracker in my pocket,

I'm afraid they decided, without telling me, to do the same tonight.

Breaker grabs a backpack from a wall hook and looks at his watch. He marches back to my cell. The girls, heavily drugged and half asleep, hug the wall to keep standing.

I step back as he approaches the cell door. "I'll be back to take care of you. You think about that. From what I've heard about you and Brad's old man, I bet you'll enjoy it."

"Yeah, right," I reply. "You can't get it up, and we both know it."

The scowl on his face tells me I've hit a button. He scrambles to unlock the cell and charges into the room. He wads the front of my button-down shirt in his fist as he pulls my face two inches from his.

"Never disrespect me, girl. I'm your lord and master from now on. You do what I say. You understand me?" His sour breath is worse than the smell of his skin if that is possible.

He spins me around, grasping the shirt collar, and, with a jerk downward, the buttons pop from my shirt and scatter on the floor. My arms are still in the sleeves; my front is now bare except for my bra, and my hands are trapped behind me.

Like he said upstairs, I keep underestimating this guy.

"You'll regret back talking me, girl," he screams. "I'm gonna have you right here and now. Get down on your knees." He shoves me to the floor. Grabbing the front of my bra with one hand, he reaches into his front jeans pocket with the other. A mental picture of Glenna's bruises flashes through my mind. My body shudders when the knife snicks open in his hand. The warm blade of the knife slides between my breasts, and I close my eyes, knowing these are my last seconds on earth.

Yanked upward from the floor as he violently slices the bra from the center, I sprawl backward on the floor when the elastic pops. I roll away from him, but he is too fast. Trying to scramble to my feet, he reaches for my jeans to yank them downward.

This time, I'm faster.

"Leave me alone, you bastard!" Fighting back the pain of the swollen ankle holding my weight, I kick him with my good leg, first his shin, then with everything I have left in me, in the balls. With a *humph* sound, the air is forced from his lungs. The knife pops from his hand and slides across the floor. It skitters in a spin under the bars and outside into the hall.

He bends double, heaving, his face a sickly shade of gray. With both hands clasped together, I slam them into the back of his head. He sprawls face down on the floor. My ankle is unable to hold my weight any longer, and I drop to the floor and push away from him.

The cell door is open.

I crawl toward the door as banging starts on the outside door. Breaker shifts to his knees, the pain in his groin still obvious. He slowly puts his weight on one foot, then the other, barely able to stand upright.

I crawl faster.

I won't make it in time. Staggering by me on the floor, he slams the cell door in my face.

Swiping his knife from the floor, he snatches the arm of the girl nearest to him, pulling the long human chain behind him. The banging gets louder, and Breaker swears under his breath.

"I'm coming." He yells at the door.

Stopping, he turns and glares at me. Once the banging stops, he yells to the girls behind him.

"All right, we're gonna go outside and get into the vans. Cause no trouble, and you'll get no trouble."

He turns the knob and opens the door, pulling the snake of girls with him into the darkness. I close my eyes, resting my head against the barred door in relief.

58

———————

Victoria waited on the opposite side of House One, away from the men hidden in the dark. Leaving Brad's office, she caught shadows moving in the dark and headed in the opposite direction. She hugged the tree line until she reached a decent hiding spot.

Two vans came through the main gate and headed for the house. With neither van using headlights, it was apparent they were Fish's pickup crew. She knew a sheriff's patrol car waited on the county road, even though she could not see that far. It would not come onto the private property but made sure no one, whether child or minder, escaped.

Both van's passenger doors opened. The two drivers headed for the basement. A partial moon gave her enough light to see. One man pounded on the door, impatient to be done with this. Fish required four times the typical shipment, and Brad had insisted on more than four times the money for the risk.

Too bad he'd never see it. She smiled to herself.

The basement door opened, and Breaker stepped out, his arm behind him, pulling a train of girls zip-tied together. Victoria counted them as each girl stepped out the door. Brad was short. Only two, but still short. Theron would be livid.

It wouldn't matter. None of them would get what they wanted tonight.

Breaker waited, holding the lead girl's arm. "Where's the money?" The second driver stepped forward, tossing a dark bag at Breaker's feet. Breaker dropped the girl's arm as he opened the bag and counted the money using his phone flashlight. He pulled the first girl in the human train forward and handed her arm to the man. The train of girls began slow steps to the van.

Victoria waited for this moment. She should have left earlier to catch a flight out of Charleston. But she needed the additional fifty thousand dollars Breaker was holding to ensure her safety. As she was to step out from behind the tree line, the sound of engines exploded into the quiet night.

Within seconds, military vehicles surrounded the men and girls in a semicircle. Behind the tactical crew, a row of police and sheriff's officers formed a tight outer circle, close enough to cut off any escape. Portable klieg lights popped on one by one, lighting the land surrounding the property in bright, white light. Victoria carefully stepped back into the shadow of the trees, still close enough to see and hear without being seen. She hoped.

"Hands up! On the ground, now!" Multiple voices yelled.

Breaker raised his arms to shield himself from the lights, stopping the girls' progress. Each girl slammed into the one in front like a child's pull toy. The two drivers froze as automatic weapons from various directions were pointed at them.

"Hands where I can see them," a voice demanded through a bullhorn. "Now! Hit the ground!"

Breaker dropped to the ground. A half dozen officers swarmed him. Instantly, a uniformed knee was on his back, his hands cuffed behind him, and his body searched for weapons. "Where are the Marshalls?" A voice shouted at him.

"Lawyer." Victoria could barely hear Breaker's voice over the activity. She smiled. For once, Breaker knew the correct response. Her smile faded. She would be law enforcement's next target. Brad's suggestion she head for the Cayman Islands had seemed flippant an hour ago. Now, it was her only choice.

She needed to get to Miami. Fast.

59

Why isn't anyone coming?

I shake the locked door to the cell. It doesn't give and doesn't open.

Now that the initial shouting is over, all I can hear are low murmurs, feet shuffling, and vehicle doors opening and closing. I see nothing beyond the bright lights streaming in the open basement door at the end of the hall.

Still, I get ready. I pull my shirt to cover me as best I can and tie a haphazard knot in front. Shaking the bars to my cell again, the door holds firm.

I wait. Impatiently—until the claustrophobia I know is coming rears its ugly head. Once it begins, the cell seems to grow smaller and smaller until I cannot stand being in this box for one more minute.

I need something to make a noise, like the lead pipe Breaker dropped in the hallway. Try as I might, it is too far for me to reach. Giving up, I scream—the loudest blood-curdling scream possible—over and over until my voice is a hoarse croak.

I sink to the floor. And wait, tears streaming down my face

from my closed eyes. I am spiraling downward and will be a puddle of incomprehensible goo if someone doesn't come soon. It has only happened once before. The night I was pregnant and alone, the night Jack told me goodbye.

I cannot let it happen again.

I hear the jingle of keys and feet slamming down the hall. I look up. A frantic Mac is desperately trying to open the door

"He said you weren't down here, damn it." Mac continued to curse under his breath with every key on the massive ring he inserted into the lock that wouldn't turn. "I'm sorry, Lee. I've been searching everywhere for you."

Once the door opens, I slam into him so hard I knock him into the far wall.

"I've got you, Lee." His powerful arms hold me, and his chin rests on my head.

"I need to see that bastard." I wipe the tears from my face and take deep breaths to get myself back on track. "He tried to rape me."

Even though it is knotted, my shirt is in tatters. My hair is wild, and my jeans are half-zipped. Embarrassed that Mac is seeing me in such a mess, I try to fix my clothes.

"I'm sorry." Mac touches the side of my face, and I wince. "It's all my fault he did this to you. I should have forced you to stay with your grandfather."

"No." My simmering anger threatens to explode. "This," I point to my face, "is only that asshole's fault."

Breaker needs the same treatment he gave me. But in this particular case, I can be patient. With the judicial system, I will make sure he gets much worse.

Mac removes his jacket and throws it around me, turning away until I can zip my pants.

"Ready?" His face is tight with worry.

"Yes."

"You need me to carry you?" he asks.

"No," I reply, "I can do this. Just let me lean on you."

"Then let's go." His arms hold me as I limp down the hall and out the door.

Stepping into the bright light, we walk around Breaker. Even though I have only one good foot, it is all I can do not to kick him in the balls again as he lays prone.

Two uniformed officers in heavy black gear lift Breaker to his feet. With one on either side, they walk him away from the vehicles' lights to a small circle of men.

"Marion Cavanaugh?" A man in a suit covered by an HSI jacket steps out of the circle.

Breaker doesn't move.

"You are under arrest for trafficking, a violation of the United States Code, Section 18, paragraph 1581."

The voice drones on with the Miranda rights. Most likely Breaker has them memorized. The men take him toward one of the cars. I reach out to touch the arm of one officer. "Wait. I need a few seconds. Can I?"

The man in the suit gives the officer a flick of his wrist. They shift Breaker to face me.

"Look at me," I say to the genuinely nasty man before me.

He quits staring at his feet, raising his head to lock his eyes with mine. A snear slowly spreads across his face. With all my strength and my hands double like I am wielding a baseball bat, I hit him. His face snaps to one side, and I hit him again, popping his face in the other direction, just like he did to me.

To my surprise, no one moves.

I lean toward him when he faces me again. "You don't like being disrespected?" I ask. "Well, you've messed with the wrong woman. Lawyer up, buddy, because I will show you what disrespect means."

"She just assaulted me." Breaker spits blood on the ground and looks at the man in the suit. "I want to press charges."

The man in the suit stares at him and then motions to the officers. Feeling Mac's hand rest on my shoulder, I step back, letting the officers take Breaker away.

It is time to find the Marshalls. I'm sure they are both running, but at some point, they will be caught. And I'll be ready. I have more than a few things to say to Victoria.

60

Three Weeks Later

Twenty years of Jack's journals are spread around me as I lay sprawled in the middle of the living room floor upstairs over the office. I read them all, every word, locked in the upstairs apartment for days. I hold the last one in my hand.

He had loved me. The journals make that clear. Yet that love was selfish, obsessed. He protected me for his benefit, not mine. He still thought of me as that teenaged Lee, the girl who set him free yet left herself bound. The girl who did everything he asked, even if she knew what he wanted, was wrong.

It has taken me these past few days to fully understand the difference between that girl and the woman I am today—the wild, unsupervised, emotionally vulnerable girl who lost a father she loved and was ignored by her mother.

Tamed by Jack with his mix of Christian rules and personal patriarchal requirements, I fell in line. Over time, he molded me into the woman, the lover, and the confidant he wanted me to be. The real Lee was forced into a mental box and locked away. Even when he left me, that malleable young woman expected Jack to return and claim her again as his.

But he didn't. His journals tell me he thought he was setting me free when he left. I was a grown woman, free to do as I wished without him. He wrote as if he were a martyr, taking the punishment of his marriage and religious life in exchange for my freedom.

But that didn't happen.

Instead, for twenty years, I have lived in the box that Jack built. I followed his rules, continued emotionally to be faithful, and waited. I ignored my grandfather's admonitions to expand my career and take risks, Clarice's suggestions to live a little, and my mother's pleas to love again. I gave up my child—our child—something I'll always regret. Yet most of all, I ignored that fifteen-year-old girl inside, the wild one who wanted to live, travel, and be free to do what she wanted regardless of anyone else's ideas, including Jack.

And then he died.

It has taken me twenty years to understand that his rules no longer bind me. I can be that same wild, adventurous person that lived inside me as a child. While it might take years, if not my entire lifetime, to understand everything Jack did to me emotionally, I am no longer in that box.

I am free.

Both Dani and Glenna are physically fine, although Glenna will carry the trauma inflicted by Breaker for the rest of her life. But she will make it. Given her strength and determination, she already shows she is the catalyst for change with the others.

The Judge and I donate our time and money for legal, counseling, and medical services for every traumatized child at Timberline Farm. HSI rescued the children in Savannah, and they, too, will heal. I will not let them hide their pain as I have.

A more recent holographic will was folded inside Jack's final journal. In this handwritten will, Jack left everything he owned to

Alex, except Willow House, which he had already deeded to me. He instructed me in the journal to make sure Victoria received nothing. An additional note permitted me to destroy the holographic will and continue under the one he signed with Heyward Kendrick. He was confident I would make the right choice.

The Judge and I visited New York. He wandered the Museum of Modern Art while I met with the dealer in Greenwich Village. Only a few pieces of Jack's art are of me, thankfully all fully clothed. Snippets of me are in several paintings, but most of the works are newer landscapes.

Leaving the art dealer with instructions, the Judge and I had dinner at Robert, one of my favorite restaurants, at Columbus Circle. With a glass of 2012 Caymus Cabernet in hand, I relaxed for the first time in over a decade.

Alex and I talked by telephone several times, and with her parents' permission, our New York trip was followed by a day in Boston for us to meet. Her adoptive parents are reasonable, hardworking people. They love Alex, have raised her, and I will not jeopardize that. I have no plans to interfere with her life and I made sure she and her parents knew this before we agreed to meet.

It was a shock to finally see her. She has Jack's significant height, towering way over the waiting people at the baggage claim at Boston Logan airport, but otherwise looks very much like me. It is obvious we are mother and daughter. I hesitated as we approached each other, worried that she would reject me, even though my arms strained to hold her. She didn't hesitate, but blasted toward me, wrapping me in a hug, her laughter—Jack's laugh—causing me to burst into tears.

Later, when showing her several selections from Jack's journals, I assured her he felt the same as me. We loved her, and had things been different we would never have given her up. Several journal passages included lovely words for the child he wished he'd known. I tore them out and gave them to her.

I made my last visit to Willow House the week after the raid. It is already listed for sale. The eventual sales and art proceeds will be deposited into a trust I set up for Alex. The trust is a vehicle mainly to protect her from Victoria, who is still missing. Alex is the only positive thing Jack and I created. She deserves all the money and to be free from Victoria's interference.

Next week, I will move to Sullivan's Island, taking the private guest suite in the Judge's house on the beach. I want to spend more time with him. My condo was rented quickly to a lovely couple, and the new renter for the upstairs office apartment, a PhD student at the College of Charleston, is patiently waiting for me to move.

I am still uncertain where I will go from here, yet I want no more closings, no more lawyers, and, except for my friends and family, no more Charleston. Dreaming of extensive travel, I want to do something different and live without the oppression of Jack Marshall hanging over my head.

Mac, hearing that I wanted a change, invited me to join his firm. He insisted Clarice come with me. The Judge thought it was a "stupendous idea." For me, the jury is still out.

Even though I have not accepted Mac's offer, Clarice and I have begun paring down my current practice. We are talking slowly to every client and have shifted the real estate litigation matters to other firms. I am introducing the builders, developers, and realtors to other suitable attorneys, and it won't be long before the remaining real estate closings on the books are finished.

Three knocks rap on the door frame, and Clarice enters the apartment.

"Done?" She looks askance at the journals scattered on the floor.

"Yes. Well, almost. I'm on the last one." I give her a smile.

"Ok, I'll leave you in just a second then." Clarice putters

around my apartment, straightening and cleaning the clutter like a mother hen.

"You can stop that now. I'm a grown woman. I can take care of myself. It's not like I'm injured or anything."

Her voice is flustered. "Well, you almost were shot. Then, locked in a cell and almost... I don't want to think about that. And if you're going to work with Mac, I don't want you—"

"Clarice, stop." She turns to me, her face lined with worry. I stand and wrap my arms around her shoulders, hugging her.

"I can take care of myself," I remind her as we part. "Just let me find the real me—"

"I know you can," she interrupts, resting her hands on her hips, waiting for me to finish.

"—the one I left behind at fifteen. I want to be that wild child, only older and more responsible. The person who sticks up for herself and others. The one who has fun and who lives her life..."

"...and stops hiding in a box," she says as she turns to go. "Oh, Dani wants lunch soon."

"I should be able to do lunch tomorrow if that works. What happened to NYU?"

"Just as you said, everything Victoria told her was a lie. It was an excellent lesson for Dani. She learned she must succeed independently, not on someone's promises. If she's meant to go to NYU, she will."

Clarice moves into the hall. "I almost forgot. Harbin called. They are charging Morris as an accessory before and after the fact. They are also considering him for Brad's murder."

"I'm sure that Victoria—if she ever surfaces, will be convicted of Brad's murder. Morris didn't do it. What did Harbin have to say about Victoria?" I ask.

"Nothing we didn't already know. That she hired that David Whatever-his-name-is, that criminal lawyer from Columbia, but no one knows where she is, and her lawyer isn't talking. Harbin thinks she is probably floating around on a boat, so she can't be extradited. She will weasel her way out of this. I know it."

It took law enforcement two days to find her trail. A video camera recorded her at a gas station outside Charleston the night of Brad's murder, with a time stamp two hours after the raid. They next found toll booth photos of her on the Florida Turnpike near Miami, then on a security tape at MIA, heading for the Cayman Islands. They lost track of her from there.

Victoria, in her usual fashion, through her attorney, accused me of Brad's death. And Kendrick's. With almost two dozen witnesses, including law enforcement, to my location on the front porch of House One, my alibi was tight for the former. As for the latter, I am still holding my breath for the GBI determination.

"It may take a while, but we'll see her in orange in the end," I say to her. "Did he mention Jack's killer?"

"You know, he surprised me." Clarice pulled at her earlobe, a habit when she was perplexed. "Harbin told me SLED was doing a full investigation. He had every intention to bring Brad's and Jack's killers to justice. He got all choked up. It was like Brad was his family or something. It was just weird."

"Yeah, well," I muse, "given what Brad did to Beth, Harbin had better get his act together. We're watching, and he knows it. Since South Carolina Law Enforcement is involved, something might get done now."

I want it all to be over.

Clarice surveys the journals strewn around the floor. "Learn anything you didn't know before?"

"That life is brief," I tell her. "And I've wasted so much of mine with hate, being unaware of my surroundings, and unmindful of my abilities. I have family and friends who are most important."

"Anything else?"

I look at Jack's last journal, still in my hand.

"I have one more thing that I believe we should do. After that,

I think I'm finally free." I grab a stack of the journals and hand them to Clarice. I pick up the other half.

"Where are we going?"

"Think, and you'll figure it out." I point to the red bowl on the table. "Grab the office keys, and I'll get the matches. Can't do this without matches." Adding the bag of things I had purchased earlier, I follow her out the door and down Archdale Street.

The Unitarian Church in Charleston's cemetery is my favorite place downtown. No, that's not true. It is my favorite place in the world—although I admit my world at this point is somewhat limited. Rather than being a manicured square of lawns and headstones, the cemetery is wild, full of flowers, ancient trees, and historical places of burial, all in a mass of luscious green.

It is the opposite of the manicured cemetery of St. Philips where Jack is buried, with its short green lawn and rows of head-stones. Except for a few rose bushes close to Jack's grave, there never seem to be any flowers at St. Philips. That cemetery reminds me of a war memorial during the day and a spooky haunt with its concrete grave covers and tall headstones at night. Visitors—and, in the middle of the night, raucous teenagers— can walk willy-nilly over the graves.

At the UU cemetery, cobblestone, sand, and brick walkways meander through the luscious overgrown grounds, giving the grave sites the privacy they deserve. It is the calmest place I know. The ghost stories of tour guides and horse cart drivers have always rung false. This small piece of land, for me, means peace.

My favorite section is in the very back. The church placed a bowl on a pedestal next to the back wall for ceremonies. A Buddhist monk guided me the first time I took part. We let the Universe, God, Whoever, or Whatever release us from a burden by writing it on a small scrap of paper. Then, one by one, we burned the paper in the bowl.

One door closes, another opens.

That was the day I met Clarice. She was talking with another woman at the Unitarian coffee held after church one Sunday, and I eavesdropped. In planning an event, Clarice turned out to be one of the most positive people I'd ever met, radiating vibes that pulled to the hidden introvert in me.

Clarice looks at the stacks of journals and then at the burning bowl. "We have enough for a bonfire. I don't think this is what they intended with this, Lee."

During the day, there are always children in the education building on the other side of the cemetery. I point in that direction.

"Yeah, well, see if the kids' teacher needs a break for an hour. We can let the kids roast some marshmallows. We'll supervise. No need to waste a good bonfire." I unfold the oversized picnic blanket in a grassy area, trying to wrangle it into submission. A gust of wind straightens out the fabric. With a *floof*, it settles to the ground in a neat square. The breeze dies, and calm settles over the cemetery. A seagull lands on the burning bowl, and I hold my breath not to scare it away. Instead of being afraid, the bird looks at me as if waiting for me to speak.

"You ready for a fresh start, too?" I ask the gull.

The bird's head bobs ever so slightly. Then, with a loud ha-ha-ha-ha and a sudden swoosh, the gull flies over my head and into the blue sky toward Charleston Harbor.

I take a long, deep breath and let it out. I thank the beautiful garden around me and ask the world for forgiveness. I then send out one small request to the Universe for the future. Taking my time, I rip the first journal into a nice fat pile of easy-to-burn pieces. Then another, and another.

Clarice's laughter bounces through the trees, followed by children's giggles, cheers, and the sound of tennis shoes on gravel. Four large bags of hotdog and smores materials are in the cotton grocery bag on my shoulder, along with the extra-long sticks I'd found online the week before. I spread them on the blanket at my feet, waiting for Clarice and the children to join me.

When we are all gathered, with marshmallows on sticks and kids ready, I light the corner of one page. The flames take hold, and the first batch of journal pages cause the fire to rise to the sky. The children clap and yell, squealing as they put their marshmallow sticks near the fire.

As I look at Clarice, she takes my hand, and the *whoosh* of the fire instantly sets me free.

ACKNOWLEDGMENTS

Even though writing is a solitary endeavor, I have never been alone through this journey. Thank you to everyone who encouraged me to begin my author career and in the writing of this book. Several friends were instrumental for the initial kick in the pants to get me started, and to them I give my deepest heartfelt thanks.

To Kimberly Brock for her encouragement and advice before, during and after the Tinderbox Writers retreats on Sullivan's Island. I'm quite sure she thought I wasn't listening.

Forever Gone would never have been completed without Rebecca Finley's bulldogged insistence that I just get it down on paper, her thrashing of the plot and the characters, and her constant friendship.

My editor, Rebecca Millar, helped me deepen the story, and I am always grateful for her help and assistance. A huge thank you to Marta Lane, for her patience in reading on an exceedingly deep level, and her give-it-to-me-like-it-is comments.

But most of all, I am at this point because of the daily support and encouragement of my family. I could not have done it without you.

ABOUT THE AUTHOR

R. S. Hampton is an attorney turned novelist, weaving suspenseful stories that unfold across various landscapes—bustling cities, quiet coastal towns, and places tucked just out of sight. With a legal career spanning three decades, her characters are often lawyers, their clients, and the people entangled in their search for truth—where morality is rarely black and white, and justice doesn't always follow the rules.

A lifelong traveler, she is drawn to places that spark curiosity, places with history, edge, and unexpected depth. Her stories are shaped by the settings in which they unfold, each becoming a character in its own right. Whether it's a courtroom in a city she once called home or a hidden alleyway in a country she's only just begun to understand, her novels reflect the intricacies of the worlds she explores.

She and her husband split their time between multiple countries, embracing a multicultural life that mirrors the layered complexities of her fiction. When she's not writing, she's usually on the move—seeking out the next place, the next story, and the next unanswered question.

For more books, updates, and contact information:
www.RSHamptonBooks.com

Help Indie Authors Succeed

Thank you for picking up this book! Whether you bought it, borrowed it, or stumbled upon it, I truly appreciate your time and interest. As an independent author, sharing stories with readers like you is a dream come true—and you're already helping just by reading.

If you enjoyed this story, **here are a few simple ways you can make a difference:**

1. Share your thoughts

Whether it's a quick review online or a conversation with a friend, your words help other readers discover this book.

2. Tell your community

Mention the book to fellow readers, share it on social media, or recommend it to your local library or bookstore.

3. Show your support

Pre-ordering upcoming books or attending events when possible can help small authors reach new audiences.

4. Stay connected

Follow me on social media or subscribe to my newsletter for updates and behind-the-scenes glimpses into my writing journey.

Every little action makes a difference, and I couldn't do this without you. Thank you for being part of this adventure!

With Gratitude,

R. S. Hampton

www.ingramcontent.com/pod-product-compliance
Lightning Source LLC
Chambersburg PA
CBHW030347120726
47901CB00007B/1945